I Was England's Only Spy Inside Nazi Germany

Noel Stevens

iUniverse, Inc.
New York Bloomington

I Was England's Only Spy Inside Nazi Germany

iUniverse books may be ordered through booksellers or by contacting:

iUniverse
1663 Liberty Drive
Bloomington, IN 47403
www.iuniverse.com
1-800-Authors (1-800-288-4677)

Because of the dynamic nature of the Internet, any Web addresses or links contained in this book may have changed since publication and may no longer be valid. The views expressed in this work are solely those of the author and do not necessarily reflect the views of the publisher, and the publisher hereby disclaims any responsibility for them.

ISBN: 978-1-4502-2567-0 (sc)
ISBN: 978-1-4502-2568-7 (ebook)

Printed in the United States of America

iUniverse rev. date: 5/11/2010

PART ONE

```
=========
   1939
=========
```

The Flappers emerged in the 1920s and 1930s – young women who were 'irresponsible', 'bold', who openly defied conventionality. Were they reacting to the butchery of The Great War followed by 20,000,000 more deaths in the Great Flu Epidemic? Opting out of society and the traditional role of the feminine woman? Acting out another small step in the Disintegration of the West? The gesture of the Flapper was to turn her back on the male-created reality.

J. M. Elliot
METAMORPHOSIS IN WESTERN SOCIETIES

I had said yes to his offer to dine and dance. It was our first time, and he picked me up in his motor. It was a couple with the top down, and on this last night of June, the air was warm as we motored across London, and I took deep breaths. He took me to a Ye Olde sort of restaurant, with smoked salmon and a dance floor. Jollity and merriment – all my 19-year-old heart could ask for. Nothing in this world gladdens me like dancing.

But he was earnest. My family, friends, and my mirror tell me that I am shapely and rather good-looking – but he was earnest. Not a quip. No raillery, no witticisms. No gazing in desire. To persiflage he was not given.

I come from an earnest home. My Spanish father, a stiff-necked Don, is a brain researcher, and they gave him British nationality to keep him working here. The British recoil at his Spanish frankness, and then timidly venture back to hear more. My German mother is a mathematician, with a Wagnerian body, which shows that my father's eyes sometimes venture beyond peoples' brains. My sister works in fighter plane design. They all enjoin me – with guilt, grief and sorrow – to make something of my 'high' intelligence, but my mental gifts tell me that daddy will support me until a husband moves in to take up my financial burden, and I can enjoy the London social seasons.

1

"You're very quiet tonight, Bruce," I suggested, composing my features in a suitably concerned expression.

"You know," he said, "Hitler, all that business."

"Hitler!" I exclaimed. Bringing up Hitler on his first date with me! "Does he concern you in some way?" I said, making my voice sound solicitous.

I had met him at Dorothy's party. He was good-looking, and both Dorothy and Winnie had told me that his father had really serious money.

"I used to be a weekend pilot, and now I've joined the RAF. We're training in super planes, but the German pilots got experience in Spain. They sent them there for a whole six months, and then rotated them back."

Aah! Is he going to suggest that he has but a short time to live, and doesn't want to die a virgin?

"Aren't you frightened?" he asked.

This date was all the way off the rails. I said, "We've got the Royal Navy, the English Channel, and thousands of brave men like yourself. Wouldn't you say we ladies are well protected?"

"Ah," he said, "You don't want to do your bit?"

"My hobby is photography – artistic photography. Portraits, street scenes, landscapes, seascapes – I've won some prizes. I'm not really terribly interested in war and female heroics. Why don't we dance?"

* * *

What a flop!

We got home about two a.m., which was not too bad, and somewhat saved the evening. Another group I knew came in, and we joined them for dancing and supper.

* * *

Next morning, I slept in until ten. I rang the maid, and asked her to draw the drapes; said I wanted only toast and marmalade for breakfast, with white coffee. We drank coffee at home, instead of tea; not that horrible Kenyan stuff, but grains imported from Brazil.

I had a shower, fixed up my hair, and went down to the breakfast room. The maid had set out breakfast on my favourite silver service, and on the sideboard had set the platter with the mail: Nothing for me, but a brown OHMS letter for mummy.

After breakfast, I took it to her study, where she had her table scattered with papers and calculations. I gave her a kiss, and handed her the envelope.

She slit it open with an onyx letter knife, and said, "Heavens! The War Office."

I raised my eyebrows.

She said, "I'm working for them, actually… but Hunts Court? Never heard of the place – ah, here's a sort of sketch. How funny."

I looked at her curiously. Mummy was 45, but looked much younger. She had blonde hair, tied in a bun, wide cheekbones, an almost unlined, creamy skin, and blue eyes. Her expression was usually vaguely absent or dreamy, as though her mind wandered through arcane equations. She was not *really* German, although we two always spoke German.

Her parents were from Germany and had emigrated to Chile in 1890. Their daughter, Christa, my mother, was born in 1894 and, as she had a French governess, she spoke French. She went to the Sorbonne in 1911 to study Advanced Mathematics, and graduated in 1915. Because of the war, she headed for neutral Madrid, and they gave her a job at the University. My father, the young Professor Fabian Madueno, fell violently in love with her; she married him in 1916. My mother took Spanish nationality and my sister, Diana, was born the next year.

In 1920, they were at London University, and their daughter Raimunda – myself – was born, a British national by birth. Five years later, my parents and sister gave up their Spanish nationality for British nationality.

So, mummy had gone through life shedding nationalities

She read out aloud to me: "It is requested that you present yourself personally at the above address at midday, July 1st 1939, in the office 2C on the second floor."

"You'll have to leave now!" I exclaimed.

We live in Queen Square, almost next to Russell Square Station, on the Piccadily Line.

Mummy said, "I think I'll get there more quickly on the Underground than motoring over. And you can't ever be sure that the car will want to start."

* * *

We had a late lunch, because mummy did not come in until a quarter-to-two. But it didn't matter because daddy came home at five-to-two, hoping for a bite, which he had imagined he would have to eat on his own.

At 47, he still had his thick brown hair, and with his brown skin and aquiline face, his great, dark eyes, he did not look like a University professor and research academic, but like a pirate on the Spanish Main. His movements were quick and sure, his eyes never still.

3

Over the soup, I asked, "What did the War Office want?"

"I can't say. They made me sign the Official Secrets Act."

My father put down his soup spoon.

"Christa! They what?"

She gave him a wry smile, and explained about the letter.

"*Por Dios!*" he cried.

We were talking in Spanish.

The wry smile remained. "That's only the half of it. They want to see Raimunda this afternoon. They have given me an envelope for you," she told me, "It's in my handbag."

"What fun," I said, "They'll want portrait photos of some Generals."

My father said, "Christa, you look worried."

My mother was obstinately silent, "Fabian, I can't say anything, except they will want to see you tomorrow."

"*Salvame Dios*," he sighed, "I'm run off my feet. They probably all need their heads examined!" and we all laughed uproariously.

My appointment was for four-thirty pm. The plaque on the door said, 'Statistical Studies', and the doorman looked like a beefy ex-sergeant. He gave me a cheerful smile, summoned up a young lady who gave me a good afternoon, very politely, and led me upstairs to a tall ceiling, dingy brown corridor. Along the corridor, we stopped at a nine-foot tall door in a dirty walnut. The young lady rapped her knuckles – the wood looked awfully hard and I wondered whether it hurt – and a voice inside called, "Come in!"

She opened the door for me, and closed it after me.

I found myself in a large office, with aged green walls – almost discoloured – and a very big and heavy desk side-on to a tall window without curtains. The carpet was thick, and cupboards stood against the walls.

The man who rose to greet me must have been 6'3" tall, with untidy white hair, receding in front. He looked about 45, and was dressed in a baggy sports coat, tweed trousers, and wore a knitted brown tie. He had a big, lined face that was ruddy, bushy eyebrows and steady, green eyes. He looked very fatherly, and his half-smile set you instantly at ease; I however felt a sudden, intense unease, and my smile was forced.

He was smoking a pipe, with aromatic smoke, and in a soft voice he invited me to take a seat on a sofa on the other side of the window. The sofa

4

was faded green, but firm, and he chose an armchair in front.

He smiled again, "I believe you like coffee. Would you like a cup? Brazilian, I assure you."

I forced myself to speak normally, "A demi-tasse, with a drop of milk."

"Ah," he said, "You understand Continental tastes in coffee. But you've never been to the Continent?"

I said, "I'm wondering whether you are a spymaster. You know a great deal about me."

"My name is Graham Bunton. I do like the 'master' bit. Any admiration sits well coming from someone as young and lovely as yourself."

He knocked on the door, and he ordered coffee.

"Well, I don't want to appear mysterious, but I would like to chat with you on matters of some import. Could you be persuaded to sign the Official Secrets Act? Otherwise, we must drink our coffee, and you must depart with our having had what I hope will prove to be a most intriguing chat."

How was I going to resist that?

I willed myself to say 'no', and get out of there as smartly as my legs would carry me, but I heard myself saying, "I will sign."

He opened a leather folder on the table, and slid it over to me, while offering me a fountain pen that stood in a holder. I signed. And in came people with jugs of coffee, hot milk, cups, saucers, and biscuits. Ginger biscuits, in fact.

"Did mummy tell you about the ginger biscuits? How I like them?"

"No, actually. I only asked her permission to talk to you. Of course, you are of age, but families – well, you know."

"Well, yes. I am sure my mother appreciated that; and I do also. We'll see what happens when you come up against professor Fabian Madueno." I grinned.

"We must cross our bridges when we come to them," he smiled.

"And what is the bridge you wish to cross this afternoon?" I asked.

He served the biscuits and poured my coffee.

I sipped the coffee. It was good.

"I believe last night with my young friend, Bruce Chambers, you, er – rather, let us say, distanced yourself from any worries about war, about Hitler."

"So Bruce is one of your – er, your... crowd?"

"He was absolutely delighted to take you dancing, and, well, er, yes, ah... sound you out. Are you annoyed at all our flattering interest in you?"

I felt my anger rising, but the word 'flattering' smoothed my feelings.

He put his elbows on his knees, and steepled his fingers.

"We have something of a problem, you see. We have spies here in Britain, spying for the Germans."

I said indifferently, "You know who all the German nationals are–"

"Mainly, they're Irish. I imagine you know, many of the Irish don't overly care for us. Luckily, we seem to have most of them identified."

"So there is really not a problem," I said brightly.

"Well, of course, there's the obverse of the coin. We have the same interest in finding out what we can about Nazi Germany, but I'm going to confide in you what the State Secret is: We have no-one over there."

I froze.

"Suppose we set you up as a Press Photographer? Do you think you would enjoy working in Germany?"

"No, I would not, I'm awfully sorry. Pressmen don't have diplomatic immunity, and if we go to war, I'll be interned for the duration, and probably find myself in physical discomfort, and lose the best years of my life."

I reached out for my handbag, and got ready to rise.

"Oh, we'd never send you as an Englishwoman," he said easily, "We've been working on several new identities – our problem is to find people to fill them."

"And why have you considered me? I don't really take life very seriously – my discipline leaves everything to be desired. I'm not very adventurous – it's simply unbelievable that you're talking to me. It's clear you don't know a thing about me, because if you did…"

"We know an awful lot about you. You've been meeting a lot of new acquaintances recently…"

He paused, and that sank in.

"You've been spying on me!"

"Assessing you – with ever growing admiration, I might add."

I was about to explode, but the 'admiration' bit calmed me down. The man was impossible!

"You have a certain insouciance, a… certain fecklessness, irreverence, irresponsibility… it all makes you, er… very disarming… really invaluable traits."

He picked up his pipe, and cleaned it out.

I said finally, "It would be suicide. There is no cover story that could ever make me feel safe. The Gestapo would be digging into my background, month after month, while every day I knew the firing squad was 24 hours nearer."

"Would you care to hear about the, er… cover story, from a point of view, shall we say, of academic interest? I should hate to cut short our conversation; I am really enjoying your company."

I held my silence for a full minute.

Then I sighed. "Please tell me," I said, begrudging my time.

"As you know, South America is one of the world's less salubrious continents. Some countries are even less prepossessing than others. We British actually control one South American enclave – Belize. With the

6

blessing of British control, it should have advantages over its neighbours, but regretfully, it doesn't. We don't look after them very well. Howbeit. Let me tell you the story of Raimunda Hurtada.

"Now, I believe that although your name is Raimunda, everyone calls you Ray. In fact, you insist on it. Is that right?"

"You know perfectly well," I said dryly. "And please, you may call me Ray." He nodded gravely.

"Raimunda Consolación Hurtada was born in Stann Creek Belize, on March 3, 1919. Her parents – Alfredo, her father, and Rosa Heredia, her mother – died in a car crash on January 1 his year. We arranged for the daughter, who was called Consuelo – from Consolación, on the insistence of the mother, although the girl preferred Raimunda – to get an offer to go to Argentina. An offer we arranged. In Argentina, we offered her work in England, in an export firm, in Manchester, where she is today, with British nationality: She wrote letters to girl friends in Stann Creek, which we intercepted. When she received no answers, she desisted. Somerset House sent her a letter suggesting that if she wished to change her name to an English name, the correct forms were enclosed. She accepted the offer. She had made friends with a helpful English lady, who strongly advised her to do it.

"However, we now have a second Raimunda Hurtada, a cover identity, who went to Argentina, and there met the editor of a Buenos Aires newspaper, EL VIGILANTE. Mr. Felix Guinjaime is of an old English family, and his newspaper is most conservative. He is in close touch with us, and on our suggestion, he is now making firm friends in Buenos Aires with the Germans there – we English and Germans are Aryan brothers, and all that rot.

"Ray did not meet Guinjaime in Buenos Aires but in Posadas. Back in Stann Creek, Ray had worked in a shop, but her secret hobby was photography, although she never said anything to the neighbors and to friends. In Posadas, Guinjaime suggested she make a tour of North Argentina, sending him photos of the country seen through a stranger's eyes. These photos were published in EL VIGILANTE."

"And who took the photos?"

"That was easily arranged."

He puffed on his pipe.

"Meanwhile, our new Ray took out Argentinean nationality, which was expedited by her influential friend, the editor Felix Guinjaime. She has an Argentinean passport."

He showed the passport to Ray.

"As you see, it lacks only the photo. We have no passport photo of you."

"A South American working for the Gestapo visits Stann Creek, finds where Ray Hurtado lives, and shows my photo around…"

"There are similarities. We would touch up your photo slightly. But no one can go around Stann Creek asking questions, I can assure you of that. They would last barely thirty minutes. Can you imagine the job to find out just where they used to live?"

He puffed contentedly.

"After publishing those photos, Ray met Guinjaime in Buenos Aires, who gave her a boat ticket for Scandinavia. She sailed in April, as the stamp in her passport shows. After two months of photography there, EL VIGILANTE sent her to England to photograph British warplanes, and photos are already appearing in that newspaper.

"Were you to be interested—"

"How do I come to speak German and English?"

"You had a German lady and a Spanish lady who looked after you when you were born. The German lady is buried in Stann Creek, and her true papers can be supplied. The Spanish lady has disappeared into South America. In Belize they speak English. Your father had a building business. His death certificate shows 'Constructor'.

"We would send you for a week to Manchester, to learn something of Press photography. You will also see the technicalities of how the photos find their way to the Printing Press, how they are etched, in the newspaper workshops. Then a Wing Commander will be with you for another week, while you take photos of planes. On July 17, you will sail for Buenos Aires, where you will spend two weeks. Try to imitate the Argentinean accent. The newspaper will then put you on a ship for Bremen; you will have introductions in Germany, in fact, to Dr. Goebbels himself, who will welcome you as a pawn in his propaganda campaign."

I sat quietly, and then exploded.

"This is total drivel!" I cried. "Madness! The Germans are the most thorough, the most systematic – their Gestapo must be the most professional, the most… inhumanly efficient machine anyone has seen ever. They sit me down with a pad and ask me to describe everything about Belize, about my Argentinean trip and Swedish tour… I'll be on my way to the firing-squad before you can say boo to a goose!"

He waved his pipe in a distantly depreciatingly gesture. "Actually," he said, taking a puff, "We'll fly you down – or is it up? – to Belize for two or three days. We've done a thick dossier on Argentina and Sweden, and a lady will sail with you, and spend each day coaxing… oh! forgive me… coaching you, and cross-examining you. She is skilled at interrogation, you see."

I looked at him.

"I can't believe a word of this. Why didn't you contact me months ago, and send *me* on the Argentine and Swedish jaunts, and let *me* take the photos?"

8

He made an apologetic gesture with his pipe.

I looked at him narrowly.

"Of course!" I cried. "You *did* have somebody. Who did take all the photos? I suppose it was a 'she'. What happened to her?"

He puffed gently.

"You *are* clever," he said, with surprise. "You look very much like your mother. Do you get it from her?"

"Mummy's not clever, except at maths. She doesn't have much common sense, she's always at sea. Like my sister, Diana. She's always up in the air with those planes. The sharp one is daddy."

"Whomsoever," said Graham Bunton.

"What happened to her?" I demanded, coldly.

"She got sick."

"Sick?" I puzzled. "People get sick, then get better."

I considered him in silence.

"She had a nervous breakdown!" I cried triumphantly. "She couldn't take it."

He sat in silence, contentedly puffing at his pipe.

"And now you pick on me. Why?"

"Would you like some more coffee?"

I nodded, and he poured me another cup

"If it's too cold, I'll ring for more."

It was lukewarm, but would do.

"Those bloody photographic magazines," I said, amazed. "They suddenly all began asking us to send in postcard size photos of ourselves. You went through hundreds of photos; I was the best match. I was the closest lookalike to the candidate who let you down. How many more cards have you up your sleeve? Have you another one from a French or British possession in the Caribbean, who has joined a Chilean newspaper? The Gestapo will be on to us in a flash!"

He smiled. "Indeed, they would be. But of this cover story, there is only one."

"So I'm going to retrace her steps through dossiers, photos and coaching – that first candidate who is now well and safe at home again."

We sat in silence.

Then I said cunningly, "You don't know who has penetrated the British Secret Service. Russians, Germans, Hungarians… they'll steal all my details, and off I go to the firing squad."

"I can give you a codename, and destroy your file. I can say that Guiajaime has found a German who is anti-Nazi, and who is supplying him with the information."

"But you'd keep just one copy on my file in your safe. Then one day – someone else opens the safe, or you're ordered to…"

9

"No copies. I just said that. We could give you a codename like CARUSO. People would think you were a man."

"WAGNER," I said, and could have bitten off my tongue. He looked at me with sleepy triumph. "Makes it sound like a German, then," I said lamely.

He said, "As I explained, you would go first to a newspaper in Manchester, then sail.

I shook my head. "My parents would collapse. Suppose there *is* a war. They'd go mad, thinking of me over there, in hourly danger."

"I told your mother that you would be sent to USA, as photographer on a top-secret scientific project. They won't even let you write letters home, in case someone is using a code. There will be a dozen stereotyped letters you can chose from, with your name printed at the bottom."

I nodded reluctantly.

Fatigue swept over me, and I sank into a sort of despondency. With lassitude, I said, "And if I go to Belize, can I get into the house?"

"Consuelo Raimunda Hurtado has kept the house, for when she wants to go back. The wife of a British Colonial officer took a maternal interest in her. She helped her to Argentina, then immediately found this position in Manchester, which was far better, moneywise. This wife is, of course, one of ours. Every week, she sends her maid to open up the house on Riverside Drive, and air it, and clean it from top to bottom. You will sleep one night there, and spend twenty-four hours inside."

I sat wearily on the sofa.

"No," I said. "The whole thing is crazy. I want to live my life out... things you wouldn't understand. I know it sounds abominably trite, but I even want to have children. My answer is no."

The steamer from Buenos Aires docked at Bremenhaven late in August. My legs trembled as I walked down the gangplank, with a suitcase. After the heat and humidity of Belize, the Bremen sun felt wan, and the breeze sharp. In Buenos Aires, we had 'winter', but the liner had sailed across the Equator, and now high summer in Bremen was distinctly cool. In a large shed, we waited for our luggage from the hold, and when I found my other two suitcases, I loaded them on a trolley, and wheeled it to Passport Control. A man in a nasty uniform, went over my papers and told me, "If you are going to reside here, you must go through the Jewish Control."

I pushed my trolley through a swing door marked 'Jewish Inspection', and showed them my papers. There were four men in those threatening uniforms the Germans are so good at; two of the pestilent creatures looked like small-time grocers who had got above themselves and the other pair like impertinent delivery-men from some London fishmarket.

They wrote it all down, carefully.

Paternal grandfather, Diego Hurtado, born 1868, with baptism certificate from the Catholic Church in Tafi del Valle. In Argentina. Paternal grandmother, Paloma Vivanco, born 1871, with Catholic baptism certificate from Rosario de la Frontera. Maternal grandmother, Marta Saladrigas, born 1870, with Catholic baptism certificate from Santa Rosa de Conlara. Maternal grandfather, Javier Villena, born 1866 with Catholic baptism certificate from San Francisco de Monte de Oro. They handled the yellowing documents gently.

Then my 'father'. Alfredo Hurtado, born 1895, with Catholic baptism certificate from Buenos Aires. My mother, Rosa Villena, born 1897, with Catholic baptism certificate from Suipacha. All in Argentina.

My birth certificate. Born in Stann Creek, Belize, March 3, 1919.

Catholic baptism certificate from Belize city (I was really only 19, born in 1920).

They nodded approvingly, but suddenly one of the small grocers said, "Isn't Belize British?"

I nodded.

He went out, a returned with an officer in black uniform.

The office went over the papers.

"You are British."

I explained, "Suppose an Indian came here. Would you ask him was he British? The British occupy India, but that doesn't make the Indians British. In Belize, the English people in the British administration keep to themselves, as does the British Army."

"So the people in Belize are Spanish?"

"My father was, and so are a lot of people. But the main population is descended from black slaves who fled to Belize I don't know how many years ago."

"You don't know!"

"Well, these slaves were stranded on St. Vicente Island in the Caribbean in the 1600's. They intermarried with Carib Indians, and finally got to Central America. They migrated to Belize and especially to Stann Creek District last century. They're very independent and easy-going."

He wrinkled his nose. "Blacks."

"Every shade from black to white, actually."

"I see you sought a newspaper in white Argentina to work for among whites."

I was at once terrified, almost aghast at what I had let myself in for, yet at the same time an icy calm had gripped me.

He nodded at the others, and walked out. They let me go through to Customs.

I immediately declared my cameras, and explained that I was a Photographic Correspondent for the VIGILANTE in Buenos Aires.

They asked me, "Do you have any film?"

I shook my head.

"The Propaganda Ministry will supply you with film, which you must return to them, for them to develop, and they will give you the developed negatives after they have been censured. You are not allowed to own your own film in Germany."

I nodded.

They searched my cameras and luggage, and waved me on.

I went out to look for a taxi.

Prince Bernd Hohenlinden was waiting for me, and I recognized him instantly, from photos. He was tall, with sharp, fine-cut features, and eyes that saw everything. His suit was immaculately cut... perhaps too well cut for

12

English taste… and he looked younger, sprightlier, than his 48 years.

"Ray," he asked in a beautiful English accent.

"Prince Hohenlinden, what a wonderful surprise," I answered in German.

From now on, I was *Ray, Raimunda Hurtado.* How I was going to miss Raimunda Mudueno…

"I see you had a good trip," he said, crisply. "Sea air suits you. You look beautiful," and he looked at me with fatherly severity. "Are you frightened?"

I nodded.

A chauffeur stepped forward, took my trolley, and rolled it to a black Mercedes. We got in the back seat, and the Prince pushed the glass partition between ourselves and the driver closed.

"You can trust Volker, our driver, with your life," he told me, "But what Volker doesn't know, he can't reveal under torture."

The Mercedes drove slowly away from the dock.

"You don't feel I've come here to betray you?" I asked him, almost stuttering, not knowing how to put such unfamiliar thoughts, feeling the fool as I spoke.

His clear blue eyes looked frozen. "We are not betraying Germany," he said in his precise, marvelously cultivated English. He rasped, "We are betraying that guttersnipe, that Austrian street lout. We cannot betray Germany, because Hitler will destroy Germany, and we are trying to save it. The Kaiser tried to destroy us, although he carried Queen Victoria's blood. You know, there are stories of Victoria's mother – lots of them. The grooms and I don't know who else. What do you make of them?"

I looked at him horrified. "Never heard a word."

"You know what the Kaiser did?"

I gasped, "Millions of dead."

"There are stories of couplings we know of in our circles that have not gone into history books. At least the planes were cloth and wooden contraptions in the Kaiser's day, and didn't fly over Germany. But the machines we are building today… You English and Americans are joined by a common tongue, and when both of you come to bomb Hitler, the bombers WILL ALWAYS GET THROUGH. Germany will be flattened. And that includes Berlin. You are still willing to sacrifice your life?" I was not, but I nodded dumbly.

"We are an ancient family, and will survive. But between horse grooms and Austrian street louts, I don't think there's much to choose."

He gave a charming smile.

"I allowed myself to get carried away, and have been a poor host. Did you enjoy Belize?"

"A paradise. I couldn't tear myself away, knowing I was coming to

13

Nazi Germany. The seawater! Like clear, greenish glass. We swam at South Water Caye – they're offshore islands, part of the longest coral reef outside of Australia, so they say. The British Army has rigged heavy nets to keep out the sharks. They've got these giant whale sharks…"

He sat very erectly. "Now you're going to see human sharks such as you've never imagined. And you're going to do them unimaginable harm," he said, putting his hand over mine, to encourage me. "You have the rings?"

I showed him the ruby ring on my finger, and then twisting clockwise, unscrewed the top.

He nodded, very pleased. "You'll put your microdot photos there to carry them to the Argentinean Embassy in Berlin."

Then he asked, "And how is the head of the SIS?"

"The SIS?" I exclaimed.

He gave me a piercing look.

"The British Secret Service. You did not meet the Head? I won't tell you his name, and then you will show your innocence if it ever comes to interrogation or torture. You don't know what SIS stands for?"

"No."

"Then I won't tell you. How many people did you see?"

"One man."

He nodded. "Graham. I must bow to Graham. How delightfully English – an utter amateur, utterly unknown." He smiled again. "Don't you worry my dear; you are going to wield such a power as no one will ever believe."

He was in high, good humour.

* * *

We drove very fast, on a very wide road, separated by a thick railing from another wide road alongside, where cars drove the opposite way. I didn't see one traffic light – not one crossing where we had to stop.

The Prince told me, "We call this sort of road an *Autobahn*. You can drive hundreds of kilometres without a crossing to stop you. After the Great Depression, you had an economist in England called Keynes, who said the way out was to prime the economic pump by spending money on public projects. Governments listened to him, and it worked. Hitler's economic advisers told him to do the same, because we had hunger, unemployment and a most massive inflation. He ordered them to build the Autobahns, which began the German turnaround. But Hitler wasn't worried about pulling Germany out of its morass. He says that in wartime, one bomb on the railway tracks can block a railway line. One locomotive can pull fifty wagons loaded with war material, but a strafing plane can fill the locomotive with holes. You

14

can't stop tens of thousands of military trucks on the Autobahns – you make a hole in the Autobahn and the trucks simply detour onto other roads, and then come back on it again. You bomb an Autobahn bridge – the trucks detour to the next secondary bridge away from the Autobahn."

What a Teutonic, boring sort of conversation to offer a girl of 20! Was life going to be grim and earnest all day long in this country? No! I wasn't going to stand for this. I was getting on the first train to Paris.

My charming but didactic Prince, obviously with his mental arteries hardened beyond his 40-plus years, forged on, unstoppably. I was the wrong girl in the wrong place.

"The German people adore Hitler because he put them all back to work, with their pockets full of money… that is *real* money. But Hitler didn't just prime the economic pump with Autobahns. Unwittingly, he followed the precepts of your Mr. Keynes to perfection – he's spending public money on a huge armament industry. It's about four times more than the English and French governments estimate. The happy German people don't realize where he is leading them – to war and to death, to a new destruction of Germany. Germany is mighty – but it cannot fight England, France and America. Capitalist America will sign a Treaty with Communist Stalin, you'll see, and how ca we fight England, France, America – AND RUSSIA? Roosevelt is Machiavellian – that American President Roosevelt is cleverer than all the European leaders put together."

Oh, my goodness! What country was this?

Squirming for respite, in a small voice, I asked, "Please, what do you mean by 'prime the pump'?"

Gratified, Prince Bernd smiled.

"In earlier times, and today out in the country, you need to pump water by hand. The pump has leather seals, and if you don't use the pump, the leather dries and lets the air out when you pump. You don't get any water. So you pour in half a bucket of water to soak the leather to make it swell. And Hitler did just that."

He settled back comfortably on the rich upholstery.

I was only 'twenty' years-old, and my head was reeling. The roadside looked peaceful – fields and trees. Yet menace hung over the land that gave me a knot in my tummy. I couldn't handle this. In Berlin, I could catch a train to Paris…

"Did you get some training in Press photography?"

"They took me to a Manchester newspaper. We covered an auction, then a Trade Union meeting. Had to take the Union boss, sitting at a table, then the other leaders sitting along the table beside him. We covered a fire, and then took the Mayor standing with the building behind him. We photographed a woman who feeds stray cats. I had dinner with a Wing Commander, and photographed some of his Hurricane fighter planes."

"A sturdy workhorse, the Hurricane," said the Prince. "But it might not stand up very well to our best Messerschmitts."

"What do you do?" I asked.

"Raw material procurements," he said. "I'm one of the Heads at that show – very big place. Means I get to talk to a lot of people who matter in German war production. Tell me, how was the ship?"

I laughed hollowly.

"Both sailing to Buenos Aires and coming back, we had a cabin with a lounge and a sleeping cabin that were separate. Each part had two portholes, thank goodness. I sailed with a Miss Constance Ancram, and she had me at it eight hours a day. We'd work two hours, then go up on deck. Generally, we could open the portholes, and look at the sea and smell it. How she drilled me! She had these thick folders she worked from."

"So you know all about the Falls at Iguazú and Monconá, in Argentina?"

"The Monconá Falls are on the *Misiones* frontier with Brazil. They stretch for about three kilometres and are indescribably beautiful. The Iguazú Falls are about the same length, but the water falls 70 metres – there are about 300 falls there, with that great cloud of mist, and the rainbows. The frontier with Brazil goes along the Devil's Throat. The forest is incredible – thousands of different sorts of plants, huge trees, orchids, creepers, ferns–"

"Very good indeed," he said relief in his voice. "You were joking with me as you told it, but keep it fresh in our mind, always. Your life depends on it – it's what stands between you and torture… death."

I looked out at the landscape beyond the Autobahn. This was lunacy!

In the late afternoon, we reached Berlin, and drove to the suburb called Potsdam. We drove up the Neuer Garten road, with wide public gardens on one side, and pulled in to a short side street. A high wall led to large wooden gates; the chauffeur got out, unlocked them and pushed them open; we drove in. He got out again to close them, and drove us up a winding drive through wide lawns with trees, to a house built with severe German elegance. A wide arched doorway in the middle of the facade, and on each side floor-to-string course windows, divided into dozens of panes, crowned by flat pediments. On the second floor, there were more tall windows, but with pointed pediments, and across the rooftop a stark stone balustrade.

We got out stiffly, and the chauffeur opened the boot. A manservant came out and the Prince introduced me.

"This is Reinhard. He and his wife Valeria have been with us many a long year."

"Welcome to Berlin, Miss Raimunda," said Reinhard, a little lugubriously, yet his stare was frank. He relaxed faintly. "Anything you need, Miss, just say the word."

He and Volker carried my luggage into the house, and up a wide, curved staircase. We followed behind, and the Prince said, "As with Volker, you can trust your life with Reinhard and his wife."

Reinhard would know that I was a Press photographer from Buenos Aires, but he knew there was more to me than met the eye. Yet he approved... feelings I couldn't properly put into words.

Years ago, someone had decorated the bedroom in pale green, pale blue and pink, with Bavarian woodcarvings on the head of the bed and the wardrobe..

"It's... so restful," I exclaimed. "I love it."

The Prince smiled, and went to a carved door, opened it to show the bathroom.

"When you're ready, come downstairs. The family are impatient to meet you. My two daughters have stayed with Felix Guinjaime in Buenos Aires. They were there twice."

He left me with a stiff but gracious smile.

This was my cover story. They were returning my Editor's hospitality to them in Buenos Aires.

* * *

My legs trembled violently, and I dropped with a thump on the bed. My arms and hands shook, and I had a painful knot in my midriff.

I tried to think, but my head spun. I quietened down, and thought, horrified, how many people knew my secret. Graham Bunton had promised he would keep a file on WAGNER in his safe – no more. Yet Constance Ancram knew, and so did Felix Guinjaime in Buenos Aires. Prince Hohenlinden knew, and there was my contact in the Argentinean Embassy, Ruben Zorrequieta. FIVE people. How long would anything stay secret?

I calmed down. I had to give the microdots to Ruben, in the Argentinean Embassy, who would somehow forward them.

And how as to make the microdots? I needed a darkroom. I had two telescopic lenses, that could be turned backwards, but they wouldn't screw on to my cameras backwards. Prince Hohenlinden had to give me another camera and a third telescopic lens...

I changed my dress to something darker and more formal, but from Buenos Aires, cut with a Spanish flair; combed my hair, put on a dash of perfume, took a deep breath, and went out on to the landing; The entry below was floored in a very dark, highly polished wood. I went down the curving staircase, and at the bottom stopped. Disconcertingly, I was lost, but then I heard voices over to my right. I crossed to a tall, richly carved door, and knocked. No one heard me, so I opened it cautiously, feeling awfully rude. I looked in, and a tall young man in the uniform of a Major on the German High Command, very blond and an aristocrat to his fingertips, smiled and exclaimed, "Raimunda! Do come in and join us." He strode over quickly and offered his arm. I put my hand on it, and everyone turned to look at me. My escort said, "I'm Claus, the eldest and wayward son of the house. Welcome to the family."

He led me to a distinguished, severely dressed lady, and said, "This is my mother, Princess Jutta."

The Princess smiled. "He isn't wayward at all. He's much too serious, and sets us all an example," and everyone laughed. I made a slight curtsy, and the Princess took my hand and said, "Please, no formality. You must feel at home here with us." I warmed to her graciousness. "My husband didn't tell me how handsome you are. You are going to turn heads in Berlin."

"Oh, dear, no. I have come here to work," I said mischievously. "Felix Guinjaime demands all my devotion."

"Felix!" exclaimed a young lady, standing close by. Everyone laughed. "That story won't wash here," she laughed. She said, "I'm Doris," and we smiled at each other. I knew Claus was 25, his sister Doris 24 and the other sister Thoma, 23. Doris was tall, slim, blonde hair and the bluest eyes – finely cut bones to her face. The dress she wore was a marvel of cut and style, unmistakably Germanic in its simplicity. Doris took the arm of a dark-haired woman beside her and said, "My sister, Thoma."

Thoma was a classic, aristocratic beauty, dressed more carelessly than her sister, and she said, "I've been looking forward so much to meeting you. Doris and I have been twice to Buenos Aires, as guests of Felix, so we know something of Argentina. But nothing of Belize." She paused, waiting.

"A little paradise on earth," I confessed.

Claus stepped forward. "Ray, please let me introduce Richterin Prieguity, the fiancé of my sister Doris."

Richterin, in a Luftwaffe colonel's uniform, clicked his heels and gave me a grin. "You're a brave girl leaving an earthly paradise to come to our dear Hitler's Germany."

18

I grinned back. He was in Luftwaffe Technical Planning. "From fishing boats and a transparent sea to the technical marvels of Luftwaffe bombers," I joked.

He said meaningfully, "Our fighters are better than our bombers. Göring was building long-distance, four-engine bombers, but Hitler kept hounding the poor man. 'How many bombers have you built this month? How many? How many?' and drove Göring to desperation. So now he has to build two-engine planes with a lower ceiling, because they take only half the time."

My heart was thudding in my chest. A SIXTH person knew. And he was telling me to send that to London.

"How complicated," I said gaily. "Two engines – four engines – how bewildering," and everyone smiled, some in admiration, others knowingly. These people were far, far ahead of me.

Claus introduced me to another young man, wearing a uniform I didn't recognise. He was tall slim, breathtakingly good-looking in the German way, and he gave me a stiff smile.

Claus said, "Ray, meet Count Holger Zorndorf, a close friend of the family."

Graf Zorndorf clicked his heels. I gave him a melting smile, and unexpectedly, he smiled broadly.

"That's a handsome uniform," I said, and heartily regretted my dumb remark. I may have flushed.

"I'm in the Berlin Anti-Aircraft Artillery," he told me, with an unreadable smile. "All this fuss on my shoulders means I'm a Lieutenant Colonel. We call it Flak." He gave a very English sort of depreciatory shrug. "We have cannons of 88mm and 128mm, guided by a primitive sort of Radio Detection and Ranging apparatus. If the English come, we can shoot them down while they stay at 5,000 metres or lower."

I heard a singing in my ears, and felt dizzy.

The two sisters were looking at me intently.

They all knew. TEN people or MORE!

He went on, after a pause. "This radio detection – the English have nicknamed it Radar."

I shook my head. "It's all Greek to me."

I had to transmit this to London. How could I, if I didn't understand a bloody word?

Holger said, in a lazy, aristocratic drawl, "We Germans are rather good at engineering. So we send out electromagnetic impulses at one point two and twenty Hertz – well, you follow those numbers with nine zeros. Let me see... it was May 18, in 1904, in Cologne, and a certain Christian Hüslmeyer made the world's first demonstration. He put his gadget on the Hohenzoller Bridge

19

over the Rhine, and managed to bounce echoes off a tug, and make the echoes sound a bell. Oh dear, I must be boring you."

Now they were testing me. Damn them.

"It's fascinating," I said sweetly. "How far off was the tug?"

"Only a few hundred metres," he said, approvingly, and everyone moved closer, smiling. "Well, next thing, Hüslmeyer goes to Rotterdam and makes it work on a ship two kilometres away. He called it his Telemoviloscope, but it fell into oblivion. With the coming of our dear Hitler, all that changed. A certain Dr. Rudolf Kühnhold, director of the *Nachrichtenmittel Versuchs Anstalt* managed to get a wavelength of 13.5 cm at 2220 MHz. He tried it on the Hindenburg Pier at Kiel, but he wasn't lucky. He was working with 100 mWatts, and it wasn't nearly enough. But then the Dutch firm, Phillips, saved the day. They put on sale a thermoionic radio valve that broadcast 50 watts at tenths of metres. They called it the Magnetron.

"On March 20, 1934, they tried again at Kiel, on the battleship *Hessen*. No problems. So, in October, 1934, on Navy land at Peizerhaken, on Lübeck Bay, they put up this funny contraption, high in the air; and they register a boat twelve kilometres away! When the boat moves off, they keep getting an echo! Then they see a W-34 seaplane has just taken off. They were getting the seaplane. That night, at a celebratory party, Dr. Schultes suggests sending pulses instead of a constant signal. A constant signal heats up the Magnetron, while with short bursts, they can use, short, higher surges of electricity. He also suggested that when the waves bounced back, they could be registered on a Braun oscilograph – well, that's a thing called a cathode ray tube and then they could

measure the distances.

"Telefunken got onto it at Gross-Ziethen and Müggelsee, researching Ultra High

Frequency rays. Dr. Wilhelm Rhunge was in charge, and in 1935 he used this so-called radar on a Junkers JU 52. He was able to read the plane's position, speed, size and direction.

"The Navy came up with a system they called – well, they call *Freya*. The Luftwaffe, working with Telefunken, has a more advanced system they call *Wülrzburg*."

An elderly lady came into the room walking very erectly with a stick. She was imperious, and came straight to me, and looked me up and down critically.

Prince Bernd said, "Ray, allow me to present my mother-in-law, the Princess Gabriele Pfaffenhofen."

"You *are* good-looking," she said to me. "And you look awake. You and I shall have breakfast together tomorrow morning, by ourselves, and get to know each other better." She patted my hand. "Is that acceptable?"

"Oh yes," I stuttered. She asked me was it acceptable. What class, as our Yankee cousins would say?

After dinner, the Prince led me to his study, bookshelves up to the ceiling on the long walls. Floor-to-ceiling glass doors, with a score of panes, led to the back garden.

We walked along the inside wall; he reached into a shelf, and pulled open a door, books and all.

"This was a bathroom, which I have changed into a darkroom for you." He switched on a red light. Inside, facing us, were shelves, and a bench with developing dishes, and a stand with a Photo Enlarger. On the right hand side wall, were cupboards holding materials?

He ushered me in and closed the door.

"Now, while you're working, you naturally throw the bolt. You don't want someone coming in, letting in light, and spoiling what you're doing, do you? You see this bolt? And the handle soldered on to it? Look – I can turn the handle CLOCKWISE – and it *unscrews*. Suddenly, I can push it much further into the door frame…"

The left hand wall was bare, except for a vertical strip in the middle to fix the wall plaster in place. But now the Prince pushed, and half the wall swung inwards, on hinges hidden behind the vertical lath. He pushed it right around till it lay flat against the inside of the other half of the wall; he switched on a light, switched it off, and switched on a red lamp. On the far wall stood shelves, and a work bench with all the equipment – developing tank, rinsing tank, washing tank, drying tank, clips, chemicals, drop bottle, fan, frames, printing paper – while on the right-hand wall, on other shelves, he showed me cameras and telescopic lenses.

"This is where you can make your photographic micro dots. You see this stand, Mat and its baseboard. You take your film and put it into this Enlarger. But the lens unscrews, and this telescopic lens from the shelf can be clicked into place, backwards. Your larger telescopic lens will click into it, backwards also. Then you find that using this attachment, you can screw this telescopic lens backwards into yours. This bar on the upright – you adjust it to take the weight of the lens. Never, ever leave your telescopic lens here – without it, there is nothing suspicious here of handling microdot photography. Now, here alongside, you have a second stand. You see this

21

camera here – this is a tube camera, adapted to photographing documents. Today, in Germany, you cannot buy film, and you are not allowed to have any film which the Propaganda Ministry does not give you. You must take every inch of that film back to the Ministry for them to develop. They will hand the developed film back to you, censured, and then you can legitimately use the outside darkroom to develop your pictures. But I have a good supply of film, hidden in the house, which is full of hides and secret compartments; I will give you the film as you need it. If you don't know where the film is, you cannot incriminate yourself."

He rubbed his jaw.

"You send your pictures to Buenos Aires with the Diplomatic Bag, as I understand it?"

I nodded. "I deliver the microdots to the Embassy."

The Prince said, "Sometimes you must compose your own text. Everything you heard before dinner, you will have to write up yourself. I will help you, writing down all the details about the radar business. But often you will receive technical plans, and those you will have to photograph directly."

I shook my head. "I insist on sending everything in code. The Embassy courier could be drugged on his way to Spain or Lisbon, and the bag searched. If they find original documents, that's it. They will track down the person who 'borrowed' them. But code – that could be the Embassy reporting to the Argentinean government. The confusion remains for the Gestapo…"

The Prince gnawed his lip.

"Plans of tanks, planes, artillery – they are priceless."

"No one is going to build them in Britain or America. What they want to know are the performance figures, the strength of the armour, the numbers to be built, and where they will build them. I will never send *proof* of spying. If they find microdots, they can never be sure that some groups in the Embassy are conspiring against other groups, or that Argentinean communists are not sending out reports."

He nodded unhappily.

"Would you care to go to your room, and encode your report? I will call by in a few minutes, with details on the radar. Can you remember the rest of it – the Flak, the bomber ceilings, and Göring's woes?"

"I remember."

"Another thing. There are bells at the three doorways to the house. If we get unwelcome visitors, the bells will sound through the house. If you hear a bell in here, dismantle your lens, take your telescopic lens and close the door. Screw tight the handle. Put your lens in your handbag, and go to work in the outer darkroom with ordinary work."

My code used a copy of *Lorna Doone*, which the Prince had in his library. He had hundreds of books in English. Written by R.D. Blackmore, my copy was illustrated by Wilmot Lunt, and published about 25 years ago. Graham Bunton had the same edition. To encode I wrote 45/7. That meant page 45, seventh line. I took the first five letters...

The paragraph read: 'But all this time while I was roving over the hills or about the farm...'

So I took, BUT AL from 'But all...' and wrote out the rest of the alphabet, omitting B, U, T, A, and L.

B	U	T	A	L	
C	D	E	F	G	
H	I	J	K	M	
N	O	P	Q	R	
S	V	W	X	*	* = Y, Z

Now I repeated the vertical first line but on the right-hand side; and the top line on the bottom.

B	U	T	A	L	B	
C	D	E	F	G	C	
H	I	J	K	M	H	
N	O	P	Q	R	N	
S	V	W	X	*	S	* = Y, Z
B	U	T	A	L	B	

My message began: 'anti air artillery', so I took *A* as being at the bottom right-hand corner of a square. For example...

<u>W</u>	X		<u>M</u>	H	
T	<u>A</u>	ie: A = W	R	<u>N</u>	ie: N = M

Every five letters, I made a break, to continue with another group of five:

W M V C W C K,
a n t i a i r   and so on.

For a full stop, take top left-hand letter, in this case 'B'. Pair it with any letter that is not the 'C' directly below, its natural pair. For a comma, take the first letter on the second line, in this case 'C' and pair it with any letter that is not 'H', its natural pair just below.

* * *

They transmitted the message in groups of five. Who got the message at the other end broke it up into lines of 18 letters – four groups of five minus two letters. The groups of five were to mislead.

The Prince knocked on my door, and handed me the stuff on 'radar', written in a copperplate hand.

I finished encoding, and took out a German portable typewriter from my cupboard. Typing, I always felt, was demeaning, with so many millions of women eking out a straitened living at the machines, but I had mastered a hunt and peck way of it, so now I typed out a letter to Felix, my editor, praising Germany, should the letter fall into the wrong hands.

Downstairs, in the darkroom, I photographed my encoded sheets in microdot. I took down a sapphire ring with me, and unscrewed the stone. Inside was a fine, razor-sharp tube, which fitted into a metal guide. Putting a coin over the top end, I pressed down sharply, lifted out the tube, and nestling inside was my microdot. I unscrewed one of my rings – this one was garnet – and with a long pin, gently pushed the microdot out of the tip of the tube, into the cavity under the garnet stone. I had four encoded pages, which gave me four microdots. A small vize held the ring upright. I screwed the stone back onto the ring – at the Argentinean Embassy, I would exchange the ring for an identical one, with a certain Ruben Zorrequieta. Would he put the microdots on my letter to the Editor? I hoped not; I was praying he had some other game worked out.

I dragged myself upstairs, and fell into bed, exhausted.

* * *

The maid woke me at half-past-eight, pulling open the drapes. She told me, "The Princess Pfaffenhofen expects you for breakfast in the summer house, at quarter-past-nine."

"Goodness. Where is that?"

"If you care to ring, I'll come and show you the way." The maid showed me a bell-push on the night table.

I stumbled out of bed, and rushed to the bathroom for a hot shower. I came out and sorted through my dresses in a nervous flurry, but for the life of me couldn't decide what to put on. I finally chose a summery, breakfast-y floral skirt with a peasant blouse, and combed my hair this way and that, getting more and more exasperated with what the mirror showed me. I

24

wondered whether a touch of Cologne Water would be allowed so early in the day, and decided not to.

The maid showed me down, and I found the Princess at a metal garden table, among foliage of plants in huge wooden tubs. On a beautifully starched tablecloth was set out a silver breakfast service.

"Sit down, my dear," said the Princess comfortably. "How rested you look. I can see you have had a good night."

Her grey hair was impeccably coiffured, and her dark grey dress had been ironed without starch, a concession to the August 'heat' of Potsdam district.

"Do you feel the heat?" she asked me.

"After Belize, this is pleasantly cool," I laughed. "But it was colder in Buenos Aires, because they're in their winter. On the ship crossing, we crossed the Equator, so I found myself sweltering again."

"Would you like bacon and eggs? Perhaps with a sausage or two?"

"I'm ravenous," I confessed, "But I don't dare put on weight. Bacon with one egg, perhaps."

"And toast? And jam? And white coffee?"

My mouth watered in an unladylike manner.

The Princess rang a bell, spoke to the maid, and in a few minutes the food was set before us. I had to hold myself from devouring the food, from bolting it down.

"I don't know what's the matter with me. I don't usually have an appetite like this."

"Nerves, just nerves. Your nerves have been burning up your body's reserves. I want to tell you how happy I am to have you here. My son-in-law tells me that you can do incalculable harm to Hitler, that guttersnipe."

I paused, uncertain.

"Say it," she commanded.

"I never realized so many people would know..."

"Think nothing of it. You need them to help you, because without them you can do nothing. You are dealing with families who have held aristocratic rank, titles, for hundreds of years. Families who are the elite of Germany," said the old lady, firmly. "My family held a Principality for hundreds of years, and we looked after our people personally. We knew their names. That was before Bismark came along, at the time I was born. In 1868, he was ready to go to war with France, just to unite Germany and undo *our* power, that of the great aristocrats. The railways, you know. That appalling man understood railways – that they were a military weapon that would let him move a million men to the French frontier in days. He panicked Germany with the French business, and in 1871, Germany *was* united, and he was the First Chancellor. Until the Kaiser dumped him. But it suited the Kaiser's ambitions all too well. Now we great families must look out for all

Germany. All its young people are our charge, and we are failing. Five million Germans will die. One million Englishmen and Frenchmen. Twenty million Russians. It's going to be a holocaust. Do you know that word?"

"Very apt. The fiery sacrifice. You are talking about almost thirty million dead, for heaven's sake."

"It's coming. Germany will be destroyed. Will be devastated. Will be flattened. And we of the great families who hold Germany in our charge cannot stop it. Only when British and American troops occupy Germany, put all those Nazis before firing squads – although I would ignominiously *hang* the lot of them – will democracy come back to this land. Perhaps by then our aristocratic influence will be done or perhaps not, because we can always work behind the thrones."

I began on my toast, with hot white coffee. I couldn't take all this in. I'd never had a conversation remotely like this in London, and my mind was at a loss trying to keep up with her.

We sat in silence.

Finally, I ventured, "I'm afraid of being recognized. In London, once my photo appeared in *LADY* and another time in *COUNTRY LIFE*."

The Princess pursed her lips and looked at me thoughtfully.

"Now you look a cross between an English and an Argentinean girl. You must manage to look more German… mmm. Luckily, your clothes are all from Argentina. I think that perhaps… mmm… tie your hair back in a bun, German-style. You have a lovely neck, so you'll be able to show it. Try to think of yourself as a German maiden who is trying to signal to all men, 'Look, I'll make a wonderful Hausfrau. Come and get me.' You have that independent, challenging English girl look. Try to be more submissive – well, you know what I mean. Look more German, *seem* more submissive. For someone to recognize you from a photo, you have to look almost exactly as you were in the photo, same mood. Of course, police photos – that's another matter. They are trained and experienced in picking up people from quite bad photos – but they are *alert*, they are *watching*."

I nodded and felt relieved.

Another silence followed, and grew a bit uncomfortable for me. Older people can sit contentedly through long silences.

I joked, "Your son-in-law has strong feelings against the Kaiser, and says his lineage is tainted."

Princess Gabriele snorted. "And so it was. And the Prince may well speak out, because our lineage is not. I think Queen Victoria's mother was Belgian, I'm not sure, but, oh dear, how that woman slept around. Do you know what the word porphyry means?"

I shook my head, and she said, "Porphyra is a Greek word for purple dye. Porphyogenite meant a son of a Byzantine Empress born in the porphyry room of the Empress – a son born to the purple. But there is a

26

porphyry disease where the urine comes out the colour of porphyry rock – reddish-purple. It often causes madness. Charles the First of England – the one whose head Cromwell cut off – had a sister who married a Prince of the Hannoverian Palatinate. He was a bearer of the disease, although he didn't have it himself. The Stuarts didn't carry the disease, and after the English threw out the Catholic Stuart, James the Second, you brought in a King from Holland. When his daughter died without succession, you brought in George the First, descendent of that sister of Charles the First who married the Hannoverian Prince. George the First carried the porphyry disease, and his grandson, George the Third actually went mad from it. Well, one of the Georges, I'm not sure which one. King William, Victoria's supposed father, carried the disease. All the descendants of the brothers and sisters of King William suffer porphyry to this day. But of the hundreds of descendants of Queen Victoria, not one has the disease."

"That doesn't mean anything!"

"I'm afraid it does, because the disease strikes a minimum of fifteen people in every hundred, and often more. But here we have not one person in hundreds–"

I shook my head.

The Princess cackled happily. "Never fear. In this house, you are among blue-bloods, not a shadow of doubt. No hostler's offspring here."

She poured us more coffee.

"How old is mankind?" she asked me. "One million, two million years? Man is born with three instincts and one urge. The urge is to procreate. The first instinct is to kill. The second, to eat your enemy. Have no doubt about it – for two million years, man has been a cannibal. If you can't kill and eat another man, the third instinct is to steal his food, his weapons and his women. About seven thousand years ago, civilization came. We built cities, discovered the wheel. In the first civilizations, in the Fertile Crescent, they skinned their enemies alive – a frustrated cannibal instinct, I suppose. But they did stop eating them. Today, we have made a second advance, after a long seven thousand years. Democracy. What do you think democracy is, Ray?"

"Everybody's equal."

"Stuff and nonsense, my girl. Listen to what I say – five men in a hundred are born to goodness. The other ninety-five are born with these simian instincts – instincts inherited from chimpanzees and gorillas. Five of those men are born to lead. The other ninety are weak followers. The leaders will excite the other ninety to kill and steal because all the leaders want to kill and steal – but Democracy stops them. Democracy has checks and balances, which democratic leaders will try to dismantle. But they don't stay in power long enough. They are tyrants, all of them, but after four or eight years, they are voted out. Not so Hitler. He will lead the German people to unimaginable

27

baseness, urge them to kill and kill – and have them killed in their turn by the millions. The democracies should have stopped him – but democratic leaders can't. Those weak populations of voters don't see their danger. When they vote for a leader, they judge his face, the speeches he makes at rallies, or on the wireless. They don't look for *goodness*, for those good five men in every hundred. They don't look for *nobility*. They see a murdering cannibal and thief, and realize he is identical to themselves, so they vote for him."

I was ready to topple from my chair.

The Princess patted my hand, reassuringly.

"You think about it. Reflect. But now, my dear, I believe you have to go to the Propaganda Ministry, to make yourself known. They will give you film and take you somewhere, and tell you where to point your camera."

She patted her lips with an embroidered serviette.

I pulled my blonde hair back in a submissive Fräulein bun, and eagerly accepted Volker's offer to drive me to the Propaganda building on the other side of Berlin, in the Wilhelmstrasse, in front of the Foreign Ministry and the Reichskanzlei, between Pariser Platz and Vossstrasse. In the car, I worried about what I knew of Dr. Joseph Paul Goebbels, the lame demon who had put Hitler in power with his propaganda campaign, and unleashed this hell. Born in 1897, a childhood illness crippled his left leg and with his short stature, he didn't attract women. But he pursued them relentlessly, because women are irresistibly drawn to power, and got into so many scandals that his wife almost divorced him. Hitler had to step in. That was last year – the scandal over the Czech actress Lida Baarova. He lived in luxury, with young actresses around him. The Ministry paid his bills, and his position drew the young women. Now in power, Hitler didn't need him as before, but he was Berlin Party Gauleiter and a Reich Minister. Graham Bunton told me he broadcasted non-stop, but his vituperative language carried no weight – not like the BBC, that he wanted to outshine. Graham said that if war came, the military communiqués would count, not Goebbels blather, and he was sure the communiqués would be taken out of Goebbel's hands.

Of strict Roman Catholic parents, the father a manual worker, he studied literature, history, Germanics and philosophy at the universities of Freiburg, Bonn, Würzburg, Cologne and Munich. At Heidleberg, he studied Goethe and Shakespeare with the famed Jewish professor Freidrich Gundolf, but Goebbels did not impress him, and Gundolf didn't admit Goebbels to a select academic circle. Luckily for Gundolf, he died in 1931.

Goebbels waded into the *embroglio* between the Strasser brothers and Hitler on how much socialism the Nazi Party – the National Socialist movement – needed. He made his demand that 'the bourgeois Adolf Hitler shall be expelled from the National Socialist Party.' In 1926, he saw the light, changed his tune and worshiped Hitler 'as either Christ or St., John.' This, I thought wearily, changed world history. He wrote in his Diary, 'Hitler, I love you!' And he won the elections for Hitler.

He rivaled Hitler as a speaker, with his resonant, bass voice coming out of that skinny face and skinny neck. Always in a trench coat too big for him, he organised mass meetings and demonstrations, and flooded Germany with his vitriol, in newspapers and on the wireless. He introduced the 'Heil Hitler' greeting.

Hitler gave him the Berlin SA, the *Sturmabteilung* or Brownshirts, unemployed ex-soldiers, and with these murderous street-fighters, he fought the Jews and communists; and the city was his.

In 1933, Hitler brought him into the Cabinet, and Goebbels formed the Reich Ministry of Information and Propaganda. He took over Germany's world famous film industry, but now for me the films are a bit flat. Most of Germany's great artists fled, including Thomas Mann; I know Richard Strauss and the conductor Furtwängler are still here.

He had manufactured cheap wireless sets, and here in Berlin had a new thing called television. It's like motion pictures, but on a small screen in your house; you can only see it in Berlin. He talks to all Germany on these radio sets.

He studied American advertising exhaustively, and applied every dirty trick our Yankee cousins use to sell lavatory paper, washing powders, and the latest car to roll out of the factory. He said people could be turned any way you wanted them to, especially when they didn't realize they were listening to propaganda, and not the truth. Outside of Germany, it seems to me that he's failing dismally.

So this is the man whom Hitler named in 1929 as *Reichspropagandaleiter der NSDAP* or Reich head of propaganda for the Nazi Party, and who reigned in the building where our Mercedes came to a stop.

* * *

An armed guard stopped me, and with as severe a mien as I could muster, I told him importantly that I was the photo correspondent of EL VIGILANTE in Argentina, and had come to present my credentials. I should have been terrified, venturing into this Nazi stronghold, but it was a bit of a lark. The guard sent me to a desk, where an unsmiling woman, also wearing a bun, told me to sit.

As I waited, looking about the foyer, a tall young man bounded in. He had a classical face, with a high, domed, bald forehead that gave him an air of intellectual distinction which women must have swooned over – as I began to. His eyes were sincere and clever under strong eyebrows. He saw me, stopped, and glory be, he examined me and crossed over to my side. I gazed up at him, transfixed.

"Hello!" he exclaimed. Are you new here? You're not German, are you?"

So much for my hair in a bun.

"I'm from Argentina," I croaked, then got my voice under firm control. "Photographic correspondent."

"My name is Adam, Adam von Trott zu Solz, and I've just joined our distinguished Foreign Service in that musty building across the street. When they finish giving you the runaround here, why don't you come over? We can have lunch together. What languages to you speak?"

"English and Spanish."

He said in English, in a beautiful Oxford accent, "Oh, I say, how jolly. You've been in England, I suppose, what?"

"No such luck," I lied. I wasn't going to talk about 'photographing' the 'Hurricanes' for 'two weeks' to anyone.

"You speak it marvelously well, you mystery woman. You must tell me how you learnt it. Cheerio! See you later."

The woman at the desk gave him a melting smile, as he hurried by her, and went up the stairs.

A young lady came out of the lift, smiled at me, and asked me to accompany her. We went up a couple of flights, along a corridor and into an office where four people were working at tables. She introduced me to a hefty, florid Herr Schneppen, who told me to sit. He took my credentials, and went through them carefully, taking notes.

Then he looked up, and with a serious expression, said, "Welcome to Germany." He added, "Do you have any plans as to what you want to photograph?"

"I've just arrived," I said.

"Generally speaking, we will suggest what we would like to see published in Argentina. You are not obliged to do what we would prefer, but we would appreciate your cooperation. If you have ideas, where possible tell me first. If there is no time for that, simply bring your film here, for the censorship to decide. How will you get your prints to Argentina – or will you send the film?"

I said, "I prefer to send the prints. Often, I take a shot, but I use only one corner of it, to heighten dramatic effect."

He nodded, with a slight, approving smile.

"The Argentinean Embassy will help me, sending the prints in their diplomatic bag."

"Excellent," he said, and then with curiosity he asked me, "In time of war – and let us hope there will be no war – how will the diplomatic courier travel?"

"By train to Spain and Portugal, or crossing over to Sweden, Norway or Finland, to catch a steamer sailing under a neutral flag. After publishing the pictures, EL VIGILANTE will sell them to an Agency that distributes all over South America."

His eyes lit up. "Marvelous!" he exclaimed. "The Ministry will be very happy with your coming here."

I said carefully, "I have a hobby – portrait photos. I would like to make portraits of the Nazi leadership. Copies would be for the leaders to keep," I added hastily, "And other copies would be published in the newspapers."

He smiled ironically. "So you're going to put Heinrich Hoffmann out of business."

"Hoffmann?"

"Photographer to the Party since 1921. His photos of the 1923 Munich Beer Hall Putsch are the only ones. He introduced Eva Braun to Hitler," he added warningly. "He's published books of his photos."

I jiggled my shoulders. "No two people ever cook alike. The food always tastes different."

"Ah! How true!" He stirred in his chair. "So you want to meet Dr. Goebbels?" he said slyly.

I shrugged.

"Before anything else, we have refugees here in Berlin from the Civil War in Spain. Germans and Spanish. That should interest South America. They're housed in an old school. If I send someone with you, could you go around there now? I take it that your cameras are in that big bag?"

I found women and children. Some were German wives married to Spanish husbands; or German wives married to Germans; or Spanish wives married to Germans. As I took the photos, I wrote down their names, and asked where their husbands were.

Some men were in the army; others had found jobs. Speaking in

Spanish, which my woman escort from the Ministry didn't seem to understand, I asked each time, "Can't you find an apartment?"

"My husband gets about 300 marks. With dependants, tax is only a 40 marks, but 260 marks aren't much to live on. You can't pay rent on that."

Another woman said, "Our house was blown up by a bomb. We lived in Barcelona, and the Italian bombers bombed and bombed it."

I thought, THE BOMBERS WILL ALWAYS GET THROUGH. I thought of Guernica. "So Barcelona is no more. It was flattened?"

The woman said impatiently, "No, heavens no! Barcelona's still there. The bombs knocked down a building, or wrecked one wall. One bomb even flattened a six-storey place. I would never have believed it possible."

"But Barcelona's still standing?"

"Of course it is. They hit a building here, a block of flats there, and killed about 2,000 people. Bombing is war against ordinary people, especially women and children. They didn't hit any factories, and didn't kill any soldiers in Barcelona, as far as I know."

I turned away, stunned, but breathed a sigh of relief. Berlin would not be flattened. And if Graham Bunton had any influence, he would keep the bombers away from Neuer Garten park and the buildings close to it, in Potsdam.

I saw a girl of four years, with a sad face, and shot her twice. Her mother told me they came from Valencia. She told me, "Little Elfie, here, went to another girl's party yesterday. Lovely house. The little friend had a lot of dolls you can dress and undress, and when Elfie came home, she had dolls' clothes hidden in her pockets. We went back to the house. I made Elfie say she was sorry, and give back the clothes."

I knelt down. "Do you like dolls?" I said. The girl nodded. "Tomorrow, I'll send some to you."

I wrote down her full name. I felt fierce.

* * *

Outside, in the street, I carefully wrote down the address.

We drove back to the Ministry.

Mr. Schneppen was waiting for us, and took us to the darkrooms; we waited in the red light, while the technicians worked, talking about Argentina and Germany, then went outside, and they served us coffee. Herr Schneppen had a strict smile for so rotund a man; he is one very serious German, but enjoys a joke.

They finally came out with the prints, and he perused them intently. "Good," he said. We went back to his office, and he phoned from his desk. After a short exchange of words, he hung up, turned to me and said, "Dr.

32

Goebbels will see you now."

He took me up personally; inside Goebbels' huge office, he introduced me, and left.

The little man with his tight, thin face, protruding nose and chin, wide, receding forehead with the thick hairline far back, gave me an intense look that stripped the clothes from my breasts; his eyes stripped naked my crotch, then swept side to side measuring my hips. They snapped back to my face.

"You are very good-looking." His voice boomed in the big room. He came round from behind his desk, limping quickly, and showed me to a sofa. He sat facing me in an armchair.

"You have a lovely neck."

I didn't know what to say, but watched the expressions that flickered, bewilderingly, across his face.

"I am a newspaper photographer, but I love doing portraits. Would you allow me to do some portrait photos of you? They could be published all over South America."

"Ah," he said. "Perhaps we could have dinner together tonight, and you bring your cameras."

"With you and your wife and children! That would be lovely!"

He blinked once, then considered me with hooded eyes.

I knew his wife, Magda Quant, had divorced a Jewish businessman, and her six children were Hitler's favorites at *Berchtesgaden*.

"My wife does not like to be photographed," he said dryly. "But perhaps the two of us."

"I'm Spanish," I said severely. "I'm sorry, but we are brought up with a strict Catholic morality."

"My parents were Roman Catholics, so I understand." His eyes were cold. "You are from Belize, which is British."

"The British administrators and Army live their lives apart from the people."

"The people are Spanish?"

"There are Spanish, Indians, and descendants of black slaves who escaped from St. Vincent Island. English people who have intermarried with them."

"My God! Mixed blood! The worst that can happen! But you are clearly of pure blood. You could be Aryan. Do you know about Arthur, Comte de Gobineau?"

He was going to instruct my mind instead of invading my body, "No, nothing. Could I take shots of you while you talk?"

He smiled. "Go ahead."

There was so much I wanted to capture in his face.

His face was contradictory, with a look that was piercing, then atavistic; a thug who fought with the sheer intelligence in his features; the face of an unstable lunatic who tried to wipe clean his lineaments with the erudite intellectual.

Goebbels said smoothly, "The Comte was a French diplomat, born in 1816 to an old aristocratic family. Alexis de Tocqueville, the French Foreign Minister, made Gobineau head of his secretariat in 1848-1849. De Tocqueville fell, and Gobineau secured diplomatic posts in Bern, Hannover, Frankfurt, Teheran, Athens, Rio de Janeiro, and Stockholm. That let him observe many races of men. He left Stockholm in 1877 and lived the rest of his life in Rome. Gobineau's misfortune was that he was an aristocrat in an age when the tide was flowing away from aristocracy. He published extensively, but his fellow Frenchmen couldn't make up their minds about him – whether he was a charlatan or a startling new thinker. He was the latter, and now he is the dominant philosopher of the twentieth century, guiding its fate. Because above all else, he was a racist. De Tocqueville told him: 'At best your fame will be an echo from across the Rhine.' "

I moved slowly, taking photos very slowly.

"It was a true prediction, but here in Germany, Gobineau is no echo – he is a thunderous voice, guiding us.

"His most important work is his *Essai sur l'inegalite des races humaines*, published in parts in 1853 and 1855. Incredibly, in France they took no notice of it. In this work, Gobineau tells us that all human races are unequal – in their physical make-up and in their minds. But a pure, primordial race degenerates when foreigners of other races pour in and mix their blood with the original nation."

"I'm listening," I said, "but now could you look towards the window."

He went on, "The belief in the inequality of races is one of the oldest ideas in the world. In every age, everyone knew it was true. It is only the races who cut themselves off from defilement who built civilizations. Gobineau asked us, very cleverly, why didn't the North American Indians, living on a continent of great wealth, invent printing or the steam engine? If they have a brain as good as an Englishman's which stayed undeveloped, why didn't they build a civilization? Then he asked whether the inferiority of some races was because of the infertility of the earth or the harshness of the climate. He showed this was not so – the difference springs always from the brains, from biology. He told us that civilization is thanks to a mixture of materialism and intellectuality, of a complex swirl of ideas that mix some people's morality with wealth and political organization. He said our civilization arose from the mixing of the blood of Germanic tribes with ancient races. The richness of the inventions which have made possible our modern societies spring from our Germanic ancestors.

"He rejected the ideas of earlier writers who said many races filled the world – he recognized three only. The White Caucasian and Semitic; the Black Hamitic; and the Yellow Altaic, Finnish, Tartar and Mongol. He told us

34

that races betray different muscle strengths and beauty. The Englishman's fist is stronger than that of all other Europeans; the French and Spanish are far better at standing up to privations and exhaustion. To quote him, 'The French have certain physical qualities that are better than those of the Germans, which allow them to withstand with impunity the snows of Russia as well as the burning sands of Egypt. Here, I don't agree with him. The German soldier is the world's master. The French did not brave with impunity the snows of Russia, because 600,000 of them died, although mainly from disease.

"Gobineau has taught us that the White race is superior to the others, and among the White race, the Aryan stands supreme. All civilizations have come from the White race, and no civilization can stand without the Whites. Europe shows no brilliant civilization but that the Aryans do not stand out in it.

"Great civilizations need the most noble blood. But when inferior races come in and impregnate noble women, the civilizations degenerate and are swept to the dust heap of history.

"In Germany, we have seen that Gobineau is a colossus who bestrides this century. Richard Wagner espoused him. Ludwig Schemann wrote, 'All good Germans consider Gobineau as one of the most extraordinary men of the nineteenth century, one of the greatest God-inspired heroes, saviors to set us free, who He has sent since ancient times'. Did you see the greatness of Bismark's Second Reich? What was that but our racial supremacy!

"His ideas were seized upon by Alfred Rosenberg and Hitler himself in *Mein Kampf*. Rosenberg published *The Myth of the Twentieth Century* and in his book recognized the superiority of the Germanic Nordic race, and said we must keep it from Etrusco-Syrio-Judaeo-Asiatic-Catholic ascendancy."

I was getting a nagging feeling that he wanted me to know that, if he couldn't get me into bed, it didn't matter to him as I would only defile his seed.

I took another photograph.

He went on, "In *Mein Kampf*, Hitler taught us that the State had to centre its concern on race and on keeping the race pure. *Mein Kampf* does not hesitate to borrow from from Gobineau's *Essai* – Hitler says straight out that races are 'culture bearing' and 'culture destroying'. We have founded the Third Reich on Gobineau's teachings."

I said, "I've finished." I rolled the film, and gave him the spool.

"The artistry of photo portraiture," I told him, "Often lies in touching up the film itself with a dark pencil. If you choose some prints, could you let me have the film to touch it up?"

He smiled. "I'll send the film to you at Prince Hohenlinden's home. Please make the changes you wish, print them, and leave the prints in a sealed envelope with Herr Schneppen. I will have the film developed now, and we shall see what surprises you have for me."

He pressed a bell, and ushered me courteously to the door.

I walked down the stairs instead of taking the lift, to get myself under control. Pure blooded races were inbreeding!

That's what it was – *inbreeding!* My father's hobby was the study of inbreeding and hybrids – he would get on that hobby-horse and bore me to death. A bee in his bonnet. I should have listened. He said hybrids had vigor and inbreeding degenerated. Once he talked about the stunning beauty of Euroasiatic women – where the father was an Irish locomotive driver and the mother a Hindu, in India; or in Malaya, an English father and the mother a Malayan; or in China, a Scots engineer for father and the mother Chinese; in Japan, an American father and an Japanese mother; or in Batavia, a Dutch father with a Batavian mother. Their beauty, he said, took men's breath away, which earned a scowl from my mother. Then he said to look at me – the offspring of a Spaniard and German. The most beautiful girl in England, he called me. How I wish I could have had that notoriety. They would never have chosen me to send to Germany.

I left the building, and crossed over to the foreign office. I told the armed guard I wanted to see Adam von Trott zu Solz. They sat me in the foyer, and took my identity document.

After a few minutes, Adam appeared with another man, also in his thirties.

Adam said, "Have you finished with the *Leopold Palast?* Was it a lot of bosh?"

His companion said in German, "That's enough of showing off. In German please, so I can follow." He smiled at me engagingly. "Not that it matters," he told me. "Adam's a very superficial thinker. You'll find out how much you enjoy talking to me." The smile reached his eyes.

"Do you want to talk or to eat?" Adam asked me.

"I'm hungry," I confessed. "And I need to sit down with a glass of wine."

They led me down the Wilhelmstrasse to a restaurant in the Leipzigerstrasse.

"Here, we're close to Gestapo headquarters," joked the friend. He quoted two lines of poetry:

"There are times when lunacy prevails.
And then it's the best heads that get the axe."

"Who wrote that?" I asked.

"I did," he said. "I am Albrecht Haushofer. Adam tells me your name is Raimunda."

"Yes," I said.

"Adam is very distinguished company," he told me in a conspiratory voice. "He was a Rhodes Scholar. In 1931 he went to Mansfield College at

36

Oxford, and then to Balliol as a Rhodes Scholar. His grandmother was the granddaughter of the first Chief Justice of the United States. His father used to be the Prussian Minister of Education."

I batted my eyes at them.

"Poor little me," I pretended to gasp. "All I know is how to read and write."

They laughed, and Adam said, "How long have you been here?"

I said, "It seems a couple of years, but really, I do believe I arrived just yesterday."

I told them about myself.

"You're staying at the Prince's home! Amazing!"

I said to Adam, "Are you a poet too?"

Albrecht said, "Four years ago, he published a new edition of Heinrich von Kleist, the poet who attacked Napoleon's tyranny. Adam compared that tyranny to today's tyranny in Germany, and wrote, 'the divine destiny of man has been trampled down into the dust.' "

I looked about me in fright. I said, "Be careful, please. I am sure the Gestapo is watching me, and if they hear you, they'll arrest you."

They both laughed.

"I'm in the Foreign Ministry, and in the *Abwehr*. Albrecht will join the Foreign Ministry any day now."

"What is the *Abwehr*?"

"The Secret Service."

I remembered Miss Ancram on the ship, and said hesitantly, "Once I read in Buenos Aires that the head of that is SS General Jokst."

"Those people are in the Berkaerstrasse in Schmargendorf, a West Berlin suburb. They guard them like Fort Knox, with Waffen SS. They are the Secret Service, while we of the *Abwehr* are military intelligence. They consider us creaky and old-fashioned. They do foreign spying – they forge passports, have the *Funkspeil* for radioing agents in the field. There's no end to the mischief they get up to. The Secret Service, or SB, owes its allegiance to the Gestapo, that is, the SS, or Secret Police, who gave it birth. It belongs, like the Nazi Party, to Hitler.

"Now we are backed by the General Staff of the Army. We obey the High Command of the *Wehrmacht*, and answer to the Commanders-in-Chief of Services, who are not going to hand over one iota to the Gestapo and its SD."

I quavered, "You shouldn't be telling me this. These are State secrets."

"I suppose so," said Adam. "Only about half a million people know all this."

"Who is in charge of your group?"

"Admiral Canaris."

"And do you spy on the British Secret Service?" I asked breathlessly, sipping my wine.

"Oh, dear, that lot," said Adam. He drummed his fingers.

"Well, let me explain. In 1937 and last year too, the American Institute of Pacific

Relations gave me a job, on China. The State Secretary of the Foreign Office, Ernst Freiherr von Weizsäcker he is into Oriental Studies too, so he's given me this job in the Foreign Office. In October last year, with my American contacts, I went to Washington to tell them about the resistance to Hitler, and to ask them to help. Hopeless."

"Resistance to Hitler," I said weakly.

We were in an alcove, away from the rest of the diners. I don't think anyone could hear us. It was an expensive restaurant.

Albrecht grinned at me. "They know us here, and seat us well away from the ordinary terrified Germans."

I gulped.

Adams went on, "I've just got back from London and Oxford trying to get support for another German government. I had senior contacts in Oxford, but generally they suspected me of being a secret Gestapo man. Other people who know me well told me about how hopeless everything is in England. The 1914-1918 trench warfare has sunk so deeply in the British military mind, they think of intelligence as purely tactical – planes flying over enemy trenches, you know. They decoded the German High Seas Fleet radio messages in the last war, but the Senior Naval Officers so despised intelligence gathering as against seamanship, the Battle of Jutland ended in a draw. They could have sunk the German Fleet at Jutland, but their thinking was hopelessly antiquated. All they've done since then is that Lord Louis Mountbatten has set up the Naval Y Service – he did that in 1927 – to intercept enemy wireless messages and try and decode them. The British Army is pathetically behind the times – if they oppose us on European soil, we'll sweep them to one side within weeks, maybe even days. They have no intelligence as to the strength of the German Army. Their RAF is the new junior Service, but they have no Intelligence, and their ideas are pitiable. They think the war will be won by bombs – and the RAF has not the planes, nor any way of finding targets in Germany to smash German industry.

"What our intelligence files in the *Abwehr* do show is that the British have a fighter called the Spitfire which might do better than anything we have. But where will they get the pilots from? We sent our pilots to fight in Spain, to learn all those tricks and skills to keep you alive. Will the Spitfire keep the raw British pilots alive for their first three weeks, which is time to learn the elementary tricks? At the end of the Spanish Civil War, the Republican pilots surrendered, and Franco shot a lot of them. He's locked up the rest in prisons. The Royal Navy should have got all those pilots out to fly their fighters and teach the young British pilots. These Spitfires are all that

38

stand between the murderous street thug and the thousand years of barbarity he promises us. Hitler will extinguish the lamp of Europe for a thousand years."

They brought us soup, and we tucked in.

Adam said, "Quite simply, in England, the politicians and the military don't see the difference between political and military intelligence. You can't do without political intelligence; so they don't see the current that is sweeping them to destruction. They just don't know who Hitler is and what he's going to do to them, what he *wants* to do. The British Prime Minister is Chamberlain and he doesn't like people bothering him after dinner. If he goes down to Chequers, there's only one telephone, and it's in the 'butler's pantry'. Germany is full of uniforms, and you've seen the *Unter den Linden* – flags and banners flapping in the breeze. *The only phone is in his butler's pantry!* Their Civil Service doesn't work together. The Foreign Office, the War Office, the Admiralty and the Air Ministry are all jealous of their own scraps of intelligence, and they never co-ordinate when they go to the Chiefs of Staff."

We finished our soup, and waited for the next course. They brought us vegetable salad – lettuce, horse-radish, olives and pickles.

Adam went on, "Public opinion there could not be worse. They are smug behind the English Channel and the Royal Navy. They just aren't interested in what is going on outside their own country. Five years ago, millions voted blithely in the Peace Ballot for the abolition of war aircraft. Abyssinia, and Franco in Spain, are 'quarrels in a far-away country between people of whom we know nothing' – as Chamberlain said last year, most detestably. Winston Churchill is a voice crying in the wilderness, trying to warn them. Sir Hastings Ismay told me that he is sure war is coming, 'but in England we are living in a world of the imagination.' Sir Robert Vansitt told me that the English public 'is an insular electorate whom none dares to educate.' He said the appalling casualties in the trenches in the last war make everyone believe it could not happen again, because war is unthinkable.

"They've got a very popular talker on the wireless there, C.E.M. Joad, who told them that 'a bomb will flatten a square mile of a city.' The bombing of Barcelona gives the lie to that, but the Spanish Civil War went in one ear and out the other. London has only 6,000 hospital beds to cope with any air raids. Professor J.B. Haldane has told them that every single person within earshot of an exploding bomb will die from burst eardrums – as though no city in Spain was ever bombed, to show what *really* happens.

"They've got what Hitler's doing right before their noses, but they are obsessed with peace. Baldwin didn't dare put rearmament in his 1935 election manifesto. They are all convinced that appeasement will placate the Austrian street lout. At Oxford, I met a student who had come back from a year at a German university. He was horrified, and tried to warn everyone. They said that he'd settle down with time, grow up, given time. There's not going to be time."

We finished our salads, and waited for the waiter to clear our plates.

"Do you suppose there will really be war?" I asked. "What is happening?"

"What is happening!" cried Albrecht. "You don't know!"

"I've been at sea till yesterday, and now I've been run off my feet, I'm a woman, remember, and I'm not clever like you two are. I only take photos, and that doesn't need brains."

I lowered my eyes modestly, and to my incredulous delight, saw them preen. Thank goodness men are... well, men.

"Five days ago, Hitler signed a non-aggression pact with Russia, with Stalin," said Albrecht, staring at me. "You know?"

"Somebody said something about it on the ship, I think," I said vaguely, "Why, does that matter?"

"Now Germany is no longer encircled, Hitler can attack all Europe – France, England, the Middle East..."

I looked at him, horror-struck. If there *was* a war, how was I going to get out? With war, the Gestapo would be down on everyone like a ton of bricks – down on *me*.

"Seven days ago," Adam corrected him.

"*Five* days ago," said Albrecht, "The press here suddenly published stories about the mobilisation of Poland, and its coup against Danzig, our Danzig corridor. Those evil Poles with, all that cavalry – all those horses to scratch the paint on our tanks. After all the newspaper hullabaloo about the threatened Polish attack, over Danzig, Sir Neville Henderson – you know who he is?"

I shook my head. Miss Ancram had mentioned him on the ship, but I couldn't remember.

"The British Ambassador. He talked to Hitler, and flew to London. But the reservists were already crowding out the Berlin railway stations. You're soon going to have man-scarcity in Berlin. There'll always be the boys from the tanks just outside Berlin, not to mention us two." His eyes twinkled at me. "War or no war, the night-clubs are chock-full. However, Henderson came back and they ushered him straight into Hitler's study in the *Reichskanzlei* – not before, I imagine, Neville Henderson saw the roofs of Berlin bristling with anti-aircraft guns. Intelligence reports tell us that London has about 40 of these A-A guns. Henderson also knew, before he talked to Hitler, that certain foods – bread, meat and fats, mainly – will be rationed. Cocoa, eggs and flour are okay; because we have lots of that. They are rationing soap, coal, shoes and clothes. Have you got your cards?"

I shook my head.

"Our dear Propaganda Ministry has 500 souls laboring 24 hours a day – with 300 officials. Someone, probably, at this moment, is getting your cards

40

ready.

"However, Hitler assured Belgium, the Netherlands, Luxembourg and Switzerland that he'll respect their neutrality, but Holland is mobilising.

"Well, when I say that they ushered Henderson straight in, I'm not being altogether accurate. He landed at the Templehof Aerodrome, and drove his own car – famous in Berlin for its number plate '6' – to the British Embassy, in the Wilhemstrasse, near where it joins the Unter den Linden. In fact, he drove right past the Chancellery where Herr Lout was conferring with Field Marshal Goring, Dr. Goebbels, General von Brauchisch, General Keitel and *Gott* knows how many other military men. He stopped in the British Embassy a couple of hours, and then walked the 200 yards to the new Chancellery. An envoy from a puny, impotent Britain that once had the greatest empire the world has ever seen. Meanwhile, the troops went through Berlin to Poland, using moving vans, delivery wagons, grocery trucks.

"Henderson and Hitler talked yesterday, but as you see, the street lights in Berlin still burn brightly. They say the British are offering a long-term settlement in Europe.

"How little they know Hitler."

We were enjoying veal done in breadcrumbs, with potatoes, turnips and cabbage.

* * *

As we sat in silence, I thought: when I had asked about the British Secret Service, Adam had said 'that lot!' Confusion galloped around inside my head. What 'lot' was I with – the Foreign Office, the Army, the Navy…?

I was bursting with questions, but I didn't want to give myself away. I forced myself to ask, "What is Neville Chamberlain like?"

Adam said, "Vansittart told me that Chamberlain was utterly ignorant of strategy, as was the rest of the British Cabinet. He said he was 'an earnest and ignorant provincial, bound to err, and with no idea of what the Germans were like.' Of course, the Foreign Office is hopeless in handling its intelligence, and can't tell Chamberlain anything."

I saw my opening, and struck.

"Isn't there any sort of Secret Service, on its own, apart from the Foreign Office and the rest of them?"

"It's called the SIS, and it reported to the Foreign Office, which, as I say, had no idea of what to do with what it learnt from SIS. Now the Secret Service reports to the Joint Intelligence Committee, as of this year. But the SIS's discredited, because Goebbels has planted all sorts of wild stories – on Monday, Germany invades in Czechoslovakia; on Tuesday, Germany attacks Holland; on Wednesday, they will cross the Austrian border against Hungary.

41

Well, Germany *did* finally attack Czechoslovakia. But meanwhile, the SIS had made awful fools of themselves."

My knees trembled under the table, and then knocked together. I was terrified I would change colour, show something in my face.

Adam went on, "They have low salaries – the Ten-Year Rule. The boss, Admiral 'Quex' Sinclair, is dying from cancer. No agent can ever get into Hitler's inner circle, and even if he did, he has no wireless, certainly not here in Germany, to send messages. With the *Anschluss* last year, the SIS lost Austria, which was its base for spying on Germany. The agents are of the worst sort you can imagine," and I swallowed uncomfortably. "They pick men from the London Clubs, and eschew university men and intellectuals. They don't go into their backgrounds, and I think communists from Cambridge have infiltrated them. You get a farmer like Frederick Winterbotham who has a smattering of German, and they take him. Well, he *was* university graduate, but having been a farmer saved him from that stigma. They say you can't understand most of their reports, their way of writing are so confused."

He looked at me sharply, and my pulse raced.

"Speaking of wireless transmissions, how do you get your photos to Argentina?"

"Through the Embassy. If war breaks out, the diplomatic courier will carry them by train to Portugal, and send them by ship."

"But now?"

"They fly from Berlin to Buenos Aires"

"Yesterday, all civil aviation was stopped in Germany."

"Then by ship."

"We need to send a document abroad, for publication. If we bring it to you tonight, could you take it to the Embassy tomorrow?"

I was carrying 110 incriminating documents through Berlin. But I could code it, and make a microdot.

"Certainly," I said indifferently.

When we got up to leave, they asked me whether I needed a car.

"I'm going back to the Propaganda Ministry. How can I thank you for such a lovely meal?"

"We can go night-clubbing together."

"That would be marvellous."

42

In the Ministry, I went to Schneppen's office, and asked him for film. "What do you want to photograph?"

"The streets. The queues of people for their ration cards. It's all so orderly and quiet. No one shows any worry about war. Have you seen them at the Cafe Kranzler at the corner of Unter den Linden and Freidrichstrasse? Sitting at the outside tables. All those square fluted columns in Unter den Linden with the huge eagles on top, and all the swastika flags."

He nodded with stiff approval. "I'll have to write you out a Special Pass to take photos in the streets. Do you have any passport photos?"

I had about 15 in my handbag. I gave him one.

"You must sign for the film. Remember, it is a criminal offence not to return it here – undeveloped, remember."

I nodded eagerly. He wrote my pass, affixed my photo, and then stamped over the pass and the photo.

"Good hunting."

* * *

I photographed a queue in a street running off Wilhelmstrasse, that took me across Mauerstrasse and over to Freidrichstrasse. I went up Freidrichstrasse to the Kranzler Cafe, and took more shots. An officer in the uniform of *SS-ObersturmbannFührer* stood up and strode over to me. I saw the Death's Head. A Lieutenant-Colonel.

"Papers!" he snapped, while all eyes turned on us.

He studied my pass.

"Very good," he smiled. "Argentina. Can I invite you for a drink?"

I asked for a Rhine wine.

He asked me about Argentina, and I told him about the north. I told him I stayed with Prince Hohenlinden.

I said, "Do you feel like a stroll? I really should be working."

"How much do they pay you?" he asked, curious.

"About 500 marks, but only 300 are sent to Berlin. I suppose I'll pay a lot in taxes."

"Taxes start off at about 30% plus. You'll probably pay about 100-110 marks."

"The newspaper has deposited 5,000 marks in my name for expenses, so I suppose I'll make do."

"Let us stroll then," he said. "You should not be taking photos in the street without a soldier or officer with you."

His name was Rutzel, and we wandered along to Parisier Platz and down Potsdamerstrasse to Potsdamer Platz, where we turned into

43

Saarlandsstrasse, and then into PrinzAlbrechtstrasse.

"These are Gestapo Headquarters," he told me. "I'll get a car to drive you home."

I accepted gratefully.

* * *

We stopped outside the big wooden doors, and the driver rang the bell. He spoke into a voice box, and the doors unlocked electrically. The driver pushed them open, and we drove up to the front entrance.

The Prince waited for us on the steps, and welcomed us. He invited the SS officer in for a drink, and we went to the library. Valeria brought us schnapps, and the Prince handed me a big envelope.

"From Dr. Goebbels himself," he smiled, and the *SS-ObersturmbannFührer's* eyes widened.

I took out the photos, and was very pleased. In two of them, touching up the film with pencil would bring out the erudite intellectual.

An embossed card from Goebbels said, "Very good work."

I handed the card to the Prince, who gave it to Rutzel. Then I handed around the photos.

I said, "I'd love to do portrait photos of *ReichFührer* Himmler. I was thinking of asking Dr. Goebbels to help me."

Rutzel said, "I will give him your message." He smiled. "With all this talk of war and rumors of war, possibly you will have to wait a couple of weeks."

"I'm in your debt, "I told him.

He was inordinately pleased at the Prince accepting him into his home.

After he left, I said, "I apologize abjectly for bringing the Gestapo to your door..."

"You have done brilliantly," he assured me. "We are under some suspicion, although we have voiced not one word of criticism. We stay well away from the anti-Nazi groups. You could call it cowardice, but we could not help you now if we did not have our hands clean. Never hesitate to bring Nazis here. We'll swallow our bile, and play the part we must play."

He stood, looking out the tall window, at the back garden, then turned and sat down.

"Tell me about your day."

He listened to my recital, and then frowned.

He said, his voice strained with alarm, "You must never see Adam von Trott again. He belongs to the Kreisau Circle of anti-Nazi aristocrats. Albercht Haushofer openly declares that Nazism is a catastrophe for Germany. Next year, he'll probably become a professor of Political Geography at Berlin University, where I'm sure he'll be more outspoken. They must be discussing your lunch in the Gestapo Headquarters at this moment."

The phone rang, and the Prince answered it.

"My son Claus will not be home till very late, or may have to spend all night at Headquarters. He used a code expression."

The Prince went to the fireplace, fiddled about, and the marble mantelpiece swung open. He reached inside, and took out a piece of paper.

"They are going to invade Poland on September 1st. Can you encode this, make a microdot, take it to the Embassy, and see if they can broadcast it tonight."

Dumbly, I took the paper.

"Go up to your room. If you hear the alarm bell, flush it all down the toilet."

Upstairs, I read:

'Germany attacks Poland on September 1st.

'Britain must declare war because Hitler proposes to postpone war till 1943-5, when he will have jet aircraft, inter-continental bombers and rockets. He plans on building an atomic, nuclear bomb, but the German moderator of commercial graphite contains boron, so they must use heavy water, which is limited in supply and mainly made in Norway. Germany must be pushed into war now, to interrupt jet plane development. The first prototype flew four years ago.'

445/11

B	U	T	W	H	B	
A	C	D	E	F	A	
G	I	J	K	L	G	
M	N	O	P	Q	M	
R	S	V	X	*	R	* = Y, Z
B	U	T	W	H	B	

GERMA   NYATT   was changed to…
FTQLH   GPHSS   and so on…

I microdotted the message, put it in my ring, and Volker drove me to the Argentinean Embassy. Inside, at the desk, I asked for Ruben Zorrequieta, and they left me sitting for several minutes.

He was heavily built, with shaggy thick, reddish hair, a large, beaming face with a large nose and a fleshy mouth under a moustache. His suit and tie were German, but he wore his clothes loosely, most ungermanicly.

"I'm Ruben. Hello! I've been expecting you! You're good-looking in your photo, but much better in person. Don't you look the blonde fraulein already!"

He was leading me to the lift. From the lift, we walked along a passageway to his office, which had an outer reception room, and beyond that an inside office, barely furnished, but with tourist posters on the walls.

He motioned me to an armchair and said, "I don't dare have an office that opens straight on to the passageway. When I knew you were coming, I didn't know what sort of conversations we might have, but I'm sure we won't want listeners. Do you smoke? No? Do you want some boxes of American cigarettes to hand around, you know, a sort of bribe, or to make yourself more popular?"

We were talking in Spanish, and I loved the way the Argentineans raised their voice inflexions in all sorts of unexpected places.

"That's a wonderful idea," I said. "Can you really spare them? Do you want me to pay for them?"

"Your newspaper is paying for them. Your editor has suggested that we ship Argentinean corned beef – well, in tins, of course – to the Embassy here, in case of war. He will pay for what you take. He will also pay for any food we bring from Switzerland, and which we give to you. Well, in the courier diplomatic bags, you understand. It looks like war, don't you think? You British are huffing and puffing trying to stop it, but Hitler is who he is, a maniac."

I asked, "What part of England did your people come from?"

"From Caithness, the Orkneys and the Shetland Islands. Three generations back. Believe it or not, I was a first-class cricketer, but I can't keep my hand in, here in Berlin. If there's one thing sure about Hitler, he doesn't play cricket, and that says everything about him!"

We burst into laughter.

I said, "You'll be sending my microdots in the courier bag by train to Lisbon, and then by ship to Buenos Aires. My messages will take months to arrive. My photos too."

"We've been working on that. We can take the bags by train to Switzerland, and then catch a Swiss plane to Madrid. But if war breaks out, the sky will be full of bombers and fighters. However, in Switzerland, we've got two people from English families. One is working on the radio. So we'll radio your messages from Geneva."

I asked, very worriedly, "Will the microdots be on the letters to my editor? If they drug the courier and open the bags, I'm finished."

"The microdots will serve as full stops in certain official correspondence – correspondence that will go to one man only in Geneva, or to a certain man in Buenos Aires. Impersonal, official, routine reports."

"Do you use your radio here, in Berlin?"

"We are under diplomatic immunity, but the Germans don't like us using our radio. They'll like it much less when war starts. But all the embassies are doing it. We often use plain language – Goebbels is saturating South America with his broadcasts, so we radio that certain news is confirmed, and keep our mouths shut about the rest of the rubbish. But, of course, we send short messages in code. So, are you leading up to something?"

I told him what my message was, and handed him my ring.

"This message will have to go out now. We'll send it to a certain official in Buenos Aires, who will hand it over to a friend who has a radio station. He has a wireless set there no one knows about, and will radio London. London will have this within the hour. We'll radio it on a wavelength that only our friend in Buenos Aires will receive."

He lit another cigarette.

"We can't do this very often, but we will do it when urgency demands – *cuando la urgencia lo exija*. For the rest, we must wait some days, or even a week, to send it through Geneva."

"Can't we advise London of this wavelength?"

"We have, but we haven't received any confirmation yet. The English SIS is very slow. If they receive it, we won't need our friend in Buenos Aires with the radio station any more. Of course, if war breaks out, the Germans may jam us, but I think that if we send very few messages, they'll probably leave us alone. Now, another thing, once a week, we have a dinner here, so... *te avisaré*... you should come. You can use the chance to hand over your microdots. It will help your cover as an Argentinean. We've got a very good cook. How are you settling in with the Prince?"

"It's lovely there. How much resistance to Hitler is there here?"

"A lot. But the repression is ferocious. The German people were happy with him while he gave them work and money. War they don't want, but if he wins victories, euphoria will carry them away. When things go badly, they'll turn against him in a flash. If they are bombed, that might arouse their anger, and then they'll follow him in their anger. What I can tell you most of is that the monsters are the Nazis, not most of the German people. They're terrified out of their wits. You can't say one word out of place. You have to watch the very expressions on your face. In ordinary life, you're always falling into arguments with people, having tiffs – you don't dare do that any more. You never know who will get revenge by denouncing you to the Gestapo.

47

They've got a big section just reading letters – hate mail – from neighbours. If you cross words with someone, you have to decide whether to get in first and write a letter – or are you going to send someone to a concentration camp who never wrote their letter anyway?"

Outside in the street, I stood there wondering how best to get back to the Prince's place in Potsdam.

A black car stopped in front of me, and two men in leather overcoats got out and walked up to me.

"Come with us." They led me to the car, and helped me into the back seat. One sat beside me and the other drove.

"Who are you?" I demanded. "Where are we going?"

"Silence!"

We drove to Gestapo Headquarters, which I recognized immediately.

They led me upstairs, up two floors, into an office, where they sat me on a wooden chair behind a wooden table.

After twenty minutes, an *SS-SturmbannFührer* came in, slapped a file on the table, and stood looking at me.

"The game's up," he said, "We know who you are."

My heart lurched.

"I am a photographic journalist from the VIGILANTE in Buenos Aires," I stuttered. My blood was pounding enough to deafen me.

"You are an English spy," he declared, flatly.

"Belize is English," I said, struggling to keep my voice steady. "We keep away from the English there – they don't accept us."

"You're English, not Spanish. You're from one of the Caribbean Islands – probably Jamaica. You've never been in Belize in your life."

He drew out blank sheets from the folder.

"Do you have a pen?"

I nodded

"Write down what the climate is like and read it to me."

I scribbled, and read out to him: "This month, for example – August – the temperature's around 32°. We get thunderstorms – it's the rainy season. The rainy season starts in June and it tapers off in September, when you get the 'mauger'."

"What's 'mauger'?" he snapped.

"I'm not sure, but I think it's a corruption of the English word 'meagre'. Meagre rains. Then you get a two months dry in September and October. In November, you get heavy rains and hurricanes, up to January. The temperature stands about 19-21° in January, but you get cold fronts coming down from the USA. February through to May are dry months."

I looked at him, trying to pull myself together.

"*SS-StandartenFührer*," I said firmly, promoting him from Major to Colonel, "I am an Argentinean citizen."

"Under German jurisdiction, on German territory," he grated. "Sketch me the plan of your house, and give me your address in Stann Creek. Draw me a map of Stann Creek, with the names of the streets."

"I can't draw a map of Stann Creek," I protested, half rising. "I only know some of the streets."

"Sit down. What streets?"

"Er... Commerce Street, Havana Street, ah... Stann Creek Valley Road, Alejo
Beni Street, Riverside Street, where I live, Magoon Street, er... Mahogany street—"

"That's enough. Draw."

* * *

I handed him my sketches.

* * *

He said softly, "All your birth and baptismal certificates – of your parents and grandparents – are undoubtedly false. Don't you realise we are checking those in Argentina. We have pro-German newspapers there, with stringers, and the stringers will soon be checking. Now, if you confess—"

"Those papers are authentic," I said indignantly. I heard distant screams.

"Do we have to get it out of you with torture?"

He opened the door, and two hefty thugs in uniform stood there, staring at me.

"They are authentic documents."

"What was your meeting about with Adam Trott and Albercht Haushofer?"

I sat there with my mouth open like a fish on the bank of a stream. I once saw an unusual sight – on a holiday, in the country, we came upon a lorry with its back wheels in deep, wet mud. The wheels spun, but got no purchase. And so my mind raced.

Calm settled on me, and I told him, "We talked about whether there would be war, and how unprepared the British were. They said the British were indifferent to what was happening, and hid behind the English Channel and their Navy. He told me their Air Force had all the wrong ideas and their Army knew nothing of modern warfare."

The SS man gave a thin smile.

"And you knew nothing of this?" he sneered. "This is common knowledge."

"It was very interesting. I knew nothing about this. Do you imagine we discuss these things in Argentina?"

"Was your meeting planned before you left Argentina?"

"I met him by accident in the foyer of the Propaganda Building."

"And he was so instantly charmed; he invited you to the Foreign Office?"

I sat there.

"So you have a high opinion of yourself, your beauty and your charms?"

"Alas, it doesn't matter what we women think of ourselves," I said sweetly. "I depend on what you men think, and that is something we can't control."

He gave a satisfied smile, then said, "But you do all you can to influence what men are thinking."

He paced up and down.

"And you went straight from your meeting with those two to report to *SS-ObersturmbannFührer* Rutzel. He is part of your spying?"

"He saw me taking photos in the street, and demanded to see my authorisation. When he satisfied himself, he offered to accompany me, and I accepted."

"I'll be damned for a tale," said the *SS-SturmbannFührer*. "And then you took him to Prince Hohenlinden, another member of the spy ring."

"*SS-ObersturmbannFührer* Rutzer kindly offered to drive me home. The Prince came out on to the steps when we arrived, and invited the officer for a drink. The Prince gave me photos I had taken of Dr.Goebbels, and which Dr.Goebbels had just had sent to us. Mr.Rutzer was most impressed by the photos, and said he would help me get an interview with Reichsminister Himmler."

He stopped, rigid, staring at me.

"An interview – what for?"

"To offer to do portrait photos of him."

He nodded at the two thugs, who left. Then he turned, and left the room.

Ten minutes ticked away. I needed to pee. An *SS-RottenFührer* came in, and I asked for the loo. He led me down a passage, and nodded at a door.

When I came out, he said, "Accompany me please."

He led me out of the building, and pointed to the back door of a car. I got in the back seat, and he drove me to the Prince's house. He left me at the big wooden gates.

At least I did get a lift back home.

At the evening meal, I told them what had happened. Boris and Thoma looked at me wide-eyed.

I asked about my ration cards, and Princess Jutta told me she had already collected them for me.

"If there is war," she said, "We shall have to dig up the lawn and plant vegetables."

Thoma said, "Oh, the back garden is already spoilt by the bunker."

The prince said, "A bunker means a reinforced-concrete air-raid shelter. We have deep cellars here, but if the house falls down around our ears, we may want to be able to get out. Our bunker has a six-foot thick roof, which might stand a direct hit. There are two rooms, with 18 bunks, and a bathroom.

* * *

At 11.45 pm, we listened to William Shirer, broadcasting from Berlin. The Prince had a powerful wireless hidden behind the bookcases in the library – it was a crime to listen to anything but Nazi broadcasts – and Shirer began, "Hello, the football – so to speak – of this diplomatic struggle…" and he went on to say that it had been kicked back to Berlin. He warned that the British government was standing firm, but that so was the German government. He didn't have a clue as to the reaction of the Germans to the British proposal, which I thought was a bad look-out. But, chillingly, Shirer told us that the DNB, the wireless service of the *Reichs-Rundfunk Gedellschaft*, or the R.R.G. – Germany's B.B.C. – would broadcast all night long.

He talked abut the Polish mobilisation, and told us that the German Press said that now they knew 'who was responsible' if anything happened.

William Shirer is one of the world's most famous correspondents and he broadcasts for the Columbia Broadcasting System. The Germans can't get him on their millions of cheap little wireless sets that Goebbels sold them – they get German stations, with no short wave. Besides, Shirer broadcasts in English.

At midnight, we were getting ready to go to bed, when Claus came in. After greeting everyone, he slumped into a chair.

I said, "Can I see you tomorrow, before you leave?" I looked at the Prince. "Could you join us?"

Claus sat up erectly, and gave me a warm smile.

"We'll talk now. I've got to leave at 8:30 tomorrow morning, and I'll be rushing."

"Can we talk alone with your father?"

Princess Jutta said, "Come on, girls. Out of here! Serious men's business is afoot," and we all laughed.

$$* * *$$

"Claus," I asked. "Do you have any idea how many planes Germany has today?"

"About 8,200 planes. But very few heavy bombers. Our tactics are for light fast bombers to attack with fighters covering them. We could have more, but when a production run gets under way, someone gets a bright new idea, and everything stops to retool and build in this latest advance. Quantity is always sacrificed to quality – quality comes first."

"And tanks?"

"We have some 2,600 tanks – the PZKW-IIIs and PZKW-IVs. They have a top speed of about 25 miles an hour, 4-inch turret armour–"

"I'm not sure about that," interrupted his father. "Isn't it 3.9 inches?"

"The two tanks are slightly different," said Claus. "I think the gun is 65 mm."

"I think the cannon are 70 mm," worried his father.

"Anyway," said Claus, "We plan to use the tanks like cavalry, not like static, armoured artillery. Sometimes, they'll advance at a walking pace, just ahead of the infantry, wiping out resistance. In other cases, the tanks will sweep forward in lightning penetrations, perhaps of many kilometres, while the infantry will be catching up in armoured carriers or in trucks, to occupy the ground the tanks have overrun. Large columns of tanks could thrust 30 or 40 kilometres behind the enemy front – these will be our Panzer tactics. It's a revolutionary new concept in warfare – although the original idea came from a Frenchman, called Charles de Gaulle, and an Englishman, Liddell Hart. The French plan on using their tanks as static artillery. The British have hardly any and still have no idea what they will do with them. We have dive-bombers

52

called Stukas. They will work closely with the tanks, destroying enemy forces ahead and around the tank columns, making their deep penetrations. Stukas will also clear the way for infantry on foot. They are our heavy artillery."

I nodded. "God in heaven," I exclaimed.

Next morning, in the shower, I tried to imagine I was back in paradise, in Belize. I got dressed dreaming I had danced away the night in Nice, or Cannes or Montecarlo.

After breakfast, I went upstairs, wrote my message and prepared to encode it:

> 8,200 planes and 2,600 tanks. Will attack with light fast bombers covered by fighters. Production inefficient. Interrupt production runs to incorporate new ideas. Strongly recommend England concentrate on fighter production for defense against heavy air raids and to complete a production run without new modifications. Save modifications for next run. Germans work 8-hour days. Recommend that English factories work 24-hour days in two or three shifts.

Then I described the German tanks, and the German tactics of smashing into the enemy rear.

(After the war, I found out they heeded me. In the next three years, British plane production tripled the German).

From Lorna Doone, I took page 65, line 4:

"Daring scarce to peep, I crept into the water…"

D	A	R	I	N	D	
B	C	E	F	G	B	
H	J	K	L	M	H	
O	P	Q	S	T	O	
U	V	W	X	*	U	* = Y, Z
D	A	R	I	N	D	

For numbers, I had to write the prefix BX, and when I finished, the suffix WX. I had to take the second and fourth line of my box.

53

1	2	3	4	5
B	C	E	F	G

6	7	8	9	0
O	P	Q	S	T

So, '8200 planes and 2,600 tanks…' became:

BXQCT TWXHE UXAYU BCBXC OTTWX LUXCK

When I finished, I went downstairs to the darkroom, and microdotted the message.

Coming out of the darkroom, I found the Prince reading.

I asked him, "How did you come to choose *Lorna Doone* for the code?"

"We both made a list of our English books, and the editions. We found that Graham and I both had the 1914 Collins gilt-edged, leather-bound edition of *Lorna Doone*, and we chose that. If there are air raids, we'll have to find a safe place for it."

I went back to the Argentinean Embassy with the microdots inside my ring. Ruben received me with a cup of black coffee. He was listening to the wireless; he switched it off, and told me that last night Hitler had named the Ministerial Council for the Defense of the Reich – a War Cabinet, with Goring; Hess, Frick, the Interior Minister; Funk, the Economics Minister; Lammers, Chief of the Chancellery; and General Keitel, Chief of the High Command of the Armed Forces.

He said, "They've been at it all night, there in the Chancellery."

He stretched, "Didn't get much sleep last night. Your messages went out. At last, London came through, and said your messages were to go through Buenos Aires. Our wavelength is monitored there 24 hours a day. The British say they don't have the people to monitor it 24 hours a day, waiting for perhaps one message a month. And we don't dare transmit on *their* wavelength. Not even from Geneva. We'd have Germans all over us! Your other message will go to Geneva for transmission." (my report on German Radar and the ceiling of their anti-air artillery)

I said, "I've got another message that needs to go from Geneva. It can't wait to travel to Buenos Aires."

I gave him my ring, with a small emerald, and he returned the rings I gave him last night; one ring had held the urgent message, and the other had hidden the radar/anti-air reports.

* * *

From the embassy, I went to the Propaganda Ministry, to hand in my street photos to Herr Schneppen, and give him the retouched photos of Goebbels – Goebbels as an ascetic scholar rather than a taut-faced, raving demagogue – in a well-sealed envelope. Schneppen gave me my developed films of the refugees from Spain, and said, "Good work."

So, back to the Argentinean Embassy! To hand them in for the newspaper in Buenos Aires. Schneppen had given me new film, with a Pass to go to the Tank School at Krampnitz outside Berlin.

I went back to the house, for lunch, and joined the ladies. Princess Jutta was clearly depressed. "This house is two hundred years old," she lamented, "With just one bomb..." She ate something, and continued, "The life that has been lived here for generations..."

I said, "I'm worried about bomb blast. All the windows..."

The Princess said, "Months ago, my husband ordered heavy wooden shutters, and the workmen cemented hinges into the stonework. The shutters simply have to be lifted into place."

"Will we have to put blackout paper on the windows?"

"Many rooms have heavy drapes. Months ago, I installed heavy drapes in all the other rooms. With the shutters in place and closed, and the drapes pulled, no light gets out."

We talked about the four-year-old girl from Spain who didn't have a doll. Doris said, "I'll go this afternoon. We have so many dolls in the attic! They go back two hundred years! I'm going to make her the happiest little girl in Berlin."

I coughed nervously, "My newspaper pays me 300 Marks, and they tell me I'll probably pay 100 marks or so in tax. I want to pay my share here."

"Heavens, my girl," laughed the grandmother. "You'll need 200 marks to keep yourself looking attractive and the men on their toes."

I said miserably, "If there's war, they'll stop making nice clothes. We probably won't get any make-up in the shops and we'll go mad looking for needles and thread." I smiled at them wryly. "All the men are going to get scared away. They won't look at us."

Thoma said grimly, If Walter stops looking at me, he'll know what's what." We all laughed, and finally Thoma smiled.

Doris said, "I think we should get married as quickly as possible.

Thank goodness none of our men have to go to the Front, but we could easily get killed in Berlin. Now we'll have to try and live our lives in a short time." She ground her teeth. "That Hitler!"

I said, "Will you let me pay 100 marks at least?"

Princess Jutta said, "You help undo Hitler and *I'll* pay *you* 100 marks."

Valeria came in and said, "Miss Ray, the phone for you."

It was Schneppen.

"The British Ambassador is going to talk to the German foreign Minister, von Ribbentrop. Can you get to the Wilhemstrasse and photograph Sir Nevile Henderson as he walks down to the Foreign Office? Dr. Goebbels has asked for you specifically. If your pictures are good enough, we'll use them in the German Press too. Dr. Goebbels said he was very pleased with portrait photos, and asks could you let him have the original films."

"I'll bring Dr. Goebbels' films when I'm finished in the Wilhemstrasse," I told him. "But these films will take weeks to get to Buenos Aires."

"Dr. Goebbels has arranged for your pictures to go straight to Sweden, should war break out. We can do it more quickly than your Argentinean Embassy. You are being afforded special treatment. Swedish ships can reach South America in a week or so. In case of war, they will be subject to search by the Royal Navy, as neutral ships, so we must hope the British don't find your photos, which will be easy to hide."

"Thank you," I gasped, and hurried back to ask whether I could use the Mercedes.

* * *

Reinard cut through Neuer Garten, on a graveled road to Schwanenallee, in his haste to get me there. We came out at the bridge on Königstrasse, and as we drove across Berlin, I tried to sort out what Schneppen had told me. Would the Swedes fly planes in wartime? Probably not. But if my pictures could reach the newspaper in a fortnight or less, that would be lovely. What my editor, Felix Guinjaime, had planned was a weekend supplement, a news review, with the photos, however late they arrived. He had been thinking of six-week delays. We turned into Wilhelmstrasse from Unter den Linden, and a couple of hundred people blocked the way. I'd have to get to the front of them for my photo; Henderson would walk down the right-hand footpath.

"Reinhard," I said, "Park close to the Foreign Ministry, just up from it."

He nosed the car through, and parked on the right-hand side. I got out and a *Polizei* came up to me. I showed him my credentials, and said, "Dr. Goebbels just rang me, and asked me to photograph the British Ambassador when he comes down the street.

"Have I time to go into the Propaganda Ministry and find someone to come and speak to you?" I smiled sweetly.

"No, no," he said hurriedly. "You stand right here by the car."

After a quarter-of-an-hour I saw a dapper Sir Nevile Henderson step out from the British Embassy, and stroll imperturbably, down towards me, looking ahead, unsmiling and meeting no eye. As he came close, my *Polizei* stretched out his arms, to keep people back. I said to Sir Nevile, "I think we're both missing dear old London right now," and gave him my most ravishing smile. Startled, he glanced at me, gave a fleeting smile as I took three photos.

I crossed to the Propaganda Ministry, and took the film up to Schneppen.

(Next day, a government newspaper carried the photo, with the subtitle, 'A Smiling and Confident Sir Nevile Henderson goes to talk to von Ribbentrop, sure that Germany will bow down to British proposals', which made me grind my teeth.)

I went to the Tank Park, and Oberst Ekkehart Kraske took me under his wing – he was young for a colonel, perhaps only 28. I photographed tank crews by their machines, and tried to show only smooth expanses of metal or unrevealing middle-stretches of the guns. He let me climb inside one, and the heavy smell of oil, metal and I don't know what else suffocated me. He sat me in the different seats, and explained the knobs and dials, which all went over my head. He invited me that night to a nightclub, and I accepted eagerly. He told me how he enjoyed dancing.

As I climbed out of the machine, my heart was heavy, because I knew it would pound down any British Army that stood before it.

He came just after dinner, and enjoyed meeting the family, and the girls' fiancés, Richterin and Walter. Finally, Thoma decided to come with us, with her fiancé (Graf Walter Vellinghausen). Claus came in at the last moment, and when Ekkehard saw his Oberst uniform (but of a Brigadier General) he snapped to attention. Claus returned the salute, but said, "My dear Ekkehard, no saluting here at home," and Ekkehard gave a cheerful smile.

Claus was a Brigadier General, not because he commanded a single platoon, but because of his high position in the General Staff Planning of the High Command. I tried to imagine young men back in London enjoying these high ranks – you probably needed to show a few white hairs before you made it to Colonel, let alone anything higher. Of course, the old boy network...

How I danced! Germany might be at war tomorrow, and my death a very young age very sure. I had no way of getting out of the country; and the Gestapo would no doubt catch me. If they didn't, a bomb dropped, perhaps by a London acquaintance, would end it.

So we who were about to die, danced the night away, till half-past-one in the morning, when Ekkehard drove us home in his staff car.

Next morning, on the breakfast table lay three newspapers; the Nazi mouthpiece, *Völkischer Beobachter*; the *Deutsche Allgemeine Zeitung*; and the *Morgenpost*.

Hitler has gone to war.

Today, he will kill the first hundreds, or thousands, of what will be perhaps thirty million Englishmen, Frenchmen, Russians and his own hapless Germans, not to mention Poles and God knows what other nationalities.

Stalin killed twenty million people in his collectivization. Hitler has to catch up.

But Hitler will – he will.

Hitler had issued a proclamation:

> 'Poland refused my offer for a friendly settlement of our relations as neighbors. Instead, she has taken up arms. The Germans in Poland have been victims of bloody terror, hunted from house to house. A series of frontier violations that a Great Power cannot accept proves that Poland will not respect the Reich frontiers..."

And on and on he goes. He had given this out at 5 a.m.

I ate breakfast, staring at a gray morning, with lowering clouds, then switched on the wireless and got martial music, with announcements –

> All schools are closed.
> Only military planes are allowed over the Reich.

All foreign nationals remain in Poland at their own risk.

The Bay of Danzig and all Poland must expect military attacks.

The phone rang. Dr. Goebbels had a special pass for me to enter the Reichstag session is morning.

Reinhard drove me to the Propaganda Ministry. I told him not to wait – that I'd find my way home on the Underground, and buses. With my Pass, I crossed the Wilhelmstrasse and they let me into the gallery of the Reichstag.

At last I saw Hitler. What an ugly, vulgar man! Were the Germans mad! He wore a field-grey soldier's uniform that he said he would wear till victory fell to German arms.

I crossed the street back to the Propaganda Ministry, handed in my film, and got a couple more rolls. Schneppen told me, "You've got a gift for catching people's expressions. Could you give us more reactions of people in the streets?"

I went over to the Tiergarten. Inwardly, I was seething, and I needed to sit down by myself. The newspapers talked about the German 'counter-attack' against Poland, and blamed England for pushing Poland into accepting what I just heard Hitler say was 'Germany's very generous offer to Warsaw." Hitler repeated General von Brauchitsch's cry to the German Army: 'Forward with God for Germany!' I wondered how Chamberlain would sound crying to the British Army, "Forward to glory with God for Britain! You glorious British troops!'

The wooden seat was slightly damp in the chill air.

What were England and France doing?

I was getting cold. I got up and walked about.

I passed a German housewife sitting on bench, with her shopping bag, her expression grim but empty.

I sat down beside her and introduced myself, 'I'm a newspaper photographer from South America. What do you think of this war?"

She looked at me in fright.

"You can't talk about these things," she said hoarsely. "Are you trying to get me into trouble?"

I showed her my papers, which she looked at slowly and carefully.

"People who talk too much disappear," she said. "Every street has a woman who's the Nazi supervisor. We've got one in our street and she seems to find out what everyone is doing and saying."

"That's awful," I said.

"We were doing all right. We never had it better. We went through the Depression and the Inflation, and now it was all right. Food and clothes at good prices – my husband was earning a good living. Now the Army has taken him. We don't need this war, and we don't need this Living Space Hitler talks about. He's dragging us into it, and we'll be bombed. We can't win against France and England and America. Suppose we conquer all Europe – what difference is it going to make to us? But all we ordinary Germans are going to be blamed. We'll go hungry, because war means hunger!" she said fiercely. "War means getting killed. I don't want to go to war against England and America. I don't know anything about them." She sobbed.

"Please, try and be brave," I begged her.

She gave me a smile through her tears and I snapped a photograph of her.

"What did you do that for!" she cried in terror.

"I photographed a brave woman I am proud to have talked to." I stumbled over the words, but I had said the right thing. She calmed down.

"Do you often come here?" I asked. She nodded.

"I don't have much time, but I hope we'll see each other again."

I didn't dare ask for her name.

I took photos of grim-faced people in the park, and went back to the streets. Somewhere, I had read that the Berlin crowd went wild in 1914 when war was declared.

Not this time.

I went back to Cafe Kranzler, on the Unter den Linden at the corner of Freidrichstrasse, and put on a PRESS armband that Schneppen had given me. People sat outside, defying the chill, their expressions withdrawn, sober or grim. Inside, I took more photos, getting resentful looks from the waiters. A most unfestive air.

At lunch, Prince Bernd had brought home a Professor, Joaquim Zuber. The Prince led me aside, and said, "Don't show any reaction to what he says, however angry he makes you. I must keep on bringing people like this to the house to protect my family – and now to protect you. To keep up appearances."

Professor Joaquim Zuber was about 50, a vociferous, intense man, with prematurely white hair and a narrow, very German face.

We sat down to lunch, to a general conversation. Then Zuber said he was pleased that Germany had grasped the nettle and gone to war. I listened alertly. The Prince steered the talk on to Hegel.

Zuber looked at me directly, and asked, "Do you know who Hegel is?"

I shook my head. "I've only just arrived, and haven't met many people."

He smiled indulgently – and let it be said, the rest of the table kept a straight face at my *gaffe*.

"Hegel was a German philosopher, who wrote last century. His works are voluminous – he turned his mind to religion, ethics, history and art. Now, last century began in turmoil from the revolution in thinking in the last half of the eighteenth century that preceded it. The French Revolution, the Independence of the United States. The Divine Right of Kings had gone. The Napoleonic Wars upset the social order and political thinking. Ideas of liberty seized people everywhere.

"Hegel set himself against that, as did most German philosophers. These Germans advocated the absolute power of the State, and instead of personal freedom, taught *duty* and *responsibility*.

"The Spanish character, as I understand, is intensely individualistic. Are people like that too in Spanish Argentina?"

"I would say so."

"So these concepts may clash with what you are used to. Hegel taught that man is not separate from God, but that the mind of man and God are one. Man's reason partakes of the divine reason, and this divine *Geist* is the force behind the evolution of the universe. The history of the world is but the history of the revelation of the divine vision, the divine process, to realise the world's *telos*, its true end and purpose. Man is the key, the hub of the unfolding of God's glorious struggle. God does not lie outside of creation, but *IS* creation. Man does not watch what is happening, but fully participates in the realisation of the universe. The universe becomes conscious of itself in the consciousness of man. The divine spirit realises itself within man, and one day man will be aware of the divine spirit within himself."

He pointed his knife at me, which were rude table manners. "So talk of the inalienable rights of man is nonsense. Hegel saw man in his native state as little better than an animal, a barbarous savage, a primitive, who is not aware of his own consciousness. He lives in unfreedom; he is not free to exercise any freedom. As Hegel writes, 'Freedom must first be sought out and won; and that by an incalculable discipline of the intellectual and moral powers. The state of nature is, therefore, that of injustice and violence, of untamed natural impulses, of inhuman deeds and feelings.' "

I said sweetly, "So an absolute and disciplined state like Germany is the very opposite?"

He beamed at me. "Aren't you quick in thought, and you follow me well," he coughed depreciatively, "Follow Hegel, we should say."

He chewed appreciatively. "Lovely meal," he said. Then he went on, "The state, society – an ideal state like Nazi Germany – limits 'the mere brute emotions and rude instincts' as Hegel puts it. A more advanced cultural state, as we are, limits 'the self-will of caprice and passion. Law and morality are indispensable to the ideal of freedom'. And this *ideal of freedom* is what reality evolves towards. Man must evolve to becoming conscious of the *ideal* freedom. To do that, he must consent to social control and, through his sense of duty and responsibility, free himself from the constraints of his animal existence."

I said, "So when the English call Hitler demonic, he is fact divine, because he leads such a state. He is aware of this?"

"We have told him."

"And what did he say?"

"That he always felt it within him."

"In war, the divine Hitler can win – or he can lose. If he loses, what does he say then to the German people?"

"That they were unworthy of him,"

"But a divine leader would resort to war?"

"Most certainly. Conflict drives progress, so here we can think of war as good, and peace as bad. Hegel himself writes, 'The history of the world is not a theatre of happiness... Life is not made for happiness but for achievement.' Elsewhere, he writes, 'Struggle is the law of growing; the storm of the world builds character; a man grows to full height through responsibility and suffering and pain'. Again, he tells us, 'History is a chain of revolutions in which one people after another, one genius after another, become the instrument of the Absolute.'

"The Greeks were the first to enjoy consciousness of freedom, as were the Romans – but they were not free. They had slaves and the liberty of men like Plato and Aristotle rested upon the backs of slaves. The German nations, under Christianity, are the first to attain 'the consciousness that man, as man, is free.' As Hitler understands – and *demands* – we depend on duty and responsibility. We must unite our minds with the universal mind, with that of the Spirit, through the German people, under the direction of Hitler – an incarnation of the Spirit itself. As Hegel tells us, this Spirit finds its final expression in the State – in the German State. Our customs and laws join up the individuals with the universal mind."

"The collective will," I said.

"Oh dear, no! The individual will does not matter. It is the divine, absolute will, as expressed in Hitler. Hegel derides Rousseau and Locke who say the individuals should have a say in the decisions of the state. Hegel tells us that the individual does not advise the state, but the state directs the individual. As Hegel says, 'To hold that every single person should deliberate and decide on political matters, to say that all individuals are members of the state, that they have the right to see that what is done is done according to their wishes and in their sight would be to put democracy into the organism of the state... it is to suggest that everyone is able to do this business of

62

running the state, which is a ridiculous notion.'

"Hegel tells us that the state is not a silly see-saw of democracy, but *the march of God in this world.*"

The grandmother, Princess Gabriele Pfaffenhofen, smiled at me, then at the Professor, and said, "Hegel has masterly observations on women too, very pertinent, I must say."

"Indeed, indeed," exclaimed the Professor. "He suggests that while men correspond to animals, women correspond to plants. He tells us this is because women are more placid, and given to feeling. He says women are educated by living rather than by study and knowledge. Manhood demands the exertion of thought and the strain of technical striving. Women are not made for the advanced sciences, philosophy and many forms of art. Women enjoy pleasing ideas, elegance and taste, but can never aspire to the ideal, to the *Geist*. When women take the helm in government, he says, woe betides the state, because arbitrary opinions and intuitions rule their actions."

"That was wonderful," said Princess Pfaffenhofen, placidly. "Such guidance in all our feminine weaknesses. So uplifting, listening to you, my dear Professor Zuber."

At six o'clock, Adam von Trott zu Solz rang, to invite me to a nightclub.

I was agitated. "My dear Adam, I cannot thank you enough, but I must beg of you not to ring here ever again. The Gestapo pulled me in to cross-question me about everything because they had seen me with you. I think they are watching you closely, but my situation is precarious. I am an Argentinean press photographer, a foreign resident, and to stay here I depend on the goodwill of the authorities and their indulgence, their sufferance."

I was sure the Gestapo had the telephone tapped, and were copying every word. "Please try and understand I can't do anything they wouldn't like. I am their guest."

Adam said, "I am ever so sorry, and I understand. It's all a question of conflicts between different government bodies, and you mustn't concern yourself. Well, Ray, until a better day."

The phone rang again. This time it was Count Holger Zorndorf, inviting me to a nightclub.

"And your anti-aircraft batteries?" I joked.

"I came on at seven this morning, and finish within an hour. I'm hungry, so we could go to a restaurant first."

"I'd love that," I said. "I believe Doris and her fiancé (Graf Richterin Prieguity) have a restaurant planned, and their cousin might be coming too. Shall I ask them whether we can all go together?"

"Oh, very good. I know the cousin, Eduard. He's a traumatologist at Berlin General Hospital. If they have other plans, we can go on our own. I'll come a little before eight o'clock."

Doris said she loved the idea, so we had to make agonising decisions about what dresses to wear.

Prince Brend came in and said, "Doris, darling, will you excuse Ray a moment."

I followed him to the great library.

A fifty-year-old man, in a beautiful suit, looked at me keenly as I came in. His bearing was authoritative, his face clever but polite, and his eyes read me in seconds.

The Prince said, "This is Ernst Freiherr von Weiszäcker, the Secretary of State, in the Foreign Ministry under von Ribbentrop. Von Weiszäcker was Minister to Norway from 1931 to 1933, Minister to Switzerland from 1933 to 1936."

Von Wiszäcker smiled at me. "I do hope our friend Bernd has managed to impress you. With a young lady as beautiful as yourself, I can be but grateful for anything to build me up in your eyes. Bernd, you did not tell me how lovely young Ray is. May we all sit?" and without awaiting an invitation, he settled in an armchair.

He said, "I have an extremely dangerous document here. It is the minutes of the secret Hossbach Conference. As I understand, you forward your photos through the Argentinean Embassy. Could you take this document to the Embassy for them to send it to Buenos Aires, to Tomas Machinia? I think Adam von Trott spoke to you."

Automatically, I said, "Yes."

One thing was sure. I was carrying no documents on my person through the streets of Berlin.

The Prince fetched glasses and bottles. I shook my head. Von Weiszäcker said, "This is the most secret and dangerous document today in the Reich. In the German parliament, and talking to foreign delegates, Hitler has always sworn he wanted peace. Hitler called a secret conference in the Reich Chancellery on November 5, 1937, and five days later, Colonel Friedrich Hossbach wrote the minutes. So the document bears the date of November 10, and is known as the *Hossbach Niederschrift* (in English – the Hossbach Memorandum or Hossbach Protocol). Hitler allowed only Field Marshal Werner von Blomberg, Minister of War; General Werner von Fritsch, commander in chief of the armed forces; Eric Raeder, commander in chief of the Navy; Colonel General Hermann Göring, commander in chief of the Luftwaffe; and Constantin Freiherr von Neurath, Foreign Minister – only these did he allow to be present, and he swore them to solemn vows of secrecy."

He opened his briefcase, and put a folder on the table, written on pink paper.

"Pink paper means *very top secret*," he told them. "Now the translators of the BBC programmes have to use pink paper! *Streng geheim* – top secret! I leave this folder with you."

I thought, this is another conspirator against Hitler. Did he introduce Adam von Trott to the Kreisau Circle of aristocrats, or did Adam introduce him? Yet he was a member of the Nazi Party, and on the ship from Argentina I had learned he held honorary rank in the SS.

I said, "Now we are at war, Thoma is looking for a job. Will you expand your offices and staff?"

He looked at the Prince.

"I fear that our dear Thoma does not know shorthand."

"But she can translate from English – or into English," I insisted.

I glanced nervously at the Prince, but I hadn't irritated him. He smiled at me indulgently.

Weiszäcker rubbed his upper lip.

"So, my dear Ray, you are suggesting a spot for Thoma in the A.A.?" (the *Auswärtiges Amt* – the Foreign Office.)

"I fear I'm guilty of temerity."

Very much mollified with those words, he said expansively, "Can we call in Thoma?"

Thank God, we had dressed up to go to the nightclub; and Thoma came in her gladdest rags, looking ravishing.

After the formalities, Weiszäcker said, "Thoma, my dear, I believe you are looking for employment?"

I stood up, and took the folder.

"Could I be excused, to attend to this?"

Thoma looked at me, surprised, and taking my leave, I went up to my bedroom.

What on earth was in this Memorandum? I sat down, and read.

Hitler began by saying that the 'solid racial core' of the German nation entitled it to larger *Lebensraum*, or Living Space. I sighed, and read on. Germans could not expand without crushing resistance, and the trick was to get the most at the lowest cost. Having decided to use force, the next thing was the timing – and Hitler said, 1943 – 1945; later would be to their disadvantage.

To be more exact, Hitler said the aim was to preserve the *Volkmasse* of Germans, and make their number grow; there were over 85 million, more tightly packed than any other racial core, so they had a greater right to spread than others. Could they survive on their own resources? By autarchy?

He said Germany had but limited autarchy in raw materials. They had enough coal, iron, and some light metals but didn't have enough copper, tin and others. They had autarchy in synthetic textiles while German forests lasted.

But with food – the answer was NO!

I put down the folder. So Germany didn't have enough food to fight a war. In conversations in London, I had heard people mention how Germany collapsed in 1918 because of the British blockade; we strangled them in materials – and in food. German hunger in 1918 had helped win us the war.

Where were the European breadbaskets? France, Poland – and the Ukraine! In Poland and the Ukraine, I had read that the peasant had grinding stones. With German ruthlessness, methodically, they would collect millions of grinding stones – the peasants would have to deliver their full crop, and get a miserable ration of milled flour in return. That or starve, be shot.

A great plain ran from Budapest to Beograd. Wheat? Czechoslovakia – wasn't it hilly or mountainous? Romania, on the other hand – mountains in the west, and behind them, a great plain running down into the great plains of Bulgaria. Hitler had a pact with Stalin – but Russia had no surplus grain to export. If Hitler took Russia, starved the peasants, and killed about 30 million people – less mouths to feed – he'd get the Ukrainian wheat. Was that it?

I went back to the Memorandum.

He argued that the standard-of-living had gone up in the last 30 or 40 years, so people were eating properly – eating MORE. Even the farmers themselves were eating more. Agricultural production had gone up, but it was being eaten. Production needs must be pushed up further, but the demands on the soil, despite artificial fertilizers, was too much – the soil shows signs of exhaustion.

So food must come from world trade.

The cost of paying foreign countries was 'not inconsiderable' when harvests were good, but catastrophic with bad harvests. Disaster came closer and closer with the German population growing – an excess of 560,000 births every year. And a child ate more bread than an adult.

This cannot be fixed by eating less food. As Hitler had solved unemployment, maximum food consumption had arrived. To make things worse were market fluctuations; and commercial treaties could break down. Since the World War, those very food exporting countries had often become industrialized; and the primitive urge to build empires could be seen in Italy and Japan, pushed by economic needs.

The world economy enjoys a boom thanks to rearmament, but this is not sound; and Bolshevism disturbs world economies. Countries which depend on foreign trade suffer from military weakness. Our own foreign trade is carried on sea routes which the British Navy dominates; in time of war, our weakness would show itself – a weakness not of foreign exchange but of security of transport of food supplies.

The only answer, said Hitler, might appear visionary – seizing more living space. This search throughout history has led to new nations, or the migration of ancient peoples. Satiated nations ignored our needs at Geneva; but it is our one central problem. We must seek space in Europe – not in colonies – but in European agricultural space. The history of the Roman Empire and the British Empire shows that expansion calls for breaking down resistance. There is no empty space – the attacker always comes up against a possessor.

Where can Germany gain the most at least cost?

Germany has to reckon with two hate-filled antagonists – Britain and France – who abhor a German colossus in central Europe. They oppose Germany in Europe and overseas – oppose the safeguarding of German commerce.

The Führer does not believe the British Empire is unshakeable. It cannot be compared to the Roman Empire, because the Romans had no serious competitor after the Punic Wars. It was only the disintegrating impact of Christianity that made Rome fall to the onslaught of the Germanic tribes.

Today, stronger states confront the British Empire. The British motherland could not protect Canada against an American invasion, or her Far Eastern colonies against a Japanese onslaught.

Already we can see that Britain, with its 45 million people, is not holding up:

a) Irish independence

b) Struggles in India

c) Japan's weakening of the British Empire in the Far East

d) Italy expanding its control of the Mediterranean at Britain's expense

The ratio of the population of the Empire to that of the British motherland is 9:1. This is a warning to us to sustain our numerical strength.

Germany's problems can be solved only by force, and this is risky. But Frederick the Great's campaign for Silesia, and Bismark's wars against Austria and France meant unheard-of risk.

The question is WHEN?

1943-1945: after 1945, we can only expect things to get worse. Our army, navy, *Luftwaffe* and officer corps are almost ready. Armament is modern – the danger is its obsolescence. The secrecy of our 'special weapons' cannot be kept forever. The rest of the world would have rearmed by then. Any year after 1945 could plunge us into a food crisis. The world expects our attack, and each year increases its countermeasures. We have to strike while the rest of the world was *sich abriegeln* – getting its defenses ready.

However!

The great *Wehrmacht* was aging. How long could it keep up today's sharp edge?

The German standard of living could drop and limit the birth rate.

Should we act before 1943?

France could get sucked into a war, leaving Germany free to attack the Czechs and Austria. A German-Hungarian frontier would intimidate Poland. Poland could always attack East Prussia, Pomerania and Silesia. Embroiled with its Empire, Britain would never welcome a protracted war against Germany.

Seizing Czechoslovakia and Austria means extra food for 5 or 6 million people, assuming we expel 2 million people from Czechoslovakia and 1 million from Austria. As well, we could form 12 new divisions...

* * *

I had read enough. I was not going to send this, as we were already at war. I could send it in plain language, but that would be suicidal. To encode it would take hours.

I put it in the top drawer of my dresser. I could not go to the nightclub with it there, but would warn the Prince to hide it.

It never occurred to me that Weiszäcker was buying his own insurance with this.

The Hossbach Memorandum was key evidence at the Nuremburg trials after the war. From 1943 to 1945, Weiszäcker was German Ambassador at the Holy See in Rome, and they gave him sanctuary after the war. The Allies arrested him as a war criminal and put him on trial in 1947. As had escaped execution after the July 20 Plot in 1944, the Allies refused to believe he was a conspirator. My sending the Hossbach Protocol would nave proved he was. I wanted to testify, and in London, they warned me I had signed the Official Secrets Act. They warned me that operatives of the British Secret Service never emerged in public. I wanted to talk to the Nuremburg judges in camera, but they told me the judges would instantly cite me as a public witness.

In 1949, an American military tribunal gave him seven years for complicity in Nazi crimes, but they let him out early.

In his memoirs, Weiszäcker insisted he had always opposed Hitler, and had joined the Nazi Party and accepted the honorary rank in the SS for 'decorative reasons'.

No one can imagine the terror that gripped us all; people had to do these things, He died in 1951.

His son defended him at Nurenberg; in 1985, his son became President of the West German Republic.

I met the cousin, Eduard, the doctor at the Berlin Hospital. He looks a real Hohenlinden, more than Claus. He brought greetings from his father, Count Axel. He slapped Count Holger Zorndorf – in his anti aircraft uniform – on the shoulder, and asked him was he going to keep the Polish planes away, or would the planes fill up his hospital with victims. Everyone thought this grisly humour funny. He asked me about Argentina, and asked Doris' fiancé, Graf Richterin Prieguity, whether Luftwaffe Technical Planning had come up with a way to stop bombers. It wasn't the sort of laughing conversation we ever had in London. Eduard was dressed casually, but expensively, and said they knew him at all the night clubs and would let him in. He was with a tall, blonde, buxom, and very shy nurse, who with her statuesque body didn't need to add a word to the conversation. She and Eduard went in Richterin's staff car, and Holger and I followed in Holger's staff car.

I would never have believed they could have made the streets so black. Thin slits of light shone from the headlights as we drove across Berlin. Whitewashed curbstones help. There are blue lights and, as your eyes adapt, you see more and more… but don't ask me how Holger managed.

It's impossible to imagine that people are sitting behind blackened windows, in brightly-lit rooms. At the restaurant, we blinked when we got inside. A loud hum of conversation under the lights – everyone enjoying themselves. We had a good meal, and groped our way on foot to the nightclub 200 metres away. The lights in the restaurant had blinded our eyes when we came out on to the street – we bumped into people, into the walls, and the lamp-posts. Alas, we had drunk a bottle of wine.

At the night club we couldn't dance – no more dancing in public while the war lasts. Let's hope the Embassies will hold dances, and we get invited.

On Sunday afternoon, the newspaper extras came out. The *Deutsche Allgemeine Zeitung*'s headlines read:

BRITISH ULTIMATUM REJECTED
ENGLAND DECLARES WAR UPON GERMANY
BRITISH NOTE DEMANDS WITHDRAWAL OF OUR ARMY IN
THE EAST
FÜHRER DEPARTS FOR THE FRONT TODAY

The state of war existed at midday.

The newspaper published all the official statements, and proclaimed GERMAN MEMORANDUM PROVES ENGLAND'S GUILT.

I had the shakes. So long as England does not send an army across the English Channel! If England loses its army, we will have a nightmare Thousand Year Reich.

The peasants in Poland, the Ukraine, Czechoslovakia, Hungary, Romania, and Yugoslavia and Bulgaria will be hopelessly inefficient. Who will take their lands – German farmers of the chosen race – or British serfs, whose children will not read or write?

My depression had no bottom, no seabed.

Yet my brave fellow countrymen, the bravest of the brave, had forced Hitler's hand.

Hitler cannot wait till 1943-1945, when he would have been invincible.

It was a warm Sunday for September, a lovely day. Schneppen rang and asked me to get to the British Embassy. At nine o'clock this morning, Sir Nevile Henderson called on von Ribbentrop and gave him a note from the British Government giving Germany till 11 a.m. to accept the British demand that Germany get out of Poland.

A little after 11 a.m. I watched him return to the Foreign Office, for the German reply. It was a memorandum, and said, 'The British government bears the responsibility for all the unhappiness and suffering which will now fall on the peoples everywhere.'

Further on, it says, 'The German people and its government do not want, as does Great Britain, to dominate the world.'

This was in the afternoon papers. The papers also gave the Führer's proclamation to the Nazi Party. One sentence read, 'Our Jewish-democratic world enemies have brought it to come that the British people are now at war with Germany.'

About 250 people stood in the Wilhelmstrasse with me this morning. I stayed till after noon – and about noon the loudspeakers blared that England had declared war. The people just stood there, without a sound.

I wandered up to Unter den Linden, photographing people in the street, their faces grimmer than anything I had seen. Grim and glassy, as though they thought Hitler was dragging them to destruction.

A whole crowd came out of the British Embassy, and went to Hotel Adlon, right next door. That's where the foreign newspapermen sleep – and drink.

I went in fearfully. Would someone recognise me? It was an appalling risk. The Embassy crowd stood around in the garden, drinking, without a care in the world – enjoying a sunny Sunday morning. I wore my Press armband, and took photos. They ignored me. I saw newspapermen from different countries – the British and French newspapermen had left Germany – but none apparently had ever seen me in London.

I heard them saying that the diplomatic staffs of the British and French Embassies head for the Belgian frontier tomorrow morning in a special Pullman train. Someone remarked on how correct and courteous the Germans had been with them. Someone else said that special coaches had taken American women and children to Warnemünde, to pick up a ferry-boat for Denmark. The American Embassy will represent Britain and France. It seems some 50 staffers are staying at the American Embassy, and a dozen are women, who refuse to leave their husbands.

Back home, in the afternoon, we listened to the wireless. Yesterday, they deafened us with martial music. This afternoon, it was Beethoven's Fourth Symphony, with long silences, then announcements. They warned us in an air raid to keep our windows *open*, to stop the blast shattering the glass. We were not to worry about gas coming in the open windows – gas is heavier than air, and sinks to the ground. Lots of people carry gas masks in the streets, but I don't have one. The British would never stoop to gassing civilians.

At the evening meal, the Prince said, "No one thought Britain and France would do it. Germans think that Poland is Germany's business. Britain and France stood aside with Czechoslovakia and Austria, and that misled them."

My tank colonel – Ekkehard Kraske – rang, inviting me to a restaurant. Claus said he'd come too, with his two sisters, and at the last moment, Thoma's fiancé, Walter, said he'd meet us there at the restaurant.

71

It's an awful business finding your way in the blackout. Suddenly, you go through the doors into the restaurant, in to bright lights and a lively hum of conversation!

Claus talked about grouse-shooting in Scotland, near Calander, and of another year, farther north. Ekkehard talked about the Cote d'Azur, the restaurants and the Casinos. We talked about roulette systems and then about probability in general... deep at the back of our minds, about the probabilities of our getting killed. I suppose Claus flattered Ekkehard, asking him what he thinks Britain could do. Ekkehard said that Britain would lose its army on the continent and sue for peace.

"We'll round up the British Army with our tanks as thought we were sheepdogs. Britain can't exhaust itself with another World War, not against Germany. It would lose its Empire. It would end up as another small nation, like the Scandinavian countries. As a world power, it's finished. The world today belongs to Germany, Russia, Japan and the United States."

"And Italy?" I asked him.

"Ach! Mussolini's all posture, you'll see."

I drove home alone with Ekkehard in his staff car.

He stopped in the blackness of the street and we got out, ringing the bell on the tall gate.

He pulled me to him, and held me with desperate strength, his cheek against mine. I could feel his heart thudding, and his breath.

"You're going to come out of all this alive," I whispered, putting my arms around him. "Alive."

How death petrifies us at our age! We tell ourselves it can't happen to us; but we have all our lives ahead of us, that we want to live to our very last day.

That enormity of Hitler, stepped straight out of hell!

Every day, the news came in. Polish heroes against German tanks, Stukas and bombers.

The newspaper *Nachtausgabe* carried a screaming headline: CAVALRY ATTACKS TANKS! A German communiqué said Polish cavalry 'invaded' German territory in East Prussia. The German airforces have destroyed various Polish railway lines: Kutno-Warsaw, Krakow-Lemberg, Kielce-Warsaw, Thorn-Eylau...

Could England go on fighting after they destroy our railway lines?

German troops have reached East Prussia overland.

The staffs of the British and French Embassies left on two trains. The Ambassadors each got a Salon carriage, and the rest of the staff, Pullmans, Officials from the German Foreign Office and German army rode with them. Goebbels sent me to photograph them, and my heart broke; I couldn't get on the train and go with them. Is there any other British national now in Germany – perhaps people married to Germans, or elderly people who've been residents here all their lives?

We were at a late breakfast. I had gone out to dinner with a Hungarian I had met in the Argentinean Embassy; afterwards, we went back to the Hungarian Embassy, and improvised a dance with six couples.

Reinhard came in, and with all the aplomb of a British butler, announced, "Two Gestapo gentlemen to see Miss Raimunda."

The grandmother muttered an imprecation, and dabbed her lips with her serviette. Princess Jutta took my hand in alarm.

I went out to the foyer.

In their long coats, they both looked at me for twenty seconds, and then one said, "*Reichsminister* Himmler wishes to see you at eleven o'clock. We will send a car for you at half-past-ten. Please bring all your photographic equipment."

I said, with a dry throat, "At half-past-ten. Thank you."

I hurried back to finish my breakfast, and then to dress.

Princess Jutta and her grandmother were jubilant.

I tried to marshal everything I knew about this monster.

There were three men who would never leave Hell – would spend eternities upon eternities there; Stalin, Hitler and Himmler. But Himmler had inflicted ruthlessly more torture and pain than the others.

73

I knew he was 39 years old. That his father was a secondary school teacher, his parents devoutly Catholic. In the World War, he joined the 11th Bavarian Infantry, and then went to Munich Technical College to get a diploma in agriculture. He had joined a paramilitary nationalist group and that's where Hitler spotted him. Hitler made him business manager of his Nazi Party. With Ernst Röhm, he was in the Beer-Hall Putsch, when Hitler tried to seize power. In hours after the Putsch, Hitler the unknown, hit the headlines all over Germany – and Hitler learnt that he couldn't win power by violence.

Himmler married the daughter of a landowner in 1928 – Margarete Boden, seven years older than himself. She got him intrigued with homeopathy, herbalism and Mesmerism.

He neglected his family, and fathered a number of illegitimate children. In 1928, he went into poultry-farming near Munich. Next year, Hitler named him head of is personal bodyguard – the Black Guard – of 300 men; the *Schutzstaffel*... the dreaded SS. This gave him the platform he needed to rise to absolute power. By 1933, an approving Hitler saw how he had swollen the SS to 50,000 thugs. Rumors abounded, and the British Embassy faithfully funneled them through to London. He wormed his way into business and manufacturing, the only top Nazi to accumulate a huge, undercover fortune, not known even to Hitler. He delved into the cupboards of all other Nazi bosses and meticulously recorded all their skeletons.

From 1931 to 1933, Röhm's SA Brown Shirts ran Himmler's SS, but Himmler organized another secret security gang, also to repress the German people, the infamous *Sicherheitsdienst* or SD, under Reinhard Heydrich. Hitler named Himmler police chief for Munich in 1933, and ordered him to build the first concentration camp at Dachau. In 1934, Göring named Himmler chief of the Gestapo in Prussia.

Himmler's joy was unconfined in 1934. He had to draw up a list of the Nazi Party's left wing (supposedly 'left') for Hitler's Blood Purge. Himmler unleashed his SS on a three-day massacre of the SA Brown Shirts and of Röhm himself. Three weeks later, Hitler withdrew the SS from its subordination to the SA, to raise it to independence; and in 1936 named Himmler *ReichsFührer* of the unified police of all Germany, of the SS and of the Gestapo.

Himmler now ran a juggernaut to oppress the German people... he had utterly strapped them. He was an authoritarian sadist who lusted for unlimited power over people – over their very thoughts and words. To speak out of turn meant a concentration camp or the headman's axe.

I met the Prince on the stairs.

He said, "I've heard."

I asked, "Can I make friends with a madman like this?"

Prince Bernd leant against the banister. "He has two sides that don't seem to be aware of each other. He's deeply into business and making money. When the British come to hang Hitler, Goebbels and Göring on the gallows, Himmler will have bought his freedom by clever negotiation, and paying British leaders millions. He will 'commit suicide' and there'll be not one proper photo of his body before it's buried. He'll argue reasonably and unanswerably with the British and strike an intelligent deal that no sane man can resist."

Reinhard came to the foot of the stairs and looked at us. He didn't need to say anything. The Gestapo car was here.

* * *

We drove down Wilhemstrasse in front of the abandoned British Embassy, and turned into Prince Alberecht strasse to the Gestapo building.

Inside, I saw them ring upstairs.

They took me up, and led me to a towering, ornate door. Inside, I stepped into a tall room with a marble floor, and darker marble walls. Light came from two windows. A black table stood at one end with black leather armchairs on either side. Was this his working office, or a special reception room?

The door closed behind me, and I stood there.

At the other end, the door opened, and Himmler walked forward briskly.

He was not tall. His blue-gray eyes stared at me through pince-nez glasses. He had the plump cheeks and the smile of a merry country schoolmaster. His smile was infectious and reached his eyes. At last I understood Shakespeare – 'how can he smile and smile and be such a villain?' That was one of the three or four lines I knew. He wore a moustache trimmed carefully below a handsome nose and had the receding chin of an English aristocrat.

If not a schoolteacher, he could have been a friendly bank teller. Was it true then, as Miss Ancram had suggested, basing her words on contemptuous reports from the British Embassy, that Heydrich was the evil wizard who was breathing life into this stick of a man and pushing, him to the top, then to take his place? But I remembered his empire of tax-exempt businesses… it would be a lethal mistake to under-estimate him.

He took my hand with a smile that filled his face, as though my being there was too good to be true, and showed me to an armchair. I took off my cameras from around my neck and put them on the spotless, gleaming marble floor.

He had taken in my hips, and now looked at my breasts, then my face.

I knew he felt an inferior physical specimen.

75

He was no muscular brute like his SS murderers, and could not do the route marches. He could not shoot well with his poor eyesight. The loutish Stepp Dietrich, who commanded the Hitler Guards – the *Leibstandarte Adolf Hitler* – once jeered at him to his face, and he took it in almost homosexually. This paucity of strength made him obsessed with racial purity, and he chose his SS with finicky care. He had organised a maternity home, and planned on scores more, where his SS could breed true. He had studied breeding at his chicken farm, and had not discovered the danger of inbreeding.

His eyes came back to my breasts, and he said, "Goebbels tells me you are a wonderful portrait photographer – you work with all a woman's sensibility. Yet you prefer to work than to fulfill yourself having babies?"

"You are making world history," I flattered him. "In Argentina, I would lead a nondescript life and read what was happening in the newspapers. Here I am part of it, and can meet the architects – meet men whose names will be remembered in thousands of years."

He straightened up, delighted. The man's smile was irresistible.

"Would you care to photograph me? I understand that Goebbels makes you account for every millimetre of film. How many spools are you carrying?"

"Three."

He opened a box on the black marble table, and took out three spools. "If you want to shoot three spools now, here are the replacements."

I stood up.

"Do you think you could keep talking, as I work? Although I will be moving around, I will not miss a word you say."

"Ah," he said. "Clever. All the more reason to have babies, don't you agree?"

"My work is more important, I believe, for German destiny. At least, in the immediate future."

I would like to capture a merciless expression, but it would be impossible.

"Would you consider going to the Polish front?"

"If I am ordered to, I will go," I answered, and got an expression of approval, which I captured on film. "I am not a war photographer."

"I don't want war photos. Let me explain. You know about the German Army?"

I nodded. Hitler distrusted many of its High Command.

"Years ago, I organised a small group of soldiers into the Adolph Hitler Guard. This grew in numbers, and today it forms the *SS-Panzerdivision-Leibstandarte Adolph Hitler* – a full tank division. I am also forming five more SS divisions – which will be a second army, but more racially pure and more loyal to Hitler. These divisions will be SS-Panzerdivisions: Firstly, *Das Reich* – secondly, *Totenkopf,* or Death's Head – thirdly, the *SS-Polizei*

76

Panzergrenardierdivision-Polizei Division – fourthly, *SS-Panzerdivision-Viking* – and lastly, *SS-Freiwilligen-Gebirgdivision-Prince Eugen.*

"As I say, these are not ordinary German Armymen, but men who I demand must be fiercely loyal first and lastly to Hitler. They must have no feelings, be hard as steel. They must fight for love of fighting, be blindly obedient, utterly despise racial inferiors, and those who do not belong to their ranks. This army is the *Waffen-SS* – that is, the armed SS – its soldiers feel a mystical bond for each other. Its soldiers believe that nothing is impossible for them – they can defeat anyone – especially Russians, English and Americans.

"After the World War, Germany had to organize demobilised soldiers to form the *Freikorps*, which remained loyal to authority, and saved this country from chaos. Many of our Nazis came from the *Freikorps*. In 1925, we formed the SS with two militarized groups – those militarized troops and the Death's Head formations, the *SS-Totenkopfverbände*. In 1933, I formed the SS-Bodyguard Regiment Adolph Hitler, the *Leibstandarte*, which today has grown to enormous strength, and is now in Poland, commanded by a most remarkable general, Sepp Dietrich."

I repressed a shiver.

"So this year, I have named this SS army the '*Waffen-SS*'."

After the war, I was to find that this private Nazi army was to finally number about one million men, all profoundly indoctrinated. Himmler taught them, 'This is a battle of races. Nazism rests on thee values of our Germanic, Nordic blood – a beautiful, honest society of equality for all.' He told them that other races were of a 'physique such as you may shoot them down without pity or remorse.'

He tried to form a Waffen-SS Foreign Legion, enlisting foreigners, but the non-Germans were not as good. His German *Waffen-SS* were beyond any argument among the world's very best troops. The Nuremberg Trial judges indicted the *Waffen-SS* as a criminal organization, along with the SS. The High Command of the German Army, also on trial, said the *Waffen-SS* committed all the atrocities, and that the German Army followed an indoctrination of honour and traditional warfare. High Army officers pointed out that Himmler's Army, steeped in racialism and the belief they were supermen, committed barbarities seeking racial purification.

Apart from the six divisions I have already spoken of, by 1945, Himmler had formed the following SS-divisions to make up his private army:

SS-Kavallieredivision-Florian Geyer	1942 Germans
SS-Panzerdivision-Hohenstaufen	1943 Germans
SS-Panzerdivison-Frundsberg	1943 Germans

SS-Freiwilligen-Panzergrenardierdivisionis -Nordland	1942 Germans, Scandinavian
SS Panzerdivision Hitler Jugend	1943 Germans
Waffen-Gebirgsdivision der SS-Handschar	1943 Yugoslavs
Waffen-Grenadierdivision der SS-Galiziacha No. 1	1943 Ukrainians
Waffen-Grenadierdivision der SS-Lettische No. 1	1943 Latvians, Germans
SS-Panzergrenadierdivision-ReichsFührer-SS	1943 Germans, ethnic Germans
SS-Panzergrenadierdivision-Gotz von Berlichingen	1943 Germans, ethnic Germans
SS-Freiwilligen-Panzergrenadierdivision -Horst Wessel	1944 Germans, ethnic Germans
Waffen-Granadierdivision der SS-Lettische No. 2	1944 Latvians
Waffen-Granadierdivision der SS-Estnische No. 1	1944 Estonians
Waffen-Gabirgsdivision der SS-Albanische No 1 -Skandarberg	1944 Albanians
SS-Freiwilligen-Kavalleriedivision-Maria Theresa	1944 Germans, ethnic Germans
Waffen-Gebirgadivision der SS-Kama	1944 Yugoslavs
SS-Freiwilligen-Panzerdivision-Nederland	1945 Dutch
Waffen-Gebirgadivision der SS-Kastjäger	1944 Italians, ethnic Germans
Waffen-Grenadierdivision der SS-Hunyadi No. 1	1944 Hungarian
Waffen-Granadierdivision der SS-Hunyadi No. 2	1944 Hungarian
SS-Freiwilligen-Grenadierdivision- Langemarck	1945 Flemish, Belgians
SS-Freiwilligen-Grenadierdivision-Wallonie	1945 Walloons, Belgians
Waffen-Grenadierdivision der SS-Russische No. 1	1944 Russians
Waffen-Grenadierdivision der SS-Italische No. 1	1945 Italians
Waffen-Grenadierdivision der SS-Russische No. 2	1944 Russians
SS-Freiwilligen-Grenadierdivision	1945 Germans
SS-Freiwilligen-Panzerdivision-Böhmen -Mahren	1945 Germans, ethnic Germans

78

Waffen-Grenadierdivision der SS-January 30	1945 French
Waffen-Grenadierdivision der SS-Charlemagne	1945 Dutch
SS-Freiwilligen-Grenadierdivision	1945 German
-Landstorm Naderland	policemen
SS-Polizei-Grenadierdivision der SS	1945 Germans
Waffen-Grenadierdivision-Dirlewanger	1945 Germans
SS-Freiwilligen-Kavalieriedivision-Lützow	1945 Ethnic
	Germans
SS-Panzergrenadierdivison-Nibelungen	1945 SS Cadets

Himmler went on, "As I say, I don't want you to take war photos. We have male photographers for that. I want you to capture the expressions of our *Leibstandarte* soldiers, their faces, their joy in combat, their contempt of death, their victorious, invincible glow when they are fighting. Who better than a woman for this – what woman does not feel a glow in her breast when she sees beside her a man in his instant of merciless conquest?"

I nodded humbly.

"You will be stationed at the side of Sepp Dietrich. Take all the photos of him that you can. He's a vain man, and he's living hours of glory."

I cleared my throat, and he looked at me sharply.

"I will do everything you command me to, *ReichsFührer*," I said formally. "But I have another problem. I am also answerable to *Reichsminister* Goebbels."

He smiled slowly.

"Your obedience does you credit. I have spoken to him."

I sighed in relief, and he beamed.

"Can I go and see him before I leave? I depend on his goodwill to be able to stay in Germany."

A shadow crossed his face.

"Ach! You women! Certainly, go and see him."

All this time, I was on my feet, weaving about the room, taking photos, sometimes crouching. I reached the end of the third spool.

"Do you want me to develop the films?"

"We will do it here."

"Afterwards, if you give me the film, I can retouch it with a soft lead pencil, and bring out nuances of expression that sometimes are surprising."

"The film will be sent to the Prince's home."

He rang a bell push, and escorted me to the door.

"A car will come for you at one o'clock to take you to the aerodrome."

He said to the two officers standing there, "Drive this young lady to the Propaganda Ministry, and wait for her. Then drive her home."

They clicked their heels.

At the Propaganda Ministry, I told Schneppen what had happened.

"Dr. Goebbels is expecting you. We'll go up to him now."

Goebbels motioned me to an armchair, and pointed to his desk. Before I sat, I walked around the side of the desk, and saw one of my portraits of him in a silver frame.

I gave him a ravishing smile.

"You do me much honour," I purred.

"You have been a busy little lady."

"Two Gestapo men came to me at home. Do I have your permission to go to Poland?"

"My permission! You have Himmler's."

"I work for you."

"You do not. You work for your editor in Buenos Aires."

"Well, or, I feel that with you..."

"We have a friendship?" he asked keenly.

"You are a dangerous friend for a young maiden," I simpered. "Let's say–" I stopped for want of a word.

"A wary, yet friendly, yet distant relationship?" he suggested, and we both burst into laughter.

I said, when I was able to stop laughing, "With a wary, friendly, distant supervisor I feel I should let him know what I'm doing and clear it first with him."

"Admirably put," he said. "You'd make a good propagandist. Off you go to Poland, and come here as soon as you get back. There's always work to be done."

He showed me to the door, an amused smile on his face.

"You're going to need all these manipulative skills with Sepp Dietrich," he warned me.

I left the building, and collapsed into the car.

Was I pleased to be out of Gestapo Headquarters! The *Geheime Staatspolizei* awoke terror in every German. Hitler had decreed that every single individual was suspect of dissidence, opposition or complaining. It had its own legal system that overrode any law court in Germany. It had ferreted out every last Jew and expelled them; now it hunted Marxists. You went to prison for an anti-Nazi joke or talking about the Kaiser. Everyone had heard of its cellars.

They first gave you a warning. If you didn't heed it, they put you in a concentration camp. If they thought you were a true threat, they beat you to death. Sometimes, they took you to the People's Court first – the *Volksgericht* – to keep up a farce of legality.

Two thirds of the population and land of Germany lay in Prussia, and when Göring took over the Prussian Ministry of the Interior in 1933, he threw out the old Police Division for political investigation and put in a new secret police, all Nazi Party people.

The first steps… the first steps to what may well be the deaths of tens of millions of Englishmen, Frenchmen, Germans and Russians, not to mention soldiers of a dozen other countries and their unarmed citizens. England had the mightiest empire the world has ever seen! What puny brains we have, that we can never learn.

Himmler suggested to Hitler that the tight centralisation of the Reich under the Nazi Party – for this, the Nazis passed the *Gleichschaltung* laws in 1933 – ought to apply to the Police also and offered to unify the forces. He adroitly ousted Göring, who got the Luftwaffe as a consolation prize; he took over Göring's secret police entire.

Göring had called his Nazi Secret Police the *Geheimes Polizei Amt*. Himmler changed the name to *Geheimes Statspolizei*. In 1934, Heinrich Muller took over the Gestapo; in 1936, Himmler gave the Gestapo to Heydrich, with Muller – mass-murderer Muller as he was known after the war – as operational boss. In another four years time – 1943 – it would grow to 45,000 men inflicting terror and death inside Germany and outside it – with another 60,000 agents, and 100,000 German citizens informing on their neighbours. All the names on captured SS files.

The whole SS Empire held not just the Gestapo, but the Intelligence Service – rivalling Adam Trott's *Abwehr* – called the SD; the *Kripo*, or criminal police – *Kriminalpolizei*; and a new, mystery organisation called the *Einsatzgruppen*, whose job apparently would be to murder prisoners-of-war, gypsies, marxists, state enemies, Jews and homosexuals in occupied lands.

I dressed in a grey skirt, hiking boots, with a dark green sweater over a blouse. Over that, I wore a khaki waterproof raincoat, and hoped the colours would pass SS military.

In the car to the aerodrome, and on the plane to somewhere in Poland, I drew from memory what Constance Ancram had told me about Sepp Dietrich.

An ex-sergeant major from the Great War, 'the most brutal man in Germany', William Shirer, the US correspondent in Berlin, had described him. A heavily-muscled bully, a killer, an insolent bumpkin, he took Shirer's remark, broadcast to the world, as a compliment. Born in 1892, he learned the trade of butcher – served in the Imperial Army in 1911 – and was paymaster sergeant in the Great War. Then he drifted from farm worker to policeman, waiter, foreman in a tobacco factory, petrol station attendant rising to customs official. He took offence at the drop of a cigarette stub. He joined the *Freikorps*, and was sometimes a *Freikorps* street thug, sometimes unemployed. He was no blond Aryan superman, but Hitler liked the burly tough and made him his bodyguard in 1928; then named him boss of the *Leibstandarte Adolf Hitler*, and under Dietrich they stood out within the infamous SS for their swagger and arrogance. A *Standarte*, an Ensign, is a unit in the SS or SA of some 1,200 to 3,000 men, like an army regiment.

Hitler made Dietrich an *SS-BrigadeFührer*, and used him for executions, especially in the Röhm Purge – the Blood Purge – in 1934, when Heydrich and Goebbels convinced Hitler of a faked SA – Brownshirt – revolt. Hitler sent Dietrich to murder old friends of his from the *Freikorps*, from the early days of Nazism. One after another said, "Sepp, you're not going to kill *me*. I've done nothing," which was the perfect truth. "I obey Hitler's orders. Hitler is never wrong," said Sepp, lifting the pistol to his friend's face and firing point blank. "Human life doesn't matter to the SS."

A bumpkin, a yokel, like Dietrich did not see through Heydrich's plotting – Heydrich even gave Göring the death lists in Berlin, and Göring swallowed whole the cooked-up conspiracy supposedly by the Brownshirts and the *Reichswehr* – the 100,000 strong German Army allowed by the victors after the Great War.

By then, Dietrich was *SS-GruppenFührer* – Lieutenant General – turned *SS-OberstgruppenFührer* – Colonel General. Now he was the first commander of the 1st *SS-Panzerdivision*, the *Leibstandarte*.

The plane landed on a rough aerodrome with fields stretching away beyond it.

I went down the steps, and an SS-Major walked up, clicked his heels, and invited me to sit in the back seat of a staff car.

I could hear explosions of bombs or artillery shells, and see a haze of smoke in the distance. Planes appeared and snarled very fast overhead.

"Where are we?" I asked.

"Near Warsaw. Warsaw is holding out, and two Polish columns have advanced to its relief. They've brought us here to stop them. The Poles are fighting fanatically, so we're very pleased."

He gave a wolfish grin and studied my face for my reaction.

After everything I had been through in the last two weeks, this was small potatoes, as our Yankee cousins would say.

"It looks as though I am fortunate," I said as callously as I could manage.

"*ReichsFührer* Himmler spoke very well of you. He ordered me to make you a small gift," and he handed me a tiny packet, wrapped in paper.

I undid it, and it was a Death's Head badge. I pushed it into the weave of my sweater.

He stared at my breast.

"Do you think this raincoat is all right?"

"I can give you a three-quarter length SS-Panzer coat."

"I'd love that."

We drove for ten minutes, and came to a small stone village. He led me into one of the houses, and gave me the dark panzer coat with flashes. "You can leave your luggage here. This will be your house. It has two rooms." He opened an inside door, and I saw a Spartan cot, with military blankets, and hooks on the wall.

The jacket had been waiting for me! I had done well to ask for it.

We went down the village street to a large building.

In a long room, I saw maps on the walls. High ranking officers bent over a long table.

"The lady photographer has arrived," the Major announced.

I recognized Sepp Dietrich instantly from photos on the ship to Argentina.

He was in shirtsleeves, the shirt open at the neck. A stove was going, but it was not warm in the room.

He gave me a hearty, countryman's grin, his narrowed eyes with pouches, fleshy cheeks with a line running down each side, a heavy, bony, protruding jaw, and this enormous grin from taut lips. He had meaty hands, very broad shoulders, and looked as though he was in his element, enjoying every ebullient minute of life. He exuded energy; warm, animal energy.

"You came, by God!" he cried. "You didn't make excuses! I was betting you'd be frightened."

I put my cameras on the long table.

"And you're wearing a Death's Head badge!" he whooped, as he took in my breasts. "Who gave you that?"

"Himmler. Through the good offices of the Major here."

He laughed. "This isn't going to be any portrait studio. It's getting violent here."

"You're stopping two columns which are attacking very hard," I said, awed, making my voice a little breathless. "Are they very close? Will we have Polish cavalry in the street outside?"

Everyone laughed, and I knew I was accepted.

Dietrich put a beefy arm around my shoulders, and drew me to the table. With a thick forefinger, he quickly pointed out what was happening.

Oh, those gallant, wonderful Poles! Against tanks! It was impossible, but the map showed where they were.

"Goodness," I said. "I'm interrupting you. It seems you have to act very quickly. What are you going to do?"

He stabbed his finger at the map, and then drew a line of a couple of inches.

"You wouldn't dare!" I gasped.

"That's the way I wage war," he said proudly. "Daring thrusts. The unexpected. Risks! And more risks! You are very quick for a woman. So what do you think? I go, or I don't go?"

I looked around the other faces. They were grave, they were not very happy. I looked back at Sepp Dietrich, and knew that he had already decided.

I took a deep breath and said, "It's a new sort of warfare, never seen before, isn't it?"

They nodded.

"This must be the way to do it."

"Bravo!" cried Dietrich.

These Germans were born warriors and killers. They would take decisions minutes before – or fractions of a second before – a British commander, or British tank captain would. They were like kids on a picnic, while *we* hated war, hated destruction and death. War depressed us and elated them.

Well – out of 85 million Germans, there would be two or three million men like this. I sensed the rest were just like ourselves. But the Nazis had tied up the country so *tightly*, so *ruthlessly*, and were indoctrinating the boys…

"While you work, can I take photos? Try to pretend I'm not here."

That got another round of guffaws, but excited now, they bent over their maps, looking up as they spoke to each other.

Himmler was going to love these photos.

As I worked, I realized the precision in their planning – setting up their units like pieces from a watch.

Dietrich's division stood with its back to Warsaw. Behind them, stood Reinhardt's 4th Panzer division of the regular army, facing attacks from the Polish army in Warsaw.

Dietrich faced two columns on the Bzura River. He planned a pincer movement behind Piastov, and I asked could I go.

He called in a colonel, who took me in hand.

I photographed merry soldiers, getting their weapons ready. In trucks, we rolled out behind tanks, and went about 15 miles north and turned west.

The ground erupted in artillery explosions. Polish soldiers jumped up from nowhere and threw explosive satchels into tank treads, disabling two of them.

The other tanks withdrew, and the trucks raced back. The colonel said, "We'll try higher up. Pincer movements need surprise."

A mighty explosion knocked our lorry over. The blast threw me clear, and I was lying on damp ground, dazed and half-blinded.

That damned Graham Bunton! He never mentioned this! Machine-gun bullets filled the air. I rolled over, and saw *Waffen-SS* soldiers lying still, or their bodies jerking with the bullets.

The shooting stopped.

The colonel was groaning, bleeding from the neck and right shoulder. Beside him, a private soldier, his left arm full of wounds, groaned, and turned this way and that. I wriggled over to the colonel.

I said, "We have to get out of here. Can you crawl over to those trees?"

He nodded, and I crawled to the soldier.

"Can you get over to those trees?"

He followed me. I picked up a machine-pistol from a dead soldier, unbuckled his ammunition belt, and pulled it along the ground after me.

The colonel had wriggled over to a dead medical orderly, and recovered his satchel.

From the cover of the trees, I looked out carefully, and saw Polish soldiers advance. We were lost.

A tank fired from the woods near us, and the Poles ran back.

We got deeper into the undergrowth, and I opened the satchel. I disinfected the colonel's neck and shoulder wounds, and bandaged them; with tweezers, I pulled out bits of shrapnel from the soldier's left arm, disinfected the wounds and bandaged him.

This took half-an-hour.

I asked the soldier, "Can you walk?" He nodded. He had lost the use of his hand and fingers.

"What's your name," I asked the colonel.

"Stefan. I can see, but suddenly it is through a mist..."

He was a good-looking, blond Aryan type with a great sense of humour, about 30 years old. As we were at war with Germany, I was probably committing high treason helping them, instead of shooting them with the machine pistol. But I had only one idea in my head – get back to the side of a comforting Dietrich, and bring these two with me. I'd never make a soldier – Stefan was much too nice to hurt. I could use the machine pistol against Graham Bunton – oh, indeed, I would.

I led them deeper into the wood, and turned left. The ground fell away, so I led them to the bottom, where we found a stream. We drank thirstily, and filled our canteens.

On the other side, I found a path, so I went some yards ahead, pointing the machine pistol up the path.

We broke out of the trees, and saw Polish units. I led them back into the forest, and we headed away from the Poles, across fields, with trees. I looked for streams, and found them.

The soldier sank to the ground. I let him rest; then he leant on me, and kept going.

We were halfway across a field, when a tank broke out of some trees.

Thank God, it was German. It drove over, and a Captain jumped out. The soldier's knees slowly buckled, and then he fell to the ground; he was out.

I lowered the soldier to the ground, and said, "Do you have any food?"

86

The captain came back with rations.

"I've radioed for help," he assured me.

After the colonel and I had eaten, I pulled out my pack, found my mirror and comb, and was doing my hair when three lorries rushed up.

We were back at Dietrich's headquarters before you could say cock-robin.

They took us to a field hospital, and we three stretched out on wooden planks. Two doctors went to work on Stefan and the soldier, and I sat up.

"I picked what shrapnel I could out of his arm, but there's probably more."

The other doctor turned to me from Stefan.

"You're a nurse, I see."

"Heavens, no! I was afraid that if their wounds got infected they couldn't walk."

The other doctor said drily, "You've missed your calling."

An *SS-GruppenFührer* strode in. I remembered him from the chart room.

"Are you all right?" he asked me, and I gave him one of my warm smiles.

"What happened?"

"An artillery barrage fell on us. The Poles blew up the tracks of two tanks with satchel explosives. A shell turned over our lorry. We three were able to escape."

Stefan said, "She led us out. Something's wrong with my eyes. She cleaned and bandaged our wounds as though she had all the time in the world. She had the presence of mind to scoop up a machine-pistol. When Gunter couldn't go on, she half-carried him. She walked point for us, most of the way, and looked for streams so we could drink. Joking all the way."

The *SS-GruppenFührer* snapped, "How are Stefan's eyes?"

"With luck, back to normal in a week. He got some concussion. I thought the lady was a nurse; she did such a good job. Picked shrapnel out of Gunter's arm."

"So, you were brave," the *SS-GruppenFührer* said, surprised and condescending.

"I was not," I said, "Because there was nothing to worry about."

A silence fell upon the room.

"Where is Dr. Beilstein?" demanded the *SS-GruppenFührer.*

"Right here," said a voice from behind us. "Helmut, what are you doing here?"

Helmut gave a quick account. He said, "I want Raimunda," and he gestured courteously with his hand, "Checked from head to foot."

"Ah," said Dr. Beilstein, eyeing me, "Blown out of a lorry. Come with me, young lady."

We went to another room, while he shouted for a nurse.

They took my blood pressure, listened to my chest, looked in my eyes, tapped my knees to make them jerk, and made me stand with my arms out, and eyes closed. Then they looked at my stool, urine sample and vaginal swab for bleeding. The doctor made me strip, and gave me gentle blows all over.

"Some bruising under your left arm, left side and left hip. I think the explosion blew you into the air and you came down on your feet; you let your knees bend, you flung out your arms, and fell on your left side. If your arms were not out you could have broken your wrist. No ribs broken. Are you a gymnast?"

I burst out laughing, and they joined me.

"I love dancing, but in nightclubs."

I got dressed, and went outside.

Helmut, my *SS-GruppenFührer* had gone, but in a few minutes, a Sergeant came in a staff car, and drove me to Sepp Dietrich.

When I walked into the chart room, everyone stopped what they were doing. Dietrich walked up to me, put his arms around me, and kissed me on both cheeks.

"So, there was nothing to worry about," and the room guffawed, then crowded around.

"You brought back two of my men, and wanted to take on the Polish army with a machine-pistol!" He stepped back.

"I'm awarding you the Iron Cross, Second Class. It doesn't become official unless Hitler approves, and he won't, but you'll always be able to wear it in this Division."

He turned to his Command.

"What say you, gentlemen?"

"Aye!" said some, and the others nodded. Dietrich hung the Iron Cross around my neck. (Hitler later refused to confirm it.)

He took my arm. "It's time to eat."

We went into a house next door, and a dozen of us sat at a long table.

Sepp made me repeat the entire story. I insisted, "There was nothing to worry about, or make any fuss," and the table broke into guffaws.

Later, with the conversation jumping every which way, I asked him, "Did this new idea for warfare come from Lidell Hart?"

"The German Army High Command had these lengthy meetings in the early 30s, and fleshed out Hart's ideas. A General called Lutz was the one who saw it most clearly, and under his guidance, the generals worked out the tactics and strategy. But I – I, Sepp Dietrich knew about this from the Great War, before Lidell Hart published his book.

"I'll begin at the beginning. In October, 1914, I was in Flanders, with the 6th

Bavarian Reserve Artillery Regiment. We were fighting the British Expeditionary Force, to capture Ypres, the key to Flanders.

"We pushed hard, and the British fought hard. The British and French stopped us every time, and halfway through November the war of movement gave way to trench warfare. Year after year of it – how I hated it! I got shrapnel in my right leg, and a lance cut over my left eye. More wounds after that, and a bad one to the head at the Somme.

· "In 1916, to break the stalemate, the German High Command formed infantry and artillery Storm Troopers. This was more to my liking, and they worked so well, the High Command added light mortar squads, machine-gun groups, and bombing and flamethrower teams. They called them *Sturmabteilungen*. I was in the 2nd battalion in the German 3rd Army. The lessons sank into my mind. We were too few to break through, but we did a lot of local damage."

I thought, aren't they descendants of the Teutonic barbarians!

"The thing I learnt was these storm troops were the best fighting men – and men and officers believed they were the very best of the nation's warriors. Men and officers were informal with each other, and like in my SS-division, discipline depends on respect that you have to earn. My SS-division is unstoppable in attack, and like granite in defense, and I learned that then.

"They used us in 1917 and 1918, and in November, 1917, I won the Iron Cross Second Class. Then they sent me to the Bavarian Storm Tank section. Our tanks had a cannon and machine guns. We had our German machines and captured British ones, and I was a machine-gunner in a captured tank.

"The British used their tanks as artillery support for advancing infantry, but we wanted to use ours as cavalry. It didn't work out that way," he said wryly, with that open, peasant grin of his. "It was June 1, 1918, at Chemin des Dames. Half our tanks broke down, but our own tank – we'd christened it *Moritz* – dropped into a shell hole and couldn't get out again. Revving up to get out, the engine almost seized up. The French were upon us, so Lieutenant Fuchsbauer detailed three of us to blow it up.

"On July 15, south-east of Soissons, they knocked out my tank – and finally all the rest! On October 9, we tried again, but my tank broke down. On November 1, we counterattacked near Valenciennes, won some ground, but lost it the next day.

"The war ended, but I had the idea firmly in my head – with a vastly advanced engine and thick armour, what a man could do! Germany could conquer the world!

"So I have no Staff College training. What I do have is what's in this head of mine," and he tapped his head with that engaging, euphoric grin of his.

In the plane, I felt helplessly depressed. Hitler was striding forth to his killing grounds.

My father, the brain specialist, used to talk about some people's having small lumps of grey matter in their brains that others didn't. I never bothered to listen to him, and I should have. He'd say, "I don't know what lumps they are, but they're there. One lump makes people feel responsible to others. Other people have a lump that makes them need to kill."

He talked about his own Spanish people. "We're descended from savage Iberians, conquering, crucifying Romans, from Vandals and Goths – and the Goths had a Spanish kingdom for hundreds of years – from Moors to whom war was second nature, from Spanish princes and counts who drove out the Moors after they had held Spain for seven hundred years and mixed their blood with ours, mixed their killing brains with ours. Spain has leaders and followers born to war.

"England had leaders born to war, but they, killed off each other in the Wars of the Roses. England still has its killer underclass, those men whom the Duke of Wellington said, 'They terrify me', those men he commanded in the Napoleonic wars.

"Now the Germans! The barbarians who overthrew the Roman civilisation! Leaders and underclass born to kill."

I used to make an excuse and slip out of the room, while my mother listened to him, and nodded, with sad agreement.

Hitler had tied down the country with thick ropes of terror. But how many would follow him willingly? Three or four million – each with a little lump in his brain?

The Princess Pfaffenhofen had said – what was her word? – a... a holocaust. Thirty million dead, she had said.

The thought made me ill.

After the war, I learned the numbers of Hitler's slaughter.

Military dead in the European theatre of war:

Russians	7,500,000
Germans	3,500,000
(how many of these did not want to fight?)	
Hungarians	410,000
Yugoslavs	410,000
British and Commonwealth	400,000
(for me, these ones are the worst – 400,000!)	
Italians	330,000
(most of whom were too civilized to want to fight)	
Polish	320,000
(how they threw themselves upon their invaders!)	
Romanian	300,000
Americans	290,000
French	210,000
(they fought much harder than anyone supposes today)	
Finns	85,000
Belgians	12,000
Dutch	12,000

More than 13 million. When we add China and Japan, the numbers go over 15 million.

To this, we must add 12,500,000 Russian civilians!

And another 23,000,000 civilians in Europe and Asia, leaving out Russia! 50 million people!

What puny brains we humans have.

We could not stop a couple of dozen men.

At the aerodrome in Berlin, Himmler had sent a black Mercedes.

But it was not Himmler's car! They drove me to the Propaganda Ministry, and took me up to Dr. Goebbels.

He poured two small glasses of schnapps – heavy, chunky glasses –

and we toasted my return.

"Sit down," he said. "Tell me what happened."

I gave him the whole story.

"Hitler won't approve the Iron Cross," he said. "Never wear it except when you are in Dietrich's division. It would be a criminal offence. We'll do your film right away, and send the photos to Argentina through Sweden. I'll send copies to your home."

He gave me his taut smile.

"That's some tale you have to tell. I'm going to make a story of that and publish it. Someone will ring you at your home in about an hour's time, and read out the story. You correct any mistakes over the phone – you can do that?"

I nodded.

He came over and held my arms in a grip, then let me go.

"Anything you need, ring me."

"Should I go and see Himmler?"

"Himmler will have copies of the photos within the hour. He'll ring you if he wants to see you."

They drove me home; a privilege. I saw no cars on the streets that were not military or official ones.

I had thought this was Himmler's show. Now Goebbels had taken over.

The family made a big fuss, and at the evening meal, I told them the whole story.

Claus said, "I've just found out that Sepp Dietrich went to Hitler and said he didn't want Himmler taking over his division. Hitler separated it from Himmler. All Himmler's new Waffen-SS division *will* be his except Dietrich's. Dietrich obeys the German Army High Command in the field, obviously."

"Goebbels made a song and dance about my not needing his permission if I already had Himmler's – just before I left."

"Goebbels was having his little joke on you. If Dietrich accepted you, it's because you came from Goebbels. He wouldn't look at you if you had come from Himmler. But Himmler needs the photos to show Hitler and arouse Hitler's enthusiasm for Himmler's new *Waffen-SS* divisions."

They admired my photos – young, grinning, excited soldiers, going about the business of killing. The beaming, ebullient Sepp in his chartroom, with his officers, who looked confident, enjoying their work.

92

Upstairs, in my room, I encoded a message to microdot. I took page 193, line 13, for my key: 'and I trow, thou wiltist not...' The first 5 letters were ANDIT

My message read:

> Himmler forming private SS army. First SS Panzerdivision Leibstandarte and under Sepp Dietrich. Hitler granted Dietrich request for own command not under Himmler. Answers to OKW in battle. Himmler forming more SS Panzerdivisions under Himmler's command. Das Reich. Totenkopf. Polizei, Wiking Prince Eugen, together called Waffen SS. Only superlative, fanatic killer soldiers taken. Warn British units facing them. Possibly no prisoners. Dietrich blocking two Polish columns for relief of Warsaw.

Prince Bernd had given me the command set-up of the SS; he had waited till we were alone after dinner.

My message went on:

> Under Himmler, research and maternity homes for racially superior SS babies. Berger, HQ, Jurmer, bodyguard troops, Waffen SS, concentration camp guards. Hilderbrandt, Race and Resettlement. Also Jews who have not escaped to West or to Russia query. Approves marriages of SS men. Vets entry to SS units depending on physique, Nordic looks. Pohl, Himmler's vast economic empire. Supplies concentration camps, Daluege, ordinary police, fire brigades. Heydrich, Reich Security. Intelligence dept rival of Abwehr. Einsatzgruppen extermination of prisoners war, gypsies, homos, undesirable races in occupied lands. Kripo or criminal police. Gestapo.

The Prince knocked on my door, and came in.

He said uncertainly, "I think you should tell London that possibly it is Heydrich who has pushed Himmler so high. Himmler just doesn't seem to have it in him. Everyone thinks Himmler has pulled up Heydrich, but it's very likely Heydrich has pushed up Himmler, although he's Himmler's underling. It sounds far-fetched, but I 'm sure Heydrich will supplant Himmler, and then Hitler. Or he may supplant Hitler directly. It sounds far-fetched, but warn London that if Heydrich supplants Hitler, the war will last 20 years. Hitler will make colossal mistakes, and he overrides his Army generals. He doesn't trust them. Heydrich will make no mistakes. Assassination of the top Nazi leaders looks impossible, but warn London they must somehow

93

assassinate Heydrich."

He looked at me apologetically, afraid he had dropped in my estimation.

"I'll send it." He left the room.

I wrote:

> Heydrich may well supplant Himmler, and then Hitler or supplant Hitler directly. If so war could last decades. Hitler distrusts German army generals and countermands their orders. Can expect colossal mistakes. While impossible to assassinate top Nazi leader assassination of Heydrich essential however difficult.

I had the rations for non-combatant Germans. They had not gone out on the wireless. The American Embassy would have sent off the amounts, but they were so bumbling in London...

Knowing the amounts, London could raise the British rations and compare them with the German, in newspapers and on the wireless. Make the British see how lucky they were... ha! ha!

Civilian rations. Bread 2 kilos 400g. Meat 500g. Fats 270g. Eggs, milk and cheese free choice.

Next morning, after breakfast, I settled into the library – to read an Agatha Christie detective story and pretend I was home in London.

After half-an-hour, Valeria came in and said, "A gentleman to see you."

"Bring him in here, please."

The man was tall, sharp-featured, pouches under his eyes, thin lips, and very well dressed. He did not introduce himself, and sat without being asked.

In a very cultured voice he said, "It's so good of you to see me. I'm from the *Sicherheitsdienst*."

Heydrich's infamous Intelligence Service, probing into everyone's life inside and outside Germany. It had had a list of 67,000 people when Hitler took Austria. Those who came out alive from Heydrich's hands went into Pohl's concentration camps.

When Himmler wanted to see me, I had a fright. Now my knees failed me. The SD was the stabbing tip itself of the very spearhead of the SS – they

94

protected Hitler, the top Nazis and the Party. In 1934, when Heinrich Himmler saw the black uniforms of the SS grow from 30,000 men to 100,000, he decided to build an inner service of the best of the best. Himmler boasted that 'The SD will discover the enemies of the Nationalist Socialists and will take countermeasures through the police.' On paper, the Minister of the Interior, Wilhelm Frick, ran it, but in truth it was the weapon of Himmler and Heydrich; and Heydrich did not need to go through the police. He made the SD form several of its own police forces, the SIPO, or Security Police, the KRIPO, or Criminal Police, and the dreaded RSHA, The Reich Central Security Office or *Reichssicherheitshauptant*, which gave Heydrich unlimited power. This gigantic network of intelligence sniffed out the meanest enemy. Day by day, methodical SD men handed in personal reports on the private lives of ordinary Germans and higher-ups. Heydrich was obsessive in his scrutiny. Countless thousands of reports were handled locally, and the rest sent to the central offices and to Heydrich.

As well, Heydrich had the Gestapo.

It had taken no time at all to uncover me.

"From the *Abwehr*?" I bluffed, desperately.

"No, no! From the RSHA." He looked at me. "How much do they pay you?"

It was useless to lie or prevaricate.

"Three hundred a month, and in Buenos Aires they deposit the equivalent of another 200 in my account."

"Would you consider working for us? And earn 500 American dollars a month." Five hundred American dollars a month! A fortune!

"I am a foreigner here. I have almost no contacts with Germans. I would be useless as a spy on other Germans."

He laughed. "I'm not from Prince Alberchtstrasse. I'm from the SD foreign liaison section. We handle operations abroad and evaluate reports from other countries."

Adam Trott had told me about them. They competed with the *Abwehr*, and belonged to Heydrich, who took little interest. SS General Johst ran them.

My visitor said, "We're in the Berkaerstrasse in Schmargendorf suburb. Do you know it? The Waffen-SS guards us!"

"I have to cross that suburb if I go to the Propaganda Ministry by car. Well... depending on the route."

"Would you consider returning to Argentina, and then spying on the United States for us? We would arrange newspaper cover for you to go to the United States itself, perhaps. A Buenos Aires newspaper. You might stay some months in Buenos Aires, to train. We have operatives there to prepare you."

"Five hundred dollars," I said, and then shook my head. "I'm not spy

95

material, I'm afraid. I need to be completely open – I don't enjoy secrecy. And I love the work I'm doing. World history is being made here in Berlin, and I'm photographing a tiny little part of it, but I'm right here. I'd hate to be somewhere out on the edges. Today, this is the only place in the world that matters. After being here, it would be awful to be somewhere else. I can't explain it to you. It's the usual sort of muddled woman's thinking," and I tried to look apologetic, confused, helpless and flustered at once.

He gave me an understanding smile.

He sat thinking, and then asked me, "Do you have any plans for tonight?"

"No," I said.

"I believe you enjoy nightclubs."

"Oh, I do. But now they won't let us dance," I pouted.

"Could I invite you out tonight?"

I gave him a very direct look. "I do enjoy going in groups," I said as plainly as I could. "And I must be back here at one o'clock. I have to work tomorrow. And they would all be alarmed here if I didn't arrive punctually. I don't know what the Prince would do. He doesn't go to sleep till I come back."

Which was not true, of course.

He gave me a graceful smile. "A group it will be. I will chaperone you like a brother."

"Ah!" I said, very pleased, but feeling like Little Red Riding Hood."

An hour later, two Gestapo men arrived, and asked me to present myself to Heydrich with my cameras, in an hour and half's time.

I went running to find Prince Bernd, who was not at home. I decided to speak to Princess Pfaffenhofen.

What did I know about Heydrich? The very name made me feel faint. I ran to the bathroom.

I know that he is one of the greatest criminals who have ever lived, over a reach of thousands of years of human history. Only monsters like Hitler or Himmler could have raised him so high. He's a living reincarnation of Atila the Hun, the Genghis Khan and God knows who else.

Carl Jacob Burckhardt calls him 'the young evil god of death.'

I know that he is ravenous for power. Scorns human life. Has no feeling for what is fit, what constitutes equitable law or legality. That mistrust plagues him. Honesty and virtue in someone awakes his contempt, often his rage. He runs his Gestapo, his domestic intelligence service, his extermination groups with gleeful sadism. That he lives in derisive disbelief. That he's incapable of clemency, has not an iota of humanity. I knew that he's brutishly savage when interrogating and murdering his victims. That Hitler extolls his 'cold iron heart.'

96

I found the grandmother in the morning drawing-room. The armchairs and sofa were upholstered in large red roses, with green leaves, and a pink and pale yellow background. The wallpaper harmonized with the upholstery, and the colours soothed me.

I took the other armchair, and said, "They're coming to fetch me. I have to go with my cameras to Heydrich."

"Oh dear," said the Princess, and put down her book.

"What do you know about him?"

"What I am going to tell you is a most dangerous secret. If he thought you knew, he would kill you. But knowing it will make you feel stronger. He should frighten you just the same, because with this man it is best never to forget your fear – never.

"He is Jewish. Hitler knows it and Himmler too. Both of them know Heydrich is easier to control while they can hang that sword over his head. He serves them both too well – they need him. But if they couldn't control him because of his Jewishness, he would be too dangerous altogether. He is the son of Bruno Richard Heydrich, a most gifted musician and the man who founded the First Halle Conservatory for Music. In 1916, Hugo Riemann's *Musiklexikon* printed, 'Heydrich, Bruno, real name Suss. His father was a Jew!

"Soon after they made him Chief of the whole German Security, a master-baker of Halle, on the Saale, that's where Heydrich was born, put it out that Heydrich's grandmother, who the baker had known personally, was a full Jewess. The rumor took off like wildfire. Heydrich took the master-baker to court, and won. The Press was muzzled, so the thing died away. The baker had required that the Marriage and Birth Register for Halle be produced in Court, and, just imagine! The entries for March 1904, when Heydrich was born, had vanished! Just that month!

"In 1935 and 1937, he threatened legal action against two people who announced he was a Jew. The first man backed down, and retracted his claims in a written statement. The second, he disappeared into a concentration camp, where they immediately murdered him.

"Heydrich had this crony, an SS-Sergeant Major from his Hamburg days, who stole the Registry papers. What Heydrich overlooked was his grandmother's gravestone in Leipzig, with the name of Sarah Heydrich. The two men I just told you about were going on about this. So Heydrich sends his trusty Sergeant Major to get rid of this evidence too. He put the gravestone on a lorry and tossed it into a river. This time Heydrich was very careful. He ordered them to install another gravestone marked 'S. Heydrich.' He was leaving no stone unturned."

In 1945, the Allies found this bill in Heydrich's files.

The Princess picked up some knitting.

"Now, there is another secret, and one or two men who got drunk and talked about it paid with their lives.

"When he joined the SS in 1931, he gave out that he had been a naval lieutenant who was forced out of the Navy for his Nationalist Socialist inclinations. Stuff and nonsense! The young naval lieutenant had an unsavory name and he got into an affair with the daughter of a naval architect. Lo! The girl found herself in the family way. Despite his long string of affairs, the naval architect overlooked them, and went to talk to Heydrich about the wedding. What a rebuff! Heydrich declared he would never marry a girl who gave in so easily and let him have his will of her before marriage. Senior naval officers stepped in, but Heydrich would not take the gentlemanly step and marry the girl. So Admiral Canaris – or was it Admiral Raeder? – threw him out of the Service.

"Heydrich covered up this story every way he knew how. 'The reactionary German Admiralty had thrown him out because he was a Nazi sympathiser!' The Hamburg SS took him to their hearts. They were a dumb lot of thugs, so Himmier quickly saw to it that this young man went straight to the front of them. As I just told you, he joined in 1931.

"I know of at least one case where an ex-naval officer drank too much at a party and blurted out the story. Heydrich tossed him into a concentration camp without more ado and most certainly murdered him."

I asked her, "Is he married?"

"To the daughter of a school teacher from the island of Fehmarn. She's one of those dark demon women out of the nightmare German myths. She spurs him on to seizing more and more power – her wicked ambitions consume her."

She paused, knitting steadily.

"He's the most malignant of all the German leaders, the worst fiend the Third Reich has spawned. He has no friends, no comrades. He jeers at friendship and comradeship for all to hear. He jibes at organizational probity. He trusts one thing alone – to know the skeletons in your cupboard. Then he has power over you. His search for people's secrets has been avid, unremitting. Every Nazi fears and hates him for what he might have

98

discovered about them. His secret files are the most feared documents in Germany now.

"He lacks even the most primitive feeling of morality. His life is given over to a lust for power. His 'Christian code' is personal power. The German State, Nazism, means nothing to him – he craves ever more power. Ideologies – he mocks them. Truth, justice – the only truth is when a true way opens up to new powers. The good is that which gives him more enjoyment of power. Politics and ideologies are to sway the masses. You cannot argue with him whether an act is right or wrong – for him, that's a waste of breath. A right action is one that works in getting more power.

"His life is a daily string of murders – some days, I suppose, he orders thousands to die. Soon, with this war, every day he will be ordering tens of thousands to die. He has made himself the god Shiva, the death-dealer of the worlds because he has the mind of a god to do what he has done and is doing. His intellect is that of a genius. His crimes are no evil impulse, no passionate lust, but the cold calculation of a most gifted mind.

"What does he plan on? Once or twice when he got drunk, he talked of making Hitler the President of the Third Reich, while Heydrich became the executive Reich Chancellor – Hitler the figurehead, and Heydrich, the death-dealer. He would never serve Germany, or the Third Reich. He would extend his power over country after country, over continent after continent, a colossus bestriding a globe of abject peoples in terror of him."

I excused myself to hurry back to the bathroom.

* * *

I sat rigid, in the back seat of the Gestapo car.

Heydrich could decide to rape me, and then thrust me into one of those maternity homes. He could rape me again and again, till I got preggies. After I gave birth, he could come back and do it again. Year after year, producing babies. No one, not a soul, would ever know where I had vanished to.

· At Gestapo headquarters, they took me up to his office – enormous, spartan, and decorated in variegated woods.

Heydrich stood by his desk. He came forward, and took my hand and not letting it go, led me to an armchair.

I sat and stared at him. His face had the terrible beauty of an angel, an angel cast out by God. A very large brow that seemed to house a huge mind. Slightly Mongolic eyes, a Teutonic descended from the barbarians of the steppes. A too-prominent Jewish nose. Wonderful Nordic cheek bones and mouth. Piercing eyes that reflected a cutting intuition. Blond hair. A beautiful Aryan. On his floor of the building I had seen Aryans – handsome, intense

99

blue eyes, and blond.

What frightened me was the sense of his intuition.

He could surely *feel* I was not who I said I was…

He said, "I have to have photos taken whether I like it or not, and I hate them. I hate even more the photos that Hitler's photographer takes of me."

I said, "Do I have to photograph you with an expression that shows you disdain vanity?" and laughed.

He smiled. "I have no vanity. It's a silly emotion."

"Perhaps I can photograph you showing you are not pleased?"

This time he laughed.

"Take me as you will. I don't like my face. Sometimes, when I do pistol practice, I put up photos of my face for targets."

"Don't you dare do that with *my* photos," I said with mock severity.

"I do as I wish," he snapped. He asked me, "Do you like classical music?"

"I love it."

"And Mozart?"

"I can listen to Mozart for hours. Tell me, could I photograph you while we talk?" He handed me a roll of film, and I got to work.

"No need to give me the film back. Can you develop it at home?"

"That's easy."

I was moving about, taking shots. At home, I'd touch up the film before he saw the prints, give him an Aryan nose.

"Do you miss Belize?"

"I confess I do. The sea there! The forest, the Mayan ruins…"

"Is the forest dangerous?"

"Yes. There are jaguars. But you can take a rifle."

"What sort of shop did you work in?"

"Mainly sold white linen – household linen, and cloth for making your own dresses."

"Where did the dress cloth come from?"

"Argentina, Chile, Peru, Mexico and from Europe. The European colours were more solid – well, it depended. If you dye in the thread, and then weave with coloured thread, the patterns are fantastic and last. But photography has been my hobby since I was small."

"I suppose being Spanish, you frequent the black crows?"

I laughed. "The priests?"

"You do or you don't?"

"My father never went, and I don't either. My mother did on and off."

"The great conspiracy," he said savagely, and I snapped his expressions. "Once they tried to dominate the world, and failed. Now they're trying again. They hold the keys of hell, they say! Hypocrites! Liars!

100

Conspirators! No one has the stature to smash them and their plague!"

"I avoid them," I said, as a member of the Low Church of England in good standing. My father *was* Roman Catholic and my mother Lutheran, so my sister and I had escaped into the Church of England.

"I'm having lunch with two sisters, from the Berlin Philharmonic. One plays the flute, and the other the viola. They will have two other friends there, one whose hobby is cooking."

"Do I need ration cards?" I asked mischievously.

"Not to worry."

He picked up a phone, and asked for a number. He said, "I'm bringing another guest."

He wrote on a card. "If you need ration cards, take this card to this man downstairs."

* * *

The two sisters were in their early thirties, and plied me with questions on Belize and Argentina. The other lady was older, a pianist, and the Frenchman cooked like Cordon Bleu.

* * *

Afterwards, Heydrich gave us a thirty-minute Mozart solo. He found in Mozart nuances I had never heard. He played with perfectionist brilliance but melded that with flashes of rare sensitivity.

Then the other three played – the flat held a concert grand piano – and Heydrich lived each note with utter concentration.

I believe what kept Heydrich sane was the sanity of the great composers. He was impervious to words, but he could not keep out of his soul their music that bespoke of feelings he never felt himself.

* * *

He drove me home.

"You don't want to spy on the Americans? Not even for five hundred dollars?"

"Not for five hundred dollars. I could not live, hiding who I really am. I need to live my own life and that everyone knows who I am. Here in Berlin are men who are shaping history, perhaps for a thousand years. I want to be close. Here are men who people will talk about, teach about in the

101

universities, one thousand years from now."

He gave me a sudden smile.

"How right you are," he said.

The SD Intelligence officer, Gerhard Wallraff, picked me up at seven o'clock. I wore a low-cut gown to show a trace of cleavage, and like a good Intelligence officer, he didn't miss a detail.

We met the others in a dark-panelled restaurant, with low, warm lighting. He introduced me to his two fellow-workers; Eugen Kratzer and Matthias Appel. They were with two girls who worked there too. Eugen's friend, Gisa, wore a high-necked – "I'm a Fraulein who wants to cook and have babies – dress, and she looked miffed at mine. Petra also wore a demure dress, but the good Lord had so endowed her it didn't matter what she wore. All evening, the men's eyes strayed from her to me, but I am sure I was losing out.

They asked me about Poland and about photography; they let me hold the talk for twenty minutes, and I felt myself enjoying it and relaxing. Gisa asked me why I didn't want to work for them in America, and then said, "I wouldn't really like to leave Germany myself. I grew up in Celle, so I can understand how you feel about Berlin. I love going back to Celle, but…"

"But Berlin is where the really exciting men like ourselves are to be found," quipped Matthias.

We talked about restaurants and Argentinean nightclubs and cooking.

Petra apologised for talking 'shop'. She said to Matthias, "Those reports came in from Holland. Twenty good landing zones."

"Holland?" I enquired.

"They're mobilizing," said Matthias. "If we attack them, they'll flood the frontier region, so we'll have to use parachute troops behind their front lines."

"Ah," I said wisely. "Germany needs to control the coast."

"Bravo," said Gerhard. "You should really think about our offer."

I laughed amusedly.

"Isn't Berlin where the real men are?" I quipped, and they all laughed too. I was amazed at myself. My fear had gone.

Eugen said, "Did we have any luck with Eben-Emael?"

Gisa said, "We can land on it."

102

"What on earth is that?" I said.

"It's the key fort in Belgium. Enormous," said Eugen. "We can put parachutists on top of it."

"God, don't you people have interesting lives," I exclaimed. "Are you on the Belgian desk, or something?"

Eugen said, "I'm Belgium, Matthias is Holland, and Gerhard worries about everything."

Gisa said, "But we're all day in an office. I think you're the lucky one, out on the street all day, taking photos."

"I never thought of it like that," I confessed. "But you *do* get fed up."

We talked about how people never appreciated it when they were lucky.

* * *

We went to a nightclub. They didn't let you dance in public any more, but the club put on a show with singers.

At eleven o'clock, Gerhard said, "We've got to work tomorrow, so, early to bed."

I wondered whether Eugen and Matthias would sleep with the two girls.

"Do you like dancing? They still hold dances in some embassies."

"Oooh!" cried Gisa. "Could you arrange that?"

"I'd love to," I said.

Next morning, I prepared the signal:

> Parachutists plan land on roof of Eben-Emael Belgium. For Dutch water barriers, parachutist landings at many points behind front.

I made the microdots, and went to the Argentinean Embassy. I told Ruben this was for Geneva to send. He gave me two cartons of American cigarettes.

I had now four cartons at home. I had forgotten about handing them around. At home, no one smoked; the two girls and Claus had smoked one cigarette each at the restaurant.

Walking back to the Underground, a black car pulled up. It was *SS-ObersturmbannFührer* Rutzel.

"Can I take you somewhere?"

"I'm going home – all the way to Potsdam."

"Hop in."

As he drove off, he said, "The Gestapo takes an unhealthy interest in you. You pay a lot of visits to the Embassy."

"They give me American cigarettes," I confessed disingenuously. I opened my carrier bag. "Two cartons. Do you want one?"

"You don't really smoke?"

"No, they're to give to friends."

I put Retzer at about 30. He was a Nordic type, with reddish hair, a faint, perpetual frown, and severe lips. It wasn't easy for him to relax his expression, but he had enjoyed himself the other day on my photographic foray around the streets, and now his eyes crinkled in a smile.

"The bribe is accepted," he said, with heavy-handed humour, and I was careful to laugh at his joke.

"You must never repeat one word of what I am going to say – all right?" My tummy tripped.

"You have friends in Himmler and Heydrich – well, understand me, Heydrich has *no* friends. But you're approved. What you always have to remember is that in the SS we're talking about a triumvirate, and the third man is Heinrich Muller – *GruppenFührer* Muller, Heydrich's right-hand man."

I scrabbled through my memory. Thirty-eight years old. Nothing else known.

"For Muller, there are two classes of people. Those who do not support the Third Reich, and perhaps even oppose it; and those actively support it, and work for it. You are in the second group. But Muller is a man who needs to know the skeletons in people's cupboards; he wants to get a file card on every single person in Germany one day. But he will not rest till he finds a vice of yours, some untoward thing about you."

I joked, keeping hysteria out of my voice, "Tell him I'm frigid. A compulsive virgin."

Rutzel roared with laughter. "That will do. Oh, that's very good. Are your fingernails clean?"

"Clean!"

"You can scratch my cheek and I can take the credit for zeal in investigating you!"

"Oh, that might hurt! I wouldn't hurt you for anything."

"Still, we might think about that. Or you could scratch another part of me," he suggested meaningfully.

"Or I could take a photo, and then it wouldn't hurt."

That made him laugh uproariously.

"You're only interested in camera sex. That might make him happy. Ach! Let me think about it."

* * *

At the tall, outside gates, I said, "I'd like to invite you to lunch, but I don't know about rationing."

"I'll accept, if I may. Don't worry about rationing. Your hosts will have no problem."

We drove in, and I gave him a carton, which he left on the back seat.

"I appreciate this."

The man was lonely. I thought he didn't have a wife…

Inside, I asked whether the Prince had returned.

The Prince came out, and I said I had invited Rutzel to lunch. Very warmly, the Prince invited him inside, for a nip of something before the meal. While Rutzel washed his hands, I said to the Prince, "He told me not to worry about our ration cards."

"Oh, clever work," said Prince Bernd, with a mischievous smile. "Luckily, this house has huge cellars, full of coal and tinned food."

At lunch, I gravely introduced him to the ladies, and he asked that we call him 'Karl'.

He was an interesting talker. Unmarried, he had his mother, father and brother in Prussia. The conversation turned to bombing, and he told us that the SS had organized Berlin against air raids. Each city block had its *Blockwart*, the Party watchdog over the neighbors. He made the neighbors go to demonstrations, pay up for Party publications or for charities, and he knew how many rooms with how many beds each house had. He knew exactly how many people there were, so he knew every last empty bed. He would get everyone out to clear rubble after an air raid or dig out buried neighbors.

I knew that after the Gestapo, people hated these people most, because they wrote a report on every anti-Nazi remark or joke.

The government was strengthening basements, and opening up tunnels from one basement to the next, to let trapped people escape. For people without basements, it was building – or had already built – bunkers.

We all listened with appalled awe.

* * *

After Rutzel left, I told the Prince, "I'm worried about the secret darkroom. If you knock on the connecting wall – the one that opens up – you can hear it's hollow. Could we tack two or three blankets inside, the muffle the knocks if anyone gets curious?"

The Prince nodded. "What an oversight!"

At mid-afternoon, I put down my Agatha Christie novel and went out into the back garden. A lorry was tipping rock and gravel over the air raid bunker, making a small hill about four metres high.

A voice behind me said, "A foreboding sight."

I swung around, startled. The man had to be Bernd's brother. He said, "I'm Count Alex Hohenlinden. You're our famous... photographer."

"Graf Hohenlinden," I said. "I have been looking forward to this."

Miss Ancram had told me he was 52. He had the amused eyes of a writer – reflective, observant, but amused. He was taller than his brother, but white-haired; thinner and slightly stooped.

He gestured at the stones.

"The bunker has six feet of reinforced concrete which won't stop a direct hit. Now, supposing the bomb does not have a delayed fuse, it will explode on touching the top stone and the energy of the explosion will be expended blowing all this rock and gravel over the garden – giving us an enormous task of collecting it and piling it back up again. Short of an English or German plane obliging us by dropping a bomb on it experimentally, we can't be sure the idea will work."

"Will you use the shelter?"

"Most certainly. I live next door, on the other side of that wall."

On the ship to Buenos Aires, Constance had told me. "Oh! Right next door," said I brightly. "I believe you write biography. You're the first writer I've ever met."

"And you're the first Press photographer of my acquaintance. Some of them took photos of me, but we never stopped long enough to chat."

"Press photography is pretty boring beside writing biographies."

"That's why you have such interesting hobbies," he said drily. "Would you care to see my house?"

We crossed the garden to a postern door set in the high wall, and stepped into his garden, which hardly had a lawn – shrubs filled it, with gravel pathways, broken by pergolas, garden ponds, crazy pavements and stone steps. We walked through a rockery into the back door of a house as big as

Prince Bernd's.

"I'm very fond of gardens, as you may observe," said the Prince. "My brother and his family next door are too busy. They have an ocean of lawn, a couple of trees, and are satisfied while they can look out on greenery. You may know that I am a widower, and you will probably ask yourself what one man does with so large a house and garden. As the house passes from one generation to another, it matters little that at this moment of time its occupant is solitary. I have a couple who look after me. I drive the car myself. A gardener lives in, and periodically cuts my brother's lawn next door. There's a maid, and three cleaning women come three days a week. Monday, Wednesday and Friday, they clean my brother's palace. Tuesday, Thursday and Saturday they come here. A man comes four days a week to clean our windows. We have wangled work permits for this, so that's four people less helping Hitler's war effort."

He took me into his library, an irregular eight-sided room, crammed with books, and sat me down.

"So you've bearded Heydrich in his den. How do you compare him with Himmler?"

"Hundred times more powerful – well, his energy, his mind."

"I believe he pushed Himmler up to where he is now. If you had known that mousy little nondescript individual as he was some years ago; but now the SS is in place, it best needs a bureaucratic nonentity to run it. Hitler sees through him, today, I'm convinced, but Hitler is very fond of him, because Himmler alone of all the high Party men says 'yes' to him, in everything. Hitler asks for the impossible, and the rest of them try to make him see reason. Himmler turns to Heydrich, who more or less delivers.

"Have you heard of the Duke of Saxony, Heinrich the Fowler, who lived from 876 to 936?"

"Good heavens! No."

"Himmler believes he is the reincarnation of that Duke. The Duke was never actually crowned as Emperor of the Holy Roman Empire, but we accept him as being so from 916.

He defended Germany from the Hungarians, Danes and the Wends, building castles everywhere and fortifying German cities.

"Have you heard of Dr. Schaeffer? He came back from exploring Tibet, and now Himmler has him breeding a super strain of 'winter-hardy Siberian and Mongol horses'. Himmler wants his SS to occupy all eastern Russia and Siberia and to form German Orders of Chivalry inside citadels. They will lord it over the Slavs, but depend on the 'Steppe Horse' that Schaeffer is trying to breed in the Austrian Alps. The Steppe Horse will keep them in flesh, cheese and milk without needing modern machines and petrol, as they ride out on these horses to guard German conquests on the Urals and beyond."

"Hitler has a Pact with Stalin!"

"Himmler is waiting. Meanwhile, he has alchemists working at Gestapo headquarters, making a stink in the cellars as they try to transmute base metals into gold. Himmler explained to Hitler that with the gold Germany will break free of the Western and Jewish capitalists.

"The man is obsessed with plots from the Catholic Church and by the Vatican. He believes the Vatican is in league with Jewry and Free Masonry to annihilate Germany and destroy the Nazi party."

"Where do you get all this?"

"Interviewing people. A biographer is always at it. As I was saying, Himmler is obsessed with this threat of the Free Masonry. He scarcely dares leave SS Headquarters, because of the Free Masons waiting in the streets of Berlin to assassinate him. Tell me, would you like some coffee?"

"Oh, I don't want to make you waste your coffee."

"Not to worry."

He rang, and when the girl came, he ordered coffee.

"Who do you think is the more dangerous – Heydrich or Hitler?"

"Heydrich. Do you agree?"

"Not necessarily. If Britain cannot react, behind its moat of the English Channel, or if Hitler manages to leap across the Channel and occupy Great Britain, then Hitler is the nightmare. If Germany is forced on the defensive, then Heydrich is the worst thing that can happen for the rest of the world.

"Let me explain. I interviewed Ernst Hansfstängl, known as 'Putzi' – his nickname. In the early 1920s, he was Hitler's wealthy companion. I was delving into the early days of Nazism, to write Nazi biographies for the English-speaking market. Most of Hitler's early cronies were uncommunicative, but Putzi, educated at Harvard, with an American mother from a family called Sedgwick, became a firm friend of Hitler's in 1921. He let him have money, introduced Hitler into Munich 'society'. The Nazis made him 'foreign press consultant.' When the 1923 Munich Beer Hall Putsch flopped, Putzi and his American wife, Helene Niemeyer, hid the wounded Hitler at their home.

"When I interviewed him two years ago, he told me that sometimes, in 1922 and 1923, Hitler would fantasize about killing the whole world, and leaving only a superior Germanic race. He would take fifty square miles, and lay out millions of corpses. Trucks would drive down tracks, three metres apart, tossing the dead into the free space. After three or four years, only bones would remain which could be ploughed under.

"Now Hitler is leading four or five million German soldiers into conquest, teaching them about the Master Race. What do those soldiers think?"

"That they'll enslave the other countries, and make them labor and toil."

"The indoctrination specially warns against mixing with women of inferior races. In one part of their minds do they realise where Hitler could lead them?"

"Heydrich wouldn't do this," I said. "He'd enslave."

"Hitler told Putzi he'd get rid of all Slavs, all Russians, and bring the British in to work the farms. He'd clean Europe of the French, the Belgians, the Spanish and Greeks. The Italians were cultured. The Dutch would be sent east to work the farms there. As the German Empire grew eastwards, he'd kill the Turks and the Arabs.

"Three days after that conversation, two years ago, Putzi came to see me, late at night, to say he was leaving directly for the States, that they planned to kill him for talking to me. Hitler had guessed he may have told me about those conversations. I think he drove to the Dutch frontier and crossed on foot at some unguarded place. I don't really know. But he's in the States now, safe and sound. I stopped talking to those people and they left me alone."

The coffee had arrived without my noticing, and I was drinking it gratefully, before I even saw the cup in my hand.

After the first crematoria went to work, their ovens multiplied year by year, as did their 'production' of charred ashes. First mass testing used Jews, gypsies, subnormals, homosexuals and enemies of the state. The Jews were an ideal rehearsal, a smokescreen for the eventual transport and disposal of tens of millions. The destruction of the Jews seemed an end in itself. With victory in Europe, by 1949, the Nazis would have disposed of some 25 million Europeans a year, with the figure rising each year to at least 300 or 400 million people in all.

---

* * *

Back next door, Princess Jutta told me that a van had come from Rutzel with fresh fish on ice, pate, butter, flour and cheeses.

I rang him and thanked him. As I hung up, the phone rang, so I picked it up and heard the booming voice of Goebbels. He told me that the district of Wedding had had some of Berlin's worst slums, and Hitler had rebuilt the housing there.

I said wisely, "Priming the pump."

He said, "Exactly, What do you know about economics?"

"Nothing." I laughed heartily, and he joined in.

"I'll send you a car. Wedding is north of the Tiergarten, but on the way, you go through Charlottenburg, where there's a maternity hospital. The Director is waiting for you. Could you take photos of joyous mothers with their newborn babies of the Master Race – sensitive photos – showing how they are producing Nordic babies although we are at war?"

"What an inspiring idea, Dr. Goebbels."

"If the sight awakens your *Muttertier* – 'human female reproducer, the Mother-beast' – instinct that will be to the good, do you agree?" he said lasciviously.

I was at a loss, and then said quickly, "You must not be naughty and try to make me nervous."

He gave a satisfied laugh.

"The driver then will take you to the Wedding district. Can you take artistic photos of the new workers' housing? The driver will have an address of a certain Andrea Boehr. She's 22, and has just had her second baby. She's an interviewer of job applicants in the *Reichsleitung der Deutschen Arbeitsfront* – The German Labour Front. She has agreed to receive you. She's on five-days leave, recovering from her birth, and she's used to interviewing strangers. She's very good-looking and you can photo one of the new flats from the inside… in this case, her flat."

"I'll need film."

"The driver will give it to you, and collect it afterwards."

* * *

At the Maternity Hospital, I photographed ten mothers, cuddling their newly-born, wrinkled babies. All wore their hair in plaits, wound around their heads, or falling blonde and combed. All had deeply blue eyes, and I was sorry I could never work with colour film.

They all had expressions of the three Ks – *Kinder*, *Küche* and *Kirche* – Children, Kitchen and Church, but I felt no stirring within myself, and thanked God I was English.

We had driven on a six-lane road – the Berlinerstrasse – then the Hardenbergstrasse and ordinary streets to the Hospital. Now we were on more wide avenues – the Tauentzienstrasse, Kleiststrasse, and Bulowstrasse, to turn up Potsdamerstrasse and Herman Göringstrasse, to turn off into Under den Linden to take Friedrichstrasse, Chauseestrasse and Mailerstrasse.

In Wedding, I saw block after block of new eight-storey buildings, with balconies like open drawers on Teutonic tallboys. We turned into Antonstrasse and pulled up.

On the fifth floor, I rang a bell, and Andrea opened the door and ushered me into the living-sleeping room. I saw a baby in a cradle, and a three-year-old boy playing with a wooden train. The flat was painfully clean, German-style, with the uncompromising furniture I was used to, sharp edges, sharp angles. Andrea had the prominent cheekbones of so many Berliners, with patient, sad brown eyes, a very wide mouth and prominent, beautiful lips. Her hair was short, very curled, a very light brown. She had the open, alert, highly featured Master Race face.

The driver had given me a small package of real coffee, and I handed it to her, then took out a package of flour from my bag.

"Oooh!" She exclaimed. "I've got some home-made biscuits. Would you like to try them?"

"I'd love to. But don't make my coffee very strong, because I've been drinking it all day. Can I take photos as we talk, or would that put you off?"

She shook her head, and set about the coffee. "I'm used to talking with people pushing and protesting all around me."

After she sat down, she said, "I don't know why they chose me. They obviously don't know that my husband is going to divorce me. He wasn't there when I gave birth, and hasn't come near me since. He hasn't seen his baby boy. I've been through hell, you can't imagine," and she broke down in tears.

I sat down and put my arm around her shoulders.

The living-room had a tall stove, reaching the ceiling. The room wasn't cold, but it wasn't warm either.

"Do you have coal?"

"This has been an amazing September. Führer-weather, we call it. I'm saving my coal for Christmas."

"Christmas!"

"I'll have to ask someone to take the children, but I'll make sure I have them at Christmas."

That rocked me

"Doesn't the Führer look after his babies and their mothers?"

"They want us to put our babies in the *Kinderheim*, and go back to work. I'm not going to do that, ever. My baby, Henning, would never get cuddled. He would just lie in his cot and cry all day. Don't talk to me about the Führer. My husband thinks he is Master Race, and has fathered two creatures of pure Aryan stock. Now he is with another girl, even younger than I am. He wants to fertilise her now, to produce more Hitler babies."

She broke into tears again.

"We are just *Muttertiers*."

"Your husband thinks he's some sort of stud bull?"

"It's what they have taught them," she sobbed. "We are just vessels for their seed. The most educated men will swallow any flattery, especially if it leads to between a woman's legs. Have you seen what figures Hitler, Goebbels, Himmler and Göring cut!"

"The *Schrumphf-Germanen*!" I laughed.

"Exactly," she said bitterly. "Nobody talks about the Master-woman!"

"They only get between our legs if we let them," I said comfortably. "So we are the masters of the situation."

"No, we aren't," she wept. "I was lying there in that hospital bed, waiting and waiting. The other two mothers in the room – their husbands came in with flowers and kisses and whisperings and love."

She sipped her coffee.

"They don't want a master race of women. We would eclipse their superiority. They only want female vessels, female cattle to breed from."

I said nothing. Her sanity depended on getting this out.

When she fell silent, I said, "Don't you want to have it out with your husband?"

"My father was Prussian. He brought me up never to cry, never to complain. When I did, he made me stand in front of a mirror and look at myself, snivelling and crying."

"Your father was... He's dead?"

"It's as though he is. He disowned me, and my mother too. They tried to stop me marrying Heiner. They didn't come to the wedding, and they stayed away from both my births. I never expected it of my mother, but she has failed me. Men like my father, I can understand. They step out of the house to go to work and they turn into implacable, loveless businessmen. They often come home, and cannot relight the flame in their hearts. They treat the home like the office, and the family like employees."

"And the Führer?"

"If it weren't for this Master Race business, he is a true Father to us. I want my sons to live well and how can we if we are *Volke ohne Raum* [people without room to live]? That Polish corridor – it's cutting us off from our own country, our own part of Prussia. The Treaty of Versailles was TWENTY years ago and still we suffer from it. Well, not any more. The Poles have learnt a lesson!"

She ate another biscuit. "Of course, we women aren't supposed to understand politics. We're supposed to have brains as weak as those in the babies we bear."

She looked at me defiantly.

"Do women talk about politics in Argentina?"

"My goodness, they do!"

After a pause, I asked, "Where does your husband live?"

"He's with that other... girl... in Kreuzberg. Why?"

"I'd like to see him. Go with a lady friend of mine. Your situation is impossible."

112

She got up, and in silence wrote down the address.

"He's an engineer, and gets home at seven o'clock."

I said, "I need to take photos. Can I shoot this room. What other rooms—"

"Kitchen and bathroom, through those two doors. Go ahead."

When I finished, I asked her, "Could you stand on the balcony? Think about your summer holidays when you were younger."

Out on the balcony, she said, "We went to the shores of a lake in the Bavarian mountains." As she talked about it, I took several shots. Then she cradled the baby, in the living room, and I took more shots.

The flat where her husband lived had been theirs. Her parents had given her furniture of theirs which he still hung on to.

* * *

With an excited Thoma beside me – we had not said a word to the Prince or Princess because they would not have let their daughter come – we rang the bell at Heiner's flat. A slim, pert young woman, her hair in two blonde plaits that made her look sixteen, answered. We asked for her husband, and she led us inside.

In the well-furnished living-room, Heiner came through a door, six-foot six, wide shoulders, very good-looking, with short blonde hair, a very Aryan face, and sensual blue eyes.

"Who are you?" he demanded.

"May we speak to you alone?"

The couple stared at us. He spoke to his girlfriend in an undertone, and she left us. He confronted us, much taller than we were, and did not invite us to sit.

I said severely, "We have come from your wife, Andrea. She has given birth to a beautiful boy, your son. She had a difficult time and was days in hospital. You did not visit her, write to her or send her flowers. You caused her needless suffering – very great suffering. She is struggling now with two of your sons, to regain her health and is short of money."

He drew himself up. "Our marriage is finished and now is a question of lawyers."

"Meanwhile, you pay her nothing, and show no interest in your baby."

He took a step forward and Thoma stepped back sharply. "The Führer has brought in a new age, and you both obviously belong to a time that is no more. I have done her a great honour, and given her children of a very superior race. I can do no more."

He looked at us with a charming, engaging smile.

"You don't think I'm tall enough?"

113

We stared at him, speechless.

"My shoulders aren't broad enough? You don't like my face? I think you have come here on an excuse. I think you would both like to bear children from a father like me – have children like Christian. When have you ever seen a boy of three years like Christian? We have a guest bedroom here – why don't you get undressed?"

I glared at him.

"You feel no instincts awakening in you?"

Thoma was white as a sheet.

"Yes. I do," my voice managed to say. "I'd like to buy a trophy board, cut off your balls and nail them to it. But I suppose they'd begin to smell after a few days, so I'd have to put them in a bottle with preserving liquid."

He gave me a tremendous blow at the head, knocking me to the floor.

He stooped over me.

I had much underestimated the hundreds of years of aristocratic breeding of Thoma. She picked up something and thunked him over the head. He dropped to the floor, clutching his head, and groaning, rocking back and forth.

Thoma pulled me to my feet and pushed me out of the flat and down the stairs. I was dazed and only half aware of what was happening.

Reinhard saw us and came running. He helped me into the car, and drove us back home.

Private cars weren't allowed, but the Prince had wangled big stickers in the front and back windows that made the car 'official'. Thank God.

I staggered into the house and begged them not to make a fuss.

Next morning, the side of my head hurt. After breakfast, I went for a walk – crossed Neuer Garten Park, went down to the bridge and across to Volkspark. I walked north, close to the water, and a path led me in front of a two-storey house, looking across the Havel river to the waters of the Jungfernsee. The beauty of the view stopped me. Behind me, a voice asked, "Do you like it?"

The lady seated on the porch had come down through her garden to the gate.

"I do. It's lovely. I'm a Press photographer from Argentina, although originally I'm from Belize, so I miss the jungle, the sea and the wide spaces."

I had astonished her.

"Who do you work for?"

"For a newspaper in Buenos Aires and for the Propaganda Ministry."

"Would you like to come and sit on the porch? I've got coffee, but it's not terribly
good."

"Really, the truth is, I'm thirsty. Water would do, one or two glasses."

"I've got raspberry syrup I make myself."

* * *

The long, raspberry-flavoured drink was delicious. She told me her husband was a tank captain, training at the tank school just outside Berlin. I told her I had been there, taking photos, and had met Oberst Ekkehard Kraske. She didn't know the name, and she told me her husband's. In confusion, she said, "I haven't introduced myself. I'm Annemarie Hartmann."

I told her my name, and explained I was Spanish by descent. She exclaimed, "You look Aryan! Do you know who your grandparents were?"

"All Spanish, all born in different parts of Argentina. But my great-grandparents? Perhaps many of them were German."

"Without a shadow of doubt. That would be interesting, trying to trace your great- grandparents all over somewhere as wild as Argentina."

She sipped at her ersatz coffee.

"And what do you think of the Third Reich?"

"History is being made!"

"Do you listen to foreign broadcasts?"

"I don't have a proper radio, and don't have time. I've got one of these tinny little sets like everyone else, that don't get any stations very far away."

"That's what I've got. But Göring has made it a crime to listen to foreign broadcasts. He tells us that this is not a real war like the Great War but a series of clashes and Britain will sue for peace."

"And what about France?"

"Göring tells us that France is tired of Britain fighting to the last drop of French blood. But I hate all of this. I love Germany – her beautiful cities, her castles, her museums, her literature and her music. Who can produce such music as we German-speakers in Germany and Austria! We are a country of youthful excitement. Who but the Berliners go on such rampages when they are enjoying themselves, who love restaurants and nightclubs. Now everyone is tight-lipped and withdrawn, watchful and frightened. When we have victories – Austria, Czechoslovakia, Munich, Poland – some people celebrate wildly. But we have made an ally of communist Russia, and that will bring the Americans in against us. They speak the same language as the English, it's a

115

blood bond. And those Yankees will build twenty tanks for every tank we can. My poor husband – when I think of him fighting off thousands of American tanks…"

I moved over and put my arm around her shoulders.

"You know how effete the British are. Everything will be all right. And if the bombers come, your house is in such a lonely place."

"We've bought a big steel box that's in an empty room at the back on the ground floor. It's got an electric heater inside. But if Werner has to go off and fight, I'm going to be here by myself."

"I'll come and visit you, and I'll give you my phone number. I live over near Neuer Garten."

"We Germans are very clever, but we obey like sheep. It's a horrible combination that no other country has. A really hard, decisive, ambitious leader – we meekly submit every time."

She shook her head in exasperation. "That's not what I mean either. Germans aren't meek. But they love to obey, love to escape from the house and go off to war. Well, a lot of them. They never think *they'll* get killed, but they think that with conquest they'll get a lot of things for nothing. In the Great War and afterwards, we were *flattened*. They think it will never happen to those of *this* generation. They don't think so because Göring and Hitler have told them so. How the German man listens to his leaders!"

"I suppose the English and French listen to anything they like on the radio, so they know more. They probably listen to German broadcasts. You know, Goebbels broadcasts in English," I said ingenuously.

"Listen to anything they like!"

"Like in Argentina."

"Göring said, 'From Posen to Berlin is only forty minutes by plane, but has one sole Polish plane reached Berlin? No, it hasn't. What chance does an English plane have of getting here from several hundreds of miles away?' What do you think?"

"Perhaps the English are not very good at driving planes," I soothed her.

"There was a false air raid alarm one night, did you hear it?"

"No," I said. "I was probably asleep or at a nightclub."

"Göring told us, 'That air raid alarm of last night? I got up and went to my shelter like everyone else, when in fact there wasn't an enemy plane within a hundred miles. But it's easy to understand. Everyone's jumpy. The men at the air-raid posts are trigger happy – they hear the roar of a motorbike and set off the alarm. So the men in one district after another do the same, and soon they're giving us a needless fright.' Another time, he joked about rationing. He said, 'I'm more provident than Germans were in the World War. Now I'm rationing you while we've got plenty. So even though the war lasts for years we'll never want for food!' Now he's saying, 'All we want is peace, peace with

116

honour, Mr. Chamberlain. We don't wish to fight the English people. We don't want a single inch of France. You English are the ones making war.' Another day, he said, 'My dear German people, I know that the Almighty God will bless us and sustain us. Even if He asks the sacrifice of death from us, we will render up our lives with the words – we die that Germany may live.' "

"What beautiful words," I said. Did I sound amoral? I couldn't allow myself the luxury of hate, the luxury of my emotions, indulge myself in my feelings. Did I hurt myself bottling up my hate? No. I expended my hate sending messages to London, the capital of hope, of decency, of life. I had a job to do. I was a pretty hopeless amateur, but as I was enjoying life, I had to do what I could. My messages, my warnings, would certainly be lost in the muddle over there in London, but my conscience was clear.

Annemarie said, "Did you hear the time Göring said, 'Our strength comes from the Führer. The Führer has made Germany live again. England will never understand how we love Hitler, what we feel for the Führer. We'll suffer the worst trials and sorrows for him. Nothing will ever divide us from the Führer.' But, what I ask myself is, where is the Führer taking us?"

I took her hand, and patted it automatically.

But I was thinking, the day I didn't enjoy myself, the day they saw I didn't, they'd catch me.

* * *

When I walked home, Annemarie came some hundreds of metres with me.

At home, Goebbels had left a message that he wanted to see me at two o'clock.

A car picked me up. Goebbels received me warmly, and held my hand between his.

"I loved your photos. You are so full of your youth and it shows."

A maid came in with coffee and buns with *Schlagsahne*, a sweet, whipped cream. I whooped with delight.

It was the very best coffee, strongly aromatic, that caught sharply at the nostrils.

"You think of me as a fussy bureaucrat, a state minister."

"No," I said. "You are a romantic."

"I am," he said. "The other day, I was looking at my Diaries, from when I was young. I miss those years, I miss that life, I miss that person."

He handed me a page. "I had found out this girl was half-Jewish."

June 28, 1924: I would like to go on a honeymoon with her, but the first magic has dimmed. She makes me feel sceptical... I would like to take her down to Italy and Greece, with plenty of money, a plenitude of loving, and no worries... Read Maximilian Harden's TRIALS... he's a lying hypocritical *Schweinehund*, this damned Jew. These pigs, traitors, gangsters, drink the blood from our veins like vampires... I sit in the new pergola in the garden, and lose myself in the beauty of this marvellous summer day: sunshine; soft air; the perfume of flowers; how lovely a world...

I stared at him. "As we grow older, the youth in us, the child, it never dies?"

"Not in artistic people, in people of sensibility..."

"I m glad," I said. "I would like to keep much of what I have now." I paused. "But thank you for showing me who you really are."

I was praying he would not try to touch me, and he did not.

"Now I have to leap 15 years ahead, back to the present, and get back to work. Would you care to go this afternoon to a *Hitler Jugend* Centre – Hitler Youth – and photograph those young faces so full of ideals and hope? The car will take you there."

From what they'd taught me of the *Hitler Jugend*, the Hitler Youth, I knew I was going to hate this assignment – the worst brats in Europe. When I thought of the Boy Scouts back home!

The guttersnipe had told us that his 1,000-year Reich rested on German youth – 'A violent, stormy, bullying, brutal youth – that is what I seek. Youth must not care about pain... I want no intellectual education. Book knowledge is ruin for my young men.'

At the Nazi Rally at Nuremburg in September 1935, 54,000 Nazi kids marched passed Hitler over seven hours. He told them that what he sought from youth was not what previous generations looked for. The torpid philistine (!) boy of yesteryear had given way to the tall, lean athlete, 'swift as the greyhound, tough as leather and as unyielding as Krupp steel.' The Nazis would have no degenerate youth (like in England?) but would train up a new German youth in tight discipline and perfect pride.

In 1933, Hitler had formed two groups, the *Hitler Jugend* and the *Bund Deutscher Mädel*, the League of German Girls. By 1935, I knew he had corralled some 60 percent of German youth, and God only knew how many were captive today.

On March 15 of the year in which a kid had his 10th birthday, every German child had to register. After a close search of the family's racial purity, they took him with that year's unblemished crop into *Deutsches Jungvolk* – German Young People – boys of 10 to 13. After, they moved up to the *Hitler Jugend* for boys from 14 to 18. At 18, the young man graduated into the Nazi party. At 19, he had to do six months in the *Reichsarbeitsdienst* – the State Labour Service – where they did manual work under strict discipline. From being shanghaied into hard labor gangs, they went into the *Wehrmacht* for a stint of two years military conscription.

The *Hitler Jugend* had an endless round of activities but no formal education, which was handled in the schools. All free time went in evenings in Youth Homes, public demonstrations in uniform, in modeling – model planes – arts, crafts, music, hiking and camping.

Now these boys were collecting clothes and blankets for the troops, paper and bones (!) for the war effort.

They planned the thing so that a boy scarcely saw his family – the parents didn't dare open their mouths. The Nazis took them away from their social class and wiped out class-consciousness in the forced labour and in the army. It brought young country children to the cities, made sure there were no young yokels left in Germany.

The boys I was driving to see would have the inexpressible honour of wearing the uniform, and would carry a dagger inscribed 'Blood and Honour'.

* * *

About 200 of the brats were lined up in a large hall. I took some photos, and told the supervisor I needed them to move about freely, to catch spontaneous expressions.

He dismissed them, and they milled about, talking to each other.

In the ranks, they had been stony-faced. Now they darted glances at me, as though I represented a 'sissy' threat, a 'female' seduction of their young manhood.

Others glanced at me with fleeting expressions of longing. Ah! All was not well in Hitler's youth movement. I could soon pick out those who had not succumbed – about one-third of them wanted to talk to me, and wanted out of there.

In the car, I tried to remember my Bible – didn't Jesus want the little children to come unto Him, and didn't He say, you harm one hair of their heads and it's better a millstone be tied about your neck and you be thrown into the sea? Well, Hitler had hurt more than the hair on their heads.

At home, Princess Jutta came to me and said, "With all this food we have, all this Gestapo loot dear Rützel has given us, the two girls want to have a dance. We have lots of aristocratic friends we can invite, but the Prince insists it is better we invite Rützel himself and some of these friends of yours."

"Oh! Let's!" I cried. "I'll ring, but I don't know who'll come."

I rang Ruben, who said he'd bring two girls from the Spanish Embassy. Ekkehard accepted with alacrity. I rang the lonely wife living by the waterside who I had talked to that morning, and she accepted – Annemarie Hartmann and her tank captain husband would come. I rang the SS-Intelligence officer, Gerhard Wallraff, and he said he'd come with the two girls. I had met at the restaurant and nightclub, Gisa and Petra. Gisa's boyfriend, Eugen Kratzer, would probably come too.

Princess Jutta said, "That's about ten people, or, eleven. The ballroom holds about seventy, but the food is the problem. With ourselves, that makes about sixteen. My brother-in-law and his son (Count Axel Hohenlinden, and Eduard, the doctor) will come too, so I'll invite two young men, Duke Herzgog Ehret Oshahrüke and the Margrave Markgraf Otto Zorndorf. The moment they see who our company is, they'll warn every aristocratic family of the sort of people we are consorting with, and we'll be ostracised. That is to the good, because we must defeat Hitler first and protect you as much as we can."

She gave me an affectionate peck on the cheek.

"I feel awful!"

"You do your job," she said severely. "You keep your mind on what you're here for."

Princess Jutta worried unduly about food.

Rützel, bless him, arrived with more food! Of the two Spanish girls, one only was from the Embassy, and she arrived with a leg of Spanish serrano ham. She came with an Embassy official, Guillermo Velasco, who had obviously wangled the whole leg, and assured himself a place in Jutta's heart while the war lasted. The girl was Caridad, and very pretty, as was the other girl, Clara, who worked in the German Broadcasting Commission's Overseas Spanish Service. Clara had a beautiful voice. Gerhard had scrounged a big box of delicacies. Oberst Ekkehard greeted a fellow tank officer Hauptmann Werner Hartmann with easy familiarity, and Thoma and Doris took the lonely Annemarie off to meet the ladies. The tank officers brought two bottles each of brandy, that Thoma's fiancé, Graf Walter Vellinghausen, scooped up expertly and bore off.

We were soon all gathered around, talking excitedly.

Clara spoke to me in Spanish, then exclaimed in German, "You've got a beautiful Castillian accent. You can hardly hear the Argentinian!"

"Hear! Hear!" said Ruben. "I'm very proud of the way we Argentineans mangle Spanish and she doesn't."

I repeated, effortlessly, the words I had recited so many times on the ship. "We had a maid from Madrid, and when I told her she talked funny, she told me she spoke the Spanish the King of Spain spoke, and that my mummy would love me much more if 1 spoke that way. So I ran off to mummy with that tale, and my mother told me, 'Try and talk the way she does'. I was awfully confused. 'Mummy,' I said, 'Don't you talk properly?' 'Of course I do, child, but that way is better.' 'Then why don't you talk that way?' 'Because I'm too old to learn, and it doesn't suit me. But I want you to talk that way'."

Rützel and Gerhard were staring at me, trying to find a hole in my story without realising they were. Rützel relaxed, smiled, and said to me. "You speak German perfectly!"

Clara said, "Much better than I do. But you have a slight Bavarian accent, Ray."

"By Gad! So you do!" exclaimed Gerhard.

"For the first six years of my life, I had a German nanny and we only spoke in German. My parents were very insistent. She was from Munich, and she finally went back to live with a sister and a brother there. She'll be dead by now. I think it was a village near Landsburg. Her name was Else, Else Baumbach, I don't really remember." Karl (Rützel) and Gerhard were listening to me, alert. Tomorrow morning, they'd be scouring the villages for the gravestone. Prince Bernd was looking at me with such admiration he was going to give the game away. And the young Duke, Ehret Oshabrüke, didn't take his eyes from Bernd's face. I could see Ehret adding two and two, and waiting to run to the aristocrats all over town. My heart turned to ice.

121

Karl Rützel deftly turned the conversation.

"I often wonder what Ray must think. Abroad, they talk as though Hitler jumped out of the sky and forced himself upon the German people. Germany was like a parched desert, pleading and weeping for rain. Don't you agree, Frau Hohenlinden?" he asked his hostess.

My God! He had called her Frau instead of Princess. Hitler had abolished all class distinctions. When Karl had stayed for lunch the other day, he had used the full forms of address, as I always did. I would have to watch myself. The Austrian street lout would not stand for Princes and Dukes around him, the rotten racial specimen he was.

"Germany had suffered hunger, unemployment, inflation, every form of insecurity – and above all, humiliation. The most powerful, the largest, the home of culture, the most numerous nation of Europe – its people roamed the streets, looking for food, for lumps of coal. Hitler had been in the headlines since November, 1923, proclaiming that he would liberate Germans from hunger and humiliation and chaotic government. For ten years, the Germans voted in other governments, and all of them dragged us down further and further. Our pride lay on the ground. In 1932, Hitler failed to win the elections, but in March, 1933, with misgovernment and loss of control, the government had to bring Hitler into a coalition. When Hitler consolidated his power, suddenly Germans found work and money and security. Hitler built and built and built – roads, houses, everything! Von Hohenlinden, what do you say?"

"Masterly," smiled the Prince.

The three Spanish had to be Spanish fascists. Caridad, looking admiringly at Karl's Gestapo uniform, took his arm, and asked, "Will you dance with me?"

It was smooth, tactful, and swift. Jutta turned on the gramophone, and Karl, astonished at such forwardness, especially from Spanish girls who were famed for their femininity, took her on the floor. Everyone followed. The grandmother, Bernd, Jutta, and Count Axel sat the first dance out, while Reinhard and Valeria served them canapés and drinks.

I found myself dancing with Gerhard, from SB-Intelligence. He guided me to one end, away from the others, and said quickly, "Rest your head on my shoulder and listen. The Gestapo ordered another branch of my organization to investigate you in South America. They sent an agent, an Argentinean businessman, to Belize, ostensibly to visit shops in Stann Creek, selling textiles. The British put a British Army sergeant to go with him. He asked the sergeant: did he know an old friend of his, Raimunda Hurtada? The sergeant said he did, and the businessman showed him a photo – a wrong photo. The sergeant said that was not her. The businessman apologised, and showed him a second photo which he identified. With the sergeant beside him, the businessman dared not ask any more questions of other people. Listen, I want you to lead me off the floor, to a bathroom."

We walked to a door of the ballroom, closed it after us, and walked down a passageway, very slowly.

Gerhard said swiftly, "They made the businessman, and another one from Chile, sleep in a hotel with a corporal on guard in the lobby. Our agent got out of the back of the hotel, at about 11pm, went to your house, easily opened the kitchen door, and hurried through the house, upstairs as well. You had drawn a sketch at Gestapo Headquarters, that's right? He confirmed your sketch. An Army patrol caught him, and he said he was looking for a prostitute, so they took him to a bar where he found what he wanted."

That sergeant would be Paul Glover, with whom I had had lunch. Whether he was a British Army sergeant, or an intelligence officer dressed up for e lunch, I never knew, but now I saw that our bumbling Secret Service had looked ahead.

We stopped at the door of the bathroom. "He had a camera hidden in a pen, and he photographed the sergeant in a group of people. They may call you to Gestapo Headquarters to identify him. Do you recognize him?"

He showed me the photo and I dumbly pointed my finger, picking him out from the group of strangers. "I met him one day on the beach. The wind had blown away my beach hat. He took me to lunch with some other people. But really, I was never comfortable with the English. We had other social circles – I had my friends, but they were girls. I always wanted to leave Belize, and I just wasn't going to get involved with anyone."

He nodded, and stepped quickly into the bathroom. I hurried back and sat with the family. The record ended, and Rützel invited me to the next dance.

He asked, "Where has Wallraff gone?"

"To the bathroom!" I giggled, and he smiled a little foolishly.

* * *

We danced until after midnight.

The Duke Herzgog Ehret Oshabrüke worked in munitions, like Thoma's fiancé, Graf Walter Vellinghausen – the two were friends – but Ehret worked beside Albert Speer, Hitler's bosom friend, and the second most powerful man in Germany, SS or no SS. Margrave Markgraf Otto Zorndorf was a doctor in engineering and worked in advanced weaponry. Both invited me to go nightclubbing, and I accepted in a flash. Did they know who I was? What could they tell me to pass on to London?

The war in Poland went on. We listened to William Shirer on our secret short-wave band radio. He spent days in Poland and went to the top of a hill in Gyndia. He said that two miles north, they could see a killing ground. German artillery deafened them – but the Poles had none. Only machine-guns, that never let up. He said that ten miles behind them the battleship *Schleswig-Holstein* fired its 12-inch guns over their heads at the Poles. He said that they could hardly see anything in the clouds of dust and smoke, cut by streaks of flame. Oh, where is the Royal Navy to blow that German battleship out of the water? Yet, the Germans argue that planes will easily sink any battleship. The British don't agree.

Shirer said he saw the German infantry advancing in short runs, behind the tanks. The Poles were hopelessly surrounded, but they fought and fought for several days. Shirer said they dragged out two anti-aircraft guns to fire against the tanks. Useless. He saw the German infantry advance and advance, but never saw a Polish soldier retreat.

When they surrendered, only 15,000 came out alive, Shirer told us.

God, they'll chew up the British Army like this, but we'll retreat to the sea I suppose. And then what!

What horrified Shirer was to see the German bombers dive to 50 metres to bomb and machine-gun the Poles. When I think of the British Tommies in France! Those German Stukas!

Shirer compared the German army to a fast, precise steamroller.

Day after day of this. Despair seized me. The Germans trapped the major part of the Polish Army in the giant curve of the Vistula River, near where I had been. In ten days, the Poles fought the bloodiest battle in all their history.

He said that below them, in the streets, they saw the women and children, listening to the guns. I remember his voice coming over the wireless: "The bitterness, the anguish on the faces of those women was indescribable." Will the next women to suffer bitterness and anguish be British women? I can't bear this. I want to go back to London – would they let me man an anti-aircraft artillery gun? Oh, to get my finger on a trigger!

Shirer told us when the Germans decided they had won. They captured 450,000 Polish troops, 1,200 guns (which I don't believe) and captured or shot down 800 Polish planes, the whole Polish airforce. How many days will the German pilots need to shoot down the whole RAF?

Shirer said that the Battle of Kutno, west of Warsaw (which was largely

Sepp Dietrich's doing) utterly surpassed the Battle of Tannenberg, that had knocked Russia out of the Great War. The Russians had lost 92,000 prisoners, and 28,000 dead. At Kutno, the Germans took prisoner 105,000 Poles on one day, 60,000 the next.

How many men are there in the British Expeditionary Force, and what hope has General Ironsides against my friend Sepp Dietrich, or against Guderain?

Then came a piece of news that made my heart sink. General von Brauchitsch, Commander-in-Chief of the German Army, went to the west front, the front of the *Sitzkrieg*, the phony war, the 'sit-down war.'

But in America, they talked about voting out the Neutrality Act, and bringing in Cash-and-Carry, to carry arms to England.

September gave way to October, and on October 1, oh, Glory! I heard Winston Churchill make a broadcast, "One Month of War." As I heard that throaty growl of a voice, my despair vanished. My heart was beating like mad.

The whole family sat around, intent.

Churchill said, "It has not yet come to the severity of fighting… but there are three things.

"Firstly, the heroic defense of Warsaw shows that the soul of Poland is indestructable and that she will rise again like a rock that may be for a spell submerged…"

He deplored that the Russians stood upon a line in Poland not as allies of Poland but as an invader, but he said Russia needed this buffer against the Nazi menace! Ho! Ho! as they say in European comics.

He spoke as First Lord of the Admiralty. Chamberlain was Prime Minister. "The U-boat attack upon the life of the British Isles has not so far been proved successful. It is true that when they sprang out upon us, and we were going about our orderly business with two thousand ships in constant movement every day, they managed to do some serious damage. But the Royal Navy has counter-attacked the U-boats…"

His speech was paused, cultured, his voice steady as a rock. I thought of the shrill and hysterical rantings of the Nazi leadership.

"Britain will hold," said the Prince. "Listen to him!"

"England will stay the course," said the grandmother. "We will hang all this riff-raff yet on the gallows, and return to a civilized life."

People had been talking about the *hunger war*. Britain blockades Germany; and everyone remembers the starvation of the Great War under the British blockade. What would this blockade do? Little did they know of the breadbaskets in the Ukraine, Poland, Romania, Hungary, Yugoslavia and Bulgaria – those endless wheatfields. But Germany blockades Britain with its U-boats, sinking England's foodstuffs on the high seas.

A few days ago, Shirer had interviewed a U-boat Captain on the wireless – a U-boat Captain who had sent a W/T message to Churchill giving the position of a ship full of grain he had sunk. Churchill told the Parliament the captain was a prisoner, but here he was in a Berlin studio at the microphone.

Shirer asked Lieutenant-Captain Herbert Schultze where had he been working.

SCHULTZE: In the Atlantic. (Schultze spoke in English)

Shirer asked him what luck he had.

SCHULTZE: Unfortunately I did not meet any enemy warships but I did have a part in some successes which perhaps you have heard about in the newspapers or on the radio.

Shirer asked for details.

SCHULTZE: I would like to tell you about the sinking of the British merchant ship, *Royal Sceptre*. There have been many stories abroad. Here is what really happened. The *Royal Sceptre* was bound for England with a cargo of grain. One day I sighted her. I rose to the surface and fired a shot of warning across her bows.

The *Royal Sceptre*, however, did not stop. Instead she answered by turning tail. I signalled, 'Make no use of your wireless,' and then heard the wireless operator sending out an SOS message, saying he was being fired at by a submarine and giving his position. Seeing that he was disobeying my orders, and by reporting my position was guilty of a hostile act, I was regretfully forced to stop him from doing so. The only means I had was to open fire with my gun. We scored several hits. These caused her to stop. Her crew took to the boats.

The radio operator, however, stayed aboard and continued to report his position. He was, by the way, an exceptionally fine and brave fellow. I say that here because I shall scarcely have an opportunity to shake hands with him personally. The lifeboats made no attempt to come nearer, so I had to go up to them to ask whether I had wounded anyone and if they had plenty of provisions.

'Supplies sufficient, nobody wounded,' was the answer. I then had the wireless operator fetched from aboard.

Shirer then asked when did he sink the ship.

SCHULTZE: I sank the *Royal Sceptre* only after I saw the smoke of a ship on the horizon. I called out to the men in the boats to wait till I could

126

send help. They waved, happy and friendly, and yelled, 'Hurrah!'

Shirer protested that reports said the men were abandoned and had drowned.

SCHULTZE: That is not true. I set sail for that smoke on the horizon. It was the British steamer, *Browning*. I wanted to tell them to take the crew of the *Royal Sceptre* on board. The Browning sights us. But to my surprise, the crew manned the boats in a panic. Before I can even draw closer to give my peaceful message, the crew and passengers have left the ship. I now had to make it clear to these people that they were to get aboard again to go and save the crew of the *Royal Sceptre*. The joy and relief on those boats surprised us. Did they believe us to be barbarians? Taking to the boats in a panic like that as soon as a U-boat comes in sight. The captain of the *Browning* – as I have now heard to my great satisfaction – obeyed my orders to save the crew of the *Royal Sceptre*. And also, my order not to use his radio till he should reach port. He has, I hear, reached safely the harbour of Bahia in Brazil.

Shirer asked him was there anything else.

SCHULTZE: Well, I sent Mr. Churchill a radio message.

Shirer said he thought the Captain had been captured.

SCHULTZE: Yes, that is what Mr. Churchill told the House of Commons. He even said I was being well treated. That, at least, is true enough – although he has apparently got the coordinates of my position wrong.

Author's note: From THIS IS BERLIN, by William L. Shirer, Copyright William L. Shirer Literary Trust 1999. Published by Arrow Books, Random House. The verbatim words are broadcast by a German Combatant on a wartime radio station in Berlin under the aegis of the German Propaganda Ministry.

One evening, Claus and the Prince took me aside.

They had a report on German Naval High Command worries about the future of the U-boat campaign against England. I read through it, and they answered my questions.

We were in my bedroom, and the Prince left. Claus suddenly pulled me to him, kissed me, then put his hands on my breasts. I took his hands away, sighed, and said, "Claus, don't you see...?"

He looked at me miserably. "I see," he said firmly. "Duty, first?"

"All those girls chasing you. Your problem is you've got so large a heart you love us all," I chided him, and he nodded his head sheepishly. He kissed me on the cheek, and left. My heart was beating to suffocate me. What sense did it make to die young and virginal? But in no way could I have an accident and find myself pregnant... that was a horror that put all else out of my head.

If I married a German, what would they think in London? My reports would be so suspect as to be useless.

I got out the typewriter, and chose page 555 of Lorna Doone, line two: 'upon my countenance. This vile thing Bob, being angered'

U	P	O	N	M	U
Y	A	B	C	D	Y
E	F	G	H	I	E
J	K	L	Q	R	J
S	T	V	W	X	S
U	P	O	N	M	U

My message, before encryption, read:

New Naval Command study fears Brits could form convoys of merchant ships. Estimate 6 to 10 knots. Believe zigzag course then impracticably slow. U-boats would surface to radio rendezvous 10 or 20 miles ahead for day attack. Night surface speed of U-bs 13 knots. Night attacks, all sides. No problem while Navy escorts stay within one mile of convoy. My recommendation. Form convoys, zigzag, Navy escorts three to ten miles out.

So it began: DKMDG NGWIY (New Naval Co...) and so on.

The hidebound British admiralty, despite the presence of Churchill, ignored my message. First a delay in forming convoys, then a delay in zigzagging, and for more than two years the Navy escorts stuck close alongside the convoys, with catastrophic losses. In Berlin, we were risking our lives to send reports like this. British Navy brass knew best – they even knew that planes couldn't sink battleships, till Japanese bombers sank the *Prince of Wales* and the *Repulse* north of Singapore, within minutes, leaving open Malaysia, Singapore, Hong Kong, Burma, the Dutch East Indies, the South East Pacific Islands and New

The Duke Herzgog Ehret Oshabrüke rang me and invited me to dinner at his villa in Grunewald. The house had wide grounds, and he had a married couple who cooked for him and looked after him.

Towards the end of the meal, he said, "I work beside Albert Speer, and Speer is constantly with Hitler – he's Hitler's favourite, and that makes him the second most powerful man in Germany. I can arrange for you to photograph him, and as Speer has strong artistic sense – he's first and foremost an architect and designer – he's going to like you very much if your photos satisfy him aesthetically. He could use you to photograph decorations he designs. I also work in the Ministry of Armaments under Dr. Fritz Todt, and you can take artistic photographs of munitions production too."

I tried to remember what I had learned of Speer, but Ehret went on, telling me what I quickly realized I knew, and some I did not.

"He's 34, and he carries out the dreams of the frustrated artist who is Hitler. I have seen Hitler staring raptly for hours at the plans, drawings and models which Speer had done for him. Hitler has named him General Architectural Inspector of the Reich and Hitler has commanded him to 'transform Berlin into the living and true capital of the German Reich.' as well as twenty-seven other cities. Speer is remaking them. My boss, Fritz Todt, dreamt up the idea of the autobahns, but Speer does work on roads too. In 1932, Speer joined the Nazi Party and the SS, although this is nominal. He's not political. Goebbels handed him the job of the 1933 Tempelhof Rally, and he showed brilliance, simple, fast brilliance. He put up flagpoles and used lighting in a way never seen before. So they gave him the job of making the 1934 Nuremberg rally – a spectacle no one would ever forget... and then the task of building a grandiose complex there that the war has interrupted.

"He had a hellish childhood, the same as Hitler – their mothers, especially Speer's parents humiliated him nonstop with his two brothers, so the two men can't express their inner emotions. In the middle of a crowd, they're loners. Women chase both of them, but they can't respond. They aren't homosexuals. Their mothers have frozen them, and they live their lives under an inner iron control. Yet they let emotions dictate what they do much more than reason. Now, Speer is clever, don't let me mislead you. He can take any bewildering complexity and in a few strokes reduce it to a stunning simplicity. He is a genius at cutting to the heart of the worst obstacles. Yet between Speer and Hitler lies a shadowy love – they are both dependent on it – they need it and it is given. I don't know how to put it."

I thought, how sensitive and clever Ehret was. All these attractive men around me...

"I think you're putting it very well."

"Through Speer, you may arrive at Hitler. Hitler loves women around him, but they are his inferiors. He humiliates Eva Braun. When his niece committed suicide, a big part of him died inside, and he said, 'Now, my only love will be the nation.' Any woman who speaks up is instantly expelled from his circle. He would like to meet you, but after what happened in Poland and your 'Iron Cross', which he refused to confirm, he's a bit afraid of you. It would be unbearable for him to confer an Iron Cross on a woman. But Hitler's curiosity will get the better of him. He doesn't even approve of a woman being a photographer, but the artist in him is too strong. He will want to see how you do. Well, he has seen several portraits of yours – Himmler, Geobbels, Heydrich, and he's impressed. His knowledge of art is unbelievable, and his own works are very good. When the Vienna Art School rejected his admission, it struck him to the heart – and he didn't deserve it. The man is a monster – but a truly artistic one."

"How can you work for two masters?"

"Hitler took me away from Todt and gave me to Speer, but Todt kicked up a fuss. So they sort of share me."

"What do you do, in heaven's name?"

"Todd and Speer give orders – cold orders people must jump to obey. Sometimes, it's better to convince people, smooth the path. That's my job."

I had to laugh.

I went next door to talk to Count Axel Hohenlinden, Prince Bernd's brother.

He sat me down comfortably and said, "You must think of Speer as a sort of Peter Pan. He does everything so swiftly, effortlessly, everything has been so easy and obvious for him, he's not your heavy-handed Nazi. And he doesn't worry about what people think of him.

"Because today we are at war with England and France because of what people think of themselves. A biographer discovers outstanding people with a very high opinion of themselves – and finds most other people share it. But myriads of people are of a lowly or unworthy condition, but have a very high opinion of themselves – perhaps as a compensation. Those people are dangerously touchy – or violent. Almost all violent people are people with a very high opinion of themselves that no one else shares. And this is what happened to Germany. We lost the Great War and Versailles humiliated us.

"Most Germans believe they belong to the most powerful and cultured country in the world – and the outside world shattered that, trod their image of themselves into the mud. That is why they follow Hitler – he's no Aryan superman, but he is a man whose face shows that life has disappointed him, crushed and humiliated him, yet he has sprung back, roaring and clawing. His speeches are those of a rank amateur. He is a raw speaker, but goes to what is deepest in Germans – their smashed self-image. He is going to teach the world to respect and fear Germans again, by our defeating Germany's enemies like young avenging gods. Now Hitler is no longer amateurish. He tries to speak at night, before strong lights. It changes his face. When he talks, you feel he cares about you. He exercises mass hypnosis. You feel he… well… even loves you. That if you follow him, he will bring out the giant in you, the awful massed power of all Germans working as one. He mixes frenzy with reasoning. He is pale, a victim of life's oppression, it's written in his white face. Now he lowers his voice in his love and confidence in you, then yells mad invective, declaims furious diatribes against our enemies, harangues us for our weaknesses.

"Speer has none of this. He is a Peter Pan, a self-made man, too clever for life to touch. He has no hate. He fulfills himself with his unerring solutions."

Count Axel got up and walked back and forth.

"Hitler is no physical coward. He has shown that over and again. But he shies away from bloody work. He did go in person to the Röhm bloodbath, the massacre of the Brownshirts – Goebbels and Göring tricked him, Himmler too, and he swallowed the whole tale. Röhm woke up, and half-asleep, greeted him warmly. 'I didn't expect you till tomorrow,' not knowing he was supposed to be plotting a *putsch* to overthrow Hitler!

"Hitler came back, badly excited, and called for Speer, to talk about architecture and try to calm down. Now he's just been to Poland, but he stayed away from the front."

Next morning, I was in Speer's office at nine o'clock. He was so handsome, he was heart-stopping. He looked so… strong… so clever… so relaxed… a beautiful face. I felt all my muscles tremble. A god to create beauty. Count Axel warned me he was abnormally reticent, and he gave me a nod with a fleeting smile.

"Do you want to photograph me leaning over plans? In fifteen minutes, I have to leave for Munich."

"Oh," I said, with all the wistfulness I knew how to muster. "Aren't you lucky? I've never seen Munich. Our problem is that I need you to talk as I take photographs, and your studying architectural plans don't help us, I'm afraid. Oh dear, now disappointing. What is Munich like?"

He stood looking at me, and thinking.

"Do you want to drive down in the car with me? We'd have to call in at your place, so you can pack, to sleep the night there at a hotel. I'll drive you back tomorrow, or if I have to stay longer, you can catch the train."

He was asexual.

"I'd love that." I looked at him with melting eyes. "Princess Jutta Hohenlinden will be home. Would you like to meet her and have a look at the *schloss*? See what you think of its architecture?"

His eyes lighted up. "Ah!" he said.

* * *

Princess Jutta was charming, and while I packed, she showed him all over the palace, inside and out.

We sat in the back seat of a large Mercedes, the glass partition drawn between ourselves and the driver. He encouraged me to talk about Argentina and Belize, and then I asked how he met Hitler.

"I had studied architecture under Professor Tessenow. Only six months after the final exam, he made me his assistant, although I was very young. But I was pessimistic. Spengler's *Decline of the West* made me feel I was living in the twilight of western civilization, in the days of the *Decline and Fall of the Roman Empire*. In the Roman Empire, architecture became internationalized, standardized. So, Germany's grovelling in its despair seemed but part of a world Decline, of a dying civilization with internationalized architecture, a Henry Ford civilization, if you like.

"We had a powerful Professor of the History of Architecture, Daniel Krenkler... in a lecture on Strassburg Cathedral, he showed us pictures and burst into tears! He had to stop the lecture. His pride in Germanic

132

architecture! Albrecht Haupt wrote a book on German architecture, *Die Baukunst der Germanen*, and that made me think that if we were treading a downward path, it wasn't racial, wasn't that we were mixed race. That had happened already back in the Middle ages. It was because we had spent our energies, driving Slavs out of Prussia or exporting our culture to the world. That was why I saw poverty, unemployment and hopelessness all around me, just the same as in the late Roman Empire, with its decline of morals, wealth and energy.

"Then Tessenow wrote that there could be misunderstood 'super heroes' living all around us, whose view is so lofty that they smile at the worst horrors because they see them as just passing. He said that nations, perhaps, which have gone down into hell will arise for their next stage of magnificence. Tessenow likewise taught that style springs from the womb of the people. People always love their native land and no real culture can ever be international. That is only Henry Fordism. Culture is local. When I heard that Hitler denounced internationalism in art, I liked that very much.

"Then Tessenow told us that someone had to come who knew how to think simply. He said our thinking had got far too complicated. We needed an uncultured peasant who would settle everything thanks to his uncorrupted mind. A man with the force to push through his simple ideas."

He turned to me. "Am I boring you?"

I spoke in my most breathless voice. "I'm fascinated. I've never been so interested in my whole life."

Still asexual. But now I felt friendship, a cool sort of friendliness.

"So what happened next was that Hitler gave a talk to the students of Berlin University and the Institute of Technology. It was in a beer hall called the *Hasheide*. Stained walls, an air of indigent seediness, where the poorest workmen went to get drunk. That day it was so packed, students were turned away. They'd stuck in a bare platform, full of professors. I was with Tessenow, close to the lectern.

"In comes Hitler, and his own followers among the students go wild. That had a bit of a shock impact on me: on posters and cartoons, he always dressed like a tin soldier, swastika armband, and forelock dancing over his forehead. Here he wore a tailored blue suit, respectability itself. He had a reputable air of unassuming strength. What I didn't know then is that he has this incredible skill in adapting to people and to audiences.

"The yelling and applause went on and on, so, as if sheepish, he diffidently and slowly checked it and when at last he could speak, it sounded more like a lecture on history − no spouting bombast, no crazy agitator waving his arms. All the ovations didn't make him depart from his sobriety of address.

"I was thinking, but what's this? He was frank, well, open, letting us into his deepest feelings and fears about the future. He could be satirical, he

133

could be self- conscious, he could be half-funny. He had charm. His timidity slowly disappeared, and now his passion grew, his hypnotic insistence… his hypnotic… entreaty.

"I could never afterwards remember what he said, but the fervor, the frenzy among his listeners was as solid as a wave of the ocean. Opponents couldn't get a word in, and this gave a hypnotic sense of total agreement, of every heart beating as one. We were all one sole being, and everything we wanted, he was giving it voice. He was leading the students of the two greatest centres of learning in all Germany by his hand.

"Afterwards, all the students got together over glasses of beer. I couldn't. I had to be somewhere silent, on my own. I drove my small car along by the Havel, and got out at a pine forest, and walked into it.

"Here was the answer to Spengler. A new burst of civilisation to last a thousand years, as he promised. Here were new insights, new beliefs, and jobs to put our hands to. Spengler had his answer, and Spengler's prophecy of a new Roman Emperor had come to pass."

He turned to me, "Do you understand?"

I put all my adoration into my eyes, "I do, I do! Please, don't stop!"

"I had seen no answer to the hazard of communism taking us over. No answer to unemployment… to hunger, misery. Hitler said he could solve all that, quickly, surely, through the labour of the German people, urgently and rightly directed. I found my way back to my car, and drove home.

"The effect Hitler had had on me, Goebbels reinforced a few weeks later. He spoke to a demonstration at the *Sportpalast*. Every word crafted, every phrase carefully turned in advance, his delivery a lesson in rhetoric. He had the crowd boiling like a cauldron, a cauldron! A raving insanity of joy and hate! Then I saw hoe Hitler spoke from the heart."

"Today, I know that Hitler does the same thing as Goebbels. They slip the leash on their audiences, wipe away the veneer of… respectability? conformity? uncertainty? – and release primal energies which are building a new Germany and leading us to victory."

"So you were sitting so close to his lectern, and he never knew how important you were to be?"

"Goebbels gave me the job of rebuilding and redecorating his new Ministry of Propaganda. This is 1933, just after they came to power in March. A sketch lay on a table, showing decorations for a rally at Tempelhof Field on May 1. 'This looks like drawings for a rifle-club gathering,' I cried, disgustedly. Goebbels' secretary, Hanke, told me, 'If you think you can do better, it's all yours.'"

I remembered years ago, in London, photos in the newspapers of monster Nazi rallies. How we had looked and dismissed them disdainfully. What had happened to our wits!

Speer said, "I dashed off a drawing of a big platform behind three stupendous banners, each rearing higher than a ten-storey building. Two banners would be red-white-black with a third swastika banner in the middle. My idea was risky because in a high wind, imagine! I illuminated them with powerful searchlights. They accepted them instantly."

Speer gave a lazy laugh. "Goebbels told Hitler it was his idea. But when I had finished my work for Goebbels' Ministry, they called me to Nuremberg. Now we're in July, 1933. They were getting ready for the first mass party rally – we were in power, and the rally had to show it."

He looked at me, "But it wasn't easy. I had to do something in no time at all, and on a shoestring. As the local people didn't have much idea, they flew me to Nuremberg. I borrowed from my Tempelhof Rally – this time I put a vast eagle spiked to a timber frame, like a butterfly pinned to cork. But the Nuremberg leader didn't dare to okay it. He sent me to Munich, where I discovered they took all of this to the highest levels. Like a shot, I found myself in the luxury of Rudolph Hess's office. He didn't even look at the folder in my hand – he didn't even let me speak. 'The Führer alone will decide this.' He used the telephone, and told me, 'The Führer is in his apartment. I'll get a car for you.' "

He rubbed his hand over his broad, powerful jaw.

"I thought, does architecture mean so much to Hitler? We pulled up at a block of apartments near Prinzregenten Theatre. On the second floor, they took me into an anteroom full of presents or mementos in poor taste. The furniture was no better. An adjutant came and told me matter-of-factly, as though it was of no importance, "Go in," and I found myself standing before Hitler himself, in person. He had taken a pistol to pieces – the bits all over a table in front of him. He didn't look at me, but said sharply, "Put the drawings here," and pushed away bits and pieces of the pistol.

"He looked at the drawings in silence.

"'Agreed.'

"Not another word!

"He turned back to his pistol, and I walked out... well, nonplussed, abashed, I don't know.

"In Nuremberg, they were flabbergasted, it had been so quick.

"Next thing, in the autumn of the same year, 1933, Hitler had commissioned his architect, Paul Ludwig Troost, to wholly refurbish the Chancellor's apartment in Berlin. Troost was from Munich, and he sent his building supervisor to Berlin, who quickly found himself floundering. Hitler recalled that some young architect had redone something for Goebbels in record time, by name of Speer; so he told me to act as aide to the supervisor and lead him through the intricacies of the Berlin building markets.

"Hitler, this building supervisor and myself inspected the residence as it stood. In spring this year, Hitler wrote about that inspection of the Chancellor's residence, and he said that after the 1918 revolution the place had fallen away. Roof timbers had rotted and the attics were decrepit. As his predecessors didn't manage to stay in office for more than four or five months, they didn't clean up the growing filth. They didn't worry about their prestige with other countries because other countries dismissed Germany as of small account. We found mould on the ceilings, and the wallpaper and floors rotting away. He said the place had a nasty smell. He was exaggerating, but there was but one bathroom, and a stone-age kitchen. The decoration was in appalling taste – doors painted to imitate natural wood! Up in the attic, the janitor pointed and said, 'This door takes you into the next building.'

"'What!' exclaimed Hitler.

"'A passage runs through the attics of all the ministries into Hotel Adlon.'

"'What for?'

"'With the riots at the beginning of the Weimar Republic, they besieged the residence and cut off the Chancellor from the world outside. So, he built this passage to escape along it.'

"Hitler walked through the door, and there we were in the Foreign Ministry. Poor Germany!

"'Brick this up,' said Hitler. 'I won't need it.'

"So, we got to work, and Hitler came almost every day at noon. The pleasure he got from it. The workers dropped into saying hello to him without formality – they were completely at ease with him, and he with them. They didn't stand to attention or say *Deutscher Gruss*. Hitler was so at home on a work site. This man in a few months was changing Germany beyond belief – the country was thriving, the unemployed back to work, myriads of projects, he was Germany's most powerful man, its giant, and here he was

136

with workers without any affectation. He'd go from room to room. 'When do we plaster this room? Haven't the windows come yet? Look at that ceiling moulding. Wonderful! Can't we hurry up things more? I'm stuck in the tiny state secretary's apartment on the top floor.'

"After about a month, in the middle of a tour, he said to me, 'Will you come to dinner with me?' He was so formal with me, he astonished me. A hod of plaster fell on me from a scaffolding and had ruined my suit coat. I gave a lugubrious look at my jacket, and Hitler, repressing a smile said, 'We'll arrange that upstairs.'

"Guests were waiting upstairs, Goebbels too, and his eyes widened when he saw me. Hitler led me into his private rooms, and sent a valet to bring Hitler's dark-blue jacket. 'There, put that on', he said, and led me back to the dining-room, where he seated me at his side, as guest of honour. Goebbels exclaimed, 'You're wearing the Führer's gold badge! That isn't your jacket!' Hitler rescued me. 'No, it's mine.' Hitler alone wears a gold sovereignty badge – an eagle gripping a swastika in its talons. All other party members wear the round badge that you will have seen everywhere.

"While we ate, Hitler asked me questions about myself for the first time. So I told him about the May 1st decorations for the Rally. 'Yes, I remember.' He hadn't even looked at me. 'And did you do the Nuremberg ones too?' Goebbels had told him they were his idea, and here was Goebbels sitting at the table! Yes, I did those too. No one knew I'd found out about Goebbels. 'Of course. An architect came to see me. So that was you? Oh, good!'

"Years later, Hitler spoke about those days. 'You drew my attention, seeing you every day. I was searching for a young architect to carry out my architectural plans in the far future, who could work on them after my death. I realized you were that man.'"

* * *

He stared ahead at the road. The speeding Mercedes swallowed the miles. Munich was more than 500 miles away, but the supercharged Mercedes often reached more than 100 mph.

"Every year, the lesser, pot-bellied Nazi functionaries held their rally at Zeppelin Field – they were the *Amtswalter*, so-called – and no one knew how to line them up in drill ranks, much less show their discipline, what there was of it. Hitler had already been mordant about them, and the Organization Section for Party Rallies held painful meetings.

"I had an inspiration. 'Let's make them march in darkness!' I thought, the flagbearers can form ten lanes, to funnel the *Amtswalter*, who otherwise would mill in every direction. Then I thought of aircraft searchlights, flaming miles up into the heavens. Spotlights on the banners and on a huge eagle. Around the edge of the field, searchlights. I asked Hitler for 130 searchlights, to put one every 40 feet, and Göring went through the roof. They were a good part of the national reserve; but Hitler prevailed upon him. He said, 'If we use this many just for a spectacle, other countries will believe we're awash with searchlights.'

"The effect that night beggared belief. The lights blazed up 20,000 to 25,000 feet, where they dissolved into a wide, luminosity. You felt you were within an astronomical cave a measureless cathedral or nature, the beams incandescent pillars. A cloud would float across – utterly surreal."

I said, "The Buenos Aires newspapers reported that, I remember. They said the British Ambassador, Sir Neville Henderson, commented, 'It was a cathedral of ice.' "

He nodded, very pleased.

* * *

I looked out at the countryside speeding by. The day was overcast, but, oh! to have left Berlin. I thought, yet again, how men open their souls to women, to impress us, overwhelm us. They believe in our discretion, as though they have woven a cocoon for two, but mostly women betray men, exploit this weakness, this fatal weakness. Even without malice, a woman must needs tell another woman, who will then run off to inflict the betrayal.

What a need is this in men!

* * *

"Now I found I had to be at Hitler's beck and call. I rented a studio on the Behrenstrasse, a few hundred metres from the Chancellery. We worked from early morning till ten at night, but I often had lunch or dinner with Hitler in the state secretary's apartment. He always had his chauffeur there – Schreck – they went back many years. Schreck was allowed to say what he liked. In the car, he would pull everyone to pieces, and Hitler would listen. Sepp Dietrich often turned up – your good friend from Poland. Brückner and Schaub, his two adjuncts, were always there. And whoever he invited, Göring and Goebbels showed up all the time. He used to talk about everything. Hitler told us how after he came to power, every trifling thing landed on his desk. Files piled up, and no matter how he ploughed through them, more arrived. 'Finally, I put an end to that nonsense,' he said. 'They said the country would grind to a halt if I didn't handle it all. So I swept them out of my office and warned them not to bring any more. Now I have time for thinking and for

138

giving orders.'

"Every evening they set up this primitive movie projector, to put on a newsreel and one or two movies. The men put the picture in upside down, broke the film – they were hopeless. Hitler took it in good part, while his adjuncts yelled and cursed at the operators. Hitler liked films on love, society – light films. He liked revues with lots of leg. He didn't like films on travel, mountaineering, animals or sport. He couldn't stand comedies like Charlie Chaplain and Buster Keaton.

"At the end of 1933, in winter, Göring asked Hitler's permission to use me to redecorate his residence. He'd taken over the lavish residence of the one-time Prussian Minister of Commerce – the Prussian state had poured money into it before 1914. Göring had it done up the way that made him happy, when along came Hitler and exclaimed, 'How can you stand living here! Dark as a cave! Compare it with my place – light and bright. What gloom!'

"Poor Göring. His romantic labyrinth of small rooms with stained-glass windows blocking out the light, heavy velvet drapes... oh dear.

"So Göring bore me off like a Roman warrior with a Sabine – I wasn't consulted. He said, 'You've got a free hand. Do something like the Führer's place, that's all. I don't know how many walls I knocked down – I turned the ground into four huge rooms, his study alone measuring about 1,500 square feet! He wanted an annexe in glass, and that needed bronze. Bronze was scarce, all going to the war effort, with terrible penalties for misuse. Göring used all he wanted, and loved inspecting the place with all its bronze, laughing like a child with its birthday present.

"His furniture suited his size – gargantuan stuff. A Renaissance desk of colossal size, and the back of its chair was higher than his head. Like a princely throne. He had these silver candelabra with vast parchment shades. The pride of the Kaiser Friedrich Museum was Rubens' *Diana at the Stag Hunt*, famous all over the world. He made the museum hang it on his wall that held openings for his projection room; the painting rose up out of the way."

Speer took a thermos flask of coffee, and poured us cups.

I said diffidently, guardedly, "I'd like to meet Hitler, but I suppose that's impossible."

"Well," said Speer, "He wants to meet you too, I think. But after your adventures in Poland... he's not comfortable with strong-minded women."

"Oh, I'm not strong-minded," I said meekly. "Things just happened so quickly. It wasn't fair at all."

"I'll speak to Hitler. He'll ask me what are you like, and I'll tell him you're a listener – that you haven't expressed a single opinion. Well, not yet!" and we both laughed.

His gaze grew distant, as he stared out of the window, and to my frustration, talked about 'Carlton's Tearoom'. "Hitler went there for coffee.

He liked it because the clients pretended he wasn't Hitler. Phoney luxury, the furniture copies of old authentic pieces and counterfeit glass chandeliers hanging from the ceiling."

Speer went on, "We met there time and again. How we talked! Well, this is Munich. But often I'd be in bed, when they'd phone from Hitler's residence. 'The Führer's going to drive over to Cafe Heck. He'd like your company.' I'd know I wouldn't get back to my pillow before two or three o'clock in the morning. Cafe Heck was the very opposite of the Carlton's Tearoom. No-nonsense wooden chairs and iron tables. It went back to when Hitler met up with Party comrades, but after he came to power in March, 1933, that stopped. When old comrades asked permission now to talk to him, he put them off with every sort of excuse. When they got too familiar with him, he lost his outward geniality for a surly impatience. Most now lived like princes in splendid homes, so Hitler reckoned, he had now earned the right to be left alone in the Café Heck.

"Hitler told me, 'I hope you don't mind the hours I keep, I got into this way because after a day of struggle, I'd have to get around a table with the veteran fighters; or if I'd made a speech, it left me so hopped up I couldn't sleep till the early hours.' "

I gently steered Speer back to Hitler and women.

"He needs to have lovely women around him, and he wants physical contact with them; he always holds women by the elbow. He calls my wife *Meine schöne Frau Speer* – 'My good-looking Frau Speer.' He told her that 'your husband is going to raise such buildings as the world has perhaps not seen in four thousand years', holding her elbow."

I asked, "And Eva Braun?"

He shook his head. "The way he treats her! Perhaps Eva wants it that way – doesn't want to be blazoned before the world as Hitler's unmarried mistress. Perhaps *he* has decided. Or they have worked the arrangement between them.

"Have you heard of *Berchtesgaden*?"

I nodded.

"Hitler has his Berghof circle there. Berghof is a small, timber house on *Obersalzberg*, after you drive up a 30 degree mountain road – with bad potholes that jolt the cars – beyond *Berchtesgaden*. Hitler's house – the roof has a broad, sheltering overhang – three bedrooms – pseudo German mountain peasant look – all very lower middle-class. Let me think – a brass canary cage, swastikas embroidered on pillows and cushions with words like 'eternal loyalty'. You see it?

"Hitler arrives and goes to his bedroom. He emerges wearing a Bavarian sports coat of pale-blue linen, with a yellow tie. With me, he straight away talks about building.

"Some hours later, a small Mercedes van pulls up. Three girls inside –

his two secretaries, Fräulein Wolf and Fräulein Schröder, and this modest girl with an outdoor face – Eva. The Mercedes van never drives in the motorcade – it comes up hours later. The secretaries are to help disguise Eva. She feels embarrassed at her position, so she's reserved with the circle of friends. Now she and I are friends. When we say goodbye to Hitler and go to our houses, those two are left alone to go to the bedroom, so what do people think? Well, an adjunct and a servant stay at Berghof with them."

On Hitler's fiftieth birthday, Bormann built the Eagle's Eyrie as a gift – you went up in a 100-foot lift, inside a cliff. There Hitler gazed out upon mountain-tops to where the misty horizon met the sky – while millions died, or twisted in agony from wounds, or gazed out at barbed wire. Higher up than Berghof, on the top of a peak.

Speer went on, "Well, between, say, 1934 and 1936, Hitler liked short hikes on the public tracks through the mountain forest, with his guests and three or four SS bodyguards. He let Eva come along, but only at the tail-end of the column, with the two secretaries. He calls a guest up to the front to talk to him – a signal honour – but the conversation would be disjointed for lack of breath. Hitler walked quickly. After some thirty minutes, he'd call for another person and the person he was talking to would melt away down the column.

"We'd run into other walkers, who'd get off the path with adoring or deferential greetings. Some women or girls would speak to him directly, and always he was cordial.

"We'd sometimes go to *Hochlenzer*, a small mountain tavern, about an hour's walk away, on the *Scharitzkehl*, with solid wooden tables and stools, for a glass of beer, or even milk."

Speer sat silently, watching the passing countryside.

I prompted him. "And he turned to you on the day of the Blood Purge, the Röhm putsch?"

Speer said, "Not on that day. The next. The adjunct phoned me. 'If you have any new designs, bring them right away.' Hitler was wrought up, as I had never seen him. He seemed persuaded he had escaped a danger to his life. He told me over and again how he had forced entry into *Hotel Henselmayer* in Wiessee. 'We were unarmed, didn't have a weapon, and didn't know whether those swine could open fire. One room, we found two naked boys. Ugh!'

"But Hitler likes to keep himself apart from violence. He even takes contradiction badly, and never tolerates it from a woman. You remember I told you that two secretaries would bring up the rear with Eva Braun? That one was Fraulein Schröder, Christa Schröder. She argued with him when Hitler objected to young soldiers smoking. She was in Coventry for weeks."

In Spring, 1943, Henrietta von Schirach, daughter of Hitler's photographer, Hoffman, and wife of the *Leader of the Hitler Youth*, saw arrests of Jews in Amsterdam. She demanded of Hitler did he know how they were treating the Jews in Holland? She had grown up in the Berghof, from a little girl at Hitler's knee. Hitler never let her in again.

After the war, I learned that anyone who spoke of the persecution of the Jews went straight to a concentration camp. Henrietta spoke of it to Hitler's face!

The Gestapo's machinery of repression was such that almost no one found out. Those in the armed forces who saw arrests, or saw the transports – workers on the railways – kept their mouths shut like clams.

At the Nuremberg trials, the judges were incredulous when Speer, the second most powerful man in Germany, the man closest to Hitler, said he knew nothing. Judges and prosecutors battered him without mercy – although deeply repentant – the only repentant Nazi in the dock – Speer did not move an inch. He did not know. Nor did I. Nor did anyone I dealt with.

All I heard was that they were killing enemies of the Reich and prisoners in the concentration camps and cremating the bodies. Like everyone, we thought in terms of hundreds of corpses.

After the war, allied troops had to take tens of thousands of Germans to see for their own eyes. Some Germans committed suicide back in their homes.

Speer looked at me mischievously. "Do you still want to meet Hitler?"

"Yes."

"And to argue with him?"

"Ideas are for men. I'm a woman and a photographer," I said, submission in the flesh.

He looked at me thoughtfully.

"You must understand Hitler," he warned. "Let me tell you a story."

"Oh, please do," I begged, like a happy girl.

"In autumn of 1934, Otto Meissner, state secretary of the chancellery, phoned me to go to Weimar, to join Hitler on a drive to Nuremberg. Hitler always wants to travel by rail, but we went by car. As always, he sat in front, beside his driver, in the dark-blue open 7-litre supercharged Mercedes. I sat behind with the servant, who had a box full of automobile maps, spectacles, pills and tasty bread rolls. Behind us sat his adjutant Brükner and Press chief

Dietrich. A second Mercedes, exactly the same as the first, carried five hulking men of his bodyguard, and Hitler's personal doctor, Dr. Brandt.

When Brandt negotiated his family's safety with invading American troops, Hitler sentenced him to death. Brandt escaped, but at Nuremberg, they hanged him in 1948 for "medical experiments" on concentration camp inmates. He studied survival of Luftwaffe airmen in cold seas by immersing inmates in ice water till they died.

We drove through the Thuringian Forest and came into more urban roads. Speeding through a village, they recognized us, but before people reacted, we were gone. 'Watch this,' said Hitler. 'The local party group will phone ahead and in the next village we won't get out so easily.'

Completely true. In the next village, cheering people filled the streets. Despite the best efforts of the local policeman, the car had to slow to a walk. We got back to the open road but people let down the barrier at a railway crossing to stop him and to greet him.

"By lunch-time, we reached Hildburghausen, where long years ago Hitler got himself the job as police commissioner, to get himself German citizenship – his first step in Germany itself. We went to a modest inn, and the innkeeper and his wife were over the moon. The adjutant finally impressed upon them that we wanted spaghetti with spinach, but they took so long the adjutant hurried to the kitchen and found the women in such a state they couldn't decide whether the spaghetti was done or it wasn't.

"While we sat there, thousands of people gathered and called for Hitler. 'What I'd give to be somewhere else,' he muttered.

"Under torrents of flowers, we reached the medieval gate. Teenagers closed it to our faces and children climbed on the running-boards. Hitler had to give autographs, and how they laughed, how merrily, and Hitler laughed with them.

"Out in the country, farmers came to the edge of their fields, women waved rapturously. Hitler leaned back to me and in low voice said, 'Till now, but one German has had triumphal processions like this – Luther. When he rode through Germany, how the people flocked to him, their adulation! Now they do it for me!'

"Ray, you must understand this idolatry. They all believe it is Hitler alone who has worked the economic miracle, whose foreign policy has compelled the respect of other countries, who has made us a nation of profound pride."

143

Pride, I thought. Germany is not yet a hundred years old. Before it was a mishmash of some two hundred principalities, dukedoms, kingdoms, palatinates, electorates, whatever. These people need to know *who they are*. Britain was united, even under the Romans, while the Romans faced the fearful German forests and the warring barbarians who sheltered in the forest gloom.

The great Christian monasteries did not clear the forests until about the year 1,200 AD... was that right?

We English, in *our* unconscious pride, which is so much part of our history we are no longer deliberately aware of it, have not known how to deal with our German cousins. For a second time, we are reaping the whirlwind.

How the Germans hated and envied the long centuries of French cultural history and cultivation – their thousand-year-old unity.

Speer's voice broke into my thoughts.

So, you must expect some imperiousness from Hitler, especially when the Nazis are so anti-feminist."

"I understand, and I'm listening carefully," I said, in my mildest voice.

"It is easy to underestimate Hitler. Yet he is planning on some of the most gigantic buildings ever seen on the surface of this planet.

"When I did my plans for the Nuremberg Party Rallies site, adjutant Brükner phoned me. 'Damn your plans! Couldn't you've given them to him some other time? The Führer didn't sleep a wink last night, he was so worked up!'

"The plan is for some 800 million marks. We're talking about sixteen and a half square kilometres. Two years after Hitler approved it, the drawings won the Grand Prix at the Paris World fair of 1937. At the southern end stands the Marchfield, for German Army exhibitions of lesser maneuvers – they'll have 3400 by 2300 feet for that. The world famous courtyard of the palace of Kings Darius I and Xerxes at Persepolis (5th century BC) covered but 1500 by 900 feet. Stands would seat 160,000 spectators. A statue of a woman would surmount a platform for guests of honour. In 64 AD, Nero built on the Capitol a gigantic figure 119 feet high. The New York statue of Liberty stands at 151 feet high. My statue would be 46 feet higher.

"The Marchfield will open out into a processional avenue a mile and quarter long, for the army to march down. This avenue is finished, paved in heavy, roughened granite to bear the weight of tanks and to give a grip to goose-stepping soldiers. On the right, rises a podium, where Hitler can stand with his generals. Behind this podium we will build a stadium to hold 400,000 persons. Rome's Circus Maximus held between 150,000 and 200,000 spectators.

"The Cheops pyramid boasts a base of 756 and a height of 481 feet, with a volume of 3,277,300 cubic yards. The Nuremberg Stadium will be 1815 feet long and 1518 wide, and will comprehend a volume of 11,100,000 cubic yards, three times more than the Cheops pyramid.

"And this is just beginning. In Berlin, we will build a great hall of Pharaonic size, something never seen before on earth.

"So, that's Hitler."

After the war, when I learned that Hitler planned to kill and cremate some 300 or 400 million Europeans and Slavs, with unknown millions of blacks and Arabs to follow later, I understood this megalomaniac building. When Germans alone survived in this hemisphere, a thousand years from now, these architectural behemoths would remind them of the man who brought this blessing upon them with his genius.

At school, they taught me that who doesn't learn from history is bound to suffer the repeating of it.

Hitler lived in a century with limited technology, and powerful foes.

Another monster will come, to kill all but a handful of the six billion... ten billion... people on earth, with a technology we cannot imagine, if we are not jealously vigilant.

In Munich, I went to the Propaganda offices, and signed out film. I rang Himmler, instead of Goebbels, and asked did he want any photos in Munich. He cross-questioned me about how I got there, and told me that there was a banquet, a meeting of the friends of the *Reichsführer SS*. So I rang home, got the grandmother, Princess Gabriele, and gave her the news.

"Who are these friends?" I asked her.

"Bankers and industrialists, who nearly always meet in Berlin. They're financial patrons of the SS, and now are equipping *Waffen-SS* units. Himmler can smooth the way for them, get them important contracts. Himmler sells

145

them cheap concentration camp labour for six marks a day a man. Do you understand what I'm saying?" she said in her elderly voice. "Can you hear me properly?"

"It's a perfect line, I can hear you properly, my dearest Princess."

* * *

They were expecting me, and made me most welcome.

"We never get women at these lunches," one beefy, heavy-jowled man said jovially.

"Hear! Hear!" several others cried merrily, like schoolboys on a picnic.

They asked me all sorts of questions on Belize and Argentina, and carried on incomprehensible conversation about industrial production, credits and business matters I couldn't follow. But they kept me in the conversation.

At the end, I stood up, to explain about the photos.

They tapped the crockery with spoons, and one or two thumped the table. "Speech! Speech! Silence!"

I put on a solemn look, and said, "Gentlemen, unaccustomed as I am to public. speaking–" which produced a roar of laughter.

When they let me, I explained, "I have to sign out film from the Propaganda Ministry, so these photos will go back first to Himmler and he'll send them to you. However, if he thinks some can be improved–" boisterous guffaws "–he'll send the film to me to retouch it. These aren't Press photos, but portraits and group photos to keep at home."

"So what do we have to do?" one huge man asked, merrily.

"You have to look handsome and wise."

"Wealthy and wise!" shouted another, amid more laughter.

Another elderly man said, "See young Karl here? He looks far younger than his years. Be careful not to make him too young or too clever or he'll be in trouble with his wife."

I asked, surprised, "Why?"

"Make him look too clever and too young and his wife won't recognize him. She'll think he's been unfaithful and had a son on the wrong side of the blanket," and that brought the house down, Karl enjoying it more than anybody.

* * *

So, I took their photos and received every sort of improper proposal.

146

Back home, Prince Bernd told me that we were invited to lunch next day with one of the ex-Kaiser's sons and grandsons.

Prince August-Wilhelm of Prussia, the ex-Kaiser's fourth son, lived in Potsdam too, and was full of funny stories. His brother Prince Oscar was there, an elderly gentleman in a resplendent red-and-gold uniform. Prince Luis-Ferdinand of Prussia was full of charm – he was the second son of the Kronprinz (Crown Prince) who we didn't see. Luis-Ferdinand is married to Kira, who had two babies we all fussed over. Kira is daughter of Grand Duke Kiril Radimirovitch, present head of the Romanov survivors.

Count Gottfried von Bismark Schönhausen, the great-grandson of Bismark, was there, and invited Thoma and me to his place in the country for the weekend. Doris wasn't free.

Later, I took Speer's photos and film to his studio; he wasn't there, but I got back before blackout.

Berlin streets carried every sort of Army traffic, taking troops from Poland to Western front.

At home, Heydrich had left a message, inviting me to an impromptu concert at the apartment of the two sisters, Luise and Margarete Gensorowsky, who played the viola and the transverse German flute.

I rang to accept, and an adjunct said they would send a car for me at midday.

Next day, the car picked me up, and at the apartment, Heydrich asked me about Speer. I told him all about the architecture and Hitler's reactions. The sisters were enthralled, but Heydrich must have known much of it.

We had roast chicken with champagne, and the concert transported me.

He drove me home in his own car, and asked me about the bankers' and industrialists' lunch in Munich. He seems to know every move I make. I explained some of the jokes, and then he described several of them, asking did I remember? I did. He asked me for my personal reactions – who seemed

147

more clever, more responsible, more honest. As a woman, I had formed instantaneous impressions, and it was these he wanted. I told him my reactions could be a bit silly and certainly unreliable, but he wanted my very first uncritical, unthinking feelings.

He chided me, "If I stop to analyze when I'm playing the violin, what's going to happen?"

We sat in the car, parked outside Prince Bernd's gate.

I asked him what he knew about Hitler's peace offer. He said that Hitler would offer a Polish protectorate, centered on Warsaw, holding about 15 million of Poland's 25 million people. He said, "Moravia and Bohemia are now Protectorates but with no autonomy. Poland would have some autonomy."

All Germany was hanging on the peace proposal and on the answer from England and France.

"What will England and France do?" he asked me, to my amazement.

I said without thinking, "France alone could accommodate Germany, but as a South American, it seems to me Britain is still living in a world of the Treaty of Versailles, of the trenches of the World War. I'm sure it believes in the 'Imaginary Line'."

He looked at me strangely. "The Maginot, you mean… and you don't?"

"I was in Poland. I saw the tank and planes."

"South American… you know, the further away, the clearer you can see. Not always, but all too often. Anything else?"

"You play the violin incredibly – speaking as an uncultivated South American."

That made him laugh.

He tapped the man sitting next to the driver, who got out and opened the door for me.

Friday afternoon, Thoma and I went to Stettiner Banhof railway station, to go to *Reinfeld* Gottfried Bismarck's place in Pomerania. The train took six hours instead of three – trains were carrying troops and material from Poland to the West. Gottfried had sent a carriage and horses, and we travelled clippity-clop to *Reinfeld* in darkness. At 2 AM, we reached the house, to find Gottfried, with manful patience, waiting up for us, with a supper and unending fresh milk, straight from the cows! Paradise! Fine table service, in silver.

Gottfried has a plump, very handsome but unassuming, un-Germanic face – rather like a young, upper-class English academic.

Next morning, at 10, Gottfried's maid roused us out for hot baths, and then a late, non-ersatz breakfast. We were doing well at prince Bernd's – he bent the rationing I don't know how, and had supplies stored in the cellars. When the tinned meat arrived from Argentina, I suppose we would do even better at the Prince's palace. But Gottfried gave us freshly baked rolls – no shortage of flour perhaps – with unlimited homemade butter and homemade jam. The coffee was Brazilian. Also rashers of bacon – did he keep pigs?

His wife, Melanie Hoyos, joined us. She is half-Austrian, half-French. A prominent jaw and a large nose, for a petite, trusting face, but her expression is practical. We were all talking at once, she was so glad to see us.

Reinfeld is a cross between a small country mansion and a country gentleman's working farm-house – simply whitewashed, sensible furniture and full bookcases.

He took us out for a long walk in the woods, talking about the war and Germany, gently sounding me out. I saw instantly that he belonged to the aristocratic resistance, and he knew all did not fit well, my living at the Prince's, an unpretentious Argentinean photographer, who brought the SS into the house without the Hohelindens turning a hair. I sympathized with his frustration. We carried fowling pieces – I had shot grouse in Scotland – and gave myself away by nonchalantly bringing down a plump bird for the table.

"Good shot," observed Gottfried.

"Everyone in Argentina shoots," I explained.

He thrust out his Bismarckian lower lip, and then gnawed it, while Thoma gave us a wicked grin.

At lunch, I found out he was the Iron Chancellor's youngest grandson, not a great-grandson.

In the afternoon, he took us riding. I hadn't ridden since the beginning of the year, so I chose a quiet horse, and soon my bottom and leg muscles told me I was out of practice.

Sunday morning, we went to a Lutheran Church, and I felt the tension, the unhappiness of the worshippers. One widow had lost her only son in Poland, and the pastor implored God to give her comfort, and for us to embrace her in loving care. He called upon the Almighty to protect us all, to keep our vision clear and just, and to bring back to Germany a peaceful and fruitful life. Full of emotion, the congregation sang the hymns with a power I had seldom heard. I don't think the SS can like Lutheran pastors.

We had an early lunch, pork followed by yesterday's bird, with beans, turnips, potatoes and cabbage. In the afternoon, we stalked deer, without getting near. Then I saw one move between two trees, and took quick, steady aim, and fired. It dropped by the second tree trunk. What a fluke! We rushed

149

it, and found it dead.

Gottfried said, "You've put venison on the table for months. That was a long shot!"

"Beginner's luck," I told him. "Don't ask me to do it again, because you'll be wasting your ammunition."

"What on earth do you hunt in Argentina?"

"Just target shooting. It's a rifle club, with awfully good-looking young men. If they chase the girls who are good shots, what is a poor female to do?"

Gottfried, more frustrated, nodded understandingly.

In the summers of 1936, 1937 and 1938, a Scottish landowner had invited me as a house guest, to the deer stalking, and my aim had been so wild that hilarity was unanimous and unabashed. The eldest son declared his desperate adoration, and to get me away from the crowd, offered to take me out on the empty moor, to shoot stones off the top of rocks, sticking out above the moor grasses. We used a .22, and also, each day, with a special protective shoulder pad, fired three times a 303. The eldest son's declarations of lovesickness gave an innocent girl insights into men's wiliness and lures; I wasted about 700 bullets, such was the measure of his love, but did improve my shooting, while enjoying his every word.

The Bismarck children were gorgeous, overfed, which was wise in this uncertain Germany. A tiny boy, with red hair, transfixed you with his blue eyes like the Iron Chancellor, his great grandfather, was wont to do.

In 1944, Gottfried was in the July 20 Bomb Plot that almost killed Hitler – in it, up to his neck. Three Gestapo men strode into *Reinfeld* and arrested him. Later, two Gestapo men and a woman arrested Melanie. A woman on the estate had denounced Melanie to the Gestapo that she was *asozial* – that she varnished her toenails and took breakfast in bed. Melanie was very weak, and they put her in prison hospital. The first day she tried to get up, she fell and broke her chin.

They took Gottfried to the dreaded People's Court from which no one emerged without a death sentence – the *Volksgericht*, presided by the crazed Roland Freisler, who insulted and hurled every invective at defendants, not allowing them to speak in their defense. There was no appeal.

And here ended the Iron Chancellor's high essay – his youngest grandson on foot in the *Volksgericht*. Photos show him there, after agonizing torture, unmoved, unafraid, and sentenced to death.

His brother Otto went to Göring.

Hitler saved Gottfried.

In prison, cells 1 to 100 held those to be executed.

Gottfried had cell 184. His good friend, and my acquaintance, Adam von Trott, had cell 97.

Adam was hanged naked, by piano wire, and his protracted death agonies filmed. Hitler re-ran the films all one night.

Balliol College, Oxford, raised a memorial to Adam, together with other Germans who died. Adam, the Rhodes Scholar, friend of Peter Fleming...

We caught a train at 10 AM on Monday, and were in Berlin by half-past-three. We rang from a public phone for Reinhard to come, when a black Gestapo Mercedes pulled up. It was Karl Rutzel, who I greeted gratefully.

"I've just called for Reinhard to come. Let me ring him back."

I rang back to tell him not to come, and climbed into the car in the front seat, He had already loaded our suitcases. Thoma sat in the back.

"So who have you been visiting?" he asked severely.

I told him about our weekend.

"We have a report that you are a deadly shot."

"Target practice in Buenos Aires and in the Argentina countryside,"

At last, they had trapped me. I couldn't talk about any rifle-club in Buenos Aires because with a radio message, they could check within 24-hours. I said I had always used a .22.

He was satisfied, but asked lots of questions, in a friendly, curious way which I found skillful. Then he mentioned casually that I seemed to have made friends with Heydrich, so I told him about the concerts. We invited him for tea, and he accepted. It was a lively meal, as we talked about our visit, treating Rutzel like one of the family.

The Prince brought up an old wine from the cellars in honour of the occasion, and at 8.30 pm Rutzel begged to be excused.

Claus came in after nine, and asked me to keep him company as he ate.

"What do you know about tanks?" he asked, between mouthfuls.

I ticked off on my fingers. "Some tank captains are handsome. They run on tracks. They have a big gun..." I giggled. "I mean the tanks, not the captains—"

He grinned, "How do they 'run on tracks'?"

"The tracks spin round and round."

"Not really. The track lies flat without moving.

151

"The tank runs along the flat track and pulls it up behind it. With wheels, a two-ton truck touches the ground over some 600 cm^2, and the pressure per square centimetre is more than 3 kilograms. So it sinks into soft ground. A tank reduces the pressure from three kilograms to so many grams.

"Now, the gun. Whether its shell will go through the armour-plating of another tank depends first on its calibre. Make a shell twice as wide, and it will pierce twice as well. The second thing is the speed at which the shell leaves the barrel. That's called muzzle-velocity. Double the muzzle velocity, and you increase by four times the impact on enemy armour. Our armour is 30 mm thick.

"In Poland, they didn't lose because they were short of material. They even had British tanks. They lost because of a revolution in military strategy and tactics. Over thousands of years, military techniques have suffered revolutions, such as when the Roman checkerboard formation of three lines – the two groups behind covered gaps opened in the first ranks – defeated the Greek shock-troop phalanx or wedge, which couldn't adapt to battle conditions like the Roman checkerboard. Do you follow me?"

"I'm with you."

"Firstly, our tank crews are exceptional. We chose them for physical strength and coordination, for their calm under stress. They are obsessed with the shame of Versailles. They are elite on the same level as our Luftwaffe pilots. We have the Mark III tank. They made only 55 of the 'D' model with a 37 mm gun, before changing to the 'E' with a 50 mm gun. The barrel is short, which means that the explosive has less time to push the shell faster. Hitler has demanded a longer barrel for years, to increase that *muzzle velocity* I told you about a moment ago."

"Double muzzle velocity and you penetrate armour four times as much."

"Bravo. The father of our military revolution is General Lutz, who asked for a 50 mm gun for our PzKw3 medium tank, but the 37 mm was the only one being made for the infantry. For our medium PzKw4 tank, however, they fitted a 75 mm gun, but with low muzzle velocity. So in Poland we used the Mark II, with a 20 mm gun, the Mark III with a 37 mm gun and the Mark IV with the 75 mm low velocity gun, plus the 'E' model with the 50 mm gun.

"You've got three trades in a tank – driver, gunner and radio operator. What we have done is make each man of the crew master of the three. We have trained the men exhaustively, over the years, so that each man can act as commander and tactician."

I listened with a sinking heart. The British Army in France and Belgium...

"The tank battalions are not alone. With them travel an infantry brigade in lorries, and other lorries towing anti-tank and field artillery. No heavy artillery, because that's the Luftwaffe's job.

"What we have found in Poland is that mechanical failure cut us down by 30%; battle losses were 217 this time.

"After Lutz, Guderian was named General of The Panzer Army and in Poland he commanded two of the six Panzer divisions. Those two were in the Fourth Army that struck straight for Warsaw from Pomerania.

"So what is the military revolution? The first to write about it were Lidell Hart in England and Charles de Gaulle. By 1929, in Germany, Colonel Lutz and von Reichenau and Majors Guderian and von Thoma had thrashed out a practical doctrine to use in field exercises. In 1929, Guderian wrote: 'tanks maneuvering by themselves or with infantry can't ever decide the battle. My studies of the exercises carried out in England and our own mock-ups have convinced me that tanks can't decide the day until other wheeled arms come up to scratch in speed and cross-country efficiency. Tanks are primary, but the support groups are indispensable.' Fortunately, for Germany, the British, French and Russian armies are keeping tanks as a support for infantry, as in the Great War.

"The Panzer division is not just tanks, but motor-bike platoons, motorized anti-tank gun platoons, field gun platoons, armored cars and light tanks for reconnaissance or for mopping up.

"Britain had Brigadier Hobart, who commanded the British Tank Brigade. He had the same ideas as Guderian, and maneuvered his tanks and motorized infantry by radio control, making them a devastating combat weapon. The British Army quickly quashed Brigadier Hobart. The German Army tried to stop Guderian in a similar fashion, but an enthusiastic Hitler pushed Guderian forward."

I had trouble breathing. In his quiet, dull, lecturing way, Claus was spelling out the destruction of the British Expeditionary Force in France and Belgium; it would be the most ruinous defeat in the whole history of the British Army – unless I was very much mistaken. Would Britain crumble and slide out of history, just like the Ancient Greeks before the brutal, stolid Romans?

"Ray, I've written it all down for you. Here you are."

He stood up stiffly, very military, and I got to my feet. He took my two arms and drew me halfway to him.

"Ray! Help me save my Germany."

His voice choked, "Try to understand. Germany is *mine*, is *ours*. It's not his. They will turn this country into a cow-pasture. They will take away Pomerania, East Prussia, Silesia, Bavaria, Alsace Lorraine and the Rhineland. They could push the Czech frontier almost to Berlin." (it now runs only 25 miles from Dresden, the Polish frontier only 85 miles from Berlin)

I went up to my room, and got out my typewriter.

DEFEAT POLAND NOT LACK MATERIAL BUT MISUSE.

VICTIM NEW MILITARY REVOLUTION FIRST LIDELL HART, DE GAULLE, THRASHED OUT BY LUTZ GUDERIAN...

It was the longest message I had sent, and I was working till one a.m. to encode it. I warned the British Army, I warned them I spelled it all out.

I microdotted the message, put it in my ring, and went to the Argentinean Embassy.

Ruben Zorreguieta exchanged my ring for another exactly the same, and made me a cup of *real* coffee.

"Some tins of Argentinaan corned beef, Chilean *mejillones* – shell fish – in spices, Chilean *berberechos* and *almejas* – I think they call them whelks in English – and Argentinean crab meat have arrived. As you can't walk across the city carrying that, I'll send an Embassy car."

My mouth watered.

"My editor's paying?"

"Your editor says he'll pay whatever in question of food. He's worrying about how you feel. Are you still frightened?"

"Not, well, really frightened... I'm tense and anxious, because I'm living in a... Looking Glass world. They made me walk the gangplank to topple me into an ocean of evil... but I have to pretend that I don't see it... well, that it doesn't matter...you know, I'm not aware. I have another name, and that gets at me. I get enraged, so angry, but I have to be casual, charming, very feminine – always, that little bit submissive. I have to talk to monsters, and they're ordinary people like myself. If we can send them to the gallows, they'll go feeling they're the victims... our victims. It's all madness, with not a voice of sanity among them. It's like living in a looney bin – you lose track of yourself..."

"There's a dance at the Chilean Embassy. Do you want...?"

"I'd love to! This nonsense of not letting us dance in the nightclubs! It's awful!"

"You're invited, and I'll send a car for you."

Driving in Berlin was a luxury – I enjoyed every second of it. You saw almost no other traffic – official cars, police and Army vehicles only.

When I packed in Buenos Aires, I had wanted to put in seven ball

154

gowns – they let me bring only five. I left the other two at the newspaper; and now I decided to send for them.

The Chilean Embassy stood just off the Tiersgarten. They introduced me to the Chilean Ambassador, Morla, who was charming and relaxed. I danced with a Chilean attaché, and he told me that Morla was Ambassador in Madrid in the Spanish Civil War, and he ordered his staff to give refuge to more than 3,000 fascists, although the Chilean Government had sided with the Spanish Government. The Republican Government protested and complained – but for three years, those 3,000 fascists lived and slept and ate inside the Embassy. They slept on floors, stairs, tables – wherever. I danced with another attaché, and he told me the same story. Then he told me that the Duke of Alba, a descendant of Charles I and II of England, came to the British Embassy asking for refuge, and with the most polished manners, they put him into the street; the Republicans shot him.

Such rage seized me! Those chinless wonders of the British Foreign Office… I could have shot them down in cold blood! I knew exactly how the Duke of Alba felt…

Some fascists attended from the Spanish Embassy. We stopped dancing to listen to one of Spain's greatest *virtuosos* of the guitar – Angel Iglesias, although I don't know whether 'Iglesias' was a stage name or not. After, I talked to him at the buffet table, and he told me that in August, he had embarked in Melbourne, Australia, on a German liner. The second day out, the captain had offered him a full suite instead of his small cabin, if he would play for them every evening.

The liner docked the day after the Declaration of War. He fulfilled a contract for two weeks of concerts, and then the German government begged him to stay on in Germany during the war.

A very tall, aristocratic Spaniard stood beside us listening, and then said, "Angel, please introduce me."

Angel gave a plump smile. "I haven't had the pleasure myself," so I introduced myself.

Angel said, "This is Don Alfonso Dalmau Aiguallonga, Grandee of Spain, Knight of the Sovereign Order of Malta, Member of the Devoted Order of Calatrava, Knight of the Royal Corps of the Nobility of Catalonia, Marquess of Altamira and Count of Noguera Ribagorza."

"Hello," I said weakly.

Alfonso shook his head reprovingly at Angel.

"You speak Spanish. Where are you from?"

I told them about myself.

"You have a Castilian accent, hardly any Argentinean at all."

I explained about Belize, and my Castilian nurse; then explained that I lived in the *schloss* of the Hohenlindens.

I invited them to lunch, next day.

155

Angel said that tomorrow night he had a concert in Hamburg, but the Grandee of Spain accepted.

I said, "I thought you wore a heavy gold chain with a golden fleece hanging from it."

"It's a bit of a nuisance to dance with," said Alfonso Dalmau, drily.

He was in his late thirties, extraordinarily good-looking, with a high brow and a nose I had seen in paintings of the Hapsburgs by Velazquez – or did the Hapsburgs come later?

I danced with Alfonso, and excused myself to go to the 'ladies', to check up on my appearance.

When I came out, a tall, solid, dark man in a diplomatic uniform asked me for a dance. He was Hungarian, from Budapest, from the Hungarian Embassy, and he gave me his name – Tibor Haraszti.

"You don't need to introduce yourself," he smiled. "I know who you are."

He steered me to one end of floor where there were no dancers – at the opposite end to the buffet table.

"You're Raimunda."

I nodded, smiling.

"Raimunda Madueño, late of London."

I nearly fainted, but he held me up, and said, "Breathe slowly and deeply. That's right. Slowly, slowly."

"The British Secret Service – we communists have penetrated it and we found messages arriving from a most mysterious WAGNER. We found they came from Buenos Aires, where more communists have penetrated the government. They found messages came from the Argentinean Embassy in Berlin, and in Geneva. Communists have penetrated the Berlin Argentinean Embassy, and they asked, 'Who is new who has appeared at the Embassy, in late August?' Really, one person stood out: you. We photographed you and sent the photo to Moscow. In 1937, your photo appeared in LADY magazine, at a party of Debutantes, at their Coming Out. So you see, we have found out that you and I are in the same business. The Nazis don't know about you, and they don't know about me. Our problem is that our communist infiltrators in the British SIS know that your messages are arriving, but they don't know what they are saying. Let us step outside a moment on the balcony, so we don't attract too much attention."

I hung on to the balustrade, feeling ill.

"All I ask is that you share everything you have with me."

I said, "I will not carry any incriminating material across Berlin."

"How do you bring it to the Embassy?"

I lied. "I write out my messages there."

"Tomorrow, I will give a dinner at the Hungarian Embassy. Afterwards we will dance, then go to a small salon. I'll ask my colleagues to

156

cooperate, to help me try and make a conquest. In the salon, you will show me the code, your code."

"What do I get in return?"

"What I have, I will give you – verbally, if you insist. If you ever have to make a trip outside of Germany, please tell me. I can be of great assistance. Let us go back inside. I'll see you tomorrow at 7 pm at the Hungarian Embassy."

I danced until midnight, without knowing whom I danced with.

I set the alarm for seven, and after six hours sleep, awoke bleary. I washed my face, combed my hair put on a dressing gown and hurried downstairs. The Prince and Claus were breakfasting, and looked at my dressing-gown, astonished.

The Prince called for another coffee cup, while I explained what had happened. The two men looked at each other.

The Prince said, "What is more natural than that you awaken envy. You live in a *schloss*, eat and dress well, have a glamorous job. You enjoy the very highest connections. What would be more natural than people denouncing you to the Gestapo as a spy – pure envy? The Gestapo will expect it, and ignore it. But why should the communists denounce you! You hold Haraszti's life in the very palm of your hand. He runs that amazing risk on orders from Moscow. Either Moscow wants your information very badly, or they need to use you."

"And suppose the Gestapo see the LADY magazine photo?"

"The Gestapo is very good – but Moscow are consummate professionals. They have a Slavic subtlety beyond our thuggish Gestapo. It's altogether beyond my powers of imagination to know what Moscow is after, but we shall surely find out in good time. They are in a position to command you, but you can do equal damage to them.

"Now, what about breakfast?"

I was starving.

* * *

I thought I would go back to bed, but at 8 o'clock the phone rang. It was

157

Andrea Boehr, the abandoned mother, whose husband, Heiner, had knocked me to the floor.

"I have a house," she said. "This morning, I'm not going to the *Arbeitsfront Abteilung* – well, they've given me a couple of days off to move in. Could you come at ten o'clock?"

She gave me an address in Charlottenburg, on Grausstrasse. She had clearly moved up in the world.

The house had a view of a park, and was two-storey.

I had brought cakes, and a tin of Argentinean corned beef, and we sat down to coffee.

"I've had to give my children to cousins and to friends. Christian is with friends of mine, Hans and Ruth, and my baby Henning are with cousins of mine."

"What a wonderful house!"

"I have these Jewish friends, and they just passed a law that all Jews must leave Germany. It's awful – they send them to concentration camps in Czechoslovakia and Poland, to do slave labor. They work and get no pay. They make them sell their houses, and I've bought this for a song. I had to get   a loan, but I'll give it back to them if things ever change. Their names are Moses Blümer and Rachael, but they don't want to

leave. I'm hiding them upstairs. Well, not hiding, but they live upstairs without ever going out where someone could see them. Do you think it's very dangerous? And I don't know how we're going to manage for ration coupons."

I said impulsively, "I can help with the food – for the moment. If no one knows they're here, then it's safe. But if the Gestapo decides to track them down, this is the first place they'll search."

"Oh, my goodness!"

"We'll think of something," I said, knowing the thing was hopeless. "Can I meet them?"

We went upstairs. Moses was about fifty, a very successful accountant, who had bought this wonderful house. He was thin, but with a thick crop of hair, and clever eyes that now looked at the floor. Rachael was plump, motherly, her face drawn with awful lines.

At last I had come face to face with naked fear – not my own, but in someone else.

Don Alfonso Dalmau Aiguallonga had arrived when I got back. The Prince, his wife, the grandmother and the daughters were all over him. He greeted me with great charm, and over lunch – with Chilean tinned luxuries – the grandmother asked me was I upset.

I told them about the Blümers, the Jewish couple.

Don Alfonso said cheerfully, "Send them to the Spanish Embassy, and they'll give them a Spanish passport."

As one person, everyone put down their knives and fork and gazed at him. "Franco's orders," he smiled.

"They'd never dare cross the city," I breathed.

"No problem," said Don Alfonso. "I'll get an Embassy car and pick them up."

The prospect of a Grandee of Spain saving two Jews in an official Spanish car took away our collective breath.

The Prince ventured cautiously. "I don't quite understand you – Franco, you say?"

"Isabel and Ferdinand expelled the Jews in 1492 – the worst thing that ever happened to Spain. Our intellectual and commercial life languished. That contributed decisively to our decline. History has marked Isabel and Ferdinand with this stigma. Franco wants history to mark him as the person who redressed this injustice."

"And that's the reason?" demanded the grandmother sharply.

Don Alfonso said equably, "That is the most important one. There are… other considerations."

"Aaah!" said Princess Gabriele Pfaffenhonen. "Pray, do continue."

"Franco has made offers to England and America. As he does not want Germans on Spanish soil, he will deny them passage to Gibraltar. And as he is sure France will fall, and quickly, he will allow British airmen, perhaps one day American airman, who have been shot down, and who reach the Spanish frontier, to proceed freely to Barcelona – the British to go to the British Consulate in Calle Junqueras, where the British consular officials will issue them with British tourist papers. In exchange, he asks America to send wheat and powdered milk to help feed the Spanish people. America has agreed. We are, of course, talking about secret negotiations. Now, Franco has about two and half million men under arms in the military and the *Policia Nacional*, which is paramilitary. Spain has a serious manpower shortage in the fields and factories. So he has ordered all Spanish consulates and embassies in Europe to issue Spanish passports to Jews. Secretly, he has prepared passports which will in one sole passport cover one thousand Jews. This passport announces that they are under the protection of the Spanish State and Army."

"Army!" I cried, incredulously. "He can't send his army into Europe."

Don Alfonso smiled. "Dictators are obsessed with their armies. So if you do not respect our 1000-person Passport, you fail in respect to our army. And that would make Franco very... *cabreado.*"

"Cabreado?" enquired Princess Jutta.

"As our American friends – who are the soul of vulgarity – say, 'pissed off.'"

I blushed.

He continued, "So Franco has asked Roosevelt to feed the Jews who reach Spain, and Roosevelt has agreed. Britain, the States, Australia, Canada, have set stringent quotas against the entry of Jews. So suppose Franco takes in five million Jews – two million of them will be able-bodied men, to work the fields and factories, and America will feed them. The question is, will the Germans supply the rail transport and will the Germans let them go? As the Germans will make men and women alike work as slaves in factories, can Germany lose three million factory hands and still win the war?"

"And what will Franco do with them after the war?"

"Franco is very clear on the question of money. Anyone who makes money in Spain is welcome, be he brown, black or brindle. Spain had a modest Industrial Revolution in Catalonia – mainly in the textile industry – so we have almost no middle-class. If the Jews largely form a middle-class, Spain will go forward 50 years in one bound.

"However, the thing is, Franco does not want the German Army, and he does not want British fliers. If in return for getting rid of them, he gets shipments of food, and then gets further shipments of food for a massive Jewish immigration, he has done good business. So, what we can do is... after lunch proceed to my Embassy, get a car and go and collect the Blümers."

At four o'clock, I had the spell-binding experience of climbing stairs behind a Grandee of Spain, to address a middle-aged Jewish couple.

Moses and Rachael thought it was a trap. They looked ashen. Andrea said, "Raimunda here is Argentinean. You can trust her. She has promised me food. You must believe me."

I said, "Don Alfonso is a Grandee of Spain."

They stopped breathing.

Don Alfonso loosened his tie and shirt collar. He pulled out a chain of chunky gold links, with the Golden Fleece hanging from it. Moses took it in his hand, and felt it.

He turned to his wife. "Solid gold. Very solid. This is a Golden Fleece. Go quickly and pack."

Andrea said, "I'll help you," and followed her.

Moses turned to Don Alfonso. "It's dangerous for us to cross Berlin."

"I have an official Embassy car with a Spanish flag."

"You are a Righteous Gentile."

"You know of the Expulsion of Jews in 1492 from Spain?"

"I know."

"Well, now many Spaniards wish to be Righteous Gentiles. How many other Jewish couples do you know?"

"Several."

"After we leave your wife and the luggage at the Embassy, we will go collecting everyone we can. They will each receive a Spanish Passport. I will travel with you all to Switzerland."

"Switzerland will not let in the Jews."

"You will be a Spanish citizen with a bona fide Spanish passport. We will cross Switzerland into France, and take the train down to Port Bou, which is the frontier railway station inside Spain. Don't you worry. Spain pays its accountants well."

At seven o'clock, I was in the Hungarian Embassy, praying the dinner would be *paprika* – plenty of spicy beef.

It was.

Afterwards, we danced, and at nine o'clock, Tibor Haraszti led me along a panelled corridor to a room with cozy furniture, red hangings and an inlaid table.

I sat in an armchair, by the table.

Tibor came with pencil and paper, and I showed him my secret code.

"Oh dear," he said. "We need a copy of Lorna Doone, illustrated by Wilmot Lunt, published by Collins in Collins' Illustrated Pocket Classics, Leather, gilt-edges, the thin-paper edition, probably printed in 1913 or 1914."

He leaned back in his armchair, rubbing the thick skin of his face.

"How would you enjoy a trip to Switzerland?"

With irony, I told him, I would.

"As you may well imagine, Moscow and London do not exchange

161

Intelligence. Further, as we have the Berlin-Moscow Pact, Moscow cannot send Intelligence to London about Germany. So what we can do is the following – a handsome, sturdy bank employee from the Credit Suisse in Geneva will visit the Swiss Embassy in Berlin. Axel Baer is his name, and you will both fall in love. On the spot. Cupid's little arrow. Alas, he must go straight back to Geneva, but if you are asked you will explain how he passionately begged you to come and see him in Geneva. As your heart languishes in tune with his, you will notify the German authorities that you are off to Geneva. Once there, you will leave the railway station and go to the cafe of Hotel de Cornavin, and sit inside as close to the door as you can."

He pushed a photo over to me.

"This is Liska Czimer. She should already be seated inside. She will drop her handbag, and you will hurry to pick it up for her. She will invite you to her table, and you will begin chatting. She will help you take a room in Hotel de Cornavin – I think it has seven stories – and then you will ring your true love, Axel. When he finishes work, you will go to a restaurant, then dancing. This is Friday night. Next morning, he will collect you downstairs, at the Cornavin, in the cafe. You are having breakfast there, when Liska walks in, and you invite her to join you. When Axel comes, you introduce him, and Axel will say, 'I wanted to show Ray my flat, but I didn't have a chaperone. Would you act as our chaperone?' and off you go. At his flat, he will give you material to send to London, for you to encode."

"I'm not carrying anything across Geneva. Nothing on my person."

"Ask Ruben for your contact inside the Argentinean Embassy in Geneva, together with the wireless-transmission wavelength. Tell Ruben that his friend will receive a message in an unknown code, that you will decode to send to Buenos Aires for retransmission to London. What is the matter in London, that you can't transmit to them directly?"

"They can't monitor the wavelength 24-hours a day."

"Is that a joke!"

I shook my head.

"Don't they know they are at war?"

"I think they imagine England will have a quick and easy victory."

"My God!"

He breathed heavily, then pushed papers over to me.

This is the code we will use in Switzerland. We write out the alphabet and number each letter like this:

	1	2	3	4	5	
6	a	b	c	d	e	4
5	f	g	h	I	j	5
4	k	l	m	n	o	6
3	p	q	r	s	t	7
2	u	v	w	x	yz	8
	5	6	7	8	9	

"For the first 4 letters, we work anti-clockwise. First letter the numbers on the top and left side; second, left side and bottom; third, bottom and right side; fourth, right side and top. Then the next four letters, we work clockwise from top. Let us take RAIMUNDA. First anti-clockwise:

R	A	I	M
3 3	65	85	63

And now clockwise:

U	N	D	A
18	68	86	61

Now, to the first letter in each four, add 77; to the second in each four, add 44; to the third add 33; and to the fourth, add 55.

"That gives us 110z109z118z118z. Now repeat the cycle of 77, 44, 33, and 55 for the next four 95z112z119z116z.

"When you are decoding, subtract 77, 44, 33 and 55 from each group of four."

"I understand," I said. "77, 44, 33 and 55. Anti-clockwise, clockwise, over and again."

"Now I'm going to give you a code phrase to remember – TO BUY CHEAP. Give it to Liska. She'll know."

SUPPLEMENT

ALTERNATIVE EXPLANATION

"For the first 4 letters, we work anti-clockwise. First letter, the numbers on the top and left sides:

	1	2	3	4	5
6					
5					
4					
3					
2					

Second letter, left side and bottom:

6					
5					
4					
3					
2					
	5	6	7	8	9

Third letter, bottom and right side:

					4
					5
					6
					7
					8
5	6	7	8	9	

Fourth letter, right side and top:

1	2	3	4	5	
					4
					5
					6
					7
					8

Then the next four letters, we work clockwise from top. Let us take RAIMUNDA. First anti-clockwise:

```
R                A                I                M
1 2 3 4 5                                         1 2 3 4 5
6                6 A                      4                        4
5                5                    I   5                        5
4                4                        6            M   6
3   R            3                        7                        7
2                2                        8                        8
                 5 6 7 8 9        5 6 7 8 9

= 33             = 65             = 85             = 63
```

"So you need to insert that phrase, TO BUY CHEAP, into the code generator."

```
        1   2   3   4   5
6       t   o   b   u   y   4
5       c   h   e   a   p   5
4       d   f   g   i   j   6
3       k   l   m   n   q   7
2       r   s   v   w   x   8
        5   6   7   8   9
```

"You understand that the 'y' in BUY represents 'yz'?"

"Yes, I know about that. I have to carry in my head TO BUY CHEAP, and remember numbers 77, 44, 33 and 55."

"In Switzerland, Liska will give you another phrase to bring back to me."

"And will Switzerland accept German marks? Am I supposed to pay for this?"

"I'll give you twenty dollars. Liska will give you two hundred, when you see her. That will cover your hotel and expenses for three days. What I need to know is the wavelength for your contact in the Argentinean Embassy in Geneva."

"How am I going to give you that? I'm sure the Gestapo watches everything I do. I can't come back here to the Hungarian Embassy, and our meeting somewhere else will be suspicious."

"You are rather exaggerated," he sighed. "Give the wavelength to Liska when you see her."

I wanted to get up at seven o'clock to tell the Prince what had happened, but I forgot to set the alarm when I got in after midnight. I slept till nine, when the maid awoke me, to say that the Propaganda Ministry was calling, I ran out to the telephone on the hall table.

It was Schneppen. "If it is suitable for you, we shall send a car at ten. Dr. Goebbels would like you to go to a farm and take photos of agriculture under the Third Reich."

"Half-past-ten," I begged. "I got to bed very late, and have just woken up."

"Ah! Burning the candle at both ends," Schneppen said with heavy humour. "What it is to be young and single."

The first time he had unbent with me.

"The driver will give you an envelope containing one thousand marks. Dr. Goebbels wants to show his appreciation for the work you are doing. Naturally, your editor pays your salary, but this is a mark of his estimation."

"Tell him I can't thank him enough. I appreciate that very much indeed."

"I will convey your thanks to him," said Schneppen, with approval.

Miss Manners. A well-brought up young London lady. But I just loved the thought of one thousand marks.

Now I couldn't go to the Argentinean Embassy to see Ruben Zorreguieta and tell him everything – and to get the wavelength.

We drove about 45 minutes out of Berlin. The day was cloudy, but no rain.

The farmer and his wife greeted me nervously. He was blond, good-looking, thin and wiry – the wife, buxom, a lovely face, strong shoulders. Goebbels had chosen well.

They sat me down at the kitchen table, and gave me delicious cakes and ersatz coffee. When I finished, I said, "Could we talk while I walk around taking photos of you both? ... Is the farm a good business?"

He said, "Things are much better than in 1933 when the Nazis came

166

in. The newspapers used to compare us to The Peasants' War in the fifteen hundreds or the Thirty Years War, things were so bad."

Ulf Hommel might be just a farmer, but he had a good education. I took half a dozen shots as he talked, his face coming alive.

His wife said, "We were paying high interest. Our income, the money we made that year," she explained, in case I didn't understand the word 'income', "was the worst since 1924. We were in debt. It was awful. So, in 1933, Walter Darre came in as Agriculture Minister and gave us the Reich Entailed Farm Law so that all the farms up to 125 hectares – he gave them to the farmer, as his own. He made the land an inheritance, that you can't sell, mortgage or divide. It goes intact to the eldest son when you die."

"Do you have children?"

"They're at school. Two boys and a girl," his wife, Else, said proudly.

Her husband said, "The Nazis are the best thing that has ever happened to Germany. The only bother is that a farmer has to prove his blood is pure Aryan back to the year 1800, and getting those papers wasted a lot of time. Anyway, Darre guaranteed us prices, and in two years the prices had gone up by a fifth. Like a lot of other farmers, I've seen my farm grow. I had 97 hectares in 1933, and now I've got 203 hectares. But the farm laborers aren't so happy, because they pay better wages on the Autobahns or in the factories. And for the farmer, well, since 1935 the rises have been slow – but don't say I said that," he pleaded anxiously.

"You can say what you like," I told him. "I'm from Argentina and I never repeat anything I hear. If I did, no one would talk to me."

"That's very sensible," said Else, pleased.

"However, now they're sending us women workers; we've got three of them. They're very cheap, and they say they'll send us Polish workers, who we won't have to pay."

"Who will pay them, then?"

"Perhaps the government," said Ulf with a wink. "Slavs are *Untermenschengeschlecht* – a sub-human sort."

* * *

In the fields, I photographed the three women. Two were Brunhildes, the ideal of Germanic womanhood, brawny, buxom and broad-hipped. The third was slim, but muscular, and coped easily. Wagnerian Rhine maidens among the grain.

Women on the land! What was Hitler bringing the world to!

I got home for lunch, thinking about what I would say to Ruben in the Argentinean Embassy. First, I would have to code a message to London.

Prince Bernd's brother, Count Axel Hohenlinden, had left a message, inviting me to lunch at his house next door.

Was I never going to see Ruben!

The servant showed me in, and Count Axel greeted me warmly. He led me to an alcove, with tall windows looking out on to the garden. The maid had set a table for two, and lit a small, portable coal stove.

He asked me about my morning, and I told him. He remarked Germany was self-sufficient in food in a good year, but that Hitler thought only of German hunger from the British blockade in the Great War – hunger that thrust Germany into capitulating.

Suddenly, I said, "I live in an ocean of evil. How could all of this have happened?"

He looked at me. "You're only 19… how you must feel it. It seems impossible that someone as young as you is doing… the work you are doing."

He put down his knife and fork, and gazed into the garden.

"Hitler for years was a lost soul in Vienna and Munich till the Great War. There he found a direction for his life. The German Army encouraged initiative among the privates and NCOs, so *Gefreiter* Hitler – the Corporal – learned to think for himself, He was a trench runner, and had to run under British and French machine guns; they wounded him twice, gassed him, and temporarily blinded him. First, he got the Bavarian Military Cross of Merit 3rd class and a Regimental citation for Bravery in the Face of the Enemy. He came out of the war with nothing less than the Iron Cross first class, a surprisingly high decoration for an ordinary enlisted man. He wears that whenever he can.

"What you have to understand is that trench warfare stalemated, so the German command picked elite infantrymen to form trench assault raiders. In 1915, Major Eugen Kaslow had the job of trying out steel helmets, body armour and portable cannon; he formed a small party called *Sturmabteilung Kaslow*, a storm troop party. He and Hauptmann Willi Rohr formulated tactics to break into the French and British trenches. At Verdun, Rohr formed three-man teams known as *Stosstruppe* – shock troops – to attack trenches from the side. The first man had a knife-edged entrenching tool and shield taken from a machine-gun, the second carried packs full of short fuse stick grenades, and the last man had a knife or bayonet. These teams created so much havoc, they formed *Sturmkompanie* – storm parties – and by 1918 *Sturmbataillonen* were all over the front, armed with a portable 37 mm *Sturmkanone* – storm cannon – light machine guns, light mortars and flamethrowers.

"The German newspapers painted these storm troopers as heroes and they gave themselves romantic names, and wore different badges – of hand grenades, steel helmets or bayonets. But the most popular was the *Totenkopf* – the Death's Head badge, or a skull and cross-bones. These were men who scorned danger and death, who played with death. And they were to be the semen—"

I blushed scarlet.

"I'm sorry… to be the father-spirit of the new Germany. On the ground, they were the best. And a new, dare-devil elite piloted the fast fighter planes in the air. Men like Hermann Göring, Eduard Ritter von Schleich, the Black Baron, and the world famous Red Baron – Manfred Freiherr von Richthofen. These men were to imbue the spirit of Hitler's Reich – men of violence.

"Of pure violence."

"I know," I said. "Sepp Dietrich told me they did the same thing with a few tanks – hit-and-run."

"Hitler gave every importance to the War. In the young National Socialist Party, you *had* to have fought in the front line in the war, to be any sort of a leader. He used the names *Strosstrupp, Sturmabteilung, Schutzstaffel* and the rest for the Nazi paramilitaries.

"Well, imagine Germany in November, 1918. Defeat, Chaos. The Kaiser abdicated. The armed forces disbanded. Demobilised left-wing soldiers in the streets, calling for a Bolshie revolution.

"Right-wing troops joined together in *Freikorps* units. These were patriotic men who believed in the old values of Germany; from the Middle Ages. Volunteers had joined the *Freiwillingenkorps* to save the medley of Germanic states. In 1918 and afterwards, the *Freikorps* men still had their uniforms, weapons and trucks. An officer would stick up posters, asking men to come to a place at a certain time, to join his *Freikorps* – all very informal. Men called officers by their first names.

"The first step for France, England and America to reap the whirlwind.

"The *Freikorps* paid scant attention to the government. They were loyal to each of their commanders, who they called their Führer.

"These men kept order, beat up the Bolshies, kept the streets safe and guarded public buildings. The Treaty of Versailles tried to dissolve them, and set up – on paper – the *Reichswehr*, or new Weimar Republic army of 100,000 men, and not one man more. The *Freikorps* men who couldn't get into the new army, gravitated to the right-wing paramilitary groups – lead by men like Himmler, Sepp Dietrich, Reinhard Heydrich, Kurt Daleuge—" (who the Czechs hanged in 1946) "–Karl Wolf—" (*OberstgruppenFührer* in the SS, who tried to surrender his troops in Italy to the Allies. The Allies freed him from prison in 1949) "–and others.

"In March, 1918, the Bavarian idealist, Anton Drexler, unfit for war service, set up a workingmen's organization that was anti-Semitic and against foreigners. In January, 1919, he registered it as the German Workers' Party. Hitler joined, with card number seven on the committee. Drexler, Hitler and Gottfried Feder drew up a 25-point program which they adopted on April 1, 1920, the day they changed the name to the National Socialist German Workers' Party, the NSDAP or Nazi Party. It had a strongly Socialist leaning, which Röhm later espoused, till Hitler killed him to purge the Party of its left-wing bent. In 1921, Hitler took over the Party, and Drexler dropped out of sight. He's still alive. Feder was Hitler's economic adviser in the early days, but five years ago, Hitler fired him from the Economics Ministry. Feder's theory was that physical capital like factories, mines, roads, railways should be independent of international money finance. In May, 1919, Hitler heard Feder speak to the new party, and he wrote in Mein Kampf:

> 'For the first time in my life I saw the meaning of international capitalism. After I had heard Feder's first lecture, the thought flashed through my mind that I had found the essential suppositions for founding a new party... I felt a powerful prophecy... in Feder's lecture.'

"Hitler believed he saw a way of running the German economy and defying Jewish international finance.

"Other founder members were Frohm – Ernst Frohm – whom Hitler was to murder, Dietrich Eckart, a morphine addict who died shortly after, and Franz Xaver Ritter, who vanished from public view.

"Between 1919-1920, about 250 Freikorps roamed German cities. We're talking about perhaps 70,000 men. They each had their badge, but the most popular were the swastika of the Ehrhardt Brigade and the death's head, taken from the Great War Storm Troops. Half a dozen of the big corps wore the *Totenkopf* on their helmets and trucks. In the war, the *Totenkopf* was a symbol of derring-do; now it stood for anti-Bolshevism, for age-old Germanic values.

"When Hitler got out of hospital, after his gassing, and was demobbed, he wended his way to Munich, and in 1919 joined the Bavarian *Freikorps*, which the war-hero Franz Ritter von Epp had put together. Ritter led it in the bloody overthrow of the new Munich Marxist government.

"From Hitler's platform in the small, new Nazi party (which he'd taken over from Anton Drexler), he made rabble-rousing speeches, and roused the *Freikorps*. Hauptmann Ernst Röhm, Franz Xaver Ritter's adjutant, also led his own *Reichskriegsflagge Freikorps* (German war flag corps) and he sent Hitler a stream of officers and men. Hitler took note of the commies, and copied them – he loaded lorries with his men, who drove with rowdy shouts through the streets. But the commies dressed as civvies – Hitler's men sat stiffly to attention and wore *Freikorps* uniforms. They looked the very image of law and order, and people cheered.

"What Hitler wanted now was to stop his party's small discussion circles and get into mass meetings. His first big meeting pulled in about 2,000 people, on February 24, 1920… at the Munich *Hofbrauhaus Festaal.*

"Hitler had begun to roll.

"He drew his 'protectors' from temporary volunteers for this meeting – they wore the field-gray of the Munich *Reichswehr* and carried pistols, but he realised this wasn't good enough. He needed blind loyalty. At the end of 1920, he built a permanent Nazi group, the *Saalschutz* or small Praetorian Guard – literally, a salon guard. This didn't last long – in 1921, a new corps swallowed it, the *Sturmabteilung*.or SA, work of Ernst Röhm and Lieutenant Hans Ulrich Klintz. The job of the SA was to beat up political hecklers and opponents at meetings, and to battle the reds.

"Low in the sky of mankind now hung a small cloud, no bigger than a man's hand.

"Hitler's *Saalschutz* was to defend – the SA was to attack. But Hitler had little control over the SA, whose thugs did not understand politics. They were loyal to their own Fuhrer. On October 15, 1922, almost the whole SA fought a battle in Coburg with the commies who ran the town. Some 800 men of the *Sturmabteilung* broke the Red Front, and Hitler made his first important headlines."

I interrupted him. "I remember! The Bible… Noah's Ark and the Flood! The Flood
began with a cloud in the sky near the horizon, no larger than a man's hand."

"You asked me where did this ocean of evil come from. The Flood had a small beginning."

He pointed to my plate. "Would you like a second helping?"

"In the rationing! I don't dare put on weight, anyway."

"To be slim is admirable. But not be skinny."

"I'm not skinny!"

"I am merely concerned at your becoming so."

"Well, if it will make you feel easy in your mind, perhaps a little bit more…"

He laughed, and rang the porcelain bell on the starched tablecloth.

He sat back, thinking. The maid came in, and he asked her to serve me more. When she left, he said, "Hitler had his first national rally of the NSDAP on January 28 1923, when some 6,000 new SA recruits marched before Hitler, and he solemnly presented standards for what were the first

171

four full SA regiments. Next month brought so many recruits, he formed a fifth regiment.

"Now, he decided he had to ensure their personal loyalty, and to control them himself, so he appointed a new man in Nazi politics, air-ace Hauptman Hermann Göring, as Commander-in-Chief of the SA. Göring held the German equivalent of the Victoria Cross, the Order '*Pour le Merite*'. He had been the last commander of the von Richtofen Squadron, with 22 dogfight victories. Göring is a grown-up little boy – he's indolent and spoilt, slave of his likes. It was Röhm who really kept the SA up to scratch, and Göring or no Göring, the SA wasn't devoted to Hitler.

"So Hitler set up a small Praetorian Guard outside the SA as his personal bodyguard, and here we have the birth of the SS.

"It was March, 1923, and Hitler formed a Munich troop called the *Stabswache* from twelve old cronies who swore him an oath of allegiance. They had no loyalty to the SA, much less to the *Freikorps*.

"Two months later, working from the *Stabswache*, he created the *Strosstruppe Adolf Hitler* of 100 men, with military uniforms and two trucks... and they aopted the death's head emblem. Hauptmann Julius Schreck and Lieutenant Josef Berchtold led it. Headquarters were the Torbäu pub, and among the bodyguard now were Sepp Dietrich, Rudolf Hess, Ulrich Graf – now a Major General, I believe, on the Western Front – Emil Maurice, the gunman who killed several in the Röhm Blood Purge, Julius Schaub and Christian Weber.

"Hitler saw the Weimar Republic in 1923 as mercurial – he decided to strike. His SA and *Freikorps* allies could grab power at least in Munich, and then perhaps march on Berlin. Mussolini had just done it with his March on Rome. In November, he put the 15,000 of the SA on red alert, and on the 8th, he saw his chance. The Bavarian Prime Mini ter, the local army commander and the head of police went to the Munich *Burgerbräukeller*; there Hitler could grab them in one fell swoop.

"He ordered Rohm's *Reichskriegsflagge* to capture the *Reichswehr Ministry–*"

I said, "The *Reichswehr* was the 100,000-strong army that Versailles allowed...?"

"Exactly. Off went the troops, led by an army officer cadet, Heinrich Himmler, who bore an imperial war banner. Hitler surrounded the *Burgerbräukeller*, arrested the three Bavarian leaders – and thrust them into a small room...

"From which they escaped!

"They rushed off to organise an armed attack against the Nazi *putsch*.

"By November 9, Röhm's SA was under siege at the War Ministry, by regular *Reichswehr* units. So Hitler and Göring put together a relief column of 2,000 SA, and with them marched the great General Erich Ludendorf of the

Great War. At Ludwig bridge, they found a police line, and swept it aside. But a second police line at the Odeonsplatz had decided not to move. Ulrich Graf, of the personal bodyguard – *Strosstrupp Adolf Hitler* – walked forward and cried, 'Don't shoot. His Excellency General Ludendorf is here!' But these were police, not troops, and no respecters of Ludendorf. They fired a volley. Josef Berchtold fell under the bullets, and Andreas Bauriedl in his death throes clutched the swastika banner and soaked it in his blood. They swept up the banner and fled with it – it's sacred today, the *Blutfahne*. The Blood Banner.

"Hitler had linked his left arm through the right arm of his close friend, Max Erwin von Scheubner-Richter, and as Max fell dying; he pulled Hitler down with him. Ulrich Graf threw himself on top of Hitler and took a dozen bullets which would have finished off Hitler for sure. By a miracle, Graf pulled through. The police had shot dead sixteen Nazis, and dispersed or captured the rest.

"And so ended the era of the *Freikorps* which had lasted five years, to the very day Hitler realised the way had to lie through politics.

"Hitler went to prison, but he had made headlines all over Germany. The government banned the NSDAP and broke up the SA and *Strosstrupp*.

"But Hitler had made headlines all over Germany. They gave him five years, but he conducted his own defense, and his words made – as I say – headlines all over Germany. He declared he alone was responsible for the *putsch*. He said, 'This is my stance: rather would I be hanged in a Bolshevik Germany, than die under French swords.' He said that the masses in the streets with their swastika banners would become one with those who today fired on them. They would form companies, then battalions, which would grow into regiments, and the regiments into divisions. 'Even if you find us guilty one thousand times, the goddess of the eternal court of history will laugh and tear into pieces the verdict of your court. She pronounces us not guilty.'

"His words made him a national hero.

"He served only nine months. He breakfasted in bed, walked in the garden, dictated *Mein Kampf* to Rudolf Hess, agonized over his mistakes, and pinpointed them; in *Mein Kampf*, a confused book, he shows his Darwinism. The fittest will survive. We can see it today in the Party. Hitler usually doesn't give clear orders. He lets the underlings fight it out among themselves, and waits to see who comes out on top – who has the best idea, or who manages to overrule the other. Law-of-the-jungle bureaucracy as it were."

Count Axel sat in silence, as we took dessert.

Then he smiled. "Hitler was incredible," he mused. "Two days after the putsch, on November 11, he issued a proclamation:

'Comrades! We stood on the field, shoulder to shoulder, all of one

173

mind. Nevertheless, on the orders of (traitors) the police of Augsberg drew a bead on Germany's leaders, Ludendorff and Hitler, and fired at these liberators of the people. From only thirty metres, the tank *Hindenburg* spilled the best of German blood. I, Hitler, was wounded; Ludendorff, surely protected by God, was untouched. Yet twenty of our best lay dead, and they wounded about a hundred men, women and children. Our enemies suffered not one loss. Comrades! Do you want to be one with these murderers or will you strive to liberate Germany? Do not fight for treacherous Jews. Let your German loyalty bring you over to our side...' "

At three o'clock, I was home, encoding my message to London.

WHEN THREE KNOW A SECRET IT IS SAFE IF TWO ARE DEAD, MOSCOW HAS IDENTIFIED ME FROM LADY MAG DEB PHOTOS 1937. COMMIE INTEL AGENT HUNGARIAN DIPLOMAT... MY MISSION NOW TOO DANGEROUS. A SCORE KNOW MY SECRET, IN SWITZ MUST ESCAPE TO ENGLAND...

I set out all Tibor Haraszti's demands, and that I was "to fall in love" with Swiss Axel Baer.

I microdotted it, rang Ruben, who said he would wait in for me; I reached him at 7.30 pm.

He brought a burning Yugoslav plum brandy, and poured about one centimetre into tiny glasses.

He steepled his fingers.

"You're still only nineteen. No one in their right mind would think London would send a nineteen-year-old girl. In fact, the London SIS is a bit of a laughing stock. They couldn't find out what times their own Underground runs, I shouldn't be surprised. Now, Moscow Intelligence – the *Komitet Gosudarstrennoy Bezopasnosti* – runs that. They call it the KGB – does that ring a bell?"

I shook my head.

Then I said, "She might have spoken of it on the ship – I 've got a vague sort of recollection..."

"It's in Dzerzhinsky Square in Moscow, and I fail to see what benefit Dzerzhinsky Square will find in trying to betray you. They clearly want to decode your information. And they want you to send something to London from Switzerland and God knows what that could be. Just let me find the wavelength they want."

He searched around.

"You can't write this down. You'll have to memorise it. Well, write it down now, and I'll give you a few minutes. Repeat it out loud and write it down over and again. Can you relate it to any birthdays?"

He waited patiently.

When I was ready, he said, "Give that to this Liska woman. Next, your contact in our Embassy in Geneva is Maximo Murphy de la Rua."

"Murphy!" I cried. "That sounds Irish and the Irish are little enamoured of us."

"Maximo, on his mother's side, comes from an old, aristocratic, landed English family. One son was a rake, a black sheep, and they sent him to Argentina. Maximo is still a little rakish – you slap his hands hard!"

"I will," I said solemnly, and we both laughed.

"On his father's side, he comes from landed gentry in Northern Ireland, and he's extremely proud of his English blood. But trust not another soul in the Geneva Embassy. I think Argentina will stock and refuel German U-boats – or already have begun. Imagine how Maximo and myself feel…"

I nodded.

"Don't worry about a thing. Here they know that in Belize the ordinary people feel friendly to the British and are anxious to cooperate. But it's perfectly clear they will feel they are from Belize rather than feel they are British. Some may rush off to volunteer, but most will not put their lives at risk. They will help… no, the Gestapo has a pretty clear idea about Belize. I've been checking. Besides, you're Spanish, of Argentinean origin, so here they think you're an outsider in Belize, even though supposedly that's where you were born."

We took cautious sips of the burning brandy.

He spoke out loud. "I wonder what *real* reactions of the people in Belize are to this war and to Britain? We'll never know. Anything the British print will be propaganda, luckily for you. Here, they won't believe a word of it, no matter what they print."

He smiled.

"The British would never manage to persuade a nineteen year old girl from Belize to spy for them! They wouldn't even try. The very idea is so preposterous…!"

I got home late, but they gave me supper. The Prince and his son Claus listened, sober and intent, as I told them about Switzerland. I had never seen the Prince lose his cool, German, aristocratic aplomb, but now he got up and paced the room once, then sat down stiffly.

"Switzerland! What does Moscow want!"

Afterwards, Claus said, "I have something for you. They have prepared a rough draft, which may become a Führer Directive next month. They have prepared the plans for a military invasion of Spain and the taking of Gibraltar, following the fall of France. They calculate France will have fallen before winter, next year. The Spanish Army is to be incorporated into the German army. Franco will be invited first to co-operate, and military action will follow if he does not."

* * *

I went up to my room at 10 pm, and felt so tired, I decided to encode the message in the morning.

Next morning, I was up at 8 am and dressed for breakfast; at 8.30 the phone rang. It was Speer, who invited me to visit a tank factory, and take photos.

They flew me to the Ruhr, and I got back at 4pm, after lunch in the factory canteen. I went to Speer's office, and left the film with his secretary. From his office, I phoned Schneppen at the Propaganda Ministry.

I said, "I apologise for not advising you in advance, but they rang at 8.30, and the car arrived shortly after. I was busy changing my clothes, and getting my cameras ready. They flew me there and flew me back."

Schneppen asked, "Could you request copies from Speer?"

"He's not here, but I'll leave him a written message."

"Ach! Excellent."

176

I wrote to Speer, 'My supervisor at the Propaganda Ministry, Hanns Schneppen, begs for copies of my photos today. Could you help me, because I have to keep sweet with Schneppen and Goebbels? They do treat me very well, and I never want to have to say no to them. Yours, Ray.'

I got home, encoded the message about Spain, and took it to Ruben at the Argentinean Embassy. When I got home, the Swiss Embassy called, and invited me to a dance on Saturday night.

The radio was full of the German U-boat that sank the *Royal Oak* and the *Repulse* in Scapa Flow. When the Prince came home, he carried the afternoon newspapers. The 2 pm edition said that the U-boat had *sunk* the *Repulse*, while the 5 pm edition said they had torpedoed it – nothing else. I wondered whether they had missed, or perhaps they had hit but it was still afloat.

The family sat around comfortably, chatting, before dinner was served. I told them about my flight to the Ruhr for Speer, and a stunned silence fell.

"Speer has nothing at all to do with armaments," stuttered Princess Jutta.

"Exactly," said the grandmother.

The Prince breathed, "This must have come from Hitler."

"Exactly," said the grandmother.

"Hitler must have liked your photos of Speer," ventured Thoma.

"Exactly," said the grandmother.

"So he wanted to see more of your work," said the Prince in a taut voice.

"Exactly," said the grandmother.

"You're very exact tonight," grumbled the Prince.

"I think we can all be pleased," said the grandmother, comfortably.

After dinner, we went back to the armchairs and sofas, and the Prince showed us some new ration cards.

"These are for a year's clothing. One hundred points. Two pairs of socks, two handkerchiefs, a set of underwear, a pair of gloves, a tie – if you buy an overcoat, that takes sixty points, which leaves you only forty with which to choose between socks and underwear, or a shirt... it's hopelessly inadequate."

Princess Jutta said, "We must go shopping quickly. How long do you think the war could last?"

Claus said, "Five to eight years. It depends on how long America takes to come in. They're already sending arms, but 3,000,000 Americans in uniform is another thing. We don't know what the bombing will do. It could stop war production dead – and the production of socks and overcoats too – and then we'll be lucky, with Hitler soon on the gallows."

The Prince said, "In a couple of days, they'll restrict the sale of galoshes to certain members of the public who have to work out in the streets – postmen, that sort of thing."

"We'll buy eight pairs of galoshes for each one of us," said Princess Jutta. "Forty pairs of socks each – well, stockings for the ladies – twenty-five sets of underwear apiece…"

She got a piece of paper, and jotted down a long list.

"The poor ordinary Germans," I said.

The grandmother said with acerbity, "*They* voted Hitler in, *they* manufacture his arms, *they* joyfully go off in his armies and kill people, destroy cities and leave women and children homeless and hungry. *They* still believe in a short war and in victory – and you know why! Because Hitler tells them! They are murderers afield with their tanks and planes and guns."

Princess Jutta said, "Gabriele, it's not good for you to get too excited."

"Hah!" said Princess Gabriele. "Those whom gods would destroy, they first make mad. The ordinary German is mad. And Hitler utterly so."

Doris asked me, "How are you off for clothes?"

"I've got three overcoats, but I had better buy five more. I've got about ten pairs of stockings, but I'll need more… if I may, I'll leave it in the hands of your mother, and then I'll pay you."

They had fitted me out very carefully in London before I left, and I had carried my luggage to Buenos Aires, where they had changed all the labels.

The Prince said, "In November, we get 80 grams of soap each and two hundred and fifty grams of soap flakes."

"Pooling the soap flakes in a household like this, we won't have problem," said Thoma.

"Let's wash while we can," said Princess Gabriele, ominously.

Next morning, at breakfast, the hero of the hour on the radio was a

Lieutenant-Captain Prien, who had got his U-boat into Scapa Flow. Claus told us that in the Great War the Germans twice tried to get into Scapa Flow, and lost both submarines. He said that mines, booms and steel nets made Scapa Flow impregnable. He said torpedo boats patrolled it.

After midday, (he and the crew got Iron Crosses on landing) Prien told Germany that he reached a boom, looked it over, and got around it. Inside, he saw two battleships at anchor, fired, and saw a fountain climb into the air beside the battleship to the north. He saw the other battleship explode into pieces, high into the air. "The ship exploded to pieces like atoms," he said. He didn't waste a second getting back to the boom and edging by it. In the open sea, he could hear the English depth-charging Scapa Flow.

The Germans are cock-a-hoop. For them this is a more important victory than Poland – they have hit the Royal Navy, no less!

Schneppen rang to say that Hitler would receive Prien and his crew at the Reich Chancellery tomorrow afternoon, and would I go? I said, yes. He told me, "You correspondents will get double rations, double ration cards. The same cards as men get doing heavy manual labor. Soon you'll be looking like a proper plump German Fraulein."

"I'll try," I promised dutifully.

At lunch, the grandmother said, "In the last war, now I remember… you couldn't get sewing needles, sewing thread, darning thread, pins, scissors, combs, every sort of brush…"

"Good heavens," said Princess Jutta. "I'll check everything in the house."

The correspondents met the U-boat crew after they lunched with Hitler. Hitler had given Prien the Grand Cross of the Iron Cross, and he wore it when he walked in. He wasn't quite blond – his hair was yellowish-brown – and he wasn't tall, but solidly built. He's married, with a child. And his crew – they looked like youngsters – just eighteen, nineteen or twenty! They looked like a youthful University rowing crew! Blowing up our battleships at that age… and looking as though they couldn't care less.

At eight o'clock, Reinhard drove me to the Swiss Embassy.

They watch your use of private cars very strictly, and sometimes stop you, to take note of your reasons. Foreign correspondents must travel on trams or the underground, and use cars only at night. But the Prince has given Reinhard an official satchel he always carries, and when I complained, Goebbels and Heydrich both gave me 'discretionary' passes – that is, I could use my own discretion, living in the distant Potsdam suburb.

At the Swiss Embassy, they liked my slinky evening-gown... heaven only knows how I could have worn it on a tram. I talked to someone who I think was called Tino Soldati, a new Swiss attaché, who said that the Swiss expected invasion from hour to hour.

A tall young man in an impeccably cut grey suit walked up to me and introduced himself... Axel Baer.

This was the man I had to fall in love with.

He was, indeed, good-looking, with strong cheek bones and a prominent chin – his grey eyes looked at the world with warm curiosity. He did look like a Swiss banker, but nothing like a secret Communist Intelligence agent. He wore an air of steadiness – no impulsiveness there. When I asked him how did he like Berlin, he said, "The blackout is really *black*." He gave me a wry grin, and said, "I live expecting the unexpected, and it seems I am never to be disappointed."

"What a funny thing to say!" I laughed lightly, failing to discern any compliment there.

"Well, I'm Swiss and a banker, and they're supposed to epitomize boredom!"

"And a communist," I whispered.

"Communists are regarded as fanatically drab," he whispered back.

He put his hand on my arm, and I stiffened.

"You must learn to feign liking my touch," he said dryly.

This was in the world of Mati Hara and spies.

"I'll be brave."

"Poor me," he murmured.

"Let's dance," I said, and he seized me eagerly.

It wasn't altogether unpleasant.

As we danced, he said mischievously, "Now you have to gaze into my face."

He was good-looking if a little overbearing, so I gazed and gazed, and prayed he was as unexcitable as he looked.

I had never felt so uncomfortable, so fed-up, so irritated – people tossed me this way and that but I reminded myself that was a drop in the bucket beside what the Gestapo would do.

We danced four more times, and I went to the ladies' bathroom to check up on my face and hair. They had introduced me to a young femme fatale with a Slavic face, from another Embassy – perhaps the Hungarian. She rejoiced in the name of Joli Szapary, Joli being a nickname; now she came in.

"You've made yourself a catch," she told me. "You felled our Swiss banker within instants. He's looking down your cleavage as though he's found the most promising investment portfolio in years."

"He seems to be… 'hard-working and steady'," I improvised. "I find men who understand about money very sexy."

She gave me a very sophisticated smile of amusement and disappeared into the cubicle.

* * *

We danced till midnight, and two-thirds of the dances were with Axel. He gave me his card, with his home and business addresses, and phone numbers. On the back he wrote train times.

"Catch the train Thursday afternoon, and you should reach Geneva at midday, on Friday. Lika will be waiting for you in the bar of Hotel Cornavin. We'll meet at half past-five in the bar of Hotel Wilson, in front of the lake. You must go to the Gestapo to get a Foreigner's Exit and Re-entry Pass. Do that tomorrow, because they will take three days to give it to you."

"Will Germany attack Switzerland?"

"We Swiss work six days a week for the Nazis and on the seventh day, we go to Church and pray for a British victory. Tomorrow I have to go back."

* * *

We all packed ourselves into different Embassy cars, which bore us to our homes.

* * *

Next morning, Schneppen rang and said would I like to visit bookshops, and take shots of the customers. He would send a car at ten, and the driver would

181

know where to go.

"Or do you prefer half-past-ten?" he asked jovially. "Perhaps you had another late night?"

"Indeed, I did," I confessed. "And I fell in love. He's a Swiss banker, and today he goes back to Geneva. I'm going to apply for an Exit Pass to go to Geneva next weekend. I don't know how he feels about me but I don't want him to forget about me."

"I will tell Dr. Goebbels," he laughed. "This will come as a shock to everyone. You seemed so in love with your work. What is his name?"

"Axel Baer. He works in the Credit Suisse."

"And if you go there in the weekend, you'll keep the other girls away from him. You have the making of a military strategist, young Fraulein."

He hung up, chuckling.

In the Ministry car, I remembered photos in the London newspapers of bonfires of books in German cities. At the bookshops, an official who came with me in the car introduced me to the manager, who introduced me to different clients, who were all too happy to play the part of thoughtful, intellectual book buyers. The going best-seller is GONE WITH THE WIND – *VOM WINDE VERWEHT* or THE WIND BLOWING ALL OVER. I shot other Berliners with Cronin's CITADEL, LOOK UP ALL ABOUT ENGLAND (a propaganda book), THAT IS POLAND (but published in 1928), FIFTY YEARS OF GERMANY by the Swedish explorer Sven Hedin and personal friend of Hitler's, THE WORLDS SING ETERNALLY by a Norwegian writer, and Ludendorff's famous tome on total war – DER TOTALE KRIEG. I found stacks of detective thrillers, and novels about air and submarine war.

Everyone I talked to believed the 'Sitdown War' today was a prelude to Britain and France finally coming to the negotiating table. Didn't I agree? Of course I did. I wondered yet again how many fighter planes was England turning out every 24 hours. This respite was England's only hope to build a fighter fleet.

That night, Count Holger Zorndorf, in the Berlin anti-aircraft artillery, took me to the *Marmorhaus* cinema to see Clark Gable in ADVENTURE IN CHINA. Gable could afford to be so brave – he was in no danger at all. Holger invited me to see Shakespeare at a Berlin theatre next weekend, but I told him I had to go to Switzerland. So he invited me to the opera at a theatre doing Johann Strauss's *Fledermaus*.

"I'd like to invite you to the Berlin Philharmonic concert that Furtwangler's giving, but it's sold out a week in advance."

All is certainly quiet on the Western Front!

Sunday morning, the Prince told me that tomorrow night Professor Chad Sabowise, Professor Emeritus at an Ivy League University in the States, was coming to dinner. He was writing a book on Versailles, and Hitler had received him. He wanted to meet Albert Speer, and the Prince asked me to invite Speer too. I rang Speer at his 'home' in Berlin, found him in, and Speer accepted.

This was an *Eintopfsonntag* – a One Pot Sunday. Everyone was supposed to eat a meal from one saucepan – say, a stew, and donate the money saved from a regular Sunday lunch to the Winter Relief Fund. The newspapers this morning called it *Opferosonntag* or Sacrifice Sunday. As people are already getting one pound of meat a week, a quarter of a pound of butter and so on it's already a sacrifice every day of the week.

When the Berliners go out for their Sunday stroll, thousands of uniformed SA and SS men stop them, with their collection boxes, and you put in 50 pfennigs or a mark. Then they affix a tiny Germanic sword – a sort of dagger – to your lapel, men, women and children. The driver of the Propaganda Ministry car yesterday gave me a message asking me to photograph the joyous faces of the hungry but charitable Berliners, so I joined a group of three SS toughs and worked for three hours.

At home, we ate from a huge saucepan, a rich stew, and the family outdid each other in their remarks about Hungry Hitler.

Monday morning, Heydrich rang, inviting me to lunch and a small concert. I took along two tins of crabmeat, which Luise Gensorowsky accepted with delight, and showed them to Heydrich when he came in. Heydrich brought some venison which Göring had shot, so we had a good lunch.

Heydrich said, "You've applied for a Pass to go to Switzerland? Personal reasons? Axel Baer, banker?"

Everyone stared.

"Love at first sight. I want to see whether I can stop him from getting away." Heydrich loved that. Luise, her sister Margarete and Marion plied me with questions.

"Is there anything I can bring you from Switzerland?"

The other three women suddenly looked imploringly at him. He grinned. "We four share a weakness for '*bonbon*' chocolates – chocolates with fillings. If I give you a couple of hundred American dollars, could you buy some? Don't buy the expensive boxes, nor the cheap ones either. The biggest boxes, but in the middle price-range."

"I'll never get them back into the country! The customs will confiscate them, and then eat them themselves."

A steely humour fell over his face. "I'll send a car to drive you to an airfield, and you can fly back to Berlin."

We talked about Furtwangler's concert, and how the tickets were sold out. Louise was playing the viola and Margarete the transverse German flute in that concert, and they said what a marvellous conductor he was. Then we had a concert – Marion playing the piano – and the long violin solos of Heydrich enraptured us.

That evening, Chad Sabowise arrived a few minutes before Speer. He was tall, gangling, skinny, with prematurely white hair – perhaps in his early forties. He had a bony face with deceptively vague eyes. He was delighted to meet Speer, and the two talked ten to the dozen.

We had pork chops, with roast potatoes and tinned peas and carrots, followed by white beans in tinned tomato sauce. For dessert, we had a huge apple pie with – miraculously – cream. The Prince brought up from the cellar bottles of old wine.

A feast.

Princess Jutta asked Speer, "Wasn't Hitler going to put a fantastic new avenue across Berlin?"

Speer said, "It really seems impossible we're at war, he spent so much time planning architectural wonders. My plans sometimes kept him awake most of the night, he was so excited."

He sipped at his wine.

"Well, I must amend that. I remember two years ago, he came to my Berlin showroom to see a seven-foot high model of my stadium for 400,000 people."

He said to Sabowise, "That is not to say I had to make models of all my plans, because Hitler has a truly remarkable gift to see plans in three dimensions."

Sabowise nodded.

"We turned to the plans pinned up alongside, and I warned him that the field didn't have the proper Olympic proportions."

Hitler dismissed that, unemotionally. "The 1940 Olympic Games will be held in Tokyo. But after that, for all the centuries to come, the Games will be held in this stadium, and these proportions will be the new ones."

Sabowise's eyes came alive. "When were you supposed to finish the stadium?"

"For the Party rally of 1945."

"Ah!"

"The Olympic Games in 1936 – he followed them closely, and got really excited. Your incredible black runner, Jesse Owens, upset him, taking all his prizes. Because the Germans took an astonishing number of prizes, Hitler said of Owen that as he came from the primitive jungle, his body had grown like all black people while the mind atrophied."

He gave Sabowise a sly grin, and the Yankee said, "A bad loser!"

We all laughed.

Speer said, "As for the avenue in Berlin, he wanted one that would measure one hundred and thirty metres across. The Berlin mayor wouldn't have that. Hitler replaced the mayor. He said, 'Lippert – the mayor – is useless, a fool, hopelessly inefficient, bankrupt in ideas, a nullity.' So, in the summer of 1936, he told me that he would put the whole thing in my hands, and leave the Berlin municipality out of it. He told me that back in the early twenties, long before he had any hope of coming to power, he had made sketch after sketch for Berlin. He wanted to put the Potsdam and Anhalter railway stations south of Tempelhof Field. Those empty railway tracks cutting across the city could be cleared for a monumental avenue, beginning at the *Siegesallee*, and running for three miles, with stupendous buildings along it. On the north side, near the Reichstag, he wanted a Berlin Meeting Hall that would dwarf all ideas humanity had ever had. It would be domed, and would hold St. Peter's of Rome about seven times over. The dome alone would measure about 270 metres across, and the floor would hold 150,000 inside, but standing room only! His second dream was a Triumphal Arch, 130 metres high! He wanted to chisel the names of 1,800,000 German war dead in the

185

Great War. He showed me two sketches he had made ten years ago."

We sat in an awed silence.

"Hitler feels that Paris is the most beautiful city in the world. Even Vienna, he says, has monumental style. The *Ringstrasse*, the *Rathaus*, the Parliament, the Opera House… the *Hofburg*, the museums. Hitler can draw all of these in perfect proportion from memory. His hero is Georges E. Haussman and his new Parisian boulevards that he built between 1853 and 1870. He hopes I will surpass him! That is a lot to load on the shoulders of someone!" he laughed, and we joined him. The air was electric.

Speer said to Sabowise, "I'm boring you," and Sabowise exclaimed, "Never! You are confirming the thesis of my book – the whole basic ideal! I can't believe my luck! I beg you to continue."

"Hitler told me, 'I've often thought of creating a new capital from scratch, on empty ground. But look at Washington or Canberra. The Australians call it their 'White Elephant', and when Parliament recesses, there's a rush to get back to Melbourne or Sydney. No, we must take as our model Paris. Haussmann's Champs Elysees is three hundred and thirty feet wide, so we'll make ours seventy feet wider still. When the Great Elector laid out the Unter den Linden in the sixteen hundreds, he made it two hundred feet wide. He could have never envisaged today's world with its motor traffic.' "

We talked about this over dessert, and after we were comfortable in armchairs and on the sofas, with brandy and coffee, the Prince asked Sabowise about his book.

The Professor asked us a rhetorical question.

"Who is the most dangerous guy in town?"

We looked blank.

"You get down on the wrong side of the tracks, some crummy little Bar, and seated at the bar is this guy who only finished primary school. He's got wide shoulders, thick wrists and big hands. He's pretty dumb and he's got a big chip on those shoulders of his. If he's got a very high opinion of himself, he watches you like a lynx to see whether you share that high opinion. Because if you don't, you're in big trouble. If the lower down the social scale he stands – if the higher his self-opinion – the greater the explosive force. Because the basic drive in humans is self-esteem, the most dangerous drive there is, and the source of most violence.

"You will remember our President Woodrow Wilson, whose mandate covered the Great War? Well, I say his ghost haunts us today. Because he tried to tell us that it was our inanity, our blindness that thrust the world into the Great War. The worst war the world has seen, unless this one turns out to be an even greater disaster. We thought we could handle things with the Balance of Power, as Britain had for centuries. After we defeated Germany, we thought we could crush her, and restore the Balance of Power. But Wilson

186

understood it went far beyond that. Germany could not be humiliated, its pride, its self-esteem trodden underfoot. Wilson warned us, 'I do not hesitate to say the war we have just been through, though it was shot through with terror of every kind, is not to be compared with the war we would face next time.'

"And look at what happened. The Kaiser abdicated after popular uprisings. In a railway car in the forest of Compiegne, in France, that is, a German envoy agreed Germany would lay down its arms. The German Government trusted Woodrow Wilson's Fourteen Points, which, said Wilson, would mean 'a peace without victors.' Wilson pursued a non-punitive peace, to let Germany grow into a democracy, under the aegis of the League of Nations.

"What happens? For Britain, France and Italy, the Treaty of Versailles was but an instrument to crush, to weaken, to drain Germany – to bleed off territory and wealth, to leave it so pinched and penniless it could never threaten Europe again. They humiliated the Germans, betrayed German trust – and now have got themselves into this new war.

"You cannot humiliate a country. What you *think* is humiliating, or not, is not necessarily what that *country* thinks. The three most populous countries on earth today are Russia, India and China, and all three are despised. Whenever we get out of this second European War, we'll have those to contend with. Another very powerful country, completely despised, is Japan. Mankind has had thousands of years of this. When one of Rome's enemies won a battle against them, Rome did not hate them. If they made the defeated Roman legions march under a yoke, then there was no mercy. Ancient Rome was implacable. Hitler agrees with me absolutely.

"Tonight, Mr. Speer, you have told us about these incredible architectural ambitions for Germany. This is a meglomaniacal response to unbearable humiliation. These avenues, these Brobdingnagian buildings…"

"You're not an architect," laughed Speer. "Any architect would give his right arm to build things like that. Nothing to do with humiliation. Simple intoxication!"

He gave Sabowise a sagacious look.

"The Middle Kingdom of China last century thought it was the centre of the civilized world. Five thousand years of civilization in a barbarian world – five thousand years of unbelievable art. The foreign devils stormed in, humiliated and violated China, with a technology one thousand years ahead of them. That's the sort of thing you're talking about?"

"Admirably put," said Sabowise.

"Leaving out the disparity in technology, I know how they felt," said Speer, sourly.

Next morning, a messenger came from Heydrich, with 500 dollars, and a note. "Buy two hundred dollars of good Brazilian coffee."

Half-an-hour later, another visitor announced himself: Fritz von Fehrbellin.

"I've come from Adam von Trott zu Solz and Admiral Canaris."

I felt a twinge of fear.

"As you're going to Switzerland, would you mind carrying a message for us?"

"I don't understand. I'm just an Argentinean photographer."

"As you know, the SD takes a most unhealthy interest in our side of things. We are two rival Intelligence Agencies. We have to move funds to pay our operatives – and operations – abroad. We usually work through the SNB – that's the Swiss National Bank, but someone in that Bank passes on what we do to the SD. We need to send a message to the Basler Handelsbank in Basel, without attracting attention."

I exploded. "Why are you telling these secrets? This is dangerous knowledge, and it could get me killed!"

"Because Adam told me to lay it all out to you, that it is the only way to come to any arrangement with you."

"If I'm searched, I'm dead. I won't even think of it."

"We'll give you a handbag that has a square of film hidden in the metal clasp. The clasp would have to be sawn open. We will pay you a thousand dollars. Think of the dresses you can buy in Switzerland!"

I almost swooned. A thousand dollars in dresses and jewellery...

"I'm sure Swiss dresses are pretty dowdy."

"I'll give you the names of stores in Geneva that have Paris models, and copies of Paris models. You can find copies for two hundred dollars."

My heart was beating so fast I felt breathless. Three dresses, and the rest in jewellery...

"I have to meet someone in Geneva at midday on Friday."

"Leave tomorrow, and you'll be in Basel on Thursday. You can sleep in Basel, and take a morning train to Geneva.

"You have to ask for Maurice Burckhardt at the Bank. And you must tell him 'PERSONAL WAY'. You must say that to him."

"PERSONAL WAY. That's the key to the code, is it?"

He looked at me strangely, and I could have bitten off my tongue.

I said, "I can't walk out of the Bank without my handbag."

"He'll give you an identical bag. I see you are a born spy."

"I am not," I said angrily. "I hate the very idea of this sort of thing."

He opened his brief case, and gave me a very nice, dark-brown handbag. I opened it, and inside saw one thousand dollars. I took them out, and held in my hand – one thousand dollars.

Basel was unbelievable!

In the railway station restaurant, I saw mountains of cakes, cheeses, butter, eggs, as someone in a dream. I didn't have to surrender bread coupons, or worry about my meat ones. They put down a big steak, with full garnishing, and I drooled. When darkness fell, the street lights blazed. Lights blazed from the houses, from the shop windows... oh, what bliss.

I slept comfortably, and arrived at midday at the cafe of Hotel de Cornavin. At a table just inside the door I saw a woman of about thirty – very thin, nicotine-stained fingers, untidy hair, a lined-face and intent eyes. She was carelessly dressed, and looked really older, a bit unkempt, but I still put her at about thirty. Liska Czimer?

I sat down at a table beside her and caught a waiter's eye. She turned to look out through the window at the street, and her elbow knocked her book on to the floor. I bent down, and picked it up. It was in French.

She said in French, "Oh, please excuse me. Thank you very much," which was the full range of what I knew in that language.

I said in English, "I'm afraid French is Dutch to me."

She laughed outright. "My English is not bad, but thankfully 'it's Dutch to me' is one of the expressions I know. Isn't English funny! 'French is Dutch to me'. That's really a crazy twist in a language. Are you visiting Switzerland?"

"Yes, I've just arrived."

"The French didn't give you any trouble?"

"I came in from Germany actually."

My coffee arrived and I paid for it. I glanced around casually. Five people were in earshot. At least one from the Gestapo, and another from the Swiss Secret Service. The Swiss would have her marked down, but would she be on Gestapo files? How convincing was our conversation? Were we passing this off as a chance encounter?

"Germany!" she exclaimed, baffled, a little too loud. "The Germans let you travel through their country?" she asked, lowering her voice.

"I should imagine there are restrictions on Germans, but I'm not German. Are you Swiss?"

"I was Hungarian, and I came here as a correspondent for a Budapest newspaper. We Hungarians have a great gift for languages, so I quickly picked up German and Italian. I spoke French and some English. I was able to travel all over and talk to everyone, so a Geneva newspaper gave me work. I decided to apply for Swiss nationality and they gave it to me."

"I need to find a hotel room."

"This is a good place. Would you like me to take you to reception?"

As we walked in, she said softly, "Please the wavelength and the code."

"TO BUY CHEAP." Then I gave her the wavelength.

She stood by me at the desk, while the receptionist gave me some choices of rooms and prices.

I chose my room, signed the book, and took the key with a large iron disk. Liska said, "May I come up to your room? If you like, I can show you a nice restaurant."

"Most certainly," I said.

"I have to phone. You go up ahead."

* * *

In the room, I unpacked. Someone knocked, and I opened the door to Liska. She handed me 200 dollars.

I sat on the bed and she took a padded chair.

"What is this all about?" I demanded. "Why must I come to Switzerland?"

"You must send a message to the British government. You must warn them that they must declare war on Switzerland, and we will give you the reasons."

"Switzerland," I said mildly, "We all need Switzerland for the Red Cross."

"The Red Cross! Bah! The only thing that can keep Germany at war is Swiss money."

I looked at her. A wild-goose chase. All this way.

"Switzerland is a tiny country of no interest to anyone."

She spat at me, "You don't know what you're talking about. In a couple of hours, you can go to the Argentinean Embassy and your encoded message will spell it all out. Your decoding key is HIS BREAKDOWN."

The light of the window ravaged her face.

"HIS BREAKDOWN," I repeated, floundering.

"Let us go to the restaurant," she said, and she led me through

190

surprisingly narrow, poor streets, half-shadowed even at midday.

When she saw me looking, she said, "Everyone thinks Switzerland is rich. Here you have the wealthy bankers, the manufacturers on the one hand, and the workers destroying their eyesight making watches and clockwork mechanisms on the other – that is, if they're not spending their lives beside vats of chocolate. No-one needs communism more than Switzerland."

We got to a table in the far corner, with no one near us.

"We're a hit late, so it's not crowded."

We ordered from an amazing menu choice.

Liska said in a low voice, "Without the Swiss bankers, Germany would have to sue for peace in two months. Germany depends on trade and help from several neutral countries, and no country will touch German marks. They want Swiss francs or American dollars, and Switzerland sells them Swiss francs, to buy tungsten from Spain and Portugal."

"Tungsten?"

"It's also called wolfram, because they extract it from wolframite. One ton of wolframite rocks gives you 1.5 grams of tungsten. It's got the highest tensile strength of any known metal – the highest strength above 3,000 degrees Fahrenheit, and it expands least when heated. Germany needs it for dyes, to harden the iron and steel in its tanks, and to make shells. Germany has set up dummy companies in Spain and Portugal to buy it. The Germans can't buy Argentinean beef, Brazilian diamonds for machine drilling, anything without Swiss francs."

She ate in silence for a minute.

"The Messerschmitts can't fly without tungsten," she said, and sipped some wine.

"Turkey sells them chrome – for Swiss francs. Sweden sells its steel – the war would stop in a few weeks without Swedish steel. But the Swedes demand Swiss francs. Stockholm, Madrid, Lisbon, Ankara, Buenos Aires – none of them will touch Reichmarks.

"So what does Germany give Switzerland? It keeps Switzerland warm in winter with German coal. And it gives the Swiss a river of gold."

After the war, I learned that the German Reich bank shipped some 400 million American dollars worth of gold to Switzerland during WWII. The Germans looted most of this gold from the occupied countries, including $US 12 million in gold they looted from Italy towards the end. Hitler began the war with gold reserves estimated at $US 100 million. To that the Germans added gold looted from Austria, Czechoslovakia, Danzig, Poland, Holland, Belgium, France, Luxembourg, Yugoslavia, Hungary and Italy, as each country fell in turn, worth some $US 650 million – of which, as I say – some

191

$US 400 million went into Swiss coffers, mainly into the Swiss National Bank.

Reichsbank accounts seem to show that about $US 280 million in gold, at least, went to the Swiss National Bank and the rest to other Swiss commercial banks. The Swiss National Bank, according to a report, laundered $US 100 million of gold for re-export to Spain and Portugal. Many countries were disquieted about getting Nazi gold, especially the central banks of Spain, Portugal and Rumania. They took Swiss francs, and then bought gold from the Swiss National Bank directly.

Swiss banks knew these amounts of gold far exceeded German reserves – so they knew the gold had been stolen.

Further, desperate Jews deposited up to perhaps $US 100 million in different currencies, jewels and other valuables. After the war, the Swiss refused to return the deposits to heirs without death certificates – and the Nazi extermination camps did not issue death certificates.

Most of this Nazi gold was converted into Swiss francs, which the Germans used to buy raw materials and supplies to fight WWII.

Liska went on, "Germans fit Swiss machine-guns to their fighter planes. Our timing mechanisms are used for everything – our clockwork pieces.

"Germany had about one hundred million dollars in gold reserves – that's now in Switzerland, to buy Swiss francs. But most of these Swiss francs have been spent. More gold is arriving. In Austria, they plundered the gold reserves and art treasure. They left alone the homes of Nazi supporters, but went through all the middle-class homes and those of the well-to-do, taking gold and silver ornaments, silver tableware, jewellery, rings, and gold-framed spectacles. Any painting hanging on the wall of a certain quality – they took it. Göring set up guidelines. All art Hitler didn't want was submitted to Göring. What Göring didn't want, went to the German museums. What they didn't want was sold here in Switzerland, or deposited in Swiss banks as collateral for Swiss francs. In Czechoslovakia, they went through every house, in certain districts. They stopped people on the streets. In Poland, they're doing the same. Some Polish art has just arrived. God help France if Germany defeats her! Germany has always envied France her civilization, and Germany will strip France to the last locket.

"Of course, America holds Swiss gold, and Switzerland will need it to help buy foreign currencies for Germany, but America so far has not answered our request to return it."

USA refused to ship the Swiss gold to Switzerland, for fear the Swiss would use it to help the Germans. So in the winter of 1941, the American Embassy froze – the Swiss wouldn't let them have a single piece of coal. The German Embassy was warm and cozy.

I said, "The ordinary Swiss are pro-Nazi?"

"Am I pro-Nazi! The ordinary Swiss, most of the public, are not, and they detest the Swiss Federal Council and the Swiss bankers. Most of the daily papers are passionately anti-Nazi. But the British have gold here, and the Americans too, and the English are selling it for Swiss francs to buy their own war material."

I exclaimed, "But the pound sterling is the world's strongest currency!"

"If Germany occupies England, there will be no more pound sterling, and the betting is 80 to 20 that the Germans will invade and occupy England."

I sat with my mouth open.

"The English are decadent beyond belief. We must do what we can to help them."

After the war, I discovered that the Allies bought three billion Swiss francs and the Nazis 1.64 billion Swiss francs, in WWII. The Allies paid in gold that was not stolen.

Liska went on, "Our Foreign Minister, Pilet Golaz, is saying that we must mould ourselves to the new European realities, and if France falls – leaving Britain out of it – if just France alone falls, he'll come out openly that he's on the Nazi side. What Pilet is doing is telling the Swiss bankers to take and wash Nazi gold," she went on disgustedly. "There's some sort of nasty business going on between our Swiss head of military intelligence and the Nazi SD, and I'm sure the rival German intelligence under Canaris is probably working with some Swiss bank or the other."

I kept my face a mask.

Liska looked around the restaurant slowly, idly, and satisfied, went on: "German businessman, Johannes Bernhardt, runs the *Sociedad Financiera Industrial* in Spain. He was the man who forwaded the first letter from Franco to Hitler, asking for Nazi help for Franco's new rebel army, in July 1936. The SD in berlin sends Sofindus, as they call it. 50,000 Reichmarks a month, which somehow Bernhardt converts into pesetas. Someone in Madrid can use Reichmarks. Sofindus buys war chemicals for the Germans – it sends the Spanish ammonium sulphate, often in shipments of 10,000 tons, and Bernhardt pays in Swiss francs."

"What's that for?"

"Explosives."

Between 1939 and December 1944, Portugal's gold reserves grew by almost five times – Portugal being 'England's oldest ally'. This was looted Nazi gold, mainly from Belgium and France. In 1946, Portugal tried to pay for Polish coal with this gold, and the USA, Britain and France came down on Portugal like a diplomatic ton of bricks.

In 1996, the Bank of Lisbon admitted to getting Nazi gold and said, 'In the Second World War, our gold reserves did increase, but this was in return for our sale of goods and services, such as wolfram which is used in explosives (!!!) to Germany. They had no acceptable currency, so we were forced to take gold.'

Liska said, "The second pipeline in Switzerland for Nazi gold is the Bank for International Settlements in Basel. The President is a Yank, Thomas McKittrick; the General Manager, a Frenchman, Roger Auboin; the Assistant General Manager is a German and Nazi Party member, Paul Hechler. The directors include Nazi leaders Reichsbank Vice President Emil Puhl and his Chief, Walter Funk, as well as bankers from London, Rome and Japan – oh, yes, and Brussels too. Puhl comes here all the time to talk to McKittrick. And the Bank of International Settlements shares a chairman with the Swiss National Bank – Ernst Weber."

"My God," I whispered.

"The Bank works with Nazi gold, makes a big profit, and then sends part of the profits to London and Brussels! And in June 1931, just 18 months after they founded this bank, the BIS as they call it, invested 445 million gold Swiss francs in Germany, but with the financial crisis, they cut this back to 300 million. And it's still there – still making a profit, part of which is dutifully paid to London! They provided most of a credit of one billion American dollars to Germany in September 1931, and I think this still generates profits, some of which go to London!"

We finished lunch, and I explained that I wanted to look at some dresses before I went to the Argentinean Embassy.

Liska led me to the shops, but refused to come in. "What decadent bourgeoisie attitudes you have," she snarled, looking at the dresses in the big windows.

I spent half-an-hour looking at heavenly dreams of dresses, then bent my steps to the Argentinean Embassy.

From Berlin, I had sent a message to London to say I would not return to Germany. How would they extract me from Switzerland – what sort of Pass would I need to cross France – AND COULD I CROSS FRANCE WITH MY DRESSES?

Maximo Murphy de la Rua received me warmly, and gave, me a rich cup of coffee. He was very tall and thin, with a lined face and wispy red hair – he was very thin on top. He had amused, slow eyes, and smile-lines around his lips despite the lines etching the dry, pale skin of his face. I put him at forty.

He looked me up and down and studied my expression. Not taking his eyes from my face, he said very carefully, "We have a message from London, which I translated… er, decoded for you. I'm worried how you are going to react."

My heart lurched, and I felt a helpless lassitude.

He handed me the slip.

ENGLAND IN HOUR OF DESPERATE NEED REQUIRES EACH ONE DOES HIS/HER DUTY SOLDIERS CANNOT DESERT YOUR MSSGS CAN SAVE 100s 1000s OR MILLIONS BRITISH LIVES

I sat, numb.

Maximo said gently, "You have a hell of long message here, I think they sent it here in Geneva. They warned me from Berlin." He handed me pages of numbers.

"My God!" I groaned, "I've got to see Axel to keep up my cover. I'll need all night to code – sorry, I mean decode this, and then I've got to code it for London. This hasn't attracted any attention here in the Embassy?"

"None. It came in on a wavelength reserved for myself. Messages are coming in and going out all the time, and everyone has more than enough work without worrying about somebody else's cryptic messages."

He paused, watching me carefully.

"Listen. You explain the code to me – give me the key – we'll do a couple of lines together, and then I'll decode the whole thing. Then I'll encode it for London. Do you have a key for decoding?"

"HIS BREAKDOWN. And the code works like this …"

In fifteen minutes we had decoded two lines – I recognised the beginning of what Liska had told me about Switzerland.

"Now, to encode for London, the key is 86, dash, one, stroke: 86-1/."

Maximo said, "I take it that is a book – page 86, line one."

"Indeed, and the key word is SPOKE."

"So that would be the first word on line one of page 86? SPOKE? Is that correct?"

I nodded.

195

"Good," he said. "You've kept it easy and simple to remember. That gives us:

S	P	O	K	E	S	
A	B	C	D	F	A	
G	H	I	J	L	G	
M	N	Q	R	T	M	
U	V	W	X	*	U	* = Y, Z
S	P	O	K	E	S	

"Perfect," I said miserably.

I straightened myself. "Would you please preface the message with the following:

WILL RETURN BERLIN, WAR WILL END IN TWO MONTH IF YOU DECLARE WAR ON SWITZRLND ANNOUNCE THAT SWISS FRANC WORTHLESS AFTER WAR

"Then send the rest of the message they've sent us."

"Off you run," said Morphy de la Rua. "The less time you're in the Embassy, the better; if you leave now, you've had no time to send any message or get up to anything."

I walked back to the dress shops, dazed. I had to meet Axel at the Hotel Windsor bar a little after five.

How proud I had been to be British – to be English. My friend Evelyn in London – we often made a foursome with our boyfriends – she had her grandfather, who had told me about January 22, 1901. He said it was a bleak, harsh day, raining. And Queen Victoria lay dying at Osborne House, with the future Edward VII beside her bed, and her adoring grandson, Kaiser Wilhelm II too.

The grandfather said to me, "One courtier said that when she finally sank, she sank like a great three decker ship. So, they told Prime Minister, Lord Salisbury, who had been there at her coronation 63 years before. And y'know what Salisbury had to say? He said he'd never felt anything so much in his life."

The grandfather was someone who had been high up in the British government. He said, 'We lost our great Mother Empress, the Mother of the British Empire, Mother of the greatest empire the world had ever seen.' He said to me, 'My gal, you know what Lord Curson told us? The British Empire is the greatest instrument for good the world has seen, because it performs the noble work of governing India which had been placed by inscrutable Providence on the shoulders of the British race.' Curzon said, 'It is carved in granite and hewn in the Rock of Doom, that our work is righteous and that it shall endure.' God has blessed you, m'dear, that you have bee born in this Empire to bear sons to carry it forward.'

Another time, he told me, "On June 22, 1897, they celebrated Victoria's Diamond

Jubilee with 46,000 troops in the parade. You shoulda seen 'em. The plumes. The swords! The lances! Muslim *zaptiehs* in red fezes, camel corps of Indian troops, *dyaks* from Borneo, hussars from Canada, tall Australians and shining black regiments from Africa... gold in all the colours. *The Times* printed that Victoria's empire was the 'mightiest and most beneficial Empire ever known in the annals of mankind.' Our Empire numbered 375 million souls and 11 million square miles. At the Diamond Jubilee, Britain marshalled the mightiest fleet the world had ever seen – 165 warships with 3,000 guns, stretched out over 30 miles. We had 11 new battleships, of surpassing speed and armour, and 18 new cruisers. Aye, girl, this was the apogee of the Empire."

How proud I had been! How safe I had felt. And now these incompetent, timid men in London needed to lean on me. Depended on me to help save their cringing skins.

I suddenly realised I had marched into one of the dress shops, and at my stride, and the expression on my face, the salesgirl had retreated two steps.

I breathed slowly. "I was here before. I'd like to see the pale blue dress with..."

Two ecstatic hours passed, choosing three dresses; I asked the shop to buy me a suitcase, pack them carefully, and send it to my hotel. I parted with 600 dollars. In another shop, I brought 400 dollars of necklaces and bracelets for social functions, carried these in my handbag. At a third shop, I spent 500 dollars on *bonbon* chocolates and Brazilian coffee, asked them to put it in a lightweight crate, and send it to my hotel.

At ten-past-five, I sat at a table in the Hotel Windsor, looking at the lake, waiting for Axel to finish work...

Axel came in at 5.11 pm, tall, dressed in a dark grey banker's suit, with a pearly grey tie, darker grey stripes slanting across it, and daringly, a thin red line at each edge.

"Darling," he cried, when he saw where I sat. He hurried across and took my hand in both of his.

"You look like doomsday," he whispered, leaning across to me. "You really must act the part." His smile was faintly amused.

My voice was constricted. "I asked to be given papers to go back to England, and they refused."

"I should think so...!"

Then he whispered, "We have watchers here. What are they going to think?" He sat back, searched for a waiter, and beckoned.

197

"Coffee, please."

His face cleared.

"But of course! They are going to think we made love in Berlin and that your period hasn't come. Perfect."

He patted my hand reassuringly and made cooing sounds. I glared at him, and wanted to slap his face.

"Ah," he said in a low voice. "What a good actress you are. It's obvious I haven't mentioned marriage or a home for the baby. In some months, our dossiers will talk about your hysterical delay in your period."

With a physical effort, I brought my expression under control.

"What have you been doing?"

"I've bought three dresses for about 200 dollars each."

"You are frugal – I approve," he said, infuriatingly.

I gave a wan smile, and said ruefully, "They had dresses for 2,000 and 5,000 dollars. I've got Reichmarks, but no-one wants them. I've got a few dollars, that's all. Heydrich gave me 500 dollars for *bonbons* and coffee, and the shop has crated it for me."

"Did our common lady friend inform you?"

"She did, and her code message is in the Embassy – the Argentinean Embassy. Its on its way to London."

"That's right," he said. "Keep your face near mine, and turned away from the room. We have to worry about lip-readers. What we are going to do is this: we'll go to a restaurant for a bite to eat, and then back to your hotel. You put on one of your new gowns and we'll go to a nightclub. As this isn't Germany, we're actually allowed to dance in public."

* * *

We went for a long walk around the Lake, and explored some streets, window shopping; he led me to an exclusive restaurant. He spared no expense, and I enjoyed a light banquet.

Back at the hotel, he waited in reception while I went upstairs with my new suitcase. I opened it, and studied carefully how the top dress was folded.

I put it on and looked in the mirror.

The dress was a silvered grey, with a steep neckline, rising each side to flaring wings. A special bra, with a wide, heavy strap and four clasps, held it up. My bare shoulders and my cleavage showed in warm flesh, in warm contrast to the severe colour and cut.

I put on one of the new necklaces, dark green stones with pendant, that matched the dress, and wore a bracelet of stones in a lighter green.

Over this, I put a warm overcoat that buttoned up to the neck, with a warm scarf and gloves.

We took a taxi to a nightclub, and we went to our separate cloakrooms. I met Axel just inside, and his eyes widened. He took his bottom lip between his teeth.

"You got that dress for 200 dollars! You're going to spoil the evening for every other woman here tonight. Ah, base capitalism – what one must do for the cause of the working-class!"

A very adaptable communist, thank the Lord.

I took his arm, and he led me to a table.

We danced... and danced... and all those glances I got. An hour-and-half later, four older men with their wives came in, and nodded at Axel.

"They're senior bankers," he whispered.

Half-an-hour later, they invited us to their table, but I found the wives spoke only French. The men spoke English and German, but under the scrutiny of their ladies, were formal with me. I danced with them all, and itched to know what the wives had to say about me. Still, they were at least fifteen years older than I was and the men were very aware of it...

We did not get back to my hotel till 3 am, driven in the Rolls of the eldest banker.

Axel came at one o'clock, for lunch downstairs, at the Cornavin.

He said, "There's a train at two, for Chur. We're going to Sargans, that's just before Bad Ragaz. My sister has married a wealthy businessman in watches and clockwork, who has a chalet in a tiny hamlet in the mountains up above Sargans, and they're anxious to meet you. His name is Battig – Rudolf Battig."

I sat by the window as the train wound across Switzerland. Snow had fallen in parts; fog lay across the country in others – but occasionally I saw hand-manicured fields in deep green, with chocolate-box chalets and wooden farms, a quiet beauty that twisted my heart when I thought of Nazi Berlin waiting for me across the frontier.

At Sargans, Axel's sister waited for us in a Mercedes. Her name was Luce, and she spoke only French. We kissed on the cheeks, and she smiled reassuringly. In the car, she talked nineteen-to-the-dozen to her brother.

"Does she know anything about your undercover... er, interests?" I asked in German.

"Heavens, no! Capitalists to the hilt."

The road wound steeply up through thick, tall forests. Twice, just off from the road, I saw immense bunkers vanishing into the mountain side – great curves of dark green, reinforced concrete, some twenty-feet thick.

At the top, I strained to see the sign with the name of the hamlet. The posts stood, but they had taken the name down.

The car drove on to a wide, flat plateau, white under snow. On the far side, steep, snow-covered crags rose some four hundred feet higher. Over the white, flat expanse, iron beams rose in black contrast from the ground. Luce stopped the car in front of a very large chalet, in light and dark timbers, and I asked, "What are those beams?"

"To stop German planes from landing."

Beside the road, behind us, I had seen a pillbox, with absurdly large windows. "How can you defend that pillbox with those windows?"

"It's never locked. A hatch in the floor lifts up, and a ladder leads to a large underground storage room, with mortars, dismantled mountain artillery, machine-guns, and a lot of ammunition."

"Underground!"

"A lucky bomb could blew it to smithereens on the surface."

The house was wide, with a steep roof, that far overhung the wide veranda up on the first floor, with carved wooden balusters and head posts, and a thick timber railing.

Inside, I met two lady friends of Luce's – her husband was not here. They spoke French. Luce showed me my bedroom, at the back, on the ground floor, with a floor to ceiling double – window. The snow reached just above the woodwork, and touched the outside glass. The bed was very low on the floor, with a duvet instead of blankets.

We ate in a wide dining-room, with huge windows looking across the stark iron beams in the ground to the distant crags. Everyone spoke French, and I smiled politely. Axel translated a few words.

That night, I lay in my bed, and the moon came out, shining eerily on the snow, only some inches from where my head was. I stared at it for half-an-hour, trying to understand what had happened to the British Empire and to today's Englishmen. Someone rag once told me that the cream of British intellect had died in the Great War… today, only mediocre minds lived on.

Well, my mind was mediocre enough. I couldn't make sense of anything. The snow took on a slightly bluish glitter in the moonlight. So close to my bed!

Who was there to lead us, someone who would not humiliate and grind down Germany a second time, after Hitler hung from a British gallows?

I gazed at the snow. What a marvellous place!

After breakfast, I put on my country boots, and Axel led me to the Pillbox. He twisted a lever, and lifted up the hatch. I saw stairs leading down.

He led me across the wide expanse towards the crags. I saw about a dozen scattered houses, some with cattle standing around the entrances to the ground floor.

Axel said, "They live on the first floor, and keep the cattle downstairs in winter – under cover."

A farmer forked straw out on the snow, the cows filed out into the open air to munch it.

Axel told me, "It does the cows good to spend some hours outside, and that gives the men time to muck out the stables."

My boots slipped on the icy snow, and Axel got impatient waiting for me. He took my arm, and I shook him off.

Climbing the crags was dangerous, my boots slithering and skidding. We worked through a deep cleft, perhaps only one hundred feet above the plateau floor, and at the far end he led me to a rock outcrop.

We leant over, and saw a sheer drop, perhaps of two or three thousand feet, to tiny, green fields and roads underneath us.

"What fun if we only had parachutes," I said wistfully.

"I like it better up here," said Axel drily. "Look at those rock walls all the way down – you would probably swing in against them."

"You men are so practical," I complained.

"It's women who have their feet on the ground in this world," protested Axel. "We men are the thinkers, the poets, the dreamers…"

I looked at him quizzically.

"And it's you men who go to war."

Next day, I crossed the frontier.

A tall Gestapo officer in a black uniform, with a death's head badge, stepped forward smartly, gave me a pleasant nod, and I pointed to the crate.

He had it tied to the roof-rack of a dark-blue Mercedes, and we drove to the nearby airport, where a small plane was waiting. Five officers stood around talking, and after I climbed on board, they followed, took their seats together, and went on with their intent conversation.

In Berlin, a waiting car drove me to Prince Bernd's house.

END OF PART ONE

PART TWO

The night I came back from Switzerland, I sat upstairs in my bedroom, lights off, and pulled back the blackout drapes to look out at the Stygian darkness of the garden and a Stygian Berlin. The lights shone brightly in the streets of the Swiss cities. I was back in a world of uneasy foreboding, where sullen inklings nudged at the edges of my mind, where people in the streets carefully buried their trepidation. My melancholy slowly rose to a furor of wrath against the SIS – or whatever they called themselves – in London.

In Switzerland, I had eaten all the fruit and vegetables I could, and bought face-moistening creams. In the mirror, I examined my dry, sallow skin. It was a bit better, but when I used up the creams I had brought with me, it would get worse.

* * *

Downstairs, dinner was ready, and they all waited for me. At least with our hungry fare, we ate like kings compared to the ordinary people.

I handed over the three huge boxes of chocolates, and gave Thoma, Doris and their mother bottles of face-cream.

Joyous exclamations.

While I was away, Prince Bernd had bought – for 650 marks – a television set!

He switched it on, as we had our soup. Ilse Werner was whistling a song, then went on singing it. I had been worried about one of my dresses, bought in Genéve – but now a chorus line of girls danced, showing their legs right scandalously. The camera didn't even bother with their faces, but closed in on their bodies between their bosoms and feet.

Prince Bernd said drily, "For the Nazis, you are either with them, with all your heart, or you are not. Goebbels rounded up all his malcontents in the Propaganda Ministry and put them into television, where they couldn't do any harm. I've heard they were at their wits' end over programs, and Goebbels even considered closing them down. Now they're offering entertainment to wounded troops. The Ministry has put sets in the hospitals and convalescent centres, and opened a dozen free TV parlours in the city."

"We've nothing like this in England."

"We've had it since 1935, but a set cost about 2,000 marks, and it was on only some hours a day."

The Prince switched it off, so we could talk, and they swamped me with questions about Switzerland.

* * *

Before going to bed, I took the Prince aside, and said, "I've got to go early tomorrow to the Argentinean Embassy to send a message to my editor. I've got to tell Felix Guinjaime urgently that he had sent me one thousand American dollars through the Basler Handelsbank."

The Prince said thoughtfully, "Where Admiral Canaris sent you to with his filmed documents... You really believe the Gestapo followed you there – on Swiss territory?"

"I'm sure people were following me everywhere – Gestapo, Commies, and Swiss Secret Service."

"Some procession it must have been," smiled the Prince, gently.

"It was no joke," I said, hotly.

"Now, now, where is your famous English phlegm?"

I grinned at him.

I knew he worked in raw materials procurement.

"Could I drive in with you?"

He and his son Claus were usually away before we ladies were half out of bed, in the mornings.

"I work at the Reichswirtschafts-Ministerium, but I'm under the General-Bevollmächtigter für die Wirtschaft (at the Ministry of Economic Affairs under the Plenipotentiary-General for Economic Affairs)."

I said, "I've seen that. On Behren strasse, I think."

"Number 43-45. You have been getting around."

"That's not terribly far from Grossadmiral-Prinz-Heinrich strasse," I suggested humbly.

"Number 2-4," he grinned. "No, it's not far."

206

The Argentinean Embassy stood on the corner of Grossadmiral-Prinz-Heinrich strasse and Tiergarten strasse.

I asked him, "Where do you drop off Claus? Where does he work?"

"At the OKW, of course, the Oberkommando der Wehrmacht. That's on Tirpitzufer, and on Bendle strasse, numbers 3, 13, 14, 15, 16, 17, 18 and 20. Sometimes he has to go to one place, sometimes to another. There are also offices on Lutzowufer, 3 and 12, he goes to sometimes. Tomorrow, he goes to Bendle strasse, to begin with, so the Argentinean Embassy is no problem."

"I'll set my alarm early."

"I'll tell them to call you at quarter-to-seven."

Upstairs, I got ready my microdot message for Guinjaime. This was so urgent it would be transmitted from the Embassy itself in Berlin.

From my edition of Lorna Doone, by H. D. Blackmore, I chose page 447, line 7: "the wounded upon the carriage of bark and hurdles." The first five letters were "the wo".

T	H	E	W	O	t	...first vertical line
A	B	C	D	F	a	on the left,
G	I	J	K	L	g	repeated vertically
M	N	P	Q	R	m	on the right
S	U	V	X	Z	s	
t	h	e	w	o	t	X = XY

My message read:

447/7   IF ASKED ESSENTIAL YOU SENT ME THOUSAND DOLLARS AT BASLER HANDELSBANK.

I amended that to say: ESSENTIAL YOU SAY YOU SENT ME...

My first letter was "I", in IF. I consider "I" as the top right-hand cornier of a square formed by G I
        MN
So, I represent "I" by the bottom left-hand letter: M

I F A S K E D E S S E N T I A L
M K L Q P B J B O O B S F M L Q

Next morning, the Prince dropped me off at the Argentinean Embassy. Ruben Zorreguieta had come in early and was waiting; I carried in a large box of chocolates with fillings, and a box of cigars. He wanted to know what had happened in Switzerland, took my emerald ring with the microdot inside, and gave me an identical ring back.

"Felix won't be at his desk for another four hours" (Argentina's clocks ran four hours behind Berlin's) "and I'll send it to him then. What's in the boxes?"

"Swiss cheeses for Goebbels."

He chuckled.

I decided to walk, along Tiergarten strasse to Bellevue strasse, then pick up Herman Göring strasse to Voss strasse. In Herman Göring strasse, a black car slid to a stop, a Gestapo man got out, and ordered me to get in. Inside, I saw he was a SS Sturmmann. At Gestapo Headquarters, he took me to the second floor. I sat there for ten minutes, and a SS Haupsturmführer came in, and sat on the other side of the table.

"What are in the boxes?"

"Swiss cheeses, for Dr. Goebbels. I have put a note inside, in case he is too busy to see me personally."

He regarded me with a menacing, unblinking stare.

After I had brought all those presents for Heydrich – after Heydrich had laid on a plane for me – what was he playing at now?

"You have declared that in Belize, you worked in a clothing shop –"

"A drapery," I corrected.

"And you declared the name of the owner as –?"

208

"Trudy Ush. It's on Front Street, in Stann Creek."

"The ladies found she was not there, so what do you say?"

They had schooled me carefully on this on the ship sailing to and from Buenos Aires. They would make Trudy sign the Official Secrets Act, then give her money to go to San Antonio or Punta Gorda where hers would be the only draper's. They were not going to let anyone talk to her, and easily trip her up. She would put it about that she had a sister in Belmopan.

I said, "I think she had a sister in Belmopan."

"These ladies asked next door, and that's what they told them. The ladies were not allowed to visit Belmopan, because it is a military zone. They talked to the owner of the shop next door."

They had primed me on what to say.

"That would be an ironmonger's – or was," I corrected hastily.

"Mmm – yes, indeed. Who would the owner be...?"

"Ah, that's Dusshinta Mickler. Could he help them?"

"It appears he corroborates your story about a sister in Belmopan."

He turned and left.

An orderly came in and said, "Heydrich will see you."

He took me upstairs, and ushered me into his office.

Heydrich said, "Ach! Cheeses for Goebbels! Let me see. Ah – I like the chocolates you chose for me better."

I grinned at him.

"Not everyone plays the violin like you. Not anyone!" I laughed.

"You were throwing around American dollars in dress shops?"

"My Editor in Buenos Aires."

"He sent them to the Basler Handelsbank?"

"I see I have no secrets from, you."

"And your trip above Sargans?"

"Two huge bunkers built into the mountainside. Some bridges over gorges that could be blown. The village at the top – flat ground, with steel girders sticking up to stop planes landing. An underground arms cache."

"Why won't you work for us as a spy? Five hundred American dollars a month."

"Perish the thought," I said firmly. "As the English say –"

"That's not my cup of tea," he supplied. "And your dresses?"

"They're Parisian designs, and one is daring – I don't know whether I will be able to wear it."

"We'll have a concert tomorrow night at the sisters' place, and you wear it."

"I don't want to spoil your violin playing," I jested.

He laughed outright, then capped his earlier remark in English with another, also in English. "You're no shrinking violet."

"Oh dear," I said, "I'll try to be."

"Tomorrow night at eight-thirty," and he dismissed me.

I walked out of the building, and along to Wilhelm strasse.

Goebbels wasn't free, so Hans Schneppen took the boxes to give to him later.

At lunch time, at home, I rang the Gensorowsky sisters, and Margarete answered. I told her about Switzerland and my dresses, one of which was wicked. I said that Heydrich had commanded me to wear it to their place tomorrow at 8.30 pm.

"Do you have any sexy dresses – low on the shoulders and bosom, you know?"

"Playing for the Berlin Philharmonic doesn't much encourage that sort of thing Besides, we are a wee bit older than you" (ten years difference almost) "so we'll let you have centre stage for the evening's performance and we can just come in off from the wings, as it were." She was giggling. "I can't wait and I'm sure my sister will feel the same. Do you suppose he'll bring any of his chocolates?"

"If he doesn't, you can play a lot of wrong notes."

"That's a very good idea, but I'm afraid we could never do that, no matter how stern the provocation. We'll see you then."

I wondered whether the telephone was tapped, and this conversation would go back to Heydrich.

* * *

As I hung up, the phone rang again.

It was Axel Baer from Genéve. Had I arrived all right? How was Berlin?

When I heard him, one overweening feeling gripped me – I wanted to go back to Switzerland! I said hesitantly, without thinking, "I was wondering about next weekend...?"

"Not next weekend," he said, smoothly, like a shameless male who was keeping a desperate female at bay.

A Gestapo man listening in must have smirked; I gritted my teeth. Oh, did I want to go back to Switzerland!

Axel made a couple of affectionate, understanding noises, and then said he had to get back to work.

To keep up the charade, if he did not ring tomorrow, I would have to ring him the day after.

* * *

I had taken my seat for lunch when the phone went again.

"This is Lieutenant-General Piekenbrock," he said in English. "I am Deputy to Admiral Canaris, here at the Headquarters of the Military Intelligence Service and the Foreign Intelligence Services of the High Command of the Armed Forces. Would it be convenient for you to come here?"

Heydrich's bitter rival, under Canaris.

"I'm just about to have lunch. In, say, an hour?"

They drove me to Wilhelm strasse, to the Auswärtiges Amt or Foreign Office, where I had met with Adam von Trott. This astonished me, and I supposed this was not where his office was.

Generalleutnant Piekenbrock seated me comfortably in an armchair, and I chose hot chocolate over coffee, to be on the safe side. In Berlin, one got every sort of coffee, most of it not very palatable.

Without preamble, he said, "I'm interested in the trip from Sargans up into the mountains. Our Branch One collects military intelligence, and they were on to me about your trip."

"A very long, steep road," I began, when a uniformed stenographer came in, nodded at me, and sat down.

I repeated, "A very long, steep, road. They could probably blow parts of it off the mountain, and then they can blow the bridges. Two absolutely huge bunkers, dark green like the forest – you could drive lorries in. My guess is that they hold ammo and food and uniforms for years of fighting, and probably have a field hospital in there. They might extend for miles, so Swiss troops could pop out all over the mountainside, hidden in the forest. Attacking troops would have to struggle uphill through the forest – I suppose the Swiss would mow them down from above.

"When we got up to the village, it was a flat, mountain top plateau – I could see for about a mile. They had put vertical steel girders in the ground to stop planes from   landing –"

"Or gliders," Piekenbrock supplied.

"Gliders!" I echoed, not understanding. "Without engines?"

"A plane tows them, releases them at the right moment, and they glide to a landing with about 20 or 30 troops on board.'

He loved lecturing me, and I gave him a look of full admiration. The shorthand writer frowned.

"They have a big, underground arms cache, near the houses. About a dozen houses that I saw. Mostly mountain herdsmen, but a couple of holiday homes."

He nodded, thoughtfully.

I said cunningly, 'Do you want me to go back? Any more documents?"

He smiled. "No, thanks. Now we have established contact and codes with the Bank. You know, it's more than your life is worth to ever reveal what you did?"

I nodded, frightened.

"Would you like to work for us a spy?"

"The Nazi Secret Service asked me, and I said no."

'We'd pay you 300 American dollars a month."

"They offered me 500!"

"Six hundred, then!"

"No, thanks," I laughed. "I'm afraid I don't have the make-up for a spy. I like everything in the open, I'm sorry."

He said, very Germanic and serious, "You have been a great help, and it is appreciated."

Back home, the Hungarian attaché, Tibor Haraszti, the communist spy who alone in Berlin, had discovered my true British identity – thanks to Moscow – rang me.

"Saturday night, there's a dance at the Yugoslav Embassy. I told one of the attachés there, Yojislav Djindjic, about you, and he wishes to invite you."

With the British and French declaration of war against Germany, Hitler or the Nazis had forbidden dancing in public, in the night-clubs. All the Embassies were holding dances inside their buildings, which were not nominal German territory. Haraszti must have something that Moscow wanted transmitted to London.

"The Yugoslav Legation is a bit out of the way, especially coming from where you live. You can come into Berlin along Berliner strasse, that right? Well, that takes you into Charlottenburger strasse, but only go as far as the round Grosser Stern park, with the tower. Leading off that, you'll see Fasanerie Allee which runs into Lichten strasse Allee. At the end, that runs into Cornelius strasse, and Rauch strasse runs off Cornelius strasse at an angle, almost immediately. Actually, the Legation – I'm sorry, I'm getting mixed up – it's the Yugoslav Embassy. As we Hungarians have only a Legation, I keep seeing Legations where there aren't any. So, actually, the Embassy has a back entry on Cornelius strasse. It's Rauch strasse, 17-18. You first pass the Portuguese Legation right where Rauch joins Cornelius."

In modern Berlin, I believe Lichtenstrasse Allee, Cornelius and Ranch have been separated by new parkland.

"A dance," I said. "I'd love to go. Please thank Vojislav Djindjic."

I had been scribbling like mad and got it down.

No sooner had I hung up when the phone rang again. It was Dr. Goebbels.

"Thank you for your gift," he said warmly, in his loud voice. "I didn't realise you had been thinking about me."

"I still remember your cream cakes," I told him mischievously.

"Ah!" he said. "Women are usually unconscious of the efforts we men take to please them. How did your romantic quest come out?"

"Some country or the other has a saying that the course of true love never did run smoothly."

"Ah, that was Germany. Germany has the world's best literature, notwithstanding what the English might say. Don't you agree?"

"I'm a simply unworldly *mädchen* – a *chamaca* as they say in Mexico."

"And well you might have been," he laughed. "And well you might have been. You sound to me as though you're learning much too quickly."

Still laughing, he said, 'When you want to get back to work come along here and we'll find something for you to do."

It was mid-afternoon. I felt lazy, and went to the library to read Agatha Christie.

Then I went up to my room to code a message.

WILL USE GLIDERS CARRYING 20 OR 30 TROOPS TOWED BY
PLANES. SWISS HAVE EMBEDDED UPRIGHT GIRDERS ON FLAT GROUND. RECOMMEND BRITISH FARMS PLACE UPRIGHT POLES IN OPEN FIELDS. WATCH FLAT MOORLAND.

From Lorna Doone, I took page 509, line 2: "kindest, and the best, and the noblest of all men, John";

K	I	N	D	E	K	
A	B	C	F	G	A	
H	J	L	M	O	H	
P	Q	R	S	T	P	
U	V	W	X	Z	U	X = XY
K	I	N	D	E	K	

For the numbers, I took the first TEN LETTERS from Lorna Doone.

1	2	3	4	5
K	I	N	D	E
6	7	8	9	0
S	T	A	H	B

I signal the beginning of a number with the prefix BX and end it with the suffix WX.

So, CARRYING 20 OR 30 TROOPS came out as:

CARRYING	20		OR	30	TROOPS
MJXXKCFH	BXIBWX		PX	BXNBWX and so on...

214

I went downstairs, microdotted it, and put the dot inside a ring with a blue stone.

That night, at dinner, Doris's fiancé came, Richterin Prieguity, in Luftwaffe Technical Planning.

Over dessert, he said, "Ray, I suppose you were wondering whether the British fighter pilots could stay in the air for the first three weeks, to learn the tricks and dodges of dog-fighting. I think you said you hoped the Spitfire were superior enough to keep them alive for that time.

"Well, we have the new JU88, for which the Luftwaffe had great hopes. It's got two engines, putting out about 2,000 horse, and double rudders. Göring hoped it would be a fighter-bomber, because the new Messerschmidt 109 only puts out 1,300 horse. We had a crack Squadron, Kampfgeschwader 30, at Sylt. That's on the island of Westerland, off the coast of Schleswig-Holstein, and Hauptmann Helmut Pohle commanded it. He's one of our best.

"On the 16th, they raided Scotland, the Forth Estuary, going for naval vessels anchored near the Forth Bridge and the naval base at Rosyth. Pohle led, and attacked the battleship, HMS Repulse and the cruiser Southampton. The destroyer, HMS Mohawk, was under steam, sailing with a convoy.

"Well, this wasn't Poland. British fighters attacked, broke up the JU88s. They shot down Pohle's plane into the sea off Crail, and now we've had news through the Red Cross that two crewmen were killed, and his wireless operator wounded, seriously. A local fishing boat fished Pohle out of the sea. The two dead airmen, Kurt Seydel and August Schleicher, had their bodies recovered, and were buried with full military honours.

"They shot down another bomber near the Isle of May, inside the Estuary, piloted by Oberleutnant Hans Storp, and a fishing boat rescued them all except the rear-gunner, Obergefreiter Kramer, who they haven't found.

"The secret facts are that we lost four planes, four airmen dead and four prisoners. The English know about a third plan, that crashed on the Borders, but a fourth one crashed west of Etten, near Breda in Holland.

"This changes the whole complexion of the war. We don't dare tell Göring or Hitler, but if we can't defeat the RAF, we can't invade England. These would be pretty green pilots, in as far away a place as Scotland, and they smashed our attack. Now, we will have to use the JU88s only as bombers, with fighter escorts to protect them. If we couldn't defeat those pilots, I doubt that in the long run we can win the war before America comes into it."

Deep silence fell over the table.

My heart was bursting. At least there were some chaps up to the job! I wasn't alone any more. Perhaps I wasn't wasting my time after all!

* * *

No one wanted to go to bed, we were all so excited.

Very late, we turned on our illegal, hidden shortwave radio, and got William Shirer, broadcasting from Berlin to the United States.

He said that tonight he had been chatting to Field Marshal Göring. And where did he run into him?

At the Soviet Embassy, where they were celebrating the anniversary of the Bolshevik Revolution!

He said Göring had a beer in one band, and a long cigar in the other; Shirer sounded him out on America selling thousands of planes to the Allies. Shirer wondered whether Göring would be "peeved".

Göring joked about whether America could really build planes, so Shirer riposted by asking whether Germany could build as many a month as they could in the States.

"If we could only equal your speed in making then, we'd be really weak," Göring said.

Shirer wanted to know whether he'd hit the Allies with massed aerial attacks before the Yankee planes arrived.

Göring told Shirer, "You build yours, and our foes can build theirs, and then the day will come when we'll see who has been building the best and the most."

Shirer said that the French claimed to have shot down a lot of German planes. Göring laughed and said that if they had shot down so many, then he knew it wasn't German planes.

Shirer asked him why it was that Germany had only attacked British warships. Göring told him that it gave their pilots practice.

The writing was on the wall, and Göring hadn't seen it.

Next morning, I went to the Argentinean Embassy and handed in my ring. I told Rubén, "You can transmit this from Genéve. Friday night, the Hungarian has arranged for me to go a dance at the Yugoslav Embassy. If anyone asks, I've come here this morning to ask you about the Yugoslav Embassy."

Rubén laughed. "I've been there for receptions, but I don't know anything about it. Let's say I told you that the Yugoslavs are horny."

"What's that?"

"They are men of ardour," he grinned.

At the Propaganda Ministry, I told Schneppen that Oberstleutnant Richterin Prieguity had invited me to the Generalluftzeugmeister at Jeben strasse 1.

"What does the Oberstleutnant do there?"

"He's in Luftwaffe Technical Planning."

"I'll give you three rolls of film. You photo as many joyful faces of our brothers in the air as you can."

Schneppen was growing more jocular every day.

"It's an excellent idea and Dr. Goebbels can write all sorts of captions. Imagine!"

He stopped me at the door.

"Just a moment. There's a car going that way..."

He spoke on the phone.

"You can meet the car downstairs."

I thanked my lucky stars for the lift. The place lay on the other side of Tiergarten, just beyond the Zoo, and the car whipped along the

Charlottenburger Chaussee in no time.

Richterin had talked to his bosses, and I was spoilt from the moment I put foot in the door. These good-looking boys and men, all grins, planning how to blow Europe and England to smithereens...their high, good humour was irresistible, their jollity, laughter and jokes. They obviously loved every minute of their job and were supremely sure they'd pulverise everything before them. I went through the three rolls before I knew it, and had a gallery of some of the handsomest faces in the city.

Heydrich rang to put off the concert for tomorrow.

That night, at eight o'clock, we listened to Hitler railing and raging against England. He was in the Munich Beer Hall to celebrate the 1923 Munich Beer Hall Putsch, with his Old Guard at the Bürgerbräu. He went on and on, and then ran out of steam. I suppose he'll be there all night, reliving the old days with old cronies.

* * *

I thanked Richterin when he came in.

"Actually, I didn't take you to Planning. They look after munitions, and that sort of thing, at Jebin strasse. Planning in the Ministry, we are solemn and wise, and I'm sure Goebbels will thank you for photos of delighted German youth on a killing spree rather than of we worried fogies."

When we came down to breakfast, Princess Jutta told us, "They rang my husband before he left. Last night, they tried to kill Hitler."

We stood still – stunned.

"Hitler escaped. No one knew he was going to Munich, till an hour before. He finished his speech at 9.05 –"

"That would be right," I whispered. "He warned the war could last five years. That soon there'd be surprises –. He cursed England till be was hoarse."

The Princess said, "He hurried off at 9.10 pm to catch his train for Berlin. He didn't stay with his Old Guard, as he always has, swigging beer. He wanted to get to his military henchmen in Berlin. They put the bomb in the empty attic of the Bürgerbrä Keller. It went off at 9.21."

Thoma said, "Doris and I have been there. It's an old dump, with rooms and passageways all over the place. The main beer ball is about 50 meters by about 30. The walls and ceilings are thick."

"They told your father it was a hefty bomb. About 1,000 people had squeezed into the hall, and almost all the killed and injured were buried under the debris. The explosion didn't get them. The lights stayed on and no one panicked – the rest worked pulling the beams and bricks off the victims. They put the bomb right above Hitler's rostrum, where he spoke for an hour, and now it's under two metres of heavy rubble."

I groaned, "Some black, leathery, mad-eyed demon came up out from the brimstone of Hell –"

Grandmother Gabriele said briskly, "He must have a sixth sense, girl. God help us if he has a sixth sense. No one will ever assassinate him unless they decide to die with him. Only Nazis and commies would do that."

I got the words out through gritted teeth. "WHO KNEW?"

"Almost no one," said Princess Jutta. "Some workman might have put it there on the off-chance."

"Off—chance! Bah!" said Princess Gabriela.

Heydrich! I thought. Heydrich! It couldn't be the British. London'd be lucky to kill the snails in their own back gardens.

"Oh, damn!" I said. "The rostrum under two metres of heavy detritus. That would have buried him and broken every bone in his body."

"They told my husband that Himmler has been working all night."

By midday, I had seen the newspapers. The Völkischer Beobachter – the newspaper of racial mysticism, national spiritual purity and anti-semitism, inspired by the demagogue Alfred Rosenberg whose fanatical books sold millions – promised horrendous deaths to the plotters.

The Allies hanged Rosenberg at Nuremburg, and he died in only 90 seconds, the luckiest Nazi. Most of the hangings were bungled, some taking 20 minutes of slow strangulation. The Nazis always hanged their victims in this agonising way.

The rest of the Press blames the British Secret Service. Ha! Luckily, only Graham Bunton knows about me; otherwise, the SIS would have me carrying bombs all over the city, the idiots.

Later in. the afternoon, I learned that Heinrich Himmler had travelled to Munich with Hitler – so Heydrich knew.

The newspapers are going on about that arch-fiend, Chamberlain, planting the bomb in the ceiling. I doubt whether Chamberlain knows how to load a revolver. That infernal demon of a Chamberlain has *personally* tried to see Hitler dead, they say.

We heard Shirer on our secret shortwave set, and he repeated the ranting against our pitiable Prime Minister.

Shirer pointed out that Hitler had had a last minute change in his plans. Usually, he begins his speech at 8.30 pm. and declaims on till 10 pm. Shirer said the bomb was not in the attic, but in a pillar just behind the rostrum. The explosion would have shredded Hitler. Blowing out the pillar brought down the roof. That uncanny sixth-sense makes Hitler the most dangerous man history has seen – more than the Ghengis Khan, who never commanded the destructive power of the German Armed Forces.

After dinner that evening, Claus took me aside into the library. He said, "I've got a list here of the German High Command, you can send to London."

I glanced over it.

"But they know that!" I complained, "This is an awful lot of work for me, for Rubén, and for the wireless transmitter operators."

Claus said grimly, "I doubt whether they do know it. I doubt whether they have given the matter any thought at all. I am sure Chamberlain couldn't care less, and the British High Command neither."

"I'm going to feel silly – be made to look silly," I pouted.

"My dearest Ray – it's your job. It's what you've come here for."

"I've got to get dressed. Heydrich is sending a car for me at eight o'clock."

* * *

I put on the most daring dress of the three from Switzerland – cut like a Chinese dress, with a high collar, no sleeves, and slit way up the side to show my thigh above the knee. The colour was a devil's red, with swirling black and gold strokes – the Nazi colours – and the swirls turned my prim bosom into an exuberant breaking surf. *Que balcon*, as the French would have said, where my *dons de la nature* were modest. I wore a thick overcoat, but downstairs Thoma and Doris demanded to see, and the men's eyes popped. The swirls contradicted the provocative seemliness of the high Chinese neck.

The car drove me to another address – a huge flat, with rich furniture and hangings. The Gensorowsky sisters hurried to help me off with my coat, to see the dress. Heydrich gave a slow smile. Our hostess was an opera singer, Lore Steinle, whose eyes snapped when she saw me. She was hefty, and did not need my feeble optical effects; her *balcon* was all too solid flesh, and when she drew in a deep breath, as if to go for a high note, and show me what was what, Heydrich gave a faint nod.

However, this Wagnerian maiden was in her early forties, which I felt was lucky – you don't compare draft horses with racing ponies. Heydrich seemed to follow every shade of expression on my face, so I asked him about the bomb.

"We'll get him," he said dismissively.

221

What would Hitler think, when he learned we were having an impromptu concert instead of hunting down the bomber?

Would he punish us?

* * *

Our little concert was glorious. Lore Steinle sang pieces from operas I loved, and Heydrich outdid himself on the violin.

* * *

At home, Claus had left a note, asking me to get up at seven, to have breakfast with him and his father.

* * *

My alarm went off at a quarter-to-seven, and blearily, I washed my face, combed my hair, threw on some clothes and shoes and went down to breakfast. The two men greeted me with cheerful energy at that ungodly hour.

"Well," said Claus, "Here are the lists and commentaries. The Commander-in-Chief of the Army is Walter von Brauchitsch, who's 58; Hitler named him Oberbefehlshaber des Heeres in February, last year. He fully knows of the officers' plot against Hitler, but he remarried last year, and his second wife is a fanatical Hitler fan, who gives him no respite. Hitler forked up the money for his settlement with his first wife. General Ludwig Beck has tried to persuade him several times to come over to the Resistance, but he's caught between the force of Hitler's personality and his domestic life. On August 10, last year, Hitler called his generals to his Berghof house and gave them a tongue-lashing – he flayed them – and Beck resigned in high dudgeon. Brauchitsch declared his subservient loyalty.

"Gerd von Rundsted is 68, and last year, in February, Hitler purged him from the Army. He's not a convinced Nazi, but he once told Rommel, "You are younger. You must do it." Hitler reinstated him in August this year, and gave him Army Group South.

"Fedor von Bock has Army Group 1 and he's 59. He's a rabid, hard bastard of the old school, and commanded the army that took Austria.

"Erwin von Witzleben commands Army Group II and he's 58.
He's one of the leaders in the Resistance against Hitler, and will become Commander-in-Chief of the Armed Forces when we kill Hitler. (In the July

222

Plot of 1944, they hanged him).

"Johannes Blaskowitz is 56, and commands Army Group III. He advocated this pact we have with Soviet Russia, 'a sacred though sad duty', so we could take Poland. He led his Third Army into Bohemia when Hitler took Czechoslovakia. He led the Eighth Army into Poland, towards Posen, and do you know what! can you believe it! at one point he made a cunning, tactical retreat. Hitler went berserk, and considered charging him with treason! Now Blaskowitz is commander-in-chief of the army of occupation in Poland. What he doesn't know is that many of his staff are members of the conspiracy against Hitler. (He was brought to trial at Nuremberg as a minor war criminal, and committed suicide.)

"Gunther Hans von Kluge – he's 57 – is commander of Group IV, which took the Polish Corridor in the first days of the war. Hitler purged him last year, then took him back. He's a 'non-Nazi', that's the best way to put it. He seesaws from the Resistance to support of Hitler, then back again. He's more comfortable obeying Hitler, I think.

"Wilhelm List is 59, and he commands Army Group V. He's one of Hitler's 'good' boys. (Nuremberg condemned him to life imprisonment, but released him at Xmas, 1952.)

"Then we have the unholy trio, who work alongside Hitler and are in his pocket. Well, I'll amend that. Walter Warlimont – he's 44 – is a convivial army man, who recommended the reorganisation of the armed forces under one supreme command – this was to snip off the power of the high military caste and put it into the hands of Hitler. Hitler ordered it done, and he promoted Warlimont to deputy of Jodl in the Wehrmachtsfuehrungsstab — the Operations Staff.

"The second man of the unholy trio is Alfred Jodl, 49, who comes from a family of philosophers, priests and lawyers. He's got a brilliant brain, and is Hitler's chief adviser on strategy. He's always at Hitler's side.

"The third man is Wilhelm Keitel, who's 57, and Chief of the High Command, Hitler's top military adviser, and second only to Hitler in power. He wears a monocle. They call him 'Lakai', 'Keitel the flunky'. They also call him 'the yes-donkey'. He has a middling brain, and a chilly reserve." (Nuremberg hanged him. He asked to be shot.)

Claus handed me the sheets. What a task I had!

It was Armistice Day, but no one remembered.

I finished encoding and microdotting after midday.

The phone rang.

It was Albert Speer. "Hitler invites you to lunch tomorrow," he said tersely. "At the Chancellery. A car will come at midday for you. I'll see you there," he added, comfortingly.

I ran to Princess Jutta, and to the grandmother, Gabriele.

223

Consternation!

Princess Jutta said, "You must have lunch next door, with Axel. He can tell you lots about Hitler."

Count Axel Hohenlinden was Prince Bernd's brother, and had a schloss next door.

Princess Jutta got on the phone to Axel, hung up, and told me, "He's expecting you."

* * *

As I ferreted around for the box of chocolates I had brought him from Switzerland, I tried to remember everything I knew about Hitler. Master of lies, of awakening panic and horror, of cruelty without mercy, the incarnation of Satan, he was well on the way to destroying the world I knew, giving it over to violence with techniques of war I barely comprehended. If he conquered the lands about him, overthrew Britain, he would be a mighty monolith to tyranny, the greatest in the history of civilised man. The Germans saw in him revenge, a savage overthrow of the Carthaginian peace, raising Germany to exalted power and malevolent retaliation. He was an evil Machiavelli who stood well to bring my western world to its nadir – or thrust it back into a barbarity of thousands of years ago. In his way stood my countrymen – old-womanish men – and effete Frenchmen. A black, infernal creature, sent to encompass the twilight of the gods themselves.

I crossed our garden, went through the poster gate in the wall, negotiated Axel's lovely garden walks, and rang his bell. He himself opened the imposing door, and ushered me inside.

He took my offerings of chocolates and a tin of Argentinean corned beef with delight.

At the table, as we waited to be served, I said, "Where did this man spring from? He must have had parents, grandparents...what, in God's name, spawned him?"

Axel settled back luxuriously. He loved talking, and he loved showing what he knew.

"As you know, his family wasn't German. They came from Waldviertel, a small village some 50 miles north-west of Vienna. The people there were hard, poor, suspicious. We suppose his grandfather was Johann Georg Hiedler, a mill worker who married a Maria Anna Schicklgruber, a maid, in May 1842. This marriage came five years late – after she gave birth to a boy, Alois, in 1837. We can only suppose Johann was the true father of Alois. Alois carried the name Schicklgruber till he turned 40. Alois registered Johann Georg Hiedler as his father, but on the birth certificate, they spelt

224

Hiedler as Hitler.

"Alois Hitler lost his first two wives. He chased the ladies, was a bit rootless and drank too much. He married Anna Glass in 1864 and she died childless in 1883. A month later, he took Franziska Matzelberger to the altar – they were already into an affair, and had had one son, Alois. Three months after the wedding, they had Angela. In 1884, this second wife died of TB, but Alois had a third wife ready. On January 7, 1885, Alois, now 47, married Klara Poelzl, 24, his second cousin. She was pregnant, and they had a special dispensation from the Vatican.

"Klara gave Alois Hitler six children – four sons and two daughters, but only Adolf Hitler and his sister, Pauline, survived infancy. Adolf came into this world at 6.30 pm on April 20, 1889, in the Gasthof zum Pommer, an inn in the small town of Braunau am Inn, close to the German border. Being cousins, we don't know what genetic damage there was. Adolf Hitler is basically ugly. He might be insane in several different ways. Adolf lost touch with Pauline, but kept close to his half-sister, Angela, and he had an incestuous love of Angela's daughter, Geli Raubal, in the late 1920s. Probably, but not certainly, this incestuous relation drove Geli to shoot herself in Hitler's Munich flat in 1931.

"Adolf's mother loved him very much, and he loved her greatly in return. She gave him his way, and he always carried her photo in his wallet. His father was unyielding and bossy, and Hitler hated it. His father used the whip on him to exact total obedience; his father wanted Adolf to prepare for the civil service, but Adolf wanted to be an artist. Hitler himself has said, 'I never did love my father. So that made me fear him all the more. He had a shocking temper and often whipped me.' In *Mein Kampf*, we read that his father was an ill-paid customs official and his family lived in near poverty – nonsense! Alois Hitler enjoyed a prosperous career in the Imperial Customs Service. Between 1885 and 1895, he won promotions and had an imposing uniform. He was a senior Hapsburg official and his family lived on the well-to-do scale that meant. Adolf Hitler was a well-dressed, middle-class boy, who wanted for little."

The maid served soup – thick, warming potato soup with herbs from his herb garden.

"To give you an idea how well off was Hitler as a boy, they had a commanding house in wide, landscaped grounds at Braunau am Inn, and from there, they moved to a grand apartment in Bavaria, at Passan, from 1892 to 1895. Hitler's father retired with a bounteous pension, and bought a dignified country house on nine acres of land at Hafeld, 30 miles outside Linz.

"In 1897, the family shifted to the compact country town of Lembach, to a wide-spread third-floor apartment, facing a Benedictine monastery. Then, still enjoying their privileged lifestyle, they moved to a gracious home with a big garden in Leonding, another village just outside Linz.

"This made Hitler change schools. His first primary school was at rural Lambach, where his school-fellows liked him, and he got good grades. But at his next school, at Leonding, he suddenly turned uncommunicative, resentful, with mood swings. With parents who were cousins, we don't know what insanities he could have inherited, but here we have an inkling that something is not right. Because I *do* believe Hitler is insane – well, psychologists have a word, *psychopathic*, which means that you can appear all right a lot of time, even engaging, but you can inflict unspeakable evil without feeling anything.

"Anyway, as I say, trouble began at Leonding, and his marks fell, never to pick up again at primary school.

"In September, 1900, Hitler launched on his secondary education at the private, fee-paying Realschule in Linz – a school to prepare you for commercial, technical or civil service exams. Hitler's marks wavered between 'average' and 'good', but, really, all that interested him was history – his teacher excited him with talk of German nationalism; geography – he never tired of maps; and art, about which he grew passionate. His teachers reported him a sullen, lazy student with mood swings.

"Afterwards, Hitler tells us that at the Realschule he first became a German nationalist. That may be as it may. He is also untiring, talking about the 'bitter poverty' of his boyhood. More than once in recent years he has said, 'I never trust a well-educated man, a professor or teacher. Their minds are full of rubbish. They can't see the real world, only theories.'

"However, he tells us that then his heroes became Frederick the Great and Otto von Bismark. And the fact is that outside school, Hitler played war games – also cowboys and Indians. Hitler always identified himself with the Red Indians, the crushed race. He devoured boys' books on Cowboys and Indians by Karl May, who was translated into English. He read war comics, and reconstructed the Boer war in his games – again, taking the part of the underdog Boers."

We had begun the second course without my realising it, and both of us sipped wine.

"On January 3, 1903," Axel went on, "Alois Hitler died of lung haemorrhage, but this seems to have released energies in his son, Adolf. His father's unforgiving domination ended, and Hitler now dreamed of becoming 'a great artist.' His mother, Klara, still got a little less than half of her husband's pension, and a sizeable lump sum. Further, each child got a lump sum, and 240 kronen a year till they turned 24. Hitler had been walking three miles to school every day, so now he talked his mother into letting him board in Linz. This worsened his emotional instability, and he had to resit his exams right through secondary school, till the school director got fed up with him.

226

He told him to take his final year at the Realschule in Steyr, about 25 miles away, so Hitler went into lodgings there. His mother had moved to a small flat in the middle of Linz, and sold the house at Leonding.

"Free of secondary school, Hitler lived the life of a young Bohemian, his hair long, good clothes of the sort favoured by artists and a typical moustache. A young dilettante around town, he slept till noon, and spent the afternoons in art galleries or libraries, or meeting friends in cafés. In the evenings, his good friend August Kubizek, a notable musician, took him to the opera and to concerts. Hitler loved Wagner.

"Outwardly, he was normal and balanced, and living a good life.

"But two traumas quickly destabilised him. In January, 1907, his mother had breast cancer. Her mastectomy went well, so Hitler got her to withdraw his inheritance of 700 kronen to go to Vienna to win admission to the famed Vienna Academy of Fine Arts. A school dropout, he was aiming awfully high. He rented a small flat in Vienna, took his exam, and failed dismally.

"I suppose nowhere in human history can we find human destiny so turned around by the indifferent 'no' of a few forgotten art teachers. So small a thing! It does show us how   accidents shape our fates.

"Their 'no' played havoc with Hitler's feelings. He described the teachers as 'fossilised bureaucrats devoid of any understanding of young talent.'

"Now, we must get things straight here. Hitler was a good artist, but of no originality. He could copy with technical perfection; he could paint buildings and landscapes with a high skill. He couldn't paint people. His paintings show no psychological abnormality. He has a strong instinct for architecture. His knowledge of art today is deep and often encyclopaedic. Perhaps, he could have made a career as an art critic.

"In October, 1907, came a second, devastating blow. His mother's cancer was terminal.

"Hitler hurried home to her bedside, and nursed her night and day. She succumbed on December 21, 1907.

"The family doctor was Dr. Bloch, who said, 'In all my career never have I seen anyone so devastated by grief as Adolf Hitler.' Bloch was a Jew, but Hitler said, 'I will be grateful to you for the rest of my life.' And Hitler has kept his word. Bloch is untouchable.

"In February, 1908, Hitler went back to Vienna and stayed there for five and half years. Next month, in March, his close friend, Kubizek, joined him – Kubizek had got into the exclusive Vienna Academy of Music. The two shared an apartment for months. Hitler wrote poetry, tried to write a play, and an opera set in Iceland. As before, Hitler went to the opera three nights a week, but in summer, Kubizek went home for holidays. Hitler tried yet again to get into the Academy of Fine Arts, and in October he failed. The second 'no' almost destroyed Hitler – it thrust him into a dangerous depression – and in November Kubizek came back to an empty flat. Hitler had left no forwarding address – he could not face his only friend in the world.

"Today, Hitler tells us his days in Vienna were the most afflicted of his life. He didn't try to get a real job. He kept changing apartments. By summer, 1909, his money had dwindled so he had to sleep in the open, usually on park benches. I think one of his forms of insanity had taken over. He was down and out in Vienna about three months, but he makes a lot of it in Mein Kampf. He tells us he worked as a labourer and sold paintings to buy a loaf of bread, but I don't believe the 'labouring' business for a moment. He did sell paintings. People I managed to talk to seemed to find him full of ideas, grandiose thoughts and intolerance, and pretty idle.

"In October, he got off the streets, into the Meidling men's hostel, financed by a wealthy family of Jews. He made a new friend, Reinhold Hanisch, an out-of-work servant with street 'smarts' who hailed from Berlin. Hanisch put it to Hitler that he could write to his well-off relatives and ask for money to buy artist's materials. Hanish suggested he could sell Hitler's postcards and paintings for a 50% cut, so Hitler wrote to his aunt Johanna who sent him 50 kronen. Hitler bought a winter overcoat and artist's materials.

"Hitler lodged at Männerheim, a better-class hostel, for workers with low wages, in December. You paid three kronen a week, but you could use the showers, a reading-room and a laundry. You had to stay out of your room during working hours, so Hitler painted near a window in the large dining-room.

"We can safely say that he did between 700 and 800 paintings –"

Count Axel paused, while the maid cleared our plates, and brought us dessert.

After the maid had gone, he went on, "He did paintings, postcards and drawings in black-and-white, this between 1909 and 1913, but his partnership with Hanisch came to a bad end in 1910 when Hitler laid charges against Hanisch for stealing his share of the proceeds from a painting of the Vienna Parliament. Hanisch was eight days in jail.

"The deep evil and cruelty hidden in Hitler came out in 1936. The Gestapo arrested Hanisch and he died on February 4, 1936 from 'a heart attack' in custody. A deadly rancour after TWENTY FIVE years! This is the man who leads us.

"Well, to come back to my story. By the end of 1910, Hitler was flush again. He must have been getting about 80 kronen a month from his paintings. His Aunt Johanna gave him what would have been a huge sum –

228

some 3,800 kronen. He even bestowed his orphan's pension on his half-sister, Angela. To stay on at Männerheim, you couldn't earn more than 1,400 a year, but stay he did. It was cheap, he could paint there, and he had other men to talk to.

"Politics didn't interest him. He saw himself as an artist and 'a coffee-house Bohemian'. In Mein Kampf he tells us the opposite, because he had to paint himself as a visionary politician from his earliest days, but we don't have to take his book seriously. And from what we know, he wasn't anti-Semitic, but thought of Jews as a religious group. He tells us that 'Gradually, I had ceased to be a weak-kneed cosmopolitan and become an anti-Semite.' The fact is that many of his friends were Jewish; he tried to sell his paintings through Jewish art dealers because he thought they were more honest, and he went to musical evenings at the home of a Jewish family. No, this form of his insanity festered after 1918.

"In May, 1913, he broke away from his loneliness and lowly achievement in Vienna to go to Munich, in Germany. Germany's nemesis had come to German soil.

"He came from no love of Germany but to dodge the draft – he freely tells us today that he was a draft-dodger, but he says it was only because he didn't want to join the Austrian Army. On January 20, 1914, the Austrian Army tracked him down and demanded to know why he was not doing military service. Hitler had to go to Salzburg to give an account of himself, but next month, a recruitment panel turned him down as 'unfit for service' because of a weak chest.

"Hitler tells us that his time in Munich, before the Great War, was 'the happiest and most tranquil of my life'. He lodged with a tailor's family, Josepph Popp, for 20 marks a month, and the family, some twelve years later, told me he was a loner. He painted, spent long hours in his room, and read.

"When the Great War broke out in august, 1914, Hitler later wrote that 'I am not ashamed to say that, carried away by exaltation, I fell to my knees and gave thanks to heaven from a full heart for my happy destiny of living at this very moment.' He straightaway volunteered for the German Army, and the Bavarian List Regiment took him. He spent most of the war either as a motorbike despatch rider, or carrying messages from Staff to the front-line troops on foot – very dangerous. He felt passionately about the fortunes of the German Army, and this focussed his life, fed his German nationalism. He showed himself as an admirable soldier, winning the Iron Cross, Second Class, in August, 1914, and the Iron Cross, First Class, in August, 1918 – this last, a high award reserved for professional soldiers and seldom given to a volunteer like Hitler. A Jewish officer recommended him for it.

"Fellow soldiers found Hitler a bit weird. He didn't ask for leave, never got letters. His relentless patriotism got on the nerves of some. The Battle of the Somme gave him a bad wound in the leg, and in October, 1918, a mustard attack blinded him for some days. He was in hospital when the news broke of Germany's defeat. 'Everything went black before my eyes; I felt my way, staggering, back to the ward, and fell upon my bunk, hid my burning eyes in my blanket and pillow. All of it in vain.'

"This instant awoke Hitler politically. Germany had been stabbed in the back by socialists, Jews and democratic politicians. So it's no surprise that Hitler never accepted the Weimar republic, and when this new government signed the Treaty of Versailles – which turned out to be an ignominious one, as the French and British spurned President Wilson's idealism on which the Weimar leaders were counting – the German right saw the Weimar government as traitors.

"Against Wilson's warnings, the British and French reduced the German army to 100,000 men, took 13% of its territory, all its colonies, and demanded a payment of £6.5 billion in reparations.

"In November, 1918, a seething Hitler went back to Germany but stayed in the army. Bavaria was in turmoil. Socialists deposed its king, but an army officer assassinated Kurt Eisner, a Jew, when he set up the people's republic. The workers revolted and formed a worker's republic. In February, 1919, troops with the Freikorps – patriotic thugs and ex-soldiers – crushed the workers. Gustav von Kahr finally imposed a government of the extreme right.

"Hitler was the right man at the right place at the right time...or the wrong one! He completely backed those who wanted to crush the left, and later, they backed him in his rise to power."

Back home, after a light evening meal, I put on the third dress I had bought in Genéve. It was cut like a classical Greek costume, in white, with a rectangular collar back and front, edged in burnished gold cloth that ran over the shoulders. A gold band of the same cloth lightly drew it in at the waist; below the waist, the dress fell in tiered pleats of the classic mode to above my ankles, and the same burnished cloth edged the bottom. There were oohs and aahs from the family, so I put on my ankle-length overcoat with a thick scarf.

I wore my hair in two coils over my ears – what fashion writers had taken to calling 'earphones'.

Reinhard drove me to the Embassy, and I asked for Vojislav Djindjic, the attaché, to thank him for inviting me. Djindjic introduced me to people of the Embassy staff, and Mladen Zizc, with thick black hair, a saturnine face lightly pitted from smallpox, intent eyes and a big-boned body took my arm possessively. He helped me put away my overcoat and scarf, stared directly at my dress, and led me into the first dance. He monopolised the next two, talking about the German danger in the Balkans. His big hand felt my body under the dress, and I said lightly, "Do you think the Germans will want the wheat fields?"

"Hitler will have to help Mussolini against Greece, you'll see. Cutting through Greece, Hitler will reach the Med. Taking Yugoslavia and Bulgaria, he can attack Turkey through Greece and Bulgaria. Of course," he added thoughtfully, "The wheat fields of Slovenia, Croatia, Serbia...all the maize and fruit up through Novi Sad to Subotica and the Hungarian frontier ... yes, why not?"

At the end of the third dance, he took me to a table loaded with canapes, and I saw the Yugoslavs knew about the basics of the good life. They had cured pork and smoked Danubian fish, bread and cakes. Their diplomatic bags must be heavy.

Tibor Haraaszti shouldered his way across to me, and greeted me warmly. He chatted with Zizc, then asked me for a dance.

"I see Mladen wants to bed you. Good cover. Mladen Zizc is a nightclubber, so you'll enjoy his company. The family has money, so he can afford restaurants. I've got an important message, and it's written out –"

I won't carry anything on my person."

"Listen, then."

Thank God, Zizc was dancing with a beautiful girl from the Spanish Embassy, who had apparently tried to run up a dress herself from bits of fabric.

"We have communists who are very close to Franco, posing as fascists. Franco has sent an emissary to Hitler, who arrived a couple of days ago. Franco has more than two million men under arms, and has offered to invade France with one million; in return, he wants Rossillon and Gascogne, all the south of France from the Med to the Atlantic; he wants Andorra, Gibraltar and Portugal; he wants all the French African territories, and also East Nigeria. Can you remember all this?"

"I can."

"Franco is rationing bread, legumes and rice. He has protein from his fishing fleets. Eighty percent of the people are peasants, and they have hens and farm animals. He has olives and olive oil, but he has to ration olive oil in the towns. He has fruit and vegetables and wine. Can you remember this?"

"Do you want me to repeat it?"

"All right, all right. The United States can offer him millions of tons of wheat, rice and legumes, plus powdered milk. America and Britain can guarantee him recognition and confirmation of his rule if they win the war. That would stay his hand. Seven people only know about this – the British and American Embassies in Madrid know nothing."

We finished the dance, and I next danced with Vojislav Djindjic. "Is Mladen Zizc an attaché too?"

"He's a vice-consul," said Vojislav, a little sharply, discouraging more questions.

Next morning, I slept in till ten, had a late breakfast. I understood that Hitler usually lunched late, at about two o'clock,

They had told me a car would come at 1.15 pm. I put on a white dress with long sleeves, with dirndl, Tyrolean-like green stripes running up the front like two braces. Below a wide green belt, my skirt fell in wide pleats. I wore my hair in two blonde plaits over my ears, and tried to look as though I had just come from milking a score of cows.

The car delivered me to the Reich Chancellery, and they conducted me upstairs to a large reception lounge. I saw Speer, who nodded at me encouragingly, Goebbels who gave me an astonished, but pleased smile. I recognised Bormann, then saw Himmler, who likewise gazed at me in wonder, then gave me that ravishing smile of his. Hitler was talking to Göring, and a man in uniform came over.

"I'm Lieutenant Wilhelm Brükner, Hitler's adjutant," he said. Another young man in a SS Gruppenführer's uniform hurried across, not to be left out, and said, "I'm Hitler's other adjuntant Julius Schaub. Welcome. Can we introduce you around till Hitler is free?"

"I know Dr. Goebbels and the Reichsminister Himmler," I said.

The chauffeur who had driven me came in, and I looked in surprise. Schaub introduced him to me. "This is Herr Schreck."

I pretended to pout. "I've heard about you. You made me sit in the back seat, when I could have sat beside you and you could have told me all sorts of gossip."

The three men laughed, and I saw I had made a friend in Schreck.

They introduced me to Bormann, who didn't appear to see me. Hess came in, looking a bit like a favourite younger brother who was being slowly left out of it, but his eyes lighted as he ran his gaze up and down my body.

Hitler turned around, and I thought, the man is ugly, but not in a way you can put your finger on. The pieces of his face each lay a bit in the wrong place.

He smiled at me, and his smile was amazingly engaging.

"You have come," he said, "Our Argentinean ally. Have you brought your camera?"

"No, I haven't," I said, very disappointed.

"We don't want to upset Hoffman," laughed Göring, looking at me without curiosity. (Hoffman is Hitler's photographer)

"Oh, I made sure Hoffman wouldn't be here," smiled Hitler at me. "Hoffman has just offered me a very good painting, and I told him to keep it. I can't deny him the pleasure of it when I don't have a proper place to hang it, and in his house it's priceless. I do wish someone would find me a Rottmann for my collection."

"You like Rottmann?" I blurted out. I sensed that if I showed he awed me, he would quickly dismiss me.

"His Greek and Roman landscapes at the Pinakothek – you should see his lighting effects. Still, we can't have everything we want in life. After all, we only have to go to Munich."

"Lighting effects," I sighed. "In photography, we think we have achieved something, and then find the field is infinite and we know almost nothing."

Hitler looked very pleased at that.

"And I hear you like Berlin? Why is that?"

"Because world history is being made. Because they will talk about these days thousands of years from now."

"How well put," he exclaimed. "And I believe you are popular with Sepp. I suppose now you will want me to confirm your Iron Cross."

"Oh, no," I said, looking as abashed as I knew how. "That would not be seemly."

"Ah! We will make a German maiden of you yet! Come!" and he led the way into lunch, and sat me at his side.

As we were being served, he said, "What do you think in Argentina about England?"

"We know practically nothing," I confessed. "I suppose what I think is that they are still thinking of trench warfare. I suppose they are digging trenches in Belgium," and the table laughed.

Hitler said with amusement, "And what does a young maiden think is wrong with trenches?"

"I suppose tanks can drive straight over them."

Hitler began his soup, and we all followed. He said, "All England had to do was avoid war with us, and so keep its Empire. All they needed was an airforce and their Navy to keep their Empire."

He took some mouthfuls.

"Now, the English can teach us some things. Here we must make steel so perfectly it will gleam like silver in 500 years time. They have a damaged warship – a slapdash repair, some welding there, and it's back at sea fighting. Here we have to do things so much more perfectly than anyone else, we waste a month where a day will do."

He finished his soup, and said, "Of course, Napoleon said the English were a nation of shopkeepers. They are not. They were a nation of farmers who were driven into the black industrial cities. Mussolini is so pleased that about 60 percent of his people are peasants. In Spain, 80 percent are. They are the backbone of a country, and make wonderful soldiers. Napoleon said an army marches on its stomach, but it's a whole country at war that marches on its stomach. And for that we depend on the good peasants. Having good land doesn't make a good peasant. The good peasants are the ones who end up with the good land. Your truly good peasant is a man who picks up a handful of earth, lovingly, crumbles it in his fingers, smells it. That's why Stalin killed 20 million of his very best, richest peasants. You can never grind down those men, and Stalin broke the back of the Russian people when he killed those. Now, all that are left are 'under-men', inferior, half-drunk Slavs.

"In Poland, I want to provide our German farmers each with a thousand hectares. They may feel lost, but when all their neighbours are Germans like themselves, they will settle in. If one day, Germany holds all the East down to the South as far as Greece, all German farmers will be large landholders, and after we conquer England, we will send the English to work for them as farm labourers. Most of the English today are town-dwellers, but in only a few months their hands will harden and their backs grow strong.

"The poets tell us that the peasant likes to sit under a tree and play the flute. The peasant likes to grow things, and once the English were like that. I will make them happy again, putting them back close to the soil. Centuries ago, the Englishman living on the land couldn't read or write, but food was scarce, sickness everywhere. Today, with good doctors and plenty to eat, the happiest men will be those who can't read or write, and we will not allow the children of the English to learn. The German farmers will have to in order to run their farms, but we will allow the English to return to a bucolic life of hundreds of years ago."

The man was hypnotic. I didn't even know what I was eating. I had a superstitious dread of his sixth-sense, and I felt a deep fear he was talking about *the English to me*. Well, he was talking to the table, but I was sitting *beside him*. Had he sensed I was English?

234

He paused, in thought, and no one dared speak.

He said absently, "I am reminded of my father. I used to say to my father, 'Father, I think...,' or 'Father, just think...,' and he would tell me brusquely, 'My son, I'm not paid to think. I don't need to. I'm a Hapsburg official.'

"But we must think...and think, and plan to change the destiny of peoples."

"We must, we must!" echoed Himmler.

Bormann just sat, eating, watching the others, like a man waiting one day to pounce.

Hitler turned to me and said, "You must visit us at Obersalzberg. That's where I take all my great decisions. Sometimes I lie in bed, unable to sleep, staring at the mountains under the moonlight.

"The other weekend I was there, staring at the mountains at three o'clock in the morning, when I realised how Great Britain had to avoid war with us at every cost. Now, when it loses its Empire, the Japanese will sweep south, and the white man will vanish from Asia. The Japanese will take even Australia and New Zealand and put every last white man to the sword, or simply work him to his death while starving him.

"Looking at the mountains in the moonlight, that illumination enters my mind."

He turned to me suddenly.

"And what do you think of Sepp?"

"He's impressive," I said.

"We are recruiting too much for SS. What we want is the very highest level."

He turned to Himmler. "You want to make a Waffen Army of *one million* men – the fiercest, best-trained soldiers the world has ever seen. But *one million*! Can you keep it an elite, or will you fill it with young men who want to show off? They must feel a superiority each one such as has never been seen."

Himmler nodded, not trusting himself to speak. Then he smiled at Hitler, and said, "I will give you that Army, I promise you."

Hitler said, "There have always been feelings between ordinary soldiers, recruits and conscripts on the one hand and guardsmen on the other. An army commander of mine must feel truly happy when he can say he commands an armoured division and an SS Reich Division. That combination – and the armoured division with full motorised support for the tanks – should be unbeatable."

"That and Luftwaffe support," said Göring petulantly.

"Ah, our Third Reich rests on your Luftwaffe," said Hitler expansively.

What he said next made the nerves over my back crawl. Did he have a sixth sense?

"We can learn a lot from the British. Their newspapers are so indiscreet. They are indiscreet in their private talk. We must learn to make sure that nothing of what we plan, what we are doing, creeps out to guide our enemies. I can't trust the Italians – they are dangerously effusive. They can't keep a secret. In future, I'm never going to tell them anything until an hour before. That is what Stalin does – his newspapers print absolutely nothing, because they know absolutely nothing. He makes sure of that! It's only thanks to the Spanish Civil War that we know he has a big aircraft industry, but I am making sure that no one knows we know that. The British and French ignored the Spanish War, so just suppose we found ourselves at war with Soviet Russia, the French and British in their ignorance would waste their substance rushing precious fighter planes to them, when the Soviet production of fighter planes far outnumbers what the British and French can produce. We must redouble our vigilance against spies in our midst, however well they hide from the Gestapo. They can be found and will be found."

He had finished his lunch, and stretched a little, then waited for the slower eaters.

"The British Public School system is considered so much better than ours, and it is supposed to produce a superior person to we Germans! At the Olympic Games, the British won only eight medals, and we won 33!

"We must make big changes in our system of education, for all that. When I remember the primary school teachers of my boyhood! They looked dirty, they sometimes smelt. Grease stained their collars, and their beards often were tangled. They had these airs of superiority. They were and still are the pets of the Left – 'the bearers of culture'. How absurd! Their political opinions are pathetic and they complain eternally about this and that. They are, in fact, at the bottom of the working-class. They complain we don't pay them enough, but the wage we spend on a corporal in the Wehrmacht is worth ten times more. What sort of person do you need to teach the ABC to the little boys and girls? Every year, new children appear, and they must go the same dreary round again. This is really a job for women. A mother is happy to bear one child after another and bring each one up. A shorthand-typist does the same monotonous job week after week, but only because she is a woman. Nature has fitted women for the task of teaching the ABC to tiny tots, and we have some two million women who are still celibate.

"Look at my Hitler Jugend, and the stern formation those boys enjoy. Instead of our weak and watery teachers, we need men who have gone through the Hitler Youth, then the Labour Service, followed by the Army. In the last two years of their Army service, they could attend courses at a Teachers' College; a man with twelve years Army service! Our new schools would eclipse the British Public Schools.

236

"Of course, the British Public Schools are very picky, and this slews their results. So, we will do the same. We will choose the best boys and girls from the Third Reich, to form an elite. Strongly formed character, handsome physique, quick, clever minds – imagine what we can do with children like that."

Hitler got up, and led us next door into a lounge with sofas and armchairs.

"Our new sort of instructors will form this chosen elite," he said, settling into an armchair. "They will join them in everything, including parachute-jumping and motorised manoeuvres."

He sat there thoughtfully.

"Our nation owes everything to its soldiers, and after they finish their twelve years, we must give them land to make the peasant soldiers our backbone.

"Himmler tells me that each farm would work out at some 23,000 marks, with machinery and so on, so we can do it. When I think that the German State is giving the Church 900 million marks a year! We can use this money on our new farms. With 50 million marks, the Church is more than well served. Only Spain subsidizes the Church like this – and all this goes back to the Reformation and Luther. Luther was one thing – but who came after him? Nobodies. We are wasting a fortune in these payments to a Church that is anti-Nazi, an enemy within. Who are these men who go into the priesthood, who become monks? Men in disgraceful economic poverty. When Germany picked up and there was money for everybody, many tried to escape back into the world, and the priests went after them, to drag them back. All those disgraceful lawsuits. It's natural. Who wants to vow himself to celibacy? With women it's different – they usually are moved by emotions, I should say, more than simple money distress.

"A German soldier who is ready to lay down his life cannot submit to these religious strictures enjoining abstinence. A warrior wins the right to love. I know that when I first went to Berghof, I saw how the local stock of people had degenerated. Now we have a regiment of the Leibstandarte there, and the countryside and forests are filled with bouncing babies of the very best German stock. We must send in choice regiments wherever we see degeneracy – places like the East Prussian lakes and the forests of Bavaria.

"Battle and love are intertwined, and I will not have the church interfering ..."

He poured himself a little brandy.

"We are at war, and insubordination and opposition cannot be tolerated.

"Imagine that now a riot broke out in the Reich. Do you know what I would do?

"On that very self same day I'd have arrested all the leaders of the opposition, the leaders of the Catholics too, and execute them, Then I'd shoot all the people in all the concentration camps over the next three days. Then I'd execute all the criminals we know of or have in custody.

"Killing a few thousand would be the end of the matter. When I think of our German warriors who are ready to risk their lives – to snuff out the lives of these rioters is nothing..."

I was home by six o'clock. I told the ladies of the household what had happened, and had been said, then went upstairs to encode my two messages for London – one on Hitler's generals, the other on Franco's emissary. In a third message, I said that Soviet Russia had a huge military aircraft industry of fighter planes and bombers, many times larger than the British and French aircraft industries.

At eight o'clock, the phone rang. It was my ardent friend from the Yugoslav Embassy, Mladen Zizc, of the roaming hands. He invited me to a dance at his home,

"The attache, Vojislav Djindjic, is coming, with a lady friend, and the Yugoslav journalist, Ratko Bregovic and a lady friend from the Bulgarian Legation. Do you have any friends you want to bring?"

"I'll ring you back".

1 asked Doris and Thoma, who rang their fiancés. Richterin and Walter said they would join us in forty minutes, with a staff car.

I rang back, accepting, but Mladen said, "The staff car is not a good idea at all, I'll send an Embassy car."

That was all right. If Richterin and Walter drove over in their uniforms, and left the car here to drive home later, that was not the same as being in a staff car with three ladies and have the police stop us, and make an official report against the two officers.

I would have to encode my message tomorrow morning.

Mladen's flat was large, but sparsely furnished.

He did have a table covered with canapés, and dozens of records to play.

I asked him about the neighbours.

"It's a warehouse downstairs. No problem with the noise."

To my stupor, Tibor Haraszti, the communist spy, walked in, with a girl from the Hungarian Embassy – no! – Legation! What had happened...?

Everyone acted normally, and we all danced for an hour. Then Tibor said, "Let me show you Mladen's flat. It has a nice view from the back bedroom windows."

He led me into a passageway, closed the door behind me, and walked to the far end. A doorway led into a bedroom.

He said urgently, "That bloody code London gave you is crazy. Moscow reports it's breakable, and they are working on it at the Gestapo. You know how you take the first line from your book? Take the first *two* lines. If you can't find one line with ten different letters, then write down two page numbers and two line numbers.

"In Lorna Doone, on page 322, line 2 it says: 'frame should...'"

He showed me a piece of paper, on which was written:

F	R	A	M	E	F	
S	H	O	U	L	S	
B	C	D	G	I	B	
J	K	N	P	Q	J	
T	V	W	X	Z	T	X = XY
F	R	A	M	E	F	

He said, "Suppose you want the letter 'G'. The diagonal is 'Q'.

"I'm going to the bathroom to burn these and flush them down the toilet. Any questions?"

"It's quite clear. But what's the trouble?"

"Bloody London. Bloody British! Rank amateurs! In breaking a code, you begin by supposing that a 'P' could substitute for 'O' or 'Q', and this code does that. Once they tumble, it could fall like a pack of cards. Luckily, so many messages have gone from Genéve, which everyone will automatically assume is using different codes to Berlin."

I said stiffly, "Quite clear."

Bloody Graham Bunton, Bloody London. Amateurs!

He went to the bathroom, and I went back to the dance. No one paid me any attention when I came in, *least of all Mladen*, of the possessive hands.

Mladen must work with Tibor.

Next morning, I encoded my messages with the new code. I took page 301, line 23: "lips and their legs to the proper..."

L	I	P	S	A	L	
N	D	T	H	E	N	
B	C	F	G	J	B	
K	M	O	Q	R	K	
U	V	W	X	Z	U	X = XY
L	I	P	S	A	L	

Then, in plain language, I explained the new code, but didn't say a word about Tibor and Moscow. I wrote, CONTACT IN CANARIS INTLL WARNS THAT CRIPTO BREAKERS TRY B AS SUBSTITUTE FOR A OR C, THEN C FOR B OR D ETC.

I microdotted everything, and took public transport to the Argentinean Embassy. Rubén listened gravely, then took my ring with the microdots inside, and gave me an identical ring.

He said, "In Genéve, Maximo Murphy de la Rúa at the Argentinean Embassy there has a contact in the British Embassy. He'll give him your plain text microdot. We'll send out your encoded message to Buenos Aires, as always, because it's the only sure route to Graham Bunton. If the British Embassy sends it out, God knows in what part of London it'll end up. As your plain text message is addressed to Bunton, we have to suppose he'll get it. However, to make sure, I'll encode your plain text in an Embassy code, and send it to your contact in Buenos Aires, on his wavelength, and he can forward it the way he thinks is best. So, Bunton should get your message twice – we hope!"

* * *

Prince Bernd's brother, Count Axel Hohenlinden and his son Eduard, came for lunch. After telling me all about Hitler, Axel was greedy for every crumb of Hitler's monologue. Eduard, a doctor in one of Berlin's biggest hospitals, the Krankenhaus Franziskus, at number 1, Burggrafen strasse, had been on night duty.

After we had eaten, and were seated on sofas and armchairs, I asked Eduard about the health of Hitler's dear subjects.

"We've had a staggering rise in crimes of food stealing – from food shops and railway tracks. That tells us that people aren't eating properly, and it shows. Mothers do better. You get married and the state gives you a loan of a 1,000 marks, at 3% interest. Every child you have cuts down the loan by a quarter, so that if you have four kids, you wipe out the loan. Tempted?" He smiled at me. "Over the last five years, well over a million of these loans have been handed out, but almost a million have been cancelled by a fourth child. That means a huge surge in children when the proper food isn't here. You get 10 marks a month for the third and fourth child. The birth rate has gone up 40% since 1932 – it's now 20 plus per thousand people, but health has worsened. The Party makes heroes of mothers – once a year, they hand out decorations. A gold cross for the mother of eight children or more, silver for six or seven, and bronze for four plus. We have three great women's groups: The German Women's Enterprise has, I think, six million members, and encourages women to go to their cookery classes. But where is the food! The National Socialist Womanhood has some three million members, and promotes 'the nation's love of life, motherhood, marriage, the family, blood and race.' But nothing about food and medicines. The Reich Mothers' Service is the other monster organisation and it teaches child care – presumably child care on short rations.

"The regime proclaims it is making a revolution in German health. And so it is – so it is – but not in the way they think. Since 1933, doctors have grown by another 17,000, by reducing the medical course to three years. We've lost 5,500 very highly specialised Jewish doctors, and we're losing German specialists by the thousands as they retire. We aren't producing new specialists.

"Now, that's not to say we haven't gained something. We give medical tests to couples when they marry and those who ask for family subsidies, and we pick up a lot of diseases early, especially TB. Our infant deaths have dropped, though we're not as low as the British yet. Sports in factories have made workers fitter, and five million have the Strength Through Joy certificates.

"But alcoholism and smoking is way up. Our suicides have gone from 19,000 in 1932 to more than 22,000 this year. We kill more people in road accidents than in Britain" – he was careful to not to say 'than you have in Britain' – "and industrial accidents have gone up by a third under the Nazis. You wouldn't believe how many workers can't report for work because of tummy upsets and pains – that's simply stress. Our hospital admissions have gone up from four million in 1932 to six million today. And German dental decay and infections are an epidemic. One quarter of the people don't have any toothpaste. In this decade, diphtheria has doubled, and heart disease, scarlet fever, typhoid and polio have got much worse than in Britain.

"What distinguishes us from Britain is that we have to do most surgery WITHOUT ANAESTHETIC, which means far more people die on the table, or quickly afterwards, from shock, than in Britain and America. It's awful operating with the screams, the patient tied down. They have heart attacks, heart arrest, or the body just shuts down and they die. Hitler's 'master race' is just so much nonsense. He has gone to war at the expense of the German people."

A message came that Hitler had invited me to his Eagle's Nest at Obersalzberg next weekend, and a car would pick me up at seven o'clock in the morning, Saturday.

In the morning darkness, the car drove me to the aerodrome. I leant back in the seat, looking through the glass, thinking about Hitler. I watched the outside world, *I* felt it; and it was as though *Hitler* did not. I thought of my mind as a still pond on a summer day, with myriad pin-points of light dancing on the water from the sun; Hitler seemed to direct everything to a dark, deep point within, where his mind decided, and then sent out a torrent of ideas and opinions. He heeded his inner torrent and the words poured out as he spoke; if you challenged, threatened or tried to kill him, only then I imagined would his reaction be one of instantaneous ferocity towards the real world in which the rest of us lived.

I wondered what his meetings with his top generals were like. The general would explain...would trace his finger on the map; Hitler would pause, wait for the inner voice, and trust that inner voice only. The inner voice would agree with the general, and when Hitler spoke, the general would beam. Or his voice would not; and when Hitler spoke, the general would listen non-plussed, and then probably argue vainly.

At the aerodrome, I sat in a chilly waiting-room. People came in and out, and then a lady in a heavy overcoat walked over to me.

"Are you the Argentinean photographer?"

I smiled at her. "Yes. I'm Raimunda."

"I'm Maria von Below. My husband, Claus, is one of Hitler's adjuncts. Well, his Luftwaffe adjunct, in fact."

She sat beside me. "There's been a bit of a delay."

"Have you known Hitler long?"

"Oh, quite some time. You met him for the first time earlier this week, I believe. What was your reaction?"

"Confusing. I saw his eyes light up – I think he loves having women around him, but he didn't seem comfortable talking to me directly."

"Oh, no!" she exclaimed. "He does love having pretty women around him, and to touch their elbows, or upper arms, but he also *does* enjoy talking to us. He talks about our families, how we feel, *light* things. You can talk to him about actors, the theatre, light cinema if you're a woman." She smiled engagingly "He feels he must reserve serious matters for men. But he is so courteous with the ladies, it makes him irresistible. We must face it – the man fascinates."

I said thoughtfully, "There's something erotic in a man with really immense power."

She laughed merrily. "How very well put! To tell the truth, I don't mind in the least when a lot of his talk is for the men, because sometimes I lose interest. What I love is when he talks about history or art – what he knows is prodigious, my dear, you will see."

"His feeling towards us is in no way really physical," I mused.

"No, it isn't," Maria von Below agreed. "Have you brought your cameras?"

"No," I said, surprised.

"I didn't think he would have told you to," she said. "I can't see him letting a woman take photos of him. She would have to step out of the woman's submissive place to do that – you know what I mean?"

"Oh, yes, I do," I said, surprised and thoughtful at once. "Isn't this a man's country!"

"And Spain and Argentina aren't?" she said, astonished.

"The men think that because we women want them to," I told her, seriously. "We women mostly have things exactly as we want them to be."

"For someone so young, you are amazing," Maria von Below told me. She got to her feet. "I have to find my husband."

Then Speer came in, saw me, and sat down beside me.

"Tell me again about Hitler's original house, the Berghof," I begged.

"It was an old, simple mountain house, which we enlarged. Hitler drew up all the plans himself, and he never studied architecture!"

"And if you had been his professor, what mark would you have given him? An 'A'?"

"You naughty girl," laughed Speer.

"Ach! A 'C'?"

"You are trying to put me on the spot," he smiled.

"A 'D' then?"

He put his finger to his lips. "I can't say," he said solemnly, "And we

244

never had this conversation."

On the plane, I found myself sitting next to a lady not much older than myself.

She said, "You're the young lady from Argentina, aren't you? I'm Rosa Irlinger. That's my sister, Irmgard, sitting across the aisle." I saw her sister lean forward to nod at me, and I did the same.

Rosa said, "We housekeep for Hitler, up on the mountain. Back in. the 1920s, we were little girls and Berchtesgaden was a tiny farming hamlet. There was this big alpine house, alone on the mountain, owned by that man who makes pianos – Bechstein, who was so rich I don't suppose he really knew himself how much money he had. He came up in winter to ski and in summer to hike, but very few times. Our family were his housekeepers, so we lived in the villa the whole year. Just above his stupendous house stood a small house that Bechstein owned too. A bit crude, you know, but very sturdy to stand up to the winter snow.

"For many years, a 'Herr Wolf' came to stay in that little house. Herr Bechstein gave it to him to use. Herr Wolf always had a couple of other men visitors who lived there with him, and lots of people used to labour up the path past our house, to see him.

"Now, the only phone on the mountain was at the Bechstein big house, and our mother used to run up the steep path to the little house to Herr Wolf because he kept getting all these calls.

"Then one day, after he finished talking and hung up, he asked our mother whether there was any shop on the mountain, and she told him about the general store way down at the bottom of the mountain.

"He thanked my mother very courteously, and we saw him go off, walking down. An hour later – it was no mean climb back up again – he knocked at our door and made my mother a gift of a box of chocolates, and we each got a lolly stick.

"Our mother said, 'Oh no, you shouldn't have done this, Herr Wolf! Why have you gone to this trouble?'

"'I want to thank you for so much kindness.'

"'You don't have to, Herr Wolf. We know you have no money.'

"And later, we found out he was Hitler!"

"You must be very fond of him."

"He's a wonderful man!"

"And what's it like on the mountain now?"

"It's all spoilt. Herr Bormann has built roads, and other alpine villas. It's not the quiet place it was. There's a big SS barracks too."

"And what is it like inside Hitler's house – what sort of program will we follow?"

She laughed. "Oh, no program. It's all pretty informal. But Herr Hitler doesn't like to go to bed till two or three in the morning."

"So what finally happened to that crude little house at the back of the Bechstein villa?"

"But that *was* Hitler's house! The Berghof! Today it's huge! And do you know what?" She leaned towards me and lowered her voice. "Herr Hitler did the plans for the new house himself, and he's not an architect!"

"Ooh!" I managed to show how impressed I was.

"Of course," she warned me in the same conspiratorial tone. "You're not going to see that natural mountain we knew as girls. Now all the buildings are called the Berghof too.

"Herr Speer, now, he does love nature and the quiet. First, he rented a small hunting lodge, in another village near Berchesgaden, but in the middle of 1935, Hitler told him to move in with his family into the Bechstein villa, to have him close. Now Hitler is up on the Eagle's Nest, on top of the Kehlstein mountain."

Ho! Ho! I thought. Speer must have loved that. Hitler would want him to waste all day listening to his harangues, and not let him work. I could see the back of Speer's head in the seat in front. Thank goodness for all the racket from the engines.

"Hitler put two other families in the villa, and one of them was Hitler's personal doctor, Dr. Karl Brandt."

Brandt worked in Hitler's euthanasia program, murdering German and Austrian children and adults with physical abnormalities, or mental deficiencies. Later, he experimented with concentration camp prisoners in freezing water, to help Luftwaffe pilots who splashed down in the sea. Nuremberg hanged him.

"Mrs. Speer and Mrs. Brandt are very nice, and they've become good friends. But then, in 1937 – yes, that's right, more than two years ago – Herr Speer rented a big family alpine villa from the actor Gustav Fröhlich. Have you seen any of his films?"

I shook my head, "I haven't been here all that long."

"That was when Hitler moved into the Eagle's Nest, that Herr Bormann built for him."

She was quiet.

"You'll see how you settle in," she said, comfortingly. "Herr Hitler will look after you. He's so clever. He knows the answer to all our problems. Germany was so poor and dangerous, and now everyone lives well and has money. We've got Austria, Czechoslovakia, Poland now, and he'll know what to do with Britain and France, you'll see. Argentina did the right thing, becoming our ally. How the people love him! He has looked after us all, no one could have ever believed it. Just in a few years, he has made Germany so rich, and the strongest country in the world."

I stared out the window at the clouds whipping by.

I had this intuitive feeling that Hitler didn't like professionals and intellectuals. In England, politicians are professionals...well, often people who aren't clever enough to make a go of it in business or the universities, although some are intellectuals. Here – none of the civil servants, professionals or intellectuals came near Hitler as far as I could see...if I excepted Speer. I suppose intellectuals must make Hitler see his limits, see himself as he is. No professional politician had a voice in today's Germany, and I'd bet they couldn't get within shouting distance of Hitler, those who once were. Of course, he couldn't choose his military people – they'd be thrust upon him, that was clear – but I sensed he loved amateurs. Well, that was me, all right – the very spearhead of England's amateurs, about to go into Hitler's mountain lair. For me, let me say, it made for an easy, relaxed atmosphere I felt comfortable in.

(Author's note: I am supposing Maria von Below, Rosa and Irmgard Irlinger are no longer alive. Rosa Irlinger told her story of "Herr Wolf" to Gitta Sereny which she published in her book ALBERT SPEER, published by Picador, using different language to mine. I suppose Rosa told her story also to many German newspapers and magazines, after the war)

We landed at Ainring aerodrome, and I stood beside Speer as we waited for the cars.

I asked him mischievously, "Do many civil servants come to visit Hitler here?"

He looked at me narrowly. "He hates them," he said, "You guessed, did you?"

We drove up. Hitler's home, his Berghof, *was* huge. The Bechstein villa, imposing, and I could see the ostentatious homes of Bormann and Göring.

Hitler had given me a room in the Bechstein villa, upstairs, done with Bavarian artisan woodwork and naive hand-paintings on the headboard of the bed and the doors of the wardrobe.

* * *

Soon after midday, Speer sent a message that he was waiting downstairs. He drove me from the Bechstein villa up the mountain to the great spur of rock where the Eagle's Nest stood on top. A tall bronze portal led to a marble entry, the air clammy from the rock damp, and he ushered me into a lift of polished brass.

Speer told me, "We're going up 165 feet of shaft here. You have to understand that Hitler's a night owl. He goes to his bedroom with Eva Braun about two or three in the morning; he shows up around eleven in the morning. What he does then is go through the press summaries, and listen to reports from Bormann. Usually, only Eva Braun, an adjutant and a servant stay overnight in the Eagle's Nest with Hitler."

We stepped out of the lift, and went into a living-room, and I saw a brass cage with canaries, a cactus and rubber plant. Knicknacks lay about and cushions embroidered – Speer told me – by adoring women, all with swastikas; some cushions had embroidered "eternal loyalty."

Hitler had his back to us, and was talking to three men in civilian clothes; I found later they were industrialists. Eva Braun stood to one side.

Hitler declaimed, "Never let us forget Goethe's son – a hopeless individual! Imagine I had children! The headaches! Which of them would be my successor, and would he be worthy of the task? What chances does any man have of having a son of high talent? Very few. And then think, imagine I had a woman who interfered. It would be intolerable. A gifted man can only take a woman of strong animal instincts with no mind worth speaking of."

I glanced at Eva Braun, keeping the shock out of my face.

She was impassive, as if she didn't hear, or had heard it so often before. No one paid her any attention, but had their eyes on Hitler.

"It's natural that women gravitate towards me because I'm not married. My attraction was important in our early days of struggle. Were I to marry, that magnetism would dissipate. You can see it happen to movie actors."

I realised in an unbelieving flash that Hitler thought he was irresistible.

The sitting-room was vast.

One wall was a window, looking out at the wondrous mountains, to Salzburg shrunken away in the impossible distances.

He turned around, saw me and smiled. He crossed over, cupped my elbow and said, "My beautiful Argentinean, welcome. Did you have a good flight?"

"Wonderful. And my room is very comfortable."

He turned to the company.

"Jealousy is built into the very nature of women. In very primitive times, a pregnant woman survived only with a man's protection, and now this is an ancestral memory. A woman who is not pregnant has this racial memory, and knows that one day she could be pregnant. Think of the years her child will be helpless, defenceless. So possessive women succeed, and women without men fail. But the triumphant, the possessive woman knows she cannot supinely confide in the male's bounteousness. The triumphant woman knows she must manipulate the male, sway him, hold him. That would make my life impossible. A woman can't surrender one whit of the ground she has conquered, the hero who will save her from the dangers on every side.

"Of course, when a woman finds the man who she believes will change her life, so the soldier changes *his* life when he first finds himself in battle. A youth is hardened into a man, and now we are living exciting, heroic days when German manhood advances beyond German soil. I would never make a speech to say – 'there is no death more to be desired', because I was in the Great War, and I know how a soldier feels.

"As motherhood makes a woman, so war makes a man, and if I had not been purged in the crucible of the last war, I could not take upon my shoulders the Herculean task of building a worldwide German Empire, single-handed.

"When we are masters of Europe, think of the advantages of European hegemony! We'll be four hundred million people against the one hundred and thirty million Americans. This prospect alarms Roosevelt.

"Unfortunately, our German Empire will benefit little from the collapse of the British Empire. America will get Canada, and perhaps Africa. Russia will grab India, and Japan will take Eastern Asia and all the British

249

Empire holdings there, from Australia in the south to Hong Kong in the north.

"England no longer interests me. It has no future, unlike ourselves. When I am no more, I shall leave behind me the most powerful army in world history, and the most ravening Party."

He got to his feet, to go into the dining-room. I had been warned that Martin Bormann would escort Eva Braun, and that Hitler would choose who was to sit beside him. My curiosity was feverish. Would he choose me?

He cupped the elbow of one of the industrialists.

Seated at the table, I found myself next to Eva.

Hitler said, "What an innocent idealist I was when they sent me to the Front in 1914. There I saw thousands dying around me, and I realised life was merciless, caring only that the strongest lived. Life cares only for the species, and although tens of thousands fall, it matters not while there are other men to take their place.

"I don't like to see people in anguish, I don't want to injure a single person, but when I realise the German species is in danger my feelings freeze and ruthless logic seizes my mind.

He addressed himself to his food, then said, "Of course, today we have two million more women in Germany than men. A woman's object in life is to marry and when she can't, she grows hysterical. People say, 'Isn't that old maid hysterical!' Hysterical is a word that comes from the Greek word for the womb – the Greeks said childless or unmarried women got 'their womb in an uproar.' They used to put pieces of ice inside the vagina to stop attacks of hysteria. We must encourage those two million women to do what nature is demanding of them – to have their babies without marriage, and the German state will care for them, because they are helping the German species to survive and grow.

"That is why women are more subtle than men – they read your feelings to know what you are thinking, in a way a man cannot. A woman has 'womb wisdom'. For this reason, we cannot have women in high places in government and business. Instead of following cold logic, they would be inclining this way and that according to whether they liked or disliked the people who would have to obey them. Instead of doing their job, men would have to scheme and worry about keeping on the right side of their woman-boss, and she would have different womanly moods during the day, which would make the effort almost impossible. An 'Amazon country' is impossible, where women rule. It will fall into decay and decadence, unless warriors among the men rise up and slay all the powerful women. Powerful women under the bias of their feelings can make insanely destructive decisions or commit insane acts just for the emotional satisfaction.

"We need male reasoning always, and the English have not let sound

250

reasoning govern their actions. They industrialised India, and what happened? Devastating unemployment in England. England should take a cold-blooded decision to withdraw from this war, and come in with us. Then it will save its Empire. For some three centuries England has imposed Pax Britannica on the world. But now America challenges it. If Britain comes in with us, it will postpone the American challenge for several decades. Because, believe me, what America wants now is to impose on the world a Pax Americana.

"No one seems to realise that Roosevelt is a secret Socialist. What is his New Deal but thinly disguised socialism? There is no doubt whatsoever in my mind but that Roosevelt feels a secret sympathy and admiration for Stalin and communism –"

(I must point out that on the Continent the word 'sympathy' does not mean compassion or being sorry for someone but fondness for, understanding of or identification with another person.)

"– and if presented with the chance, will deliver Europe, or what part of Europe he can, into Stalin's eager hands. Europe would not compete with America for hundreds of years, once under communism. Roosevelt is a 'silver spoon' Red.

The west had been uncritical of Roosevelt, but from my first visits to Spain I found an extremely angry attitude here. Everyone talked openly of how Roosevelt had not been ill and close to his death, but had actively betrayed Europe. Germans thought the same, and felt free to say so once inside Spain.

"To understand the Americans, to understand why they are such poor soldiers, so uncultured and so vulgar, we have to go back to their immigration.. 'Send me your poor, your huddled masses'. And that's what they got – the sweepings of Europe, the rubbish we were lucky to get rid of. The early settlers on the frontier in the Wild West built their cabins without doors! Back in Europe, they had not understood the hinge on their doors. On the frontier, they were too stupid to reinvent the hinge, so wolves and bears could burst into their primitive dwellings. On the other hand, Alexis Toqueville said they were a nation of mechanics, who one day would build a boiler big enough to blow up the whole world. We are speaking of later generations now, who can build a hinge. But that is all the Americans are – mechanics. They can fill their lives only using their hands and playing with their toys – driving their cars which cannot compare with Germany's Mercedes, playing with their telephones, listening to their radios, because they have no thoughts unless their radios or newspapers supply their brains.

"Their art was a feeble imitation of Europe's, and now they begin to develop their own, it is Coca Cola, Ford Model-T art, that history will sweep into oblivion. They are masters of advertising, so they will broadcast worldwide their gutter art and their tinny music."

He stopped, and ate in silence. Then he turned and spoke in a low voice to the industrialist beside him.

Desultory conversations sprang up around the table. I wondered whether Eva Braun would speak to me, but she didn't; I was frantically remembering what Constance Ancram had taught me, on our ships to and from Buenos Aires.

She had been Hitler's mistress since 1932. She was Bavarian, from the town of Simbach on the river Inn almost touching the Austrian border. She was the daughter of a middle-class schoolteacher, and in her late teens, Hitler's photographer, Heinrich Hoffman, employed her, and introduced her to Hitler. In 1931, Hitler's second cousin, Geli Raubal, shot herself in Hitler's Munich flat. Hitler had been her incestuous lover, and her suicide devastated him. Although Goebbels introduced him to several glorious Nordic women, he spurned them; he did surround himself with beautiful women.

In Eva Braun, he found the love he needed. She was slim, tall, with regular, pretty features – but not 'beautiful' – and she went in for gymnastics, skiing, mountain climbing and swimming. Above all, she was a dancer, which she had studied. She was interested in sports, reading novels and watching films. She grew besotted with Hitler.

He gave her a flat in Munich but later moved her into his Berghof at Obersalzburg. Now she lived in the Eagle's Nest. Hitler worried about her health and wouldn't let her use fast cars or planes.

But she was a non-person. Hitler did not let her appear in public. She spent her life waiting for him to come. Almost no German knew of her. When important guests arrived, she had to hide in other rooms, or leave the high spur of rock and go down in the lift to another house of the Berghof. In her waiting, she suffered depressed introspection, and made several tries at suicide. She killed time writing letters and her diaries, or with physical activities, with reading...

The servants had to call her "EB". Only with Hitler's closest entourage could she join in. Hitler had extended to me a strange honour, although Eva pretended not to see me.

After several long minutes of muttering with the man beside him, Hitler said, "Our only enemy is not just Roosevelt... When Britain declared war, I interpreted it as but a valiant show and hoped to negotiate. But the other month, I remember how Göring came through the door and collapsed into a chair.

"'They have taken Churchill into the War Cabinet as First Lord of the

Admiralty. Now we have war!' Because Churchill *is* a true enemy of the German people and wishes to see us destroyed, to see all Germans dead. At the end of the Great War, British and French leaders circumvented the American President, Wilson, who wanted reconciliation with Germany, a new friendship. The British and French leaders wanted only revenge, punishment, humiliation and reparations. They wanted to grind us into poverty, into the dust – and they almost did. Churchill belongs to that circle and will never rest till Germany lies a total ruin, no matter the cost of millions of lives all over the earth. Yet I still dream of an understanding with the British people – that they respect our hegemony in Europe, and we respect their Empire. Because if we fight to the finish, not only will Britain lose its Empire but it will dwindle to an insignificant island on the edge of Europe with scarcely any influence, while a mighty Germany marches on to ever greater destinies."

I realised I had finished my dessert – it had been a simple lunch – and now his words gave me a twinge of indigestion. We had begun the century with a thirty-mile array of naval might – how would we finish it? I thought of those German tanks, and my indigestion gained a little on me.

We sat there in silence.

I said to him, "I believe you have a phenomenal memory for numbers, Herr Hitler."

Everyone looked at me, and Hitler suddenly beamed.

"Indeed, I have," he said, "To the consternation of my industrialists, advisers and generals."

He looked at the industrialists, a general in uniform and at Speer. All nodded, some vigorously, others sheepishly.

"I can tell you the calibres of all our artillery, all the cannon on our tanks. All the speeds of our tanks, the thickness of their armour, the length of their cannon, their range – everything. And always I find myself in argument! I keep saying we need more muzzle velocity for the cannon of our tanks. Double the muzzle velocity and you have four times the penetrating power of enemy armour. No, they tell me. A longer barrel will unbalance the tank! We have the light Czechoslovakian tank, the Panzar Kw 38t. It weighs only 10 tons and has a gun of 37 mm. A short barrel. A pop gun! At ten tons, it has no armour! Our Panzar Kw4 medium tank has a 75 mm gun, but it's low muzzle velocity again! A short cannon! Both tanks have armour about 30 mm thick. What nonsense! They tell me the tanks do 25 miles an hour. More nonsense!

"When two battleships meet at sea, and one is faster but has a shorter range and thinner armour, what good is its speed? Only to run away with! The heavier battleship can open fire a mile earlier and the faster one cannot respond if its enemy is still out of range.

"Our tanks won in Poland, but their guns are too short, their armour

253

too thin. Army Ordnance complains a longer barrel will throw the whole tank off balance. Hah! The British Matilda tank has a maximum thickness of armour of 78mm! Seventy-eight mm! Their gun is only 40 mm, and not very high velocity. But it will destroy our 30mm of armour. The French Char B has both a 47 mm and a 75 mm gun, and its 20-ton Somua a 47 mm gun – but both tanks have armour between 40mm and 60mm thick. The French have about 3,000 machines, Canaris tells me, plus a thousand more obsolete machines. The British have about 200 light tanks and 100 Matildas in Europe – and properly handled, each Matilda could destroy a score of ours. We have only some 2,000 tanks, but my generals tell me we will outmanoeuvre those 3,000 plus enemy tanks easily. With our thin-skinned, lightly-gunned machines. Ach! It's intolerable that we are manufacturing such poor machines, even if we do win in the West against Britain and France.

"I have asked for rough sketches of a new tank called the Tiger. They want to make it 50 tons, but our enemies will build new generations of devastating tanks, so I will demand it carry armour to bring it to seventy-five tons, They complain that will cut the speed. Who cares! Another sketch is of a Panther tank – called the Panther because of its speed, Its speed! I won't tolerate that. It has the same engine as the Tiger. I have demanded a much longer gun and heavier armour, to bring it to fifty tons. You'll see we'll have to build these tanks when our enemies appear with new machines.

The Panther, at 48 tons, was easily the best tank in World War Two. It did only 30 miles an hour, with a 700 hp engine, and a 75mm gun.

"In tanks, the heavier is better, although slower. But in the air, we have the opposite. For an attack on England, they tell me we need four-engine bombers flying very high, Nonsense! We need dive-bombing Stukas, close to their targets, the English aerodromes. They tell me we need bigger, heavier fighters with very long range capability. Wrong again. Our Messerschmitt B 109 has revolutionised dog-fighting in the air. We need a lightning war in the British skies, and if we hold all the French coast, the limited range of our planes will do comfortably. We will overwhelm and demoralise the British within a couple of weeks. As I have insisted on a fast production of light bombers and our fast, short-range fighters, we have DOUBLE the numbers we would have had otherwise, and the defeat of Britain in its own skies will be a catastrophe for them."

Lack of four-engine bombers with very high ceilings, and of long-range fighters, assured the German defeat in The Battle of Britain.

Hitler led us to the sitting-room, with its immense picture-window, the staggering mountains beyond the glass.

We sat in armchairs and on sofas.

Hitler made himself comfortable in. an armchair, and said, "The problem is not one of two-engine or four-engine bombers. If our German engineers could build us a bomber that would fly at 500 mph – perhaps using another fuel than petrol – I could dominate the skies. If it could fly at 45,000 feet, it would not have to carry the weight of armament. It would fly faster and higher than any fighter. We worry first about building fighters, but they look after themselves. Bombers are what we should think about."

Germany built some 35,000 Messerschmitt B 109s during the war.

"The key to the war is the super-bomber. You'll see, the British, and Americans will build 4-engine bombers by the thousands, and we will shoot them down.

"Of course, indiscriminate bombing from great heights will not win the war. That's why I've insisted on low-flying fighters and bombers to defeat Britain quickly; one bomb on a hanger is worth fifty dropped on dwelling houses.

"The man truly guilty of the war today, in my opinion is Churchill," he went on, changing the subject without missing a beat.

"Churchill, that drunk, with his tippling cabal, with Vansittart, Belisha and the whole baying pack of them, doomed France too. When Chamberlain got home from Munich, all he had to do was call elections, and the peace party would have won in England by an overwhelming majority. I promised him peace in our time, and he proclaimed peace in our time as soon as he stepped off the plane, but he didn't understand what he needed to do. He told me he understood very well why I had to take Czechoslovakia. He let that drunken Churchill stir things up within the Parliament, and now Churchill has wrangled his way into the cabinet as First Lord of the Admiralty. The whole gang of Churchill's are pounding Chamberlain without mercy. In cases like this, I've always called for a plebiscite.

"But the British trade unions want to nationalise the land and the ownership of buildings. They've drawn up a program, and they want public ownership of industry and transport. Let them go ahead, and that could spell the end of the Conservatives and of Churchill. Sir Stafford Cripps is statesman enough to displace Churchill, bloodless though the man be personally – an ascetic against the fleshy indulgences of Churchill. A crisis now of this sort could save the situation, and we could negotiate peace. I warned Chamberlain that war with Germany would mean the loss of the Far East for Britain.

"Of course, a truly Red Britain – and don't forget that Cripps enjoys the confidence and approval of Stalin – would immerse that tiny island in such unspeakable poverty, its thirty million people would cast about so desperately they could threaten Europe.

"With their Empire, every Englishman dines well, and their comfortable life depends on their holding on to their Empire. The British have no ambitions in Europe. After their wars of hundreds of years ago, trying to hold on to their French possessions, they saw their destiny lay in an Empire beyond the seas, not in Europe, and for hundreds of years now, they have had no territorial designs on one inch of Europe. They have come to Europe to fight – and when they won – or lost – they went back to their island as fast as they could, without holding on to one field of turnips. With German hegemony in Europe, the British will face a friendlier Europe than they have in centuries – a Europe which will rigorously respect their Empire. Napoleon made that mistake. He tried to take Egypt, probably as a first step towards India. He challenged British holdings in the West Indies, challenged Britain's West Indies' sugar trade. He applied trade embargoes.

"I want to trade with the British Empire. I want British trade.

"That's why I choose Cripps against Churchill. I think Cripps thinks about the lower classes, who need the wealth trade brings to allow them to live a humane level. Churchill is an old man who splurges money on himself, who drinks and smokes immoderately.

"For me, there's nothing to choose between Churchill and Roosevelt. Roosevelt has a infirm mind and abjures America's safety. Americans always have had one idea – that one single power cannot control the Euroasiatic land mass. Roosevelt will give Stalin Europe if he can, and if he can't, he'll try to put Stalin within a jump of the North Sea. If I found myself at war with Russia, I'd make sure that Japan occupied Mongolia and Siberia – dividing the Euroasiatic landmass between our two nations, to keep Roosevelt's successor happy."

He sat quietly, and no one dared speak.

Then he said, "The British have a lot to teach us about diplomacy. I have diplomats in Tokyo, who can give no idea about the Japanese, what they want, what they plan. All my European diplomats have been just as hopeless. Now, British diplomats send an unending stream of information to London about the leaders of other countries, about public opinion. My diplomats tell me about what their barber or cleaning woman thinks. And the British have spies – spies everywhere."

I stopped breathing, but he didn't look at me.

"At last we have informants – in Holland, Belgium and France. By a miracle we know French and British tank strengths, although no one can tell us about the much-vaunted British Spitfire. We have a report of our informant having seen *eight* machine guns on the wings. *Some wings!* is all I can say. We lumbering, big-footed Germans, with our German accents, make poor spies. But the British have spies everywhere."

Today, the German newspapers tell us they lined up nine young Czech university students from the University of Prague, and firing squads shot them down. They never got a trial; and the newspapers talk about student demonstrations. The Germans arrested other students and closed the University for three years to Czech students. German students from the Protectorate will still go there. The newspapers quoted one Nazi authority as saying "we can't have joking in wartime."

Three million Sudaten Germans lived under the Czechs for some 20 years after the Great War, and the Czechs refrained from shooting a single one of them.

The papers also tell me that two Germans of 26 and 29 years, who passed on information to a foreign power, both workers, were guillotined yesterday. When I look around Prince Bernd's family, I cringe.

The Nazis have made work obligatory for Poles. I now discover that Poles never knew what work was, and the Germans will teach them. All Jews must do manual labour in places the war destroyed. The *Lokal Anzeiger* waxes furious at America flying its war planes into Canada, and handing them over. "Dirty smuggling is twice over dirty when the government itself does it," the paper howls.

258

A few days later, the Nazi mouthpiece, the *Völkisehor Bocbacher* warns that England is encompassing the annihilation of Germany and the enslavement of its people. The *Frankfurter Zeitung* in a front-page editorial this morning clamours that Britain will impose a peace treaty far worse than Versailles.

Each day, for five days, I tried to ring Axel Baer in Genéve, and each time they told me he was too busy. Gestapo Headquarters will be grinning about the course of true love never running smoothly...

Damn the man. Genéve *was* fun. But now they let us dance again in public, although the night clubs must close at one o'clock.

A few days later, Heinrich Himmler announced that the Nazis caught the leader of British Intelligence in Europe – a Mr. Best, and his nefarious accomplice, a Captain Steven, as they 'tried to cross the Dutch frontier into Germany.' What is sure, they never tried any such thing – so what happened?

I'm a jelly with fear. Do they know about WAGNER in Berlin? Will they be tortured? Can they betray me?

Prince Bernd and Claus told me I had nothing to worry about – that only London spymaster Graham Bunton knew about me.

Bunton, and about a score of other people here in Berlin...!

I asked then about the incredibly witless secret code Bunton had given me. "The Gestapo must be working on it every day. How come they haven't broken it! How long will it be – !"

Claus said, "Sometimes we Germans san be a bit square-headed. That code is so obviously addled, so brainless, I don't think it even occurred to them to try it."

On our illegal shortwave radio, we listened to the American correspondent, William Shirer, in Berlin, talk to his fellow correspondent, Ed Murrow, also of CBS, in London.

Murrow told Shirer how good it was to hear him, and Shirer said, 'the same here.' He said they didn't see half as much as they used to of each other, and Shirer reckoned there were reasons. Murrow laughed that he supposed there were a few.

Murrow said he was bouncing off lamp-posts and sandbags in the London blackout, and was going to ask New York for football pads. He said he had plenty of food, clothes, heat and whatnot. (So London wasn't doing so badly, thank God.)

Shirer said that in Berlin they hadn't seen much of the war, that he wanted to go to the Western front but they wouldn't let him. He said the Berlin lamp-posts are in the middle of the sidewalk so he was covered in bumps. (Thank God I went out at night by car most of the tine). He said the food wasn't too bad because he got a double ration (the same as myself) and that he got every three weeks a box of bacon, eggs, butter and cheese from Denmark. (Thank God I could get tins of corned beef, fish and whatnot from the Argentinean Embassy). Shirer missed decent coffee, but said that the government had promised a new substitute. He asked Ed Murrow what did the ordinary Englishman think about things.

Murrow told him people didn't talk about how long the war could last, but they're sure Britain will win, but uncertain as to how. Murrow said so many people were unemployed for ten or twelve years, but now they're working furiously in the shipyards on the Tyne and Clyde; digging in the coal mines in Rhondda; and toiling in the munition factories, which makes them very happy. The British papers warn then of a big attack in spring; but most people think the Navy and RAF will strangle Germany economically, which was how Germany collapsed in the Great War.

I felt so homesick!

Shirer said the ordinary German thought the war would be over quickly, and expects a big air war over Britain soon.

Sunday morning, December 17, over breakfast, the grandmother, Princess Gabriele Pfaffenhofen, asked me, "Is Christmas an important holiday in Argentina?"

I had studied that on the ship sailing to and from Buenos Aires.

I said, "My father, who is Spanish, told me that the Spanish celebrate Christmas Eve much more than Christmas Day itself, not like in England. They told me that in Argentina they celebrate both things."

"Ah," said the grandmother. "Here, in Germany, we celebrate Christmas Eve rather than Christmas Day, so you won't find it strange, then. It's a very important celebration, and everyone tries to have a Xmas tree with real candles, not those electric ones the shops try and sell. Nowhere in Europe is Christmas so important as here in Germany. All the cinemas, cafes, and theatres close at 8pm on Xmas Eve. I suppose the nightclubs too. Did you know that in the three Sundays before Xmas, the shops open? And that we are allowed a pair of stockings without coupons?"

She smiled sourly.

"What Hitler has brought us to. In Germany, men traditionally get a tie for Christmas, so in his goodness, Hitler has decreed that you can buy a man a tie for Christmas without coupons."

Out in the streets, I photographed boys waving Welfare Collection boxes for my coin, and they gave me, first, a coloured picture of Chamberlain with an umbrella, and then one of Churchill without an umbrella, but without a cigar either.

The clothing shops must have done a roaring business on these Sundays, but people crowded in front of their extravagant window displays, staring at the clothes – but no one went in. Clothing coupons! They guillotine you if you sell anything on the ration without coupons, and the newspapers have ghoulishly reported three or four executions. I had to wriggle my way into the bookstores; I had hardly room to breathe. Everywhere, I saw

German translations of British and American novelists, including Phillip Oppenheim – I think that was the way he spelled his name – England's master-novelist of books on intrepid British spies.

The grandmother had told us we couldn't buy a gramophone record without handing in an old one, and the Prince had joyfully collected a score of old, scratchy ones for each of us and told us to buy new ones.

And so it was,

I bought a collection of songs by Mahler for Heydrich, Wagner songs for Himmler, a tie and Mozart pieces for Goebbels. It was a moment from Unter den Linden to Gestapo Headquarters, then back to the Propaganda ministry.

For the Prince's family, I carried bags of records and books in the Underground, careful not to bump anyone, and then walked the rest.

I had bought a tie for Reinhard, and had brought a small bottle of perfume from Switzerland for Valeria. She helped me wrap up all my gifts, and put them away in a cupboard. They would lie at the foot of the Xmas tree.

I had looked at toys for three-year-old Christian, Andrea Boehr's son. Her husband had abandoned her, attacked me, but Thoma had felled him with a vase; now Andrea lived in a house bought from a Jewish accountant and his wife, who were safely in Spain.

Toys were mainly wooden soldiers, guns, tanks and fighter planes – the tin was kept for the war effort. I chose a train, a lorry and a Fokker passenger plane.

After lunch, I went to see her.

She answered the door immediately, and her face lit up.

"I'm so happy to see you!"

I sensed she was desperately lonely.

She showed me in, and offered me the so-called 'coffee'.

I had a packet of powdered chocolate from Switzerland, so we made hot chocolate.

"What has happened is so awful – you won't believe it, I can't tell anyone –"

"Go on," I urged her.

"Do you remember my mother won't have anything to do with me, because I married Heiner?"

I nodded. Heiner had knocked me down, and Thoma had felled him with a vase.

"My father, the same. My brother is on the Western Front, and my sister is in Frankfurt – she's a nurse in a hospital there – I wrote to them and they said they can't do anything, although they say they knew something like this would happen but they are on my side –"

"*What* did you write to them, Andrea?"

"You remember I work in the Labour Ministry, so I had to give my children to someone to care for them. Christian is three, and I gave him to friends, Hans and Ruth, while my baby Henning is with cousins – Petra and Wolfgang. I've been saving up my money for my Xmas here with them. Yesterday afternoon –"

She sobbed.

"Saturday, yes,' I prompted.

"I went there, to my friends, Hans and Ruth, to see my little Christian.

"Ruth said, 'We're just on our way out,' and she left as standing in the hall. She didn't ask me inside. The parlour door opened and Christian ran out into my arms. He caught as around my neck and begged, 'Mutti, mutti, take me out to play in the snow.'

'Hans appeared and didn't greet me. He didn't smile, but said in a chilling voice, 'Mutti won't do anything such thing. You're wearing your new suit and you're not rolling around outside in it.'"

Andrea stared at me. "Ruth had an operation, and can't have children. I glanced at her and then I saw she was watching Christian with his arms around my neck. Her jealousy was so plain!

"I told Christian, 'We'll play in the snow another day. Now we'll have a nice walk.'

"Ruth screeched, 'I told you we were going out!' She got herself under control. 'Please, Hans has to speak to you.' I put Christian down, and followed her into the parlour, all luxurious furniture. Hans was seated, but he didn't invite me to sit. He left me standing there, and said, 'I understand you've spoken to Ruth about taking Christian for Christmas,' I just stood there, struck dumb, because I knew what was coming. 'I'm sorry, that's out of the question. We have Christmas Day and Boxing Day all planned for him.'

"I stuttered, 'You mean I can have him only on Christmas Eve?'

"'Christmas Eve!' they both shrieked. "Christmas Eve is sacred! This is Christian's home!" Ruth cried, 'Christian is like our son. He feels part of us. You keep coming along and upsetting him. We're giving him all our love and you're confusing him.' Hans said, 'You don't pay us anything; you hardly have any rights in the matter. I think it's enough for you come for one afternoon every fortnight, but we don't think it's right you should stay with him in the house. You may take him out. It's not as though you don't have little Henning.'"

Andrea was weeping.

My head reeled.

At 20 years of age, how little I knew of the world. I had heard that children were certain grief and doubtful joy; was that cynicism, or the truth? How was I to cope with this – what was I to say to Andrea? I was a babe in the woods. Would English parents have been as cold to Andrea as hers were? I didn't imagine they would, but what did I know? In Spain, it wouldn't happen, and Hans and Ruth would have put their lives on the line speaking like that – if not Andrea, the neighbours would have lynched them. But England or Scotland? I felt people there *were* hard – yet gentler when it came to extremes like this. Germans today had this icy streak – or rather, Hitler had twisted them to think that what they wanted meant they could take it.

Dubiously, I told her, "You still have Henning."

She burst into loud tears.

I looked at her, dawningly, appalled.

"You went to your cousins," I whispered. "The same thing happened...?"

"Yes," Andrea wailed, uncontrollably. "Forgive me – forgive me...my father taught us that we should never show our feelings, or weep. That it was common... Yes, the same thing...my cousins, Petra and Wolfgang..."

She couldn't speak, strangled by sobs.

Then she quietened down.

"You could take boarders. You'd have money to pay them."

"They told us in the labour Ministry that in a few days they'll ration coal. Each house will get enough for a coal burning stove to heat one room – but not for a fireplace. Landlords with boarders must let them sit in the warm room as long as they want. I couldn't stand that."

"What are you going to do for Christmas?"

"I'll be here by myself. I'm not welcome to join my mother and father..."

I thought, she'll go mad. I couldn't invite her to the Prince's Schloss.

Then I thought – thank God, Britain has only 33 million people, and not 85 million. The rationing for 33 million will be far easier...

* * *

I stayed for another hour and a half, and gave her the toys I had bought for Christian.

264

On December 19, they called us to the Propaganda Ministry, to meet half-a-dozen pilots who had shot down 34 British bombers yesterday. I cringed on the outskirts of the correspondents; William Shirer was there and I ached to speak to him, but didn't dare. Would some correspondent give my game away? They were all eyes for the pilots.

Lieutenant-Colonel Karl Schumacher had led them. He was 43, and hefty to fit into a cockpit; he told us how the British came over with clear skies, making it easy for the German fighters to climb above them. Last Thursday, he said he'd shot down 10 out of 20 bombers only because of low cloud ceiling the bombers had hidden in. He had attacked with Messerschmitt 109s, and then slower, bigger "pursuit" planes had finished the British off. The Me-109 has only three machine guns, while the more cumbersome pursuit planes have more machine guns and cannon. He told us the battle had covered 150 miles of sky from Heligoland to the Dutch islands.

I took photos, feeling really frightened. What would happen in the air war over Britain in spring or summer? Defeat?

Back home, I begged Doris to ring her fiancé, Richterin Prieguity, in Luftwaffe Technical Planning, and beg him to come tonight.

He came at eight-fifteen, and after ten minutes of pleasantries, led me off to the library.

I told him what happened, and that Hitler had told me that perhaps the British Spitfire had 8 machine guns in the wings.

Richterin told me, 'Our Intelligence seems to confirm that."

"Why has the Me-109 only three?"

"The Me-109 has one on each wing, that is, one on each side, and one on the fuselage. You can't load the Me-109 wing with more – it suffers incredible stresses in a dive or in a very high speed turn. The machine gun and the ammunition belt add a dangerous weight."

"How fast does the Me-109 go?"

"The first ones at 292 mph. Later models have an upgraded engine and do over 300 mph. Speed is limited by the wings – you can't pull the wings off! Back before 1935, the British, the French, Fiat in Italy and Heinkel in Germany were obsessed with slower biplanes that could turn inside its opponent – could turn around a tabletop as it were. Willi Messerschmitt made a great leap – he decided on a very high-speed fighter, with a wide turn, and in Spain, he was proved right.

"He built an all-metal plane, with only one wing, and made the wing strong enough to stand up to the speed. The Me-109 in Spain – and the Russian monoplane, *Mosca* – shot down all the biplanes."

"When did they build the Spitfire?"

In 1935, too. A man called Mitchell, who, it would seem, made an even greater leap than Willi Messerschmitt, if he's put the incredible load of *eight* machine guns on his wings. That would mean that the Spitfire could shoot down Hitler's bombers without any help from pursuit planes, and that would decide the battle. Because our bombers are two-engined, low-flying planes, something like the British bombers we've just shot down. We shot down ten British bombers on one day – Thursday – and 34 yesterday. Imagine what will happen over Britain in summer, without cloud cover! Hitler will be finished.

"But they are green pilots. They didn't send them to Spain, that utter fool of Chamberlain, and the Prime Minister before Chamberlain. And the British Navy didn't take off the Spanish Republican pilots and bring them to Britain. Those two mistakes will decide the war. If the green British boys can last the first three weeks against our veterans because their planes are better, Hitler has lost the war. He won't be able to take Britain, and Britain is a great 'aircraft carrier' as it were, floating off the German coast. If the Americans fill it with their planes alongside future British airfleets, that 'aircraft carrier' will sink Germany. Today, the top Nazis, and Hitler too, are overjoyed at these 44 British bombers shot down, the blind fools. What it really means is that our bombers will be shot down too over Britain.

"If the Spitfire truly has eight machine guns, they can take out two or four of them, and put in cannon. That will be the end of our bombers."

"What did Mitchell do with the Spitfire wing to make it so strong?"

"Impossible to know. And impossible to believe! It just isn't possible! Some new metal...thank God, we haven't the remotest idea, so we can't copy it."

R.J. Mitchell put *five* beams into the wing of the Spitfire instead of just one inside... five beams one on top of the other, like the leaf-spring, the leaf-suspension, over the back wheels of a lorry. He did this in 1935. The Spitfire had eight Browning machine guns, of .303 inch. They took out two or four machine guns and put in their place Hispano cannon of 20 mm.

The Battle of Britain was decided by British engineering before it began. The first models were:

	HP	TOP SPEED	CEILING
Spitfire	1030	362 mph	32,000 ft
Me-109	635	292 mph	26,575 ft

A Rolls Royce Merlin engine of 27 litres powered the Spitfire.

R.J. Mitchell made a greater leap than Willi Messerschmitt in 1935, and foiled Hitler.

MAY 2, 1940
========

At least the temperature had gone up – between 16° and 21°. In January, the government – with Hitler's blessing – had forbidden us to take baths or showers, so in the morning, Doris, Thoma and I stripped naked in the bathroom, and washed one another's backs with wet towels. Then, shivering, we washed our own selves, still with the towels. The Germans don't have the problem with nudity we London maidens do, but a cold business it had been till these buds of May.

Today is Ascension Day, and the German Press has red-ink, banner headlines of German victories in Norway over British troops. They write, "The British sent some of their best troops. They defended, with the Norwegians, every creek, every turn of the valley to the last man or to the last bullet. They dug themselves in and raked the narrow valleys and the roads with murderous machine gun fire." I felt sick to my stomach, and out in the streets filled with people, I felt an exultation among the Germans. They had little respect for the Poles, but more for the British Army and very much for our Navy. Chamberlain tells us the British Navy is in force – in the Mediterranean! The average Berliner feels the Navy didn't dare show itself off the Norwegian coast, and that the German Army has beaten the famed British Army hands down in a fair fight.

I went home, frightened.

That night, Claus told me, "I'm going to have a quick bite, and then type a report for you to encode. We will attack Holland, Belgium and Luxembourg on the tenth of this month – in eight days. You have to microdot the message and get it to the Argentinean Embassy. They have to get it very fast to Genève, because it will be too long to send from Berlin without attracting attention."

We ate in silence. No one said a word. Claus hurried off to the library, and I sat, miserably, looking at them all.

The grandmother said briskly, "Claus should have finished his first page. Off with you, girl, you've got to play a great part now in matters of great moment, or we're all going to spend the rest of our days under Hitler and the Gestapo."

I got to my feet, with wobbly knees, and went to the library. Were my fellow Englishmen going to be much good in defending us Englishwomen?

Claus handed me the first page. I read it, and had to run to the bathroom. I came back, and then had to go back again.

Some spy.

I took my copy of Lorna Doone, page 39, line 15, "outlandish part where...", and prepared to send the most incredible message.

O	U	T	L	A	O	
N	D	I	S	H	N	
B	C	E	F	G	B	
J	I	M	P	Q	J	
R	T	W	X	Z	R	X = XY
O	U	T	L	A	O	

ALLOUT ATTACK BELGIUM HOLLAND LUXEMB MAY 10. FEINT. PLACE BEST MOBILE TROOPS AND 2000 TANKS ON 25-MILE FRONT BETWEEN SEDAN CHARLEVILLE MONTHERMÉ. PRINCIPLE ATTACK THERE THROUGH ARDENNES FOREST OR GUDERIAN AND REINHARDT WILL TRAP BEF FROM REAR.

I sat back, and thought – they won't believe this. They WON'T listen.

Claus interrupted me. "A plane of ours crashed with these plans. That they thought it was a 'plant', a trick, we're so sure that we're going ahead. It now all depends on you. They MUST believe it when *you* confirm it."

I had to rush back to the bathroom. I thought I was going to throw up.

Back with Claus, I read the explanation. They HAD to believe it after reading it.

Claus explained on his typewritten sheet – which I had to encode, all of it – that after the Polish campaign, the Old Guard in the German High Command still refused to absorb the lessons of the lightning Panzer strokes. In the attack on Belgium, they wanted to follow the 1914 Schlieffen Plan of striking through Belgium into France, north of Amiens, and then swinging down to behind Paris. The Senior German General Staff couldn't take in the striking power and speed of tank warfare, and wanted to replay 1914. They feared French military know-how, and knew how the French and British General Staffs shared the same doubts about mechanised war. They feared the French and British could well be right. Of course, the allies would expect the Germans to follow the Schlieffen route and fiercely try to stop them on all the Belgian rivers. But they will spread their tanks thinly across their Front, often an individual tank with infantry units, so that one tank will find itself facing a score of Panzer tanks.

Rundstedt's Chief of Staff, Manstein, presented another plan. The Maginot Line ran from the Swiss frontier to cover the Luxembourg frontier and stopped at the Belgian frontier. The first part of the Belgian frontier was the Ardennes Forest. North of the Forest, the frontier gave way to the agricultural plain – Flanders' mud of the Great War – and the coast.

The Forest – the Ardennes Forest – was impenetrable.

Manstein told Rundstedt that what they had seen in Poland was that tanks could – and did – speed through so-called impenetrable forests. So tanks could go through the narrow, winding cart tracks of the Ardennes Forest, or even through the trees.

Rundstedt had four Panzer Corps, and Manstein told Rundstedt they could send two Corps through the Ardennes – one Corps under Guderian and the other under Reinhardt. Guderian and Reinhardt loved it – they went wild.

Rundstedt fired Manstein.

But Manstein went to Hitler – who loved it.

Hitler insisted on watching all the War Games, and told his Generals that the Games clearly showed the Ardennes was the way to go.

Hitler ordered Guderian, with his three Panzer divisions, and Reinhardt with his two divisions, plus all the attached motorised divisions and bridging equipment for crossing the Meuse, to smash through the Ardennes.

And, sick to the stomach, I realised they had condemned to

destruction the BEF – the British Expeditionary Force of some 300,000 British soldiers. Hitler had defeated them before they fired the first shot.

After Guderian said yes, Hitler was the only one to think further. He asked Guderian, "When you cross the Meuse, then what?"

Guderian told Hitler, "Unless I am ordered otherwise, I plan the next day to push westwards. The High Command must then decide whether I go for Paris or Amiens. In my view, I should pass Amiens to reach the British Channel."

Claus said, "And Hitler mused, 'And doom the French armies in Belgium, and the BEF. Guderian, *you* shall decide.'"

While the French had some 3,000 tanks with armour up to 78 mm thick – and the British had some 200 tanks, mainly Matildas with thick armour, again, 78 mm maximum, and a 40 mm gun – the Germans had only some 2,700 tanks... 2,050 of them were Mark Is, with two machine guns and tinplate armour, and Mark IIs, with a 20 mm gun.

They had 630 Mark IIIs, with a 37 mm gun and Mark IVs with 50 mm and 75 mm guns, of low velocity. Their armour was 30 mm thick. They also had Czech 10 tonners with a 37 mm gun.

I had to encode all this and get it urgently to London – through Genéve.

I continued encoding my message.

WHEN GERMANS REACH ARDENNES THROUGH LUXEMB BELG WILL WELD METAL BEAMS TO FRONT BUMPERS OF LORRIES EQUAL TO TANK WIDTHS AND FLAG PRACTICABLE ROUTES THROUGH ARDENNES TO MEUSE TWEEN SEDAN GUDERIAN AND MONTHERME REINHARDT. GUDERIAN REINHARDT WILL TRAP BEF IN TIGHT POCKET. BLOCK BEF WITHDRAWL INTO FRANCE.

I worked till one am; the alarm woke me at seven; and I went on working almost to midday. They brought me my breakfast on a tray. I had everything microdotted at 11.45.

In the bathroom Princess Jutta wiped me down with a hot, wet towel and soap.

After a light lunch, I was at the Argentinean Embassy at 2 pm, where an appalled Rubén Zorreguieta heard my story.

"As we've had two days' holiday, a courier goes to Genéve this evening, so London will have this by tomorrow. Stop fretting. You'll see how the BEF will be waiting for them at the Ardennes."

MAY 10, 1940
=========

They called me to the Foreign Office at the ungodly hour of 8 am on May 10, 1940.

Herr von Ribbentrop read us out a memorandum to say Germany has marched into the Low Countries because Britain and France had decided to attack Germany. German troops have stormed in to protect the Low Countries' neutrality, and blame the two tiny countries for building fortifications against Germany but not against France and Britain.

The Germans have handed a memorandum to the Ministers of Holland and Belgium, requiring that their governments give orders to offer no resistance to the liberating German soldiers. Otherwise, "If the German troops meet resistance in Belgium or Holland, it will be crushed by every means. The Belgian and Dutch governments alone will bear the blame...for the consequences and bloodshed which will be altogether unavoidable."

Hitler has made a proclamation to his troops – "The hour of decision for the battle for the future of the German nation is upon us."

* * *

In the streets, people looked unconcerned, and hardly anybody spent their pennies on newspapers.

I crossed over to the Propaganda Ministry and caught Hans Schneppen arriving. He sat me down on the other side of his desk while he hung up his hat.

He smiled. "You want to ask me what I think? Who will lose irreparably will be Britain. It will lose its Empire – what three-and-a-half centuries of Empire builders have built, this decadent generation cannot even hold on to. Suppose America and Russia under Roosevelt finally crush us –

277

we will arise again, stronger than before. But now we will capture and humiliate a great English army. In Asia, 'face' is everything. The English sahib behaves like a demi-god, treats the natives like dirt, and the Empire stands on this myth. In Africa too. When we humiliate the British in the next few days that will be the end. The Asiatics will rise up. Suppose Japan attacks – it will even capture Australia."

"Japan!" I exclaimed.

"I'm just supposing. It's possible we will occupy the British Isles themselves in July."

He leant back.

"I want to join Guderian."

"What! You're crazy!" Cunningly, he added, "Why Guderian?"

"Can I see Dr. Goebbels? I want to join Guderian."

"You're the clever one, no doubt about you. And no doubt about your not joining Guderian."

"Then I'll camp here in your office."

"Then we'll arrest you and send you –" He paused.

"Where? To Guderian."

"Mein Gott! You're impossible. I'll speak to Goebbels."

"If he says no, tell him I'll come back tomorrow."

'If he says no, it's no."

"I'll appeal to Hitler."

"Bluffing, on top of everything else. Women! Hitler will be pleased, I don't think."

* * *

I marched up the street to the Reichchancellery. They let me in, unbelievably, and I left a written message for Hitler. He had gone off to the Western Front, they said.

Next day, the Germans crossed the River Maas and reached the Yssel Line, the front Dutch line of defence. They crossed the Albert Canal...its bunkers couldn't stop them. No allied fighters – the Germans threw bridges across all the water defences.

After the Great War, Belgium took Malmédy in the Ardennes from Germany, and today an exultant Germany took it back.

I went back to Schneppen, with a tin of Argentinean corned beef.

"Hah!" he cried, and made to hand it back.

I said, "Keep it as evidence against me. I want to join Guderian. I want 50 rolls of film. I want to see Dr. Goebbels, now!"

I stamped my foot.

"We can't have you terrifying Dr. Goebbels. It would be worth my neck for me to let you loose on him." He laughed. "I've spoken to Goebbels, and even argued in your favour. I'll go upstairs again, today, I promise. What clothes would you wear?"

"Dark grey slacks and a light grey shirt." I decided not to say, 'blouse', which sounded feminine and unwarlike.

'I'll mention that too," he chuckled. "We've got some work for you this afternoon, if you feel inclined," he added ironically.

"Of course I'll do it," I snapped. "Give me something to do till you send me."

"How do you expect us to send you?"

"Fly me to Luxembourg, the capital of Luxembourg."

"Go on! Have we captured it yet?"

"Probably."

"Ach! Wait till I repeat this conversation to Goebbels. And now what I want to know – and Goebbels too – is how do you know that's where Guderian is?"

"Because it's where I would be if I were Guderian."

He shook his head.

"Dr. Goebbels is not going to believe this."

"I want to join Guderian! Can I leave tonight?"

"You cannot. Off to work with you. You 20-year-olds!"

Next day, the papers reported that yesterday the Germans had taken Belgium's most powerful fort, Eben-Emael. I had sent a coded message to London, warning them that the Germans would parachute on to the roof.

London had ignored me.

Eben-Emael protects Leige, and commands the place where the Meuse joins the Albert Canal. A certain first-lieutenant Witzig landed on the roof –

whether by glider or parachute I don't know – and got from Hitler's own hands Germany's high military medal – the Knight's Cross of the Iron Cross.

He and his men made the thousand men inside surrender.

Yesterday, also, they did occupy Luxembourg, and so reached the Ardennes.

Today, our illegal shortwave wireless set said that low-flying, two-engine German bombers had pulverised, had flattened Rotterdam – left it a ruin of smoking rubble.

I sank into a daze. London – Birmingham – Manchester – Leeds – Coventry – Liverpool – Edinburgh – Glasgow. They would all disappear, with millions of dead under the rubble. Could our green pilots stop them?

I staggered upstairs to my bedroom, and feeling ill, encoded a message:

GREEN FIGHTER PILOTS WHO FALL BEHIND GERMAN LINES LOST. THOSE BEHIND OUR LINES WILL LEARN FROM THAT MISTAKE.
WITHDRAW SPITFIRES HURRICANES TO BRITAIN TO RECOVER ALL PILOTS. IMPERATIVE FULL RESERVE AGAINST BOMBER ONSLAUGHT ON BRITISH CITIES LIKE ROTTERDAM.

I microdotted it, and went over to the Argentinean Embassy. Rubén was sombre at the news of Rotterdam, and gave me a tin of corned beef to cheer me up.

Back home, at lunch, listening to the German wireless, we heard a German commentator reporting the air bombing of allied defences in Belgium. We could hardly hear him for the stunning howl of planes and bombs. I cringed. Were there British soldiers under that? Could I stand it if I travelled with Guderian – could I hold my cameras still? Hitler's choice of two-engine, low level bombers is devastating – God help my country, my England, when they show in our skies.

Where IS the British Expeditionary Force?

Next day, at 8.30 am, they rang to say they would come to get me at 9.30. They were flying me to Luxembourg, to join Guderian.

At 8.45, the phone rang again.

It was Doctor Goebbels.

"Raimunda, you are a naughty girl. You besieged me in my own Ministry. To show how much I appreciate you, I rang Hitler, who said you could go if you could take photos that they would want to see a thousand years from now. Well, that's a big order."

I laughed and cried.

"And I'm giving you fifty rolls of film."

I joked, "What can I bring you from France?"

"Now there's a question," he said.

I thought of all his actresses and mistresses. "Perfume?" I suggested.

"Ah," he breathed. "Perfect. Are you a good judge?"

"I know what I like myself. Afterwards, you will tell me."

We took off at eleven, and I found myself sitting beside an astonished Generalleutnant.

I explained hastily who I was. "I am attached to Generaloberst Heinz Guderian's Panzer Corps. What is the news?"

"Today, we have knocked out Holland. They have capitulated, or are about to sign the capitulation. We're turning our armies from Holland to Belgium. We're fighting the French First Army along the Dyle River. South, stands the French Ninth Army."

"And the BEF?'

"They're in there somewhere," he said, dismissively.

"When Guderian appears on the French side of the Ardennes, what French Army will he face?"

"The French have nothing there. We've brushed aside French screening forces inside the Ardennes and near Sedan and Monthermé, but they haven't bothered us. We've had much more of a headache organising our traffic flow than bothering about the French."

"But if the French now move up an Army Group?"

"They would need two weeks. They've got poor radio communications. It would take them two days to get moving, and they don't have lorries. To move a French Army say two hundred miles takes about two weeks.

"And to move a Panzer Army Corps?"

281

"Inside Germany? Two hundred miles? About six hours," he said unemotionally. "Of course, the French probably have more tanks than military lorries. We've been meeting them in Belgium, but they're heavily scattered. They have thick armour-plating, but when one French *char* finds itself surrounded by a dozen of our light Panzer tanks, what can it do? It finds it has German tanks in front, on each side, and behind."

"I have heard that Rundstedt didn't want to make this attack through the Ardennes."

"He's a decent man – but thick," said my companion. "You must never repeat what I have just said – I put my life in your fair, female hands."

"I know better than to repeat something like that," I said primly. "Women know better than men what can be said and not said."

"How are you getting to the front?"

"I suppose a lorry will be waiting for me."

"You can come in my staff car."

He had not given his name, and I knew not to ask him.

We landed at Luxembourg, and he dismissed the lorry driver who had been sent for me.

"Now that driver can better pick up supplies, without having to hurry to get you to Guderian."

His open staff car drove quickly to Arlon, and then plunged into beautiful, rough roads inside the Ardennes, where we motored under the canopy of the trees, close by on each side.

The Generalleutnant told me, "We have the 15th Panzer Division at Dinant, the 19th – that's Guderian – at Sedan, and the 41st at Monthermé."

"That would be Reinhardt."

"You are well informed."

"I had a talk on the phone with Dr Goebbels."

"Oh, good," he said approvingly. "We're self-sufficient for nine days, and have petrol for 125 miles."

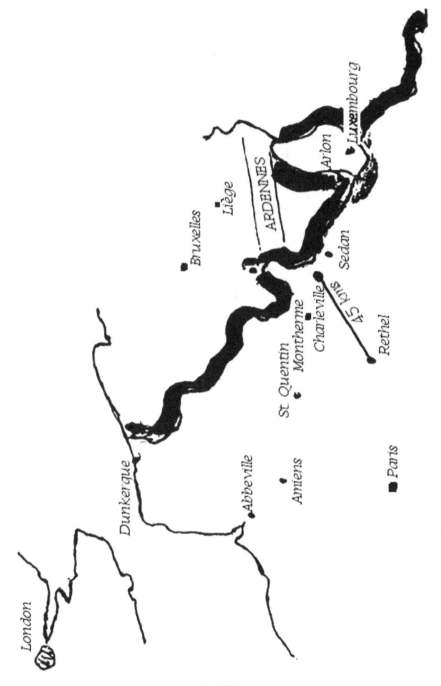

London

Dunkerque

Abbeville

Amiens

Paris

St. Quentin

Monthermé

Charleville

Rethel

45 kms

Sedan

Bruxelles

Liège

ARDENNES

Arlon

Luxembourg

283

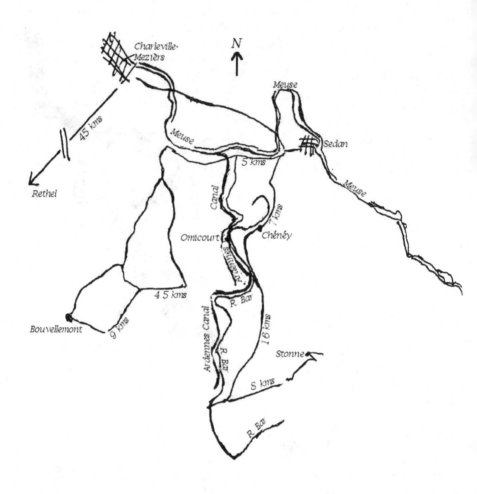

"Enough for Amiens. But Amiens isn't on the coast."

"Indeed not," he said, looking at me curiously. "So what would an Argentinean do?"

"I'd go for Abbeville."

"What? One hundred and forty miles?"

"It has the advantage of being at the head of the estuary. The sea comes in to meet you."

"I'm sorry we can't have you with us at Dinant with the 15th."

"Where is Dinant?"

"About 50 miles north of Sedan."

The day was sunny, with white clouds crossing the blue sky. Often the green foliage shut out the sky, or opened a little to let the sun slant through. The air was pleasantly cool in the open staff car, and the lorry driver had given me a Panzer jacket, with PRESS roughly printed on the front with white paint.

Guderian didn't miss a detail!

I struggled out of my grey jersey, and put on the Panzer coat – it better stopped the rush of air.

We drove fast along a narrow, twisting, dirt road, and after many miles, caught up with a convoy of lorries. There was no room to pass, so we slowed down, and followed them from about 400 yards, to keep out of their dust.

I laughed. "You don't think much of the French. And the British?"

"Their decadent aristocrats control the Army. If an aristocratic son is stupid, they try to put him in the Church, in England. If he's really hopeless, they dump him on the Army. These aristocratic sons think the world owes them everything – nothing is expected of them."

I said lightly, "And have you had to fight yet?"

"The French 213th Infantry Regiment and the French 7th Tank Battalion attacked Guderian yesterday, at Chéréy. (see P.91(C)) Gudenian has a bridgehead about five miles deep, covering the ground between Sedan and Monthermé. The tank battalion had light FCM tanks only – they've only got a 37 mm gun – and our anti-tank and flak guns knocked them out. Then our Panzers came up and finished them off. The French have got their heavy tanks – and they're the ones we would have to worry about – up in Belgium, fighting off our feint invasion."

Silence fell.

I said contritely, "If you have to go to Dinant, I'm taking you out of your way."

"Don't you worry," he said. "I had to see our Chief-of-Staff of the Panzergruppe, Colonel Zeitzler, and then would have reported to Guderian from Dinant by radio. Now I'll speak personally, which will be much better."

"What is Guderian like?"

"He doesn't like orders being countermanded," he laughed. "For this to work, it has to be done his way or not done at all. You know: 'Order – Disorder – Order!' Colonel General Heinz Guderian has always believed in independent tank groups with motorised infantry and motorised artillery since 1920 – when hardly anybody else did. He admits you can't drag along heavy artillery, so he wants Stukas to do that job. When Hitler came to power, the Führer backed him – Hitler loved his ideas. Hitler backed him and Thoma and Reichenau too; and he promoted Heinz quickly, and in 1938 named him General, as the successor to Lutz, who is the real father of these new tactics – well, that is, General of the Armoured Troops – that's what he made Guderian. Guderian teaches us high speed, non-stop pressure and advance and disruption of the enemy rear – he did it in Poland, and now we'll see whether he can do it here. In Poland, he destroyed thousands of artillery pieces or captured them, he moved so fast, and he crushed seven Polish divisions. Luckily, in the West, they think the Polish Army was a small, poorly equipped, outmoded raggle-taggle. The Poles had a formidable army, which we destroyed with our new tactics. Now, in Belgium and France, each side has about two million men, but you'll see how we destroy the French and British armies in a couple of weeks the way we did the Polish. The Poles had well over a million men, they tell me, but I don't know what the true figure was. Here we face two million men, as I say, but you see, we won't need more than a couple of weeks."

* * *

We came out of the denser woods, and the road wound downwards. At one bend, I caught a glimpse of the Meuse.

The Brigadier said, "We've crossed the Meuse – our engineers have put pontoon bridges across."

We didn't cross the river, but drove into a thickly wooded copse close by. The staff car stopped, and I followed the Brigadier along a path to two trailers. Sentries saluted and stared at me.

The Brigadier went to the second, larger trailer – the door was open.

He stepped up, greeted the half a dozen high officers inside, then took my hand and led me in.

I recognised Guderian instantly, with his high, bald front, his moustache, his piercing, bagged eyes, the prominent nose, chin and cheekbones, his sunken cheeks in a triangular face that gave him an expression of concentration, even in repose. He looked clever, controlled and strong. He stared at me, then turned to my Brigadier.

286

"Gerard, I'm astonished to see you. I expected to hear from you by radio from Dinant. You are more than welcome, and your devotion to duty, coming so far out of your way, is an example to us all." He smiled, looking back at me. All the officers burst into laughter, and looked at me too.

I smiled sweetly at them all.

Guderian said, "I believe, young lady, you were so anxious to meet me you went over Goebbels' head to Hitler. I am flattered. And I believe that Goebbels demands we capture all the French perfume we can for you to take back to him."

I felt myself blush.

"How can I thank you for letting me come?"

"I believe that Hitler has tasked you with taking photos that people will want to see a thousand years from now. Let us see whether we can make history worthy of your photos."

Now I grinned at him, and everyone grinned back.

Guderian said, "You can come and go as you wish and take your photos. I have designated an orderly to look after you, and put up your tent and so on. You will mess with us."

Gerard, my Brigadier, said, "We've been talking on the road, and Ray advises us to head for the estuary of the Somme, because, she says, the sea comes inland to meet us."

Everyone stared at me in silence.

I said nervously, "I just mentioned Abbeville – we were conversing." My voice trailed away.

Guderian said, "We are going to get on famously. As famously as you did with Sepp," and everyone laughed again.

I was with Sepp Dietrich's division in Poland.

We heard planes outside.

Everyone hurried out of the trailer, and went to the edge of the trees.

They were peering upwards, shading their eyes, and I shot Guderian close up, and then them all in a group.

About a dozen planes flew towards us, old-fashioned machines with French markings – and four with British! The flak guns exploded with deafening noise. I saw bright, smoky flashes buffet the planes, and then two caught fire. Another tipped to one side. Bombs fell on the bridges and into the river. A British bomber blew up, with drifting pieces, another dropped its nose and dived out of control towards us. A third caught fire and I saw English pilots jump out and open their parachutes. The fourth English plane

287

turned upside down, and then dropped like a stone. The French planes were on fire, or their crews were parachuting. I ran towards where the British bomber would land, and two bombs exploded near me.

I was safe on the ground while these men were dying. Where were our modern planes! Where was the BEF? That bloody General Ironside, who led the BEF?

The English bomber smashed into the ground and flames engulfed it. I could make out figures. The heat drove me back, and I took two shots without thinking.

Then two men parachuted to ground to my right, and I ran over to them. They rolled on the ground, and got to their feet.

"Are you English?"

"Indeed, we are. Who are you?"

"I'm awfully sorry, but you're prisoners. Leave your parachutes there. Would you like to come with me?"

"Never did man have a fairer captor," said the taller one. He turned to his companion. "Those bloody bridges are still there." They both examined the river.

Then they turned their faces up to the sky.

"Got every one of us. As with the two earlier raids."

I walked back towards Guderian, and they followed.

"I'm not sure captor is the right word," said the shorter man, a red head. "I would have thought that was a masculine noun."

"There's no feminine form of the word," I said.

We reached Guderian and his officers, who looked at us quizzically. Infantrymen stood to one side, with their rifles at the ready.

The English pilots gave Guderian a smart salute, despite their ruffled appearance, and he returned it gravely. He made a gesture to an Unterfeldwebel, and said in German, "Give them everything they need. Let them see a doctor."

As he led them off, they said, "So nice meeting you," to me.

Guderian joked, "You take prisoners as well as photos."

I had shot them saluting Guderian.

Back in the trailer, Guderian said, "They were determined English pilots and brave men. In 1914, in France, we faced tough peasant soldiers who wanted revenge for the Franco-Prussian War. But today, we're going to meet urban conscripts – the staggering casualties of the Great War terrify them. I promise you we won't meet many like those two Englishmen. The French armies haven't got proper communications for the hourly changes in the front we will cause – the French have badly designed fighter planes and obsolete bombers, as you just saw. Today, we have shot down 41 planes and not a single one has escaped. The French are masters of static war – a million men who *nobody* can move from where they are, unless you cut off their supplies. Stubborn men who dig in and hold on. With long, rigid supply lines."

We heard planes, and ran out.

I counted fifteen, with about six British. Me-109s appeared, and dived on them. The planes broke up in the air. Bombs dropped on the river and bridges, but did little damage. Some men got out in their parachutes and landed on the far side of the river.

Planes crossed above our heads, and ran into a storm of anti-aircraft fire, filling the sky with flashes and dark smoke. The planes caught fire or broke up and fell to earth.

By the end of that day, we had lost close on 90 planes. The RAF machines were Fairey Battles, and the French were Bréguets with some LeOs and Amiots. RAF Official History writes: "no higher rate of loss in an operation of comparable size had ever been experienced by the Royal Air Force."

In the trailer, a phone rang, and Guderian grabbed it. He listened, put it back, and said,"Colonel Balck has crossed the Bar river and the Ardennes canal near Omicourt! Gentlemen, we're rolling! From Omicourt to the Somme at St. Quentin it's open, undulating farmland – a paradise for our tanks! Next stop, the Somme river! I've told him I'm bringing up the 1st and 2nd Panzers to him. Let's go next door."

We hurried out of his trailer to the second one. I realized it had antennae on the roof, and a small petrol engine at the back chugged quietly, probably driving a generator.

Inside, I saw radio equipment stacked up the back wall, on rubber cushions and springs. Two narrow tables ran along each side, under windows, with Morse transmitter keys, microphones and telephones. A sort of typewriter with a score of cog wheels and several axles stood at the far end – a coding machine I supposed. A major saw me looking, and said proudly, "Our Enigma machine. Its messages are an enigma for the enemy."

A Polish engineer gave the British a copy of the Enigma machine before the war, and in part, the Allies won the war because they decoded all instructions to the German armed forces on all fronts. Field Marshall Montgomery, in the Battle of Alamein, knew exactly where Rommel would attack. Montgomery made the Enigma liaison officers bivouac in an unknown wadi near his caravan and never acknowledged the key part of Enigma in the battle. He told reporters he had a photo of Rommel on the wall of his caravan, and studying Rommel's face carefully, 'divined' where Rommel would attack.

Chairs stood alongside tables, and Guderian sat. He nodded at an operator, and them spoke into a microphone. "General Kirchnet. This is Guderian. Let your 1st Panzer divison roll. Look on your road map! Can you see Rethel! It's yours, my friend!"

Next day, the French attacked to the south. I went down in a lorry, but they made me stop two kilometres from the thunder of the guns. Guderian had put the Grossdeutschland Regiment to cover himself down here, and the French burst in with their heavy Char B tanks of their 3rd Armoured Division, and a battalion of light H-39, I could have wept with frustration. I was digging my fingernails into the palms of my hands. Couldn't they get anything right! The whole day long, the tanks of the 10th Panzer Division and the anti-tank guns of the Grossdeutschland Regiment fought back. They brought me rations and a water bottle at midday, and I slipped into a wood, and followed narrow, winding trails. After a couple of kilometres, shells were exploding just beyond some trees. I wriggled into some rocks, and saw burning tanks, and dead men. I saw the French Chars storm forward with the same bravery of the First World War, their cannon blazing. On they came, with shells exploding on their armour. Shells pierced one here, another there, as I shot my film. The crews staggered out of the hatches, dragging heroic wounded Frenchmen after them. The light H-39s rolled in with suicidal bravery as I shot my film – and shot still more. The shells destroyed the light tanks, and sometimes a dazed and wounded French hero would stagger out and fall to the ground. Tears ran down my face. The trap was closing on the BEF. Where was bloody Ironside? Where were the Matilda tanks? Columns of smoke rose from the tanks, and spread out to fill the air with the smell of scorched flesh. German tanks burnt everywhere.

Shells burst close by, and I burrowed into my rocks and heard shrapnel ricochet viciously.

A Panzer tank took a hit, one hundred yards below me. The captain staggered out of the hatch, and tried to pull a man after him. He had no strength; blood streamed from his head. I pushed my camera into my haversack and rushed down. Smoke spiralled up from the engine. It was going to catch fire. I scrambled up, pushed aside the captain, and pulled out the other man. Men rushed over, and lifted them both off the tank. A third man painfully climbed up inside the tank. I grabbed him and yanked. The bloody tank was going to explode – I smelt smoke everywhere. A Stabsfeldwebel raced over.

"Keep back!" I shouted. "It's going to explode."

He jumped up, caught me around the waist, and lifted me bodily off the tank. Other men pulled out the third crew member.

I found myself looking an Oberstleutnant in the face. He was laughing till the tears ran from his eyes.

"In the German Army, Fraulein, women don't give orders to Sergeant Majors!"

Everyone dispersed, and dropped into trenches.

The Sergeant Major said, "When I tell you, make a run for those trees, and then go back to Guderian. Guderian said you might be worse than the French, and the Old Man was right."

* * *

Guderian received me with a face of thunder.

I said meekly, "I've got a lot of film that has to get back to Berlin."

He called a despatch rider, who took my film, while Guderian glowered.

He turned back to his maps on the wall of his trailer with his other officers. I took close-up photos, and they ignored me.

A cable ran from the communications trailer to Guderian's headquarters trailer. At about five o'clock, the phone rang, and we all hurried to the other trailer.

Guderian spoke into a mike. "Guderian here."

There was static and hissing.

"Is that the regimental commander of the Grossdeutschland? Come in!"

We all looked at a loudspeaker on the wall.

"The French have pushed us out of Stonne. My men are physically exhausted and in no state for further combat."

Guderian said, "I have no one to send you. Hold! Push your men till they drop. Give no more ground than you must."

"Very good!"

291

We walked slowly back to the main trailer, and at 5.30, half an hour later, the phone rang.

We crossed to the other trailer.

The loudspeaker broke into life.

"I am a radio operator. The French have launched a strong attack towards Chéhéry."

A corporal said, "Message received."

Guderian said, "Give me Luxembourg."

A voice rasped out of the loudspeaker.

Guderian said, "Collect every last truck, and bring infantry. Every truck must tow a piece of light artillery or 88 mm guns."

The 88 mm was a gun that could fire against a tank, or they could tilt it up to the vertical, on cogged wheels to use as a flak gun.'

Guderian went on, "I am sending every free truck to carry infantry and guns."

The loudspeaker said, "Message received."

Guderian looked around the group of officers.

"We have to stop this First War thinking – protecting our rear in Luxembourg! We have to advance like lightning – blitzkreig! Our problem is *not* our rear. That's First War thinking. Our problem is our front! And as we fly across France before they can react, we must place a screen of infantry and artillery along our flanks. That's all we need. We can race back at 30 miles an hour to meet a counterattack to cut our line of advance in two. If we have to, we'll race back with hundreds of tanks at 30 miles an hour. But meanwhile, we have to race forward. The infantry army marches twenty miles a day, and now they're thirty miles behind us. They will catch up eventually and form an impenetrable wall. *But we're not going to wait for them! We're not going to worry about them!*"

The other officers nodded, and smiled at him, and some looked uneasy, or surprised.

He turned and smiled at me. "Young lady, you appear neither surprised nor worried. Do you agree with me?"

That broke the tension, and everyone grinned.

"You stop pedalling and you'll fall off," I said.

"Bravo!" he cried, and everyone laughed. "If we stop, we fall off."

They turned sober again, and sat on the chairs, watching the loudspeaker.

The voice came on at 6.20. "The French are attacking with enormous courage, but they don't have enough tanks, I am to report to you. Am I speaking to the Colonel-General?"

"You are," barked Guderian

At 6.30, we heard the voice.

"I am ordered to report to the Old Man that the French attack has failed."

"This is Guderian," he growled. "Message received."

* * *

We dined under the trees. I was cold, and I had to tell them about Belize and the north of Argentina. They plied me with questions, and then they reminisced about visits to England and France. They talked about the Austrian Alps, and how when Guderian raced down to Vienna to take over Austria, one third of his tanks broke down.

Every few minutes, a corporal came from the other trailer with wireless reports he had written down of maintenance and repairs to tanks and vehicles.

The communications were fantastic.

How could the French respond without this sophisticated wireless network?

Guderian said, "When we get far enough into France, we'll be out of contact with Berlin, thank God."

I looked astonished.

"We use a weak, very-long-wave transmission, so enemy receivers can't pick up our messages unless they're very close. And if they're that close, they've far too many worries to think about *our* transmissions. But they have hardly any transmissions at all. They probably use the telephone at the local bar!" and everyone chortled.

Next morning, scores of tanks arrived, with lorries full of troops, towing 88mm guns and other light artillery.

I awoke early in my tent, and asked Guderian to let me wash in the Meuse. He ordered a squad to men to go with me to protect my modesty, and

293

told them to 'face outwards' or he'd string them up by their heels. I asked could they swim after I had finished, and he said 'five minutes!' So, to the envy of all, they marched me down to the river, where I soaped myself all over, with the soldiers looking at me over their shoulders and grinning. I ran out naked, and dried behind a blanket, hung from a tree. Then they all stripped, and ran naked into the river.

Back at Guderian's trailer, I found consternation – all the officers looking at the Old Man, who was furious.

I caught up with him.

"What has happened?" I panted.

"Kleist," he barked.

Were the 350,000 British troops in Belgium saved?

The German military command had split in two.

Hitler, and his two cronies, Generals Wilhelm Keitel and Alfred Jodl, who seldom left his side. Under Hitler's influence, they were usually daring.

The OKW, the Oberkommando Der Wehrmacht – the High Command of the German Armed Forces – were more conservative and unhappy in great part with this new-fangled Blitzkreig Panzer war. They had a strong aristocratic stiffening at the top levels – the Prussian military caste – and had little enthusiasm for Hitler. However, loyalty to their leadership – now Hitler – was born into their bones. Ewald von Kleist was their unlikely scion – an aristocrat close to the Von Hindenburg family, and a monarchist to his toenails – chosen for this wild breakthrough from the Ardennes.

Guderian spoke into a mike.

Kleist's voice came through the loudspeaker. "Stay where you are for another 36 hours. The mass of the foot infantry will reach you then, to protect your southern and south-eastern flanks."

"Sir," said Guderian, "I am leaving this morning."

"You will stay where you are."

"Sir, if I behave like my opponents who think in terms of the First World War, I am lost. In 36 hours, they can summon huge forces to crush me. I must move very fast."

"You must stay where you are, till we can protect your bridgehead with the mass of the foot army. They are only 30 miles away."

"Yes, sir."

When Hitler invaded the Ukraine, the people looked upon him as a liberator from Stalin. Hitler gave orders for savage repression, and turned tens of millions would-be allies into fanatical enemies. Hitler did this right across Russia, and into the Crimea.

In the Caucasus, von Kleist refused to treat the people as

Untermenschen – human inferiors – and formed armies from the Azerbaijani, Kalmucks, Ossets and the rest of the central Asian people to fight the Russians. Stalin had never known a threat as deadly as von Kleist.

He surrendered honourably to the British in Yugoslavia; and in 1948, supinely, unforgivably, the British handed him over to Stalin. He died, probably from ill-treatment, at the Vladimirovka camp 110 miles from Moscow, in October, 1954.

Guderian was white with anger.

"Von Kleist," he gritted. "The old woman. Von Kleist, the fearful! Connect me with Colonel Zeitzler, the chief-of-staff of the Panzergruppe. Thank God Gerard went to see him."

(Gerard was the high ranking officer who bad given me the lift from Luxembourg to Guderian's trailer.)

Some minutes later, the loudspeaker blared out, "Heinz! Old Man! Have you reached the sea?"

"Kleist has ordered me to stay put for THIRTY SIX godammed hours, while the foot-sloggers catch up."

"Are you sure you understood him properly?"

"Damn it! I understood him all too well."

"I'll speak to him. Get everything ready to move, Heinz."

Ten minutes later, Kleist's voice came from the loudspeaker.

"If the French overrun you, they'll cut you off and destroy you."

"The French generals are in bed with their mistresses. They have to get their cocks out, get to a phone, find the number of a *bistro* in one of the villages near here. They need two or three days to reach a local French commander."

"If they overrun you, you're finished," shouted von Kleist,

"Do you think the French have communications like this trailer? But what good is it to us if you only use it to condemn Germany to a five-year war in Belgium."

"Are you suggesting you know more than me?"

"I'm suggesting that the French have realised by now that they have been the biggest fools in all history, trusting to the natural barrier of the Ardennes. Now they know it's no barrier at all, and they'll move entire Army Groups of a million men here if we sit on our arses and let them"

"So now I'm talking to master-strategist Guderian, the future Field Marshal."

"I'm here on the spot and know what's happening. As I'm on the spot, I know what we have to do. You can't fight a war from an armchair far in the rear, my dear Ewald."

"Heinz, you are quite impossible. Go to the devil in your own way. I'll give you 24 hours – only 24 hours – to get yourself into God knows what mess."

"Twenty-four hours it is," growled Guderian. He strode back to his commannd trailer.

"Roll west!" he shouted. "Everyone move. West!"

The officers hurried to argue over the maps in the command trailer, then hurried back to the communications trailer to send out streams of orders.

That night, we dined under the trees, wearing warm clothing. They needed to get out of the trailer, and away from maps.

We drank a tart wine they said they had found in Luxembourg. Raising a glass for a toast, a Generalmajor said, "It's unbelievable, but Nietzsche was right. To think they had to lock the man up in an asylum. But the Third Reich now is reaping the rewards from listening to him."

"Didn't he teach something about a superman?" I asked, and the Generalmajor laughed tolerant. He had a thin face, and looked intellectual, too scholarly to be here.

"People have seized the word 'superman', without knowing what Nietzsche says. 'Superman' says it all, and tells us absolutely nothing. Nietzsche said that in the last 2,000 years we have gone astray, with Christian charity towards the weak – with all religions which favour the weak and the *untermenschen* – the under humans. For 2,000 years we have defied nature by talking about mercy and the meek. Nature cares only for the survival of the strongest, of what best fits in, and before, in ancient civilisations, there was no mercy, only trials of strength and extermination. The Romans forgave nobody. The ancient Egyptians buried their victims in the sand leaving only their heads out.

"For Nietzsche, life has no meaning, it has no good and no evil. We live only in nature, and nature is cruel. Our lives are as impersonal as the earthquakes, floods, fires and hurricanes that nature inflicts on us. Only the strongest amongst us rise to the top. Look at the weak and mediocre Frenchman who confronts us today! The decadent British up in Belgium who we will soon deal with! Our lives are but to struggle and triumph...or be crushed, Nietzsche tells us, and this is exactly what is happening to us today, here near Sedan.

"Nietzsche tells us that 'no one gives to man his qualities – neither God nor society, nor his parents and ancestors, nor we ourselves... Man is not the effect of some special purpose, of a will, of an end to attain an ideal of humanity or an ideal of happiness.'

"He tells us that the only end is that of the superman rising over the mediocre. We must free ourselves of all compassion towards human frailty. Judaism has infected Christianity which teaches weakness as good, and strength as evil, so the despicable common man learns insolence towards the strong whom he envies and fears. Nietzsche teaches us that Christianity is a deadly war against this higher type of man; from the sure instincts of the superman it has distilled evil and the Evil One."

They listened enthralled. He inspired them.

"Nietzsche takes us back to pre-Socratic Greeks, whose philosophies sneered at weakness and cherished strength. He said the fundamental principle in an uncaring universe was the *Will to Power*. We have to have that Will! We have to cultivate the will to override, to control and to conquer. He wrote a book called *Beyond Good and Evil*, and in it he says, 'Life itself is *in essence* appropriation, inflicting hurt, conquest of the weak, exploitation, incorporation, severity and suppression. The incarnated Will to Power will strive to grow, to seize new ground, gain ascendancy – this has nothing to do with immorality, but is so because it *lives*, because life is precisely The Will to Power.'"

The officers sat in rapt silence.

"Nietzsche warns us that all the universe strives towards inequality. The strong alone survive. The mediocre in mankind perish. He wrote in *Thus Spoke Zarathustra*, 'Men aren't equal! Nor can they become equal! What would my love of the *übermenschlich* – the superhuman, the superman – be if I were to speak otherwise!'

"This is the superman who rises above the dirt of the masses. He recognises inequality. He struggles to overturn the religions which have stained 2,000 years and would teach compassion and mercy for the weak. He says, 'I *teach you the übermenschlich*. Man shall be overthrown! What have *you* done to overthrow him? The superman is the meaning of this earth! I beseech you, my brother, *stay faithful to the* earth and shut your ears to those who speak of otherworldly hopes! They decay and poison themselves and the earth is weary of them... Will we go back to the beasts? What is the ape to man? So is man to the superman. You have made it from worm to man. Even now, man is more ape than any ape."

Guderian stood up, and stretched.

"Goodnight, gentlemen. I'm off to sleep. Tomorrow, we have to deal with these French apes," and we all laughed appreciatively.

I was tired. My orderly had set up my stretcher in my small tent, and I crawled in between my grey-issue blankets, my towel over one of my satchels as a pillow.

* * *

Next morning, Guderian, four officers and myself drove to the front, in two staff cars. Guderian wanted to see the 1st Panzer Division.

We drove into the main street of Bouvellemount, and my heart sank as I saw the buildings ablaze. Those poor people.

We were looking for Colonel Balck, and there he stood, in the middle of the street, with his stick, his eyes bleary and smarting, his uniform covered in dust and soot.

Guderian pulled up alongside him, and Balck laughed and said, "One of my officers said the men were worn out and any attack on the village would fail. So, I picked up my walking stick, waved it in the air, and off I went. I shouted, 'Then I'm going to take the place by myself!'"

Guderian decided to keep going, and we drove along the Montcornet road, ever deeper into France. As we drove past tanks, the boys shouted, "Good show, Old Man! Heinz der Rascher! We're with you!" (Heinz der Rascher – Heinz the Rusher, the Rushing Heinz). They were calling to each other – "Look, he's here! Over there! The Old Rusher!"

The French countryside was beautiful. At Montcornet, we met General Kempf, and all the officers got together, with maps on tables under the trees, to work out routes for the three Panzer divisions thundering through the town, filling the air with the stink of exhausts. Looking at the maps, I saw with horror that advance units had reached Marle and Gercy (see p. 109). One prong was Guderian's 1st and 2nd Panzer, and Kempf's 6th Panzer.

They finished, and stepped back.

Guderian gave the order. "Don't stop, till you burn up the last drop of petrol. Stop only for empty petrol tanks."

We drove back, to meet up with the two trailers, and waiting Field Police flagged us down, and led us into a small wood, some way off from the road.

* * *

That night, I curled up in my blankets in misery. I saw 350,000 British soldiers lying twisted and dead in the streets of Calais and along the sea edge – blood staining the sea red for a mile out.

What had happened to my message? Had it been passed on? Had Ironside tossed it aside scornfully? One night, after we had eaten and sat around talking, Prince Bernd had told me of Frederick of Prussia's stricture: "You will be excused a defeat, but never forgiven that you be taken by surprise."

With Churchill Prime Minister, I thought all would change. Had *he* seen my message? Did he seriously believe the Ardennes were an impenetrable natural barrier? He was a politician...he would never have given it thought. In the Sunday Supplement of a London newspaper, once I had read that he thought he had inherited the tactical and strategic genius of his forebear, the Duke of Marlborough.

Well, he hadn't.

Spies, and soldiers at the Front, know what's what. Those at home, their mind-sets mire them in pig-headedness.

* * *

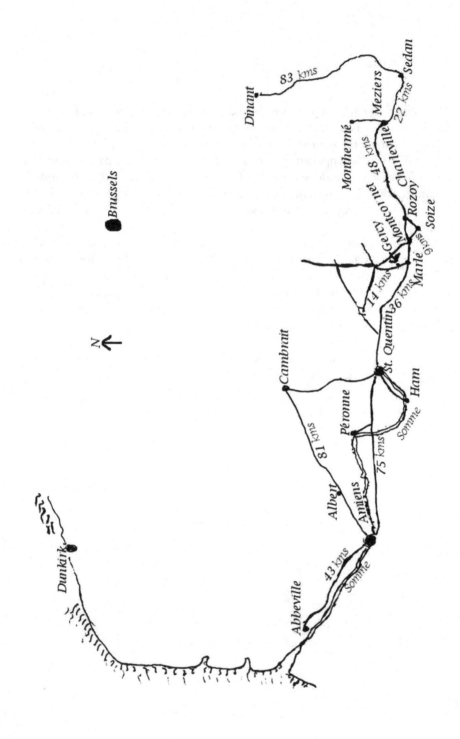

N

Brussels

Dinant

83 kms

Sedan

22 kms

Meziers

Charleville

Montcornet 48 kms

Montthermé

Gercy

Rozoy

Soize

Marle 6 kms

14 kms

36 kms

St. Quentin

Cambrait

Péronne

Ham

Somme

75 kms

81 kms

Albert

Amiens

Dunkirk

Abbeville

43 kms

Somme

Somme

At mid-morning, Guderian was beaming.

"Our advance is beautiful," he purred. "It's going just as Manstein planned."

An officer beside him said, "Manstein could plan all be pleased, but it's you who is making it work."

They were self-congratulatory, and very rightly so.

The phone rang. Guderian's face darkened. He gestured to the others and hurried to the other trailer.

He picked up a mike and said, formally, "General Kleist, Guderian here."

"You are to stop this advance as of this moment, and report to me."

"That is impossible; I will have a million Frenchmen in my path within 24 hours. I have already explained that."

"You have disobeyed orders. You were given 24 hours only."

"The 24 hours aren't up yet!"

"But you have used them only to rush to your destruction."

"We are advancing with amazing speed, and meeting no opposition. The French don't even seem to realise what is happening."

"You are racing two entire Army Corps to their destruction."

"My lorries are ferrying infantry and light artillery to leave a covering screen along both of my flanks."

"A paper screen!" sneered Kleist.

"The attack is proceeding exactly as Manstein planned it and as Hitler accepted it."

"Hitler will not accept the destruction of two entire Army Corps. Hitler will have all our heads when you sacrifice hundreds of tanks and thousands of German soldiers. Your spearheads are about 120 miles ahead of the mass of the foot infantry! You have no reserves of mobile infantry! All the mobile infantry are with you. Do you hear me?" he yelled. "One hundred and twenty miles! What megalomania has possessed you? You stop this instant, do you hear me? You will stop and report to me."

Guderian said coldly and calmly, "I wish to be relieved of my command. I wish to request permission to return to Berlin."

"Your resignation is accepted," said Kleist. "But remain where you are till further orders. Meanwhile, implement the cessation of your advance – all of it!"

"Yes, sir," said Guderian, mechanically. "Immediately."

He put down the mike, nodded at the operator, who disconnected.

Guderian turned heavily to his officers.

"You know what to do. I'll be here, outside."

He walked heavily, slowly, down the steps of the trailer, and slumped in a folding chair, set out under a tree.

Now the British Expeditionary Force was saved, I felt affectionate and sorry towards him. I picked up another chair, and sat facing him, in silence.

Finally, I said, "Can I get you coffee?"

He shook his head.

"A very small drop of brandy?"

"Thank you, no."

I went to the main trailer, and asked the orderly for a folding table, and a small glass of brandy.

He gave me a bottle of French brandy, a thick glass, and hurried out to set up the table. I poured half-an-inch of brandy, and handed it to him; he swirled the liquid round in the glass, then swallowed it.

"Where's your glass?" he asked me.

I called the orderly, and asked for coffee. What I badly needed was a cup of tea.

I said, "Hitler will be furious. He will realise that he will have no other alternative than to promote you to Field-Marshall, so there will be no one over you."

He rewarded me with a wry grin.

"How I envy you," I said, and that drew a wry smile of enquiry.

"What it must be to always be right when everyone else is wrong. Of course, sometimes, things like this happen. But what matters is to be right when everyone is wrong."

That drew a tired, appreciative grin.

We sat there in companionable silence, listening to the urgent voices in the communications trailer.

Twenty minutes later, the radioman ran out.

"General, please, quick! It's Colonel-General List for Colonel-General Guderian."

Guderian seized the mike. "Wilhelm! Heinz here."

"Heinz, you old devil! What have you been up to, throwing the French into disarray? Rewriting the military textbooks, down there by the Meuse. Must be a very inspiring river, that. Colonel-General von Rundstedt tells me to tell you that the Halt Order came from the OKW – some sort of bureaucratic thing, you know what these mixups are with officers in their headquarters in Berlin. Happens all the time – these people probably don't know whether you're at Sedan or parked in Brussels. Of course, as von Rundstedt is head of Army Group A, these people aren't overly concerned with a Panzer Division here or there. So busy lookIng at the forest, they don't worry about the trees."

A pack of lies to calm excited egos.

"However, Heinz, as commander of the 12th Army, I wish formally to state I understand your thinking in pressing on, and herewith I now authorise you to undertake a 'reconnaissance in force'. Have you got that? 'A reconnaissance in force', and if that takes you a hundred or a hundred and fifty miles, so be it. If you reach a hill and don't know what's on the other side, you are authorised to go and look – and that applies for the hill after that. However, OKW wants you yourself to stop where you are, so we stay in contact. Your trailers must not move, for the time being, or we won't be able to reach you."

"I'll leave the trailers at Soize, to keep them a bit off the main route."

List laughed. "Good hunting," and clicked off.

General Ironside's British Army in Europe was doomed.

Guderian turned swiftly to his officers.

"Let everything roll! When you are finished, take the trailers to Soize. I'm going to join the tanks."

He hurried back to the command trailer, and I ran after him.

"Is there room for a photographer?"

* * *

We drove in two staff cars and a radio car with a high aerial. On the road from Montcornet to Marle we saw tanks parked off the road, the crews asleep on the ground beside them, or nearby under trees. Everywhere, mechanics worked on tank and lorry engines, while infantry stood guard, waving cheerfuly at the Old Man. After fifteen miles of French countryside in May, Guderian pulled up beside a field with a farmhouse on the far side, and walked back to his radio car.

"I want to talk to Soize," he told the radioman.

A voice cane through with static. Guderian said into the mike, "Guderian here. Can you hear me? Stop everything, and let the tank crews rest. We'll push on tomorrow. We'll bring up petrol, it's our chance."

Through the static, a garbled voice repeated the message.

At Marle, we walked around the French town with an escort of 30 infantrymen. A large cafe served the 37 of us on outside tables.

The radio burst into life, and the radioman got up and crossed over to it.

He called out, "The French are attacking from the south and trying to cut us in two. They have what looks like a battalion – no! two battalions of old R35 tanks, and one of heavy Char Bs."

"Where? Where?" said Guderian impatiently.

After a moment, the radioman said, "Montcornet, They're smashing their way through, trying to reach Montcornet."

We drove back slowly. Two miles from Montcornet, we could hear the firing, and tank crews were waking up and climbing into their tanks along the roadside.

The radio told us they had reached Montcornet. Then another report said that a prisoner said the French commander was Colonel Charles de Gaulle.

We had pulled off the road, to let the tanks roll down to Montcornet. Guderian stretched his legs, and said, "Amazing! That Frenchman, with Lidell Hart, the Englishman, are the fathers of the whole idea of this new warfare. If we could show a flag of truce, imagine the conversation de Gaulle and I could have for the rest of this pleasant afternoon. Ah, if this were a civilised world, that is. But what I don't understand is his attacking force. It has pushed forward to Montcornet itself which is a sort of miracle. But he can't attack us with a handful of tanks only. Are they all the tanks the French would give him? Does he think they are enough? Historians will ask this question in a thousand years time while they are looking at your thousand-year photos because he is supposedly the mental giant who created the whole idea. Is the theory one thing – but on the field of battle is he impractical? Two battalions of old tanks and one of Char Bs! Mein Gott! The French have 3,000 tanks. What is the man thinking of? Apparently, he's smashed absolutely everything in his path, but now we'll have him out of there in no time at all. If only we could take him prisoner! He'd be lionised in Berlin. What a conversation we could have – but he's probably a stiff-necked Frenchman looking down a long French nose and wouldn't deign to talk to us simple practitioners of the art which he has conceived."

He cocked his head.

"Listen."

The heavy firing was moving to our right – to the south – away from Montcornet. They were driving the French off.

"Let's see whether de Gaulle escapes,' mused Guderian. "Is he in the rear or is he in a tank?"

The noise receded. Guderian got into his staff car, and we followed in a dash to Montcornet. We drove to the southern edge of town, and saw burning tanks and bodies.

A Major saw us, hurried over and saluted.

"At first, we held them with flak units. Tanks had limped into the town

304

yesterday and today for repairs, and we rushed those in. Then tanks came down the road. The brunt of the attack – lieutentants and captains held it. But how the French fought! We've lost a lot of material and men."

Guderian nodded.

"Then the French lost their belly for the fight," said the Major. "Our defence was nothing...and now they've gone off. We'd have never stopped in a situation like this."

Guderian thought out loud. "Did de Gaulle's men let him down, or did he pull them out?"

No one answered him as he looked at us.

The radioman called out from the radio car.

"A message for the Colonel-General. The first foot-infantry have come out of the Ardennes and reached Sedan. They're marching across the pontoon bridges on the Meuse."

'Huh!" exclaimed Guderian. "At last. That will keep the old women in the OKW happy. Now we'll have a wall around our bridgehead instead of a screen. Now the OKW might leave us in peace."

Next day, at midday, back in Marle, the radio reported that the First Panzer did 30 miles that morning. The radio operator cried, "We're in San Quentin, and they've taken four bridges over the Somme!"

Guderian grinned. "We're just tourists, seeing France. Touring France with an army."

Another message followed. The mass of the foot-infantry had reached Sedan.

Next day, de Gaulle attacked our headquarters at Soize, but came no closer than three miles. His 4th Division fought against the Panzers, but only 2cm flak guns defended the headquarters had he got closer.

Four hours later, overwhelming force drove off dc Gaulle and the noose fell firmly on the BEF. I felt sick. Guderian said, "Well, what was that? A few uncomfortable hours and at last our menacing visitors have departed."

Only de Gaulle tried to save the 350,000-man British army to our north. Britain owes him an imperisbible debt, I thought, a debt I imagined would never be recognised. Britain was now set fair for as huge a defeat of its arms as history has record of, and de Gaulle had fought himself to a standstill to save us.

That evening, Guderian's 19th Panzer Corps reached a line running down from Cambrai through Péronne to Ham. (See page 109(B)). We moved headquarters up to Marle.

Next day, I drove with Guderian up to Péronne, to visit the 10th, which had relieved the extenuated 1st Panzer. Here we found the irrepressible Colonel Balck, with his walking stick. He had taken a high promotion when the commander of the 1st Panzer, Colonel Nedtwig had keeled over from exhaustion. Balck forthwith offended his successor, Colonel Landgraf, of the 10th, who took over from him. Balck had merrily pushed the reeling 1st Panzer on to Amiens – he wasn't going to miss *that* attack. Landgraf angrily expostulated at him for dumping Péronne, and Balck told him, "It was me who captured it in the first place. If we lose it, you can always take it again, the way I did!"

We drove into Amiens in staff cars at half-past-midday. We held a bridgehead over the World War killing grounds of the Somme about four miles deep. Most of the houses and shops were shuttered, but now French people ventured out. I itched to go shopping, and on the main street saw a big perfume store, shuttered up. Guderian was standing, looking this way and that, and caught my expression.

'Don't even think of it," he laughed. "When you cone back on your way to Berlin. Goebbls can wait. Let's go to Albert." (See p. 109(B))

On the road, he found the 2nd Panzer, which he was looking for. They were stopped, strung a couple of miles along the road. He yelled out to the tank crews, who looked exhausted.

"We're almost out of petrol," they recited, one after another.

"That's as carefully rehearsed a story as I've ever heard," grumbled the Old Man. "You can never believe troop commanders. When they get tired, and think of a quiet afternoon, resting and tippling, with a good sleep that night, they suddenly find they have no fuel. But the petrol's there, hidden in their tanks."

He got onto the radio car, and. in half an hour some thirty lorries rumbled up, loaded with jerrycans of petrol. The tank crews looked at them in disgust.

When they refuelled he gave the order.

"Straight for Abbeville."

They got there at 5 pm, and my British Army in Belgium was hopelessly trapped.

In Amiens, I bought the perfume. The owner didn't want my DM, but four infantrymen with machine pistols persuaded him.

I drove to Luxembourg, and they put me on a plane for Berlin.

At Templof, two men from the Propaganda Ministry waited for me.

One held a huge bunch of flowers in his arms – from Goebbels. A small note in an envelope said, "Your photos are historical."

The other man took my satchel, with my last 18 rolls of exposed film, and the wooden box with the perfumes.

They went off in a car. A second car drove me to Prince Bernd's schloss in a Potsdam suburb.

It was May 20, at 7 pm, when I arrived.

Princess Jutta greeted me, and the grandmother came out. Princess Gabriel exclaimed, "You poor child."

"Flowers from Goebbels," I said. "Please, a hot bath!"

I came down from half-an-hour in the hot bath, perfumed, dressed in a bright Argentinean blouse and skirt, for a late meal at 8 pm. All the family fussed, and then Claus walked in. He stared thunderstruck, then picked me up and waltzed me around in most un-Germanic fashion, planting a kiss on my cheek.

He set me down, held me at arm's length, and then turned me around. 'You seem to be in one piece," he said at last, and we all laughed.

Over dinner, soberly, he said, "There are messages for you to encode."

"Not tonight," I objected. "I'm bone weary. What are they?"

"A Waffen-SS officer, one Wilhelm Mohnke, of the Leiberstandarte, today murdered 80 British prisoners-of-war, at Wormhoudt. He's a close crony of Sepp Dietrich, and Sepp pushed ahead in person – the British trapped him in a ditch for an hour, under heavy fire, Sepp taking potshots, and enjoying every minute of it. Mohnke was furious after they managed to get him out, and machine-gunned the British prisoners in revenge. Here's a photo. Microdot it, and send it in the Diplomatic Bag, so London will know what he looks like."

The photo showed a very tall, thin officer in the uniform of a SS-Brigadeführer, slightly stooping as tall men often instinctively do, with a receding jaw, weak face and small mouth.

"This bastard's photo will be on the way tomorrow," I promised.

Claus said, "Now, next thing. Yesterday, Waffen-SS Totenkopf troops – they panicked under a ferocious British counterattack, and murdered 100 disarmed 2nd Royal Norfolks with a machine-gun at le Paradis. I've got it all typed."

"My God," I whispered.

I put down my knife and fork.

The grandmother poured me a little liqueur, and I sipped it gratefully.

"Pull yourself together, girl," she commanded, and then turned to Claus. "What is happening? What Waffen units are there in Belgium?"

"There's the Waffen-SS Leibstandarte – that's Sepp; then the SS-Verfügungsdivision; and the SS-Totenkopf, as I've just said; and there's the Deutschland-SS – and they're fighting fanatically, pushing the British, the French and a few Belgians into a pocket against the coast. Now Guderian has cut off their supplies." He laughed. "Ray, wait till you read the newspapers of the last few days. You were fighting gigantic battles down there against the whole weight of the French Army."

I laughed outright. "The only one who took any notice of us was Charles de Gaulle, and they gave him such a small handful of tanks it was pitiful. If they'd given him 300 or 400 of the big Chars, Guderian wouldn't have got through...I don't think so. Of course, once the foot-infantry caught up, that was it. But they might have stopped the mass of foot-infantry getting very far, if they 'd had time to bring up a French Army."

We finished in silence, and went to the sitting-room.

"They've doomed the British Army," I said.

Claus nodded.

I had to tell my story of my days with Guderian, and they listened in silence.

I said, "I'm falling asleep here in the armchair. I have to go to bed."

Everyone jumped to their feet, and bade me goodnight.

Claus said, "I'll come with you, because I have something here for you."

Outside the sitting-room, he closed the double doors and handed me a thick folder.

"The German armed forces are using a code machine, something like a typewriter with lots of cogwheels that can change their positions on the axles –"

"I think I've seen it, in Guderian's trailer. The Enigma."

"That's it. We got a copy of it through to the British before the war, but now we have a new model – a little larger and much more complicated. These are photos of the plans. Microdot them tomorrow, and take them to the Embassy."

"I've only carried coded messages..." I said weakly.

He said impatiently, "It makes no difference what you are carrying, so long as they are microdots in your ring. You don't have to carry any documents or papers. There are 27 sheets here, and they're the right size for your camera."

I nodded wearily, and took the folder.

He caught me in his arms and pressed me to him.

"Please, Claus – please. That's enough."

He stood back miserably, and I climbed the stairs with all my body aching.

* * *

I woke up at 4 am, with a nightmare, and perspiring. I went to the bathroom, splashed my face, and did my hair. Then I tiptoed downstairs to the library, opened up the secret shortwave wireless, and tried different stations. William Shirer came through. He was broadcasting from Cologne.

He said that the Allied Air Force had done nothing he could see. He had driven fourteen hours along roads crowded with troops and supply vehicles without a single Allied plane showing. On the road to Brussels, German tanks and lorries thundered along, he said. He talked to six British Tommies, the only survivors of a company, and they told him that dive bombers and tanks had plastered them.

He said he drove from Aachen to Maastricht in Holland, and saw no signs of fighting. But the Belgians were another matter. He said they must have fought like 'lions'...one town after another heaped with ruin and rubble. He said the ancient University city of Louvain – whole parts lay flattened. The Belgians and English had fought three days with ferocity before the Germans steamrollered then. He saw the famous university library still smoking – all the books burnt. In the street fighting, the residential part changed hands several times and 'was a terrible sight to behold.'

He said the Germans had ordered the shops and cafes in Brussels to open, and they gave one DM for ten francs. German soldiers mixed freely with the Belgian crowds along the streets.

Forty-eight hours later, Shirer broadcast from here, in Berlin, to say he had just got back from a 450-mile drive, and how quiet the city was after the guns firing and bombs exploding. He said he had to send his reports by phone amid the sound of German flak guns and British bombs falling, and they could hardly hear them at the other end. The British bombers were aiming for a target about 100 yards from his hotel, and they droned overhead all night dropping their bombs, but no bomb exploded closer than 500 yards from the hotel and they broke no windows. He mused that if a bomb hits a building which you're in, it won't matter whether you're in the attic or the cellar.

The front was to the west of Brussels, with stubborn fighting by the allies, but he saw the Germans bringing up troops, artillery and vehicles for miles and miles along the roads without a single Allied plane. He said the Germans can bring up reinforcements and ammunition with unbelievable speed. On the other side of the Front, the German dive-bombers and fighters make the allied roads lethal.

The communiqué of the German High Command today says the allied resistance has stiffened. But the main fighting has shifted to Guderian's corridor along the Somme.

With massive reinforcements pouring along those roads I remembered so well, from Sedan and Dinant to the sea, Guderian now is driving upwards into the allied rear.

On the night of May 24, Claus came home and hurried over to me.

"Rundstedt and Hitler have decided to halt the advance in Flanders. As they get near the coast, the land is more swampy for the tanks. The British are withdrawing on Dunkirk, and it's bad country for tanks. Further, as the British and French perimeter tightens, they're afraid of the anti-tank guns and artillery. They're going to need their tanks for the 65 French divisions in the rest of France. Göring says he can wipe out the BEF from the air, and Hitler says it will be a lesson for the British to see their defeated, bedraggled army come limping back to England. Also, if he spares Britain the humiliation of taking its whole army prisoner, the English might be easier to negotiate with. You must prepare an urgent message to be sent from the Argentinean Embassy here in Berlin, telling them to send everything that floats to Dunkirk."

We had eaten, and while Claus sat down to a late meal, I hurried upstairs to my typewriter

HITLERS ORDERS STOP GERMAN ARMY MILES FROM DUNKIRK. RUNDSTEDT FEARS SOFT GROUND. FEARS REDUCED BRIT PERIMETER WITHERING ANTITANK FIRE. GÖRING SAYS WILL FINISH OFF BEF ALONE PROM

AIR. HITLER WANTS KEEP TANKS FOR 65 FRENCH DIVS IN FRANCE. WANTS AVOID HUMILATION TO EASE PEACE NEGOTS. OKW FURIOUS BUT COUNT ON TEN DAYS OR MORE TO EVACUATE. SAIL ALLCRAFT AFLOAT TO DUNKIRK NOW NOW NOW. UTTER GUARANTEE MY SOURCE.

I went downstairs to get Lorna Doone from the library.
Line 21 of page 338 read: "times, and could not bring you to it, John"

T	I	M	E	S	T
A	N	D	C	O	A

I encoded and microdotted the message by ten-thirty. The fanily had gone to bed, so I went back to my room for a restless night.

* * *

Rubén read the message gravely.
"I'll send this right away. But first, the good news. We've received some kilos of good Brazilian coffee. I'll give you a kilo, with three tins of Argentinean corned beef. Now I'll make you a cup so you see how good it is."
We sat sipping luxurious Brazilian coffee.
"Your other messages have gone out, and the miorodots of the plans for that Enigma thing are on routine documents as full stops in a diplomatic bag which will probably go to Sweden tomorrow for shipment to Buenos Aires. We're really lucky – our friend in Buenos Aires handles a lot of our boring paper work. Well, ours, and from other Embassies too, follow me? He usually takes everything to our friend at the radio station, but he has another contact in the British Embassy there, so he'll pass the plans onto the British Embassy direct."
"This message I've just brought. Do you radio that to your contact in the government, or to the radio station?"
"Something as urgent as this – to the radio station direct. Otherwise, a lot of our routine radio traffic goes to our friend in the government in Buenos Aires. He passes your messages on to the radio station. If we use the radio station wavelength for a short message, the Gestapo doesn't have time to search for it, but if we used it often, they would find it in the end. Our embassy here realises nothing. Now, your messages about the atrocities – the killing of British prisoners-of-war. I sent that to Geneva. The less examples

the Gestapo have of your code from Berlin, the harder it is for them to try and break it. But I should say that now your code is unbreakable."

I went to the Propaganda Ministry, and Hans Schneppen said, "Your photos are~magnificeni, but no! no!"

"No?" I said innocently.

"You want to see Dr. Goebbels, and as he has made up his mind you cannot go to the western front, he can't see you. He is a sensitive man, who hates saying no to you."

"The western front," I said in feigned surprise. "Now that is a wonderful idea."

"I told you – no."

"Could I leave tomorrow?"

"No."

"Well," I said sadly, "I'll come back tomorrow. I'll write a letter to Hitler."

"Hitler has been all this time at his campaign headquarters at Munstereifel. I don't know whether he's back in Berlin today, or not."

All that day of May 24, neither radio nor newspapers spoke of Hitler ordering a stop. They talked of how Guderian had cut off a million men in Belgium and northern France and was fighting his way north of Calais, the port which Britain used to supply its army.

The BBC spoke of fighting around Boulogne.

Then the Germans talked about bombing Dunkirk and Dover. Could we hold Göring in the skies, to take off the British Army in Dunkirk? Would they listen to my message? They had completely ignored my warning of 'the stab in the back' through the Ardennes, those chinless, aristocratic wonders who ordered our fate in London. Would they feel shame and. remorse? Their only thought would be their whiskey or gin and tonic in their London clubs tonight.

The German News Agency, Dienst Aus Deutschland, had its feet well on the ground. It has just said it cost but twelve days to cut the Allied armies in twain, and thus end part one of the war. Part two will depend on whether the allies can snip Guderian's noose in two – attacking from the north, while the French attack from the south. What a joke! The French would need ten days to mount that sort of attack! In the north, they're already bottled up around Dunkirk.

Will the British listen to my message, and despatch a vast armada of boats to get the BEF off tomorrow?

By the evening of this awful May 24, the tanks of Guderian were closer to Calais. The key town of Saint-Omer, twenty-five miles inland from Boulogne, Calais and Dunkirk fell late this afternoon.

At dinner time, a British radio station replayed a speech that Churchill had given seven months ago.

How unafraid that voice! I was ill with fear.

How sure that gravelly growl! How absolutely safe the man felt!

"Directions have been given by the government," Churchill said, "to prepare for a war of at least three years."

Three years! Britain would not fall.

"That does not mean that victory may not be gained in a shorter time."

The incredible confidence of the man!

I felt my appetite coming back, and addressed myself to the food in a new spirit.

"How long it takes depends on how long Herr Hitler and his group of wicked men, their hands stained with blood and soiled with corruption can keep their grip upon the docile, unhappy German people. It has been for Hitler to say when the war would begin, but it is not for him or for his successors to say when it will end. It began when he wanted it and it will end...'after the smoke of battle has cleared away, the horrid shape which had cast its shadow over a whole continent has vanished and gone forever'". He was quoting someone or the other of two centuries ago.

He was, then, not even Prime Minister.

Later, they replayed another speech, of May 19, when I was with Guderian.

The words made my spirit soar.

"This time I speak as Prime Minister, in a solemn hour for the life of our country...a tremendous battle is raging in France, and in Flanders. The Germans, by a remarkable combination of air bombing and heavily armoured tanks, have broken through the French defences, north of the Maginot Line – "

That was Guderian, and I was there.

315

"– where strong columns of their armoured vehicles are ravaging the open country. They have penetrated deeply and are spreading alarm and confusion in their track; behind them are appearing infantry in lorries, and behind them the large masses of infantry on foot are moving forward..."

I had lived that, minute by minute.

"The regroupment of the French armies to strike at this intruding wedge has been proceeding for several days –"

Oh, dear, I thought. A white lie. If I had to face the truth, why not he and everyone else?

"– largely assisted by the magnificent efforts of the Royal Air Force –"

All of whose pilots are now dead or prisoner, I thought, remembering what I had seen.

Later, he went on, talking of his new government. He said of its members, "We have differed and quarrelled in the past, but now one bond unites us all, to wage war till victory is won and never to surrender ourselves to servitude and shame –"

Prince Bernd raised his glass, and everyone else did too. He said, "As we Germans are subject to servitude and shame."

Churchill went on, "– whatever the cost and the agony may be."

Tears came to my eyes.

"This is one of the most awe-striking periods in the long history of France and Britain, and beyond doubt, the most sublime. Side by side, the French and British peoples have advanced to rescue not only Europe but mankind from the foulest and most soul-destroying tyranny which has ever darkened and stained the pages of history."

I thought despairingly of the schlerotic French armies, trying to bestir themselves like tiny-brained, one hundred ton dinosaurs, and of the huge British army in Dunkirk with its antiquated commanders.

"Behind the armies gather a group of shattered states and bludgeoned races, the Czechs, the Poles the Norwegians, the Danes, the Dutch, the Belgians...but on all of whom the night of barbarism will descend unbroken even by a star of hope, unless we conquer, as conquer we must, as conquer we shall... Centuries ago, the words were spoken: Arm yourselves, and be men of valour, and be in readiness for the conflict, for it is better for us to perish in battle than to look upon the outrage of our nation and our altars."

Churchill had carried my spirit beyond this day of May 24 to the months and years ahead. Hitler had not yet extinguished the glory of the British Empire.

Could Göring finish off the BEF at Dunkirk? They had told me the allies had about 3,000 military planes against Germany's 2,750. Doris' fiance, Richterin Prieguity in Luftwaffe Technical Planning, had told me Germany had some 1,500 bombers and 1,250 fighters.

Germany ruled the heavens with devastation.

Where were the Spitfires? Had they listened to my message and taken them back to Britain? Now they would have to surge forth to cover the skies over Dunkirk. Would those green British pilots hold their own – they would if the Spitfire was the far better machine than the Me-109. Why, oh, why hadn't they rescued the veteran Spanish Republican pilots and brought them to Britain? How many Polish pilots, blooded in the air over Poland, had reached England? Had they given them Spitfires and Hurricanes?

All day, May 25, the German newspapers and wireless said not a word about Hitler calling a halt. They did say that the Belgians, French and British bottled up in Flanders – the invincible German tank crews, infantry and pilots had sealed their doom. The German High Command communiqué this afternoon said, "The ring around the Belgian army, remnants of the first, seventh and ninth French Armies and the mass of the British Expeditionary Corps was yesterday strengthened considerably and was closed."

The newspapers say that the OKW reckon they have caught 400,000 Belgian troops, 500,000 French and 200,000 British.

Official British figures state that 338,226 British troops and 140,000 French were evacuated from Dunkirk.)

Newspapers and wireless report sources from the OKW saying 'they have trapped Britain's choice mechanised forces, the pick of its men, and the best of the French army. People in Berlin are elated – so easily has Germany defeated the flower of the British Army.

Then they told us they had taken Boulogne and encircled Calais. They said the French are making weak counter-attacks on the Somme, trying to cut Guderian's noose from the south.

317

On May 27, Calais fell. Not a word about Hitler ordering a stop. Not a word about an English fleet of large and small boats. Not a word about letting me join Sepp Dietrich outside Dunkirk. Yesterday, I handed in a begging letter to Hitler.

Today's German communiqué read, "After German troops pushed on with their advance to Gravelines, Calais fell into German hands after a hard fight." Gravelines is a small place on the coast road halfway between Calais and Dunkirk.

Calais was England's great supply port for its army. Now only Dunkirk is left – the last big channel port. And the Germans report that Stukas have blown much of the harbour works into the sea.

Calais is but twenty-five miles from England. The gargantuan German tank army is but 25 miles from the English coast.

Sepp Dietrich apparently stands at Wormhout. They ordered him to stop, but the irrepressible Sepp disobeyed orders. Hitler had to send him a direct personal order, to stop him at Wormhout. The main road runs from Lille through Armentieres to Dunkirk. Wormhout is about one mile to the left of that road, on a secondary road about 25 kms on my map from Dunkirk.

When I got home at 7 pm, the grandmother, Princess Gabriele, told me that the eldest son of the Kronzprinz, Prince Wilhelm of Prussia, died today in a Brussels hospital, from wounds in the stomach and lungs on May 13. She had spoken to his cousin, Prince Burchard, who was raging because Hitler won't let the family fight and gain a dangerous glory.

The princess sneered, "Hitler thinks they could attract the loyalty of the mass of people, bah! The whole royalty of Europe has a corrupted lineage from Queen Victoria's mother sleeping with those hostlers, and one of them fathering Victoria herself. Prince August Wilhelm, the fourth son of the Kaiser, is an active Nazi from before Hitler came to power. He's a Storm Trooper," she spat, "and his S.A. rank is Obergruppenführer. Ten
318

Hohenzollerns have been at the Polish and French fronts, one son of the Kaiser and nine grandsons, and one of those riffraff, Prince Oscar, they killed in Poland. After the Munich explosion, Prince Burchard told me today, the Kaiser, from Holland, sent Hitler a message of his 'joy' at his escape. The Hohenzollerns are a blue-blooded family, that gave us Frederick the Great, but when they married one of Victoria's brood, the stable-boy's blood, certainly untainted by porphyria, gave us Kaiser Wilhem and *his* Great War. The problem with the German people – do you know what it is? They have barely been a nation for a hundred years. Before that, for old, old centuries, they lived in principalities, tiny kingdoms, duchies, counties and palatinates. The ancient German aristocracy knew many of the common folk by name, and cared for them like children. The lowest swineherd could ask for help. Through countless generations, like children, they learned to trust and obey their fatherly overlords. While other countries have been nations for hundreds of years, we have been for less than a hundred, and now the people give that blind trust to whatever riffraff comes to rule over us. With these successes, they will follow Hitler blindly as never before. What calamities lie ahead for Germany."

Doris' fiance, Richterin Preguity, arrived, clasped Doris in his arms, gave her a chaste kiss and turned to me. He worked in the Luftwaffe, and now he said exultantly, "Our planes report thousands of ships and boats of every size and shape sailing for Dunkirk. The soldiers are like ants on the beaches and are queueing out into the water. Spitfires and Hurricanes by the score are fighting off our planes behind the beaches!"

We listened dumbstruck; and filed in silently to dinner.

Claus arrived, and we told him.

He turned to me, and said, "Do you ever read P. Wodehouse?"

Amazed, I said I did, and the rest of the family chimed in, laughing, to say they did too.

"What does this have to do with England's Dunkirk Armada?" chuckled Thoma.

"They arrested him today, at Abbeville, playing golf, and are bringing him to Berlin. They reckon we'll have more than a million French and Belgian prisoners, and they'll ask him to edit a POW newspaper, a funny, humourous newspaper, to translate into French."

Our Wodehouse was technically a British subject but an American resident. The Germans interned him as an enemy alien, but the USA asked for his release. The American Broadcasting System's man in Berlin blandished him into making five funny broadcasts for the American public – with skilful satire of the Germans – and this went out on a German radio station. That made him technically guilty of collaboration with the enemy and London warned him never to set foot on English soil again.

Count Holger Zorndorf, of the Berlin anti-aircraft flak, friend of Claus, arrived ten minutes late, full of apologies. He wanted to know all about my adventures with Guderian, and invited me to the cinema, to see a film on the bombing of Rotterdam.

Richterin said sourly, "The allies put out we killed 30,000 people. We killed 814 –that's the most exact figure we can make. German ground troops sent up flares, telling the planes to veer off and return to base. The pilots didn't see them, and it seems they literally flattened the place. Tonight, at the cinema we'll see Dutch and German newsreels. I promise you they won't do that to Berlin – we'll put up such a curtain of fire!"

Then, with some reluctance – I could see he wanted me to himself – he asked who else wanted to come. Finally eight of us went.

The grandmother said, "I don't like the sound of that at all. Churchill wants only to see Germany turned into a cow pasture. Thirty thousand dead! Is he trying to condition the British public into the senseless bombing of civilians – of women and children? Any responsible leader should recoil at the very idea. We must say that for Hitler – he devastated Warsaw but says the superior western races must be spared that sort of thing."

"Tonight, you are mordacious," murmured Prince Bernd.

The newsreels of Rotterdam stupified. In the Dutch films, you saw whole buildings sag and fall in a few seconds. Afterwards, the German ones showed acres of rubble and a flattened City.

Today, May 28, King Leopold of the Belgians surrendered. He will go on as

King, and allowed to choose his place of residence – unlike Queen Wilhemina of Holland who ran away to England. The Dutch Prince Consort has escaped too, and Aschwin Lippe, his younger brother, who fought in Poland and France has been *fristlos entlassen* – cashiered without notice. On the phone to Dora and Thoma, he told them that the family land holdings are in his brother's name, and Hitler will probably confiscate them. The man is in despair.

So half a million tigerish Belgian soldiers have laid down their arms. The press and radio here says the surrender of the Belgians makes the plight of the half a million French and British in the deadfall of Dunkirk unbelievable. Not a word about the Glorious English Armada cutting through the waters of the Channel. The German communiqué describes their position as 'hopeless', and leaves it at that.

They listened to my message in London!

Later, a new communiqué said, "Just how quickly things come to a conclusion on this battlefield cannot yet be predicted."

Hurrah! They *are* holding off.

The German radio, later, said, "King Leopold acted like a soldier and a human being."

Of course! When he knew we would get off by sea, he had no reason to kill more of his Belgian heroes.

I spent the afternoon at home, beside the phone, praying for it to ring.

It rang at 3.30pm. It was Sepp Dietrich, in person!

"So you're looking for more excitement, Ray! I can't give you any. We're stuck here, and bored to death. You'll hate it."

"Oh, Sepp, please, please, please! I can't even wear my Iron Cross outside of your jurisdiction."

He gave his deep, rough laugh.

"This is just a garden party, everyone sitting around with cups and saucers. We don't even have decent coffee. We've drunk all the French coffee we found."

"I can bring you a quarter of a pound of real Brazilian coffee!"

"You can! Bring it! A car will come in two hours. We'll fly you to Lille. A plane has to come, and I'll squeeze you on board. You'll be met at Lille and driven to Wormhout."

The line went dead, and I rushed upstairs to change and to pack.

The plane landed at Lille in darkness. A staff car drove me, with hooded lights, through military traffic to Wormhout. I put on my Iron Cross as we drove along a narrow road out of Wormhout to a country house, with two trailers under trees beside it. The sergeant led me inside, to a poorly lit foyer, where I waited while he knocked on tall, carved wooden doors. He went in, then came out, and beckoned to me.

I strode in, holding the Brazilian coffee high. Dietrich and his officers were sitting in armchairs and on sofas, in a great, gilded, beautifully decorated sitting-room.

"Greetings!" I cried. "Your Brazilian coffee, gentlemen."

Dietrich grinned at me, and a colonel cried,"What perfect timing."

Then Dietrich got to his feet, lumbered over, picked me up in a bear hug and swung me around.

He put me down, showed me to an armchair, took the coffee, and yelled a name. A corporal hurried in, and Dietrich said, "Make us all some coffee with this, and don't waste a single grain. Bring back what you don't use. This is as valuable as gold dust."

He turned to me. "Here you have us. The armchair war. Not like Guderian. You're going to find us a lot of bores after Guderian."

"But what is the enemy doing?" I asked.

"Our fighters and bombers tell us the English have sent ten thousand ships, and they're busy loading up the British and French armies."

"The Berlin wireless said they had bombed the docks."

"Exactly. So I don't know what they're doing."

322

"I have just had an idea," I said, cautiously, and all the officers grinned. Dietrich scowled.

"Hitler wouldn't recognise your Iron Cross, and if I decorate you again, he'll be on to me like a ton of bricks."

The room laughed.

"Suppose we find a spotter plane, and paint the word PRESS under the wings and on the fuselage. I'll take rolls of film for you."

A Major said, "And then Hitler would hold our General responsible if you were shot down."

Dietrich gave a wolfish smile. "That's easy. I'll go along too."

"No!" several officers shouted at once, and a couple got to their feet.

Dietrich shrugged his shoulders. "All right, then, I won't go."

I said,"I heard you were shooting it out in a ditch for an hour."

"For hours!" corrected a Colonel.

"It's no life, this of a general," explained Sepp. "Always safely behind the lines and looking at maps, and telling the others to go and enjoy a scrap."

"But I can go and get you your photos?"

"Hitler would have your guts for garters," warned another officer.

"Let him," said Sepp, indifferently. "If anything happens, she's a woman, so they won't shoot. They'll fish her out of the water, take her back and send her home to Argentina. What's going to to happen? Who shoots at a light, unarmed plane marked PRESS? I'd hesitate to send a man photographer, a German, who is an enemy for them. Ten thousand furious Tommies would riddle him with rifle fire when he came down, or came out of the water. He'd never survive. It's a damn good idea."

He picked up the phone.

"Contact the aerodromes close by. I need a spotter plane."

The corporal came in. with the coffee. It smelt marvellous, and every face lit up.

As the corporal served us, Dietrich said, "Tell us about Guderian. Everything, from the very beginning."

They had me talking till half-past-ten that night, firing questions at me. In the middle, the phone rang, and Dietrich talked to about ten different people, asking for a spotter plane painted with the word PRESS.

They finally told him it would be ready on a field about ten miles away at 11 a.m., next day.

I asked him why did he think Hitler had ordered the halt.

"Secret negotiations with the King of the Belgians. I'd swear to it. When Leopold was satisfied the French and British would get away, he surrendered. That saved us losses against the British and Belgians, saved us tanks for our jaunt through France. I would have attacked, anyway, and taken them all prisoner, much more so now I've talked to you. We could have lost some hundreds of tanks, and still we'll take France. From what you've told me, it will be a picnic...lovely countryside, good food, pretty girls, and French divisions surrounded and surrendering half-a-dozen or a dozen at a time. We can probably surround those French divisons with motorcycles."

They drove me to a field hospital where I slept in a tent with German nurses.

* * *

They picked me up at seven in the morning, to have breakfast with Dietrich and his staff officers. I wanted to shoot a roll of film, so we went to a roadsign that said DUNKERQUE, in the form of an arrow, about 18 inches from the ground. He put his foot on it, leaned forward on his knee and gave a cheeky grin. Then we walked through some streets and came to a Matilda tank, brown in color compared to the dark grey of the German tanks.

A Major told me, "It ran out of petrol, so they found a petrol can somewhere, poured the petrol over the engine and inside, and set it on fire."

The turret was blackened at the opening, but the rest was all right. Dietrich climbed on to the turret and sat there contentedly, with a proprietary smile.

"Some tankmen, the British," he said contemptuously. "The armour on this is twice as thick as ours."

After taking group photos and finishing the roll, we drove to the aerodrome.

The plane looked small and flimsy, with PRESS painted under the wings and on both sides of the fuselage.

Dietrich said,"Are you sure you want to go?"

"Nothing's going to happen to me," I laughed. "I just know it. I'rn like you – one of the lucky ones."

They introduced me to the commanding officer of the aerodrome, and he said, "I'd like to paint PRESS on your jacket."

"The paint wouldn't dry in time". -

"We'd got an old flying-jacket we painted last night. Do you want to try it on?"

It smelled very funny – oil, petrol, sweat and gunpowder. It fitted – a little large perhaps – but comfortable.

The commander said, "It belonged to a small pilot. We lost him in the fight for Brussels. He managed to land, so it's a lucky jacket."

PRESS was painted in white, as on the plane.

My pilot was Flying-Sergeant August Fehrle, an older man of about thirty.

324

"It'll be all right," he assured me. "Perhaps we should paint the Argentinean colours on the plane," and that got a laugh.

I emptied the pockets of my panzer jacket, and put everything in the pockets of the flying-jacket, including my Argentinean passport.

"Put your bag in the back," August said, "Wear your camera around your neck. If you need to change cameras, we'll fly inland. When you lean over to the bag, put it in your lap, and make the changes you want. Don't put the bag on the floor in front on you, between your feet. Only in the back or on your lap."

I turned my face up, squinting my eyes. Planes raced inland at incredible speed.

"Spitfires and Hurricanes," said Sepp.

"Why aren't they over the beaches?"

"They don't wait for our Stukas to arrive," said August. "They meet them 40 or 50 kilometers inland. If they were over the beaches, we couldn't go there today."

The formations broke up into dogfights, planes twisting, diving and climbing.

Dietrich said, "Now our Messerschmitts have arrived. Our Stukas don't have a hope against a fighter."

August handed me a lifejacket, and helped me put it on. He pointed through the window to a bundle behind his seat.

"That's a rubber dinghy, with a bottle of gas to inflate it." He opened the rear door. "You pull this metal clasp to release it from the floor, and in the water, pull this red ribbon."

My eyes went back to the aerial fighting.

"Don't they attack this field? Isn't it very close to the front?"

The commanding officer said, "This is an emergency landing ground. If a pilot doesn't want to try for his field inland – if his machine has suffered hits, if he is   wounded –" and he shrugged his shoulders. "We repair what we can here," and gestured. Suddenly, I saw planes under cotton-netting, with mechanics working, scattered over hundreds of yards. The commander said, "They don't know we're here. This netting makes us invisible from the air."

We climbed into the seats, August on the left.

He said, "We'll fly up from the south, so you point your camera straight out of your window. Keep the window open, because we'll be there in a few minutes. Is your camera ready?"

I nodded. I had telescopic sights screwed on to them.

We fixed our seat belts, and he started the engine. He waited till it heated up, and taxied us into the open, bumping over grass till we reached the earthern runway. He swung the plane around, someone waved a green flag, and he pushed forward the throttles.

The plane gathered speed, and suddenly we were in the air. August looked at me, and grinned. "That was fast, wasn't it? It's a very light plane."

He glanced through the windshield at the air battle, then banked away. "We're heading south."

After a few minutes, he banked again, and shortly, he pointed. "That's Calais."

We were flying amazingly close to the ground. Every rifle on the Dnnkirk beaches would pepper us.

He peered about. "I don't see any British fighters, so now we'll climb to a thousand meters."

I did mental arithmetic. A rifle couldn't reach us at 3,000 feet, firing upwards.

I hoped.

We spiralled above Calais, climbing.

With the needle at 1,000 meters, he headed over the sea.

Through the windscreen, I saw four planes.

"Our escort," August told me. "Two 109 fighters and two Stukas. Any warship opens fire on us, the Stukas will blow him out of the water."

I saw the coast unreeling below my window, and had my camera ready.

Then I saw the Dunkirk beaches...

100,000 men – 200,000 men – on the sands, in brown so different to the German field grey.

I was shooting fast.

Men raised their rifles to shoot vainly at us, and I photographed them.

I saw scores of queues in the water, with tiny boats loading men, one or two at a time, to ferry them to the big ships.

Puffs of black smoke burst in the sky in front of us.

I thought stupidly, "Oh, dear me. Oh, dear me. This can't be happening."

I kept shooting.

August banked out to sea, and the firing stopped. He flew south for a minute, miles from the beaches, and I saw more ships and boats and launches than I could count.

He banked back into the coast, then turned up to follow it again. Above us, our four escort planes kept station. The Dunkirk beaches rushed up again, and I frantically shot my second camera. Black clouds burst again and I saw the Stukas scream down at a destroyer.

A huge crash stopped us in middair. I saw a hole gape in the wing, and August slumped forward.

He said hoarsely. "I'll get you down, I promise."

Blood covered him, and sweat ran into my eyes. I wiped it away and found it was blood.

Oh, God! Not a scratch in the forehead! The blood could blind me.

Through the windscreen I saw a destroyer erupt like a volcano of flame, and then everything was quiet. No one else fired at us.

August looked at me. His face was awful.

"I'll get you down. I'll get you down."

We raced across the sea and hit it with a bang. We skidded and splashed.

August slumped over the controls.

"August! August!" I shouted.

I undid my safety harness and put my fingers on his neck. No pulse. I lifted up his face, and he was lifeless. I was sure his spirit floated in the cabin and I said, "I know you're here. Thank you."

I leaned over behind his seat, but couldn't get at the dinghy.

The plane just sat in the water.

I realised the sea was inside the cabin, up to the seat. The door pushed open easily, and I got on to the wing.

I pulled off my cap, and undid my hair, so it fell free, and they could see I was a woman.

We were near a cruiser. They had taught me to distinguish warships on the ship to and from Buenos Aires. Brown-uniformed Tommies crowded the rail, firing their rifles. The bullets splashed everywhere, and pinged into the fuselage. I had climbed out on to the wing, and sat there. Officers were rushing up and down, making the Tommies put up their rifles.

If I dropped into the water, behind the wing, I'd be safe, but I'd get wet. I decided to sit it out, and the shooting stopped.

Would they send a boat for me?

I stood on the wing and waved, then looked around. Everywhere were ships, with soldiers at the railings.

I had a very big audience.

The cruiser lowered a launch – a pinnace – which drove towards me, and swung around alongside the wing.

Two ratings gripped the wing with boathooks, while an officer – tall, thin, and very English, of some twenty-seven years – in crumpled whites made an abrupt gesture for me to step on board.

"Do you speak English?" he snapped.

"Indeed I do."

"Is the pilot dead?"

"He is."

"Are you German?"

"No, I am carrying an Argentinean passport. Please take me to your captain. I have to send an urgent message to London."

"At the moment you are *my* prisoner, and you won't tell me what to do or not to do."

I said slowly, "If you don't want to spend the rest of the war patrolling the Outer Hebrides on an armed trawler, with your Royal Navy career in tatters, you will take me to your captain."

He looked at me sulkily, muttered under his breath, and gave his attention to the return journey. The four sailors kept wooden expressions.

They had lowered a gangway, up which the soldiers climbed, and we went up it.

The haggard Tommies stared at me sullenly, as we picked our way through them.

The offiicer led me up to the bridge, and the captain scowled when we entered.

The officer said, "The prisoner insists she has to send a most urgent message to London."

The captain turned on me savagely, "You will be held in custody, and we'll see what's what when we reach England."

I said quietly, "I have a most urgent message to send to London. If you don't send it, it will cost you your command, and your future in the Navy. I am going to give you a phone number, and a message which you alone must hear. You will tell your radioman to encode it, and God help him if he ever repeats one word. And God have mercy on you if you don't send it, because their Lordships of the Admiralty will not."

He gestured rudely with his head, and I followed him to his cabin.

"Please give me a piece of paper and a pencil."

I wrote down the phone number.

"Your message is I HAVE WAGNER SAFELY ON BOARD HMS MYKONOS"

He wrote it down.

"Is that it?"

He showed me a chair. "Sit."

He went out.

After a few minutes, a rating came in, with a pistol on his belt, and stood stolidly.

Ten minutes later, the captain returned.

"We were to return to Falmouth. Now we must go directly to London, without waiting to pick up more troops. Can I send you some refreshments?"

"Please."

"A doctor will drop by. Are you Argentinean?"

"I'm afraid the less you know, the safer you are."

He nodded. "I understand."

He went out.

Hadn't I been bossy! So much self-assurance! After Hitler, Himmler and Heydrich, a Royal Navy cruiser captain was but a blunt old salt.

Tiny bits of safety glass had peppered my scalp, and jacket, but didn't get through the fleece flying jacket and lifesaving jacket. The lifesaving jacket would not have inflated. The shell had gone through the wing and not exploded. Bits of wing metal had smashed the second window behind me – I had ducked and turned my head backwards.

When we docked at London, two ratings led me off the ship, where two women waited.

"Where's Mr. Bunton?" I demanded.

"I am Patricia, and this is Shirley. We didn't think Mr. Bunton could be of much help to you right now. You must have left your wardrobe in Berlin."

I gulped.

All my dresses! All my things! The enormity of it hit me. My three Genéve dresses!

"We are going to take you to a country house near Cambridge, and we'll have to shop there. It won't be London I'm afraid, but with the war, there's not much to choose from anyway. We need to debrief you. We'll have a team of shorthand typists and some bods from the SIS. The house has beautiful grounds, and you can go into Cambridge as much as you want. But you can't walk around London – someone could easily recognise you."

I nodded, sourly.

"I'm worried about my family."

"Depending on what you do next, you can't let anyone know you're in England."

It was just after midday. We climbed into a black Bentley, and drove north to a country house about a mile from Cambridge.

My room was lovely, and after an afternoon-tea – with all these goings-on, a spotter plane, cruiser and a Bentley, I missed lunch entirely – we drove into Cambridge.

We went into three or four shops.

The dresses, frocks and skirts were AWFUL. Now I did realise we were at war.

We bought underwear, jerseys, toiletries, with blouses, skirts, slacks and three dresses. Walking along the street, I saw a Catholic Church.

"I need to go in a moment," I said.

They followed me, and I walked down to the back, then through a side-door, calling out.

A middle-aged priest came out, and he looked at us with our bundles.

"I wish for a Mass for the soul of a friend," I said. He led us inside, gestured to chairs, while he sat behind a table and pulled out a big ledger.

"August Fehrle, Luftwaffe pilot. Please commend him as a man who thought of others before himself."

The priest dropped his pen, startled, and gazed at us.

Patricia pulled out a folding wallet, and showed it to him. They must have been her credentials. He studied them with astonishment, and nodded.

Quietly he picked up the pen and asked, "How do you spell that?"

I spelt it. "He died today, before midday, at Dunkirk."

The priest gripped his pen tightly, and looked at us.

"His Mass will be celebrated tomorrow morning. My daughter, do you want confession?"

That shook me.

"Yes," I said.   "But not just yet. I'm still confused and shaken."

He blessed us.

Out in the street, Patricia laughed nervously. "This promises to be some debriefing."

The debriefing took five days, and each day I repeated that I would not go back to Germany.

They told me, "We can expel you as an undesirable alien, and send you to Portugal. You can go into Spain, and so return to Berlin."

I was adamant.

On the sixth day, they drove me into London, to Downing Street. We went into a building, and then followed stairs down going ever more deeply underground. The walls were dreary, and on one level, pipes ran along the ceiling, held by thick wire. Along a passageway, we came to a door, and one

331

of the two men with me knocked. I heard a growl, "Cummin," and entered a brightly lit room, with maps on the wall, a table, chairs, and armchairs.

It was Winston Churchill, dressed in a sort of outsize child's bunny-suit.

"What an amazing pleasure to meet you," he said. "Please, do sit down. That armchair is most comfortable, I assure you. These are dismal environs for someone as young and lovely as yourself, but war imposes necessity. I have read your debriefing, with ever-growing admiration and wonderment. But before we start, would you like something to drink?"

"An orange juice, Prime Minister."

He pressed a button, and an orderly opened the door. "Two orange juices, please."

"Now, that is a truly healthy drink. I incline towards champagne and brandy, myself, when I should be drinking orange juice. You would he a good mentor."

Our drinks arrived.

"Now, pray, tell me why you do not care to return to Berlin? This is, of course, absolutely voluntary, but your circumstances are exceptional – so unbelievably exceptional – you must forgive us for entreating you to reconsider."

"You have their Enigma coding machine. I have just sent you the plans for their new, revised version. That will tell you of their battle plans. I'm no longer needed."

"But you are, my dear. You are! You can give us information on the political background...wars are not simply constituted of battles, you must believe me."

"I can't live in a state of suspended animation. I'm sorry."

He rumbled, "I know exactly how you feel. But, alas, these are times of war, of heroic effort and heroic sacrifice. We put a factory worker into uniform, and beside him, we set the corner grocer and we send them forth to fight these evil powers. Can you imagine the alienation these simple men feel?"

"They are with their mates. Everyone knows their true names, who they are. Their officers know. They write letters to their families, who reply."

"But my dear, admirable Ray, you are not under enemy fire, facing instant death."

"I soon would be; when we begin air raids on Berlin."

"*Touché.* Yet I am glad to see we think with one mind on carrying the war into *their* backyards, after what they have inflicted on so many European neighbours of ours, our martyred brothers in all too close a propinquity let it be acknowledged. But I would enjoin you, with fervour..."

"Prime Minister, I am sorry but it is too dangerous. Too many people know. Their lives are in danger too, which helps keep their silence, but the day is coming when the Gestapo –"

I choked. "When I think of what they will do to Prince Bernd's family, how they could discover the secret photographic room...the risk they run is unbelievable."

"A family with whom technically we are at war. Contemplate, I beseech you, how many British soldiers have fallen in Flanders in the last few days, who are dying at this moment on the sands and in the shallows of Dunkirk."

"I have done what I can for them. But my responsibility is for Prince Bernd and his family, who are fighting Hitler, who dream of democracy and who pray for a British victory."

Churchill sat in silence, looking at me with hooded eyes.

"Tell me, what is Hitler like?"

"Hypnotic. A grandiose talker. He sees on a vast scale, but everything is out of focus with what he says."

"Could you give me a concrete example?"

"He said – oh, I don't remember. Something about Roosevelt being a sort of spiritual Red who would bring Stalin to the edge of the North Sea – something like that, but I don't remember. Hitler rivets you, leaves you confused, and afterwards you don't really know what he *did* say."

"In your debriefing, you warned us that the Communists have penetrated our Secret Service."

"They knew all about WAGNER. They warned the communists in Berlin, and one of them photographed me –"

"I know," said Churchill impatiently. "They identified you in Moscow from the LADY magazine photo. Most surely, other explanations must exists – an exegesis of less extravagent a purport for our secret affairs."

I said stubbornly, "I know what I know. That Hungarian was not involved in some complicated cover-up. If at a given moment, Moscow needs to sacrifice me, I'm finished. Suppose one of the chinless wonders here in London had a double agent to feed misinformation to the Abwehr or to the SD. He needs to instil blind faith in Berlin. The double agent betrays me, and then they will believe everything he tells them."

"How can you entertain the notion of our stooping to such infamous mischief – you are blandishing what is, in fact, a most precocious and contumacious casuistry, my dear young lady."

"And I have been in the fiery furnace and come out alive."

"Indeed, indeed," he murmured.

"When I send a message, I know it is true, because I am there on the spot. But I see you...er, London, reads it and then decides on what fits in with their own ideas. Not by what the facts are. By what they believe are the facts, what suits their ideas. Look at my message on Switzerland. We could end the war in two months, and save hundreds of thousands of British lives."

"Here you are meddling in high matters of State."

Money! I thought.

"I'm talking about hundreds of thousands of deaths."

"We cannot proceed to such a momentous step just upon the basis of your coded message. Believe me, we are studying the matter with urgency, seeking confirmation."

I compressed my lips.

"I told you about the breakthrough in the Ardennes, and the Army High Command did nothing."

Churchill said with asperity, "We had a message from WAGNER, who we believed was a turncoat Hun, and setting us a trap. Your message urged us to gravely weaken the Belgian front and sent the flower of our British infantry and mechanised forces to face an empty forest, from which you promised a Nazi horde would pour forth like savages from a North American forest."

"And it did."

"And so it did."

"So when did Mr. Bunton reveal my identity?"

"At that moment. We obliged him to."

I demanded triumphantly, "So why didn't you listen then?"

"A twenty-year-old socialite was telling our Army High Command how to proceed," he said with gentle calm.

"A socialite, a young lady of twenty years, was telling you how to keep more than 300,000 men – or 400,000 men – off the beaches of Dunkirk."

"Indeed," acknowledged Churchill, with a fatherly, forgiving smile. "So now you know, you can go back to Berlin and know you will be taken seriously."

"Prime Minister," I said, "You know how with a bank book, you deposit money, and as you spend it, your balance falls?"

"That, I grant you, is the unhappy experience of us all."

"Courage is like money deposited in a bank book. You spend your courage, and finally the account stands at zero."

"I take your point."

"What I suggest is the following. Both the SD and the Abwehr asked me to work for them in the United States as a spy. We could advise the editor in Buenos Aires that I'm on my way there. In Buenos Aires, I go to the German Embassy and ask them to send a message to Heydrich, that I am accepting Gerhard Wallraff's offer to work for them, in Washington. Washington can use me to funnel misinformation to Germany. I will ask the German Embassy in Buenos Aires to teach me how to make microdots. I will correspond with someone in Portugal, say. Perhaps the Germans will have someone in the Mexican Embassy in Washington."

"Ah," said Churchill, "You don't know Edgar Hoover. He is a dolt and clod-hopper. Imagine him with straw in his hair and sticking out of his ears, and then you will realise how little possibility your plan has of prospering over there."

"And Mr. Roosevelt?"

"Mr. Roosevelt? Ah, now, that is a thought."

"After the German Embassy in Buenos Aires makes my travel arrangements and finds me an apartment in Washington, I will insist on going to Belize, to visit my house, and have a week's holiday, swimming and lazing. In Belize, I will explain what the plans are so the Americans will be prepared when I arrive."

"An interesting idea, and well thought out."

I heard Mr. Churchill'a speech on Dunkirk – he had given it on June 4.

He said, "When a week ago today, Mr. Speaker, I asked the House to fix this afternoon as the occasion for a statement, I feared it would be my hard lot to pronounce the greatest military disaster in our long history. I thought that perhaps 20 or 30 thousand men might be re-embarked. It certainly seemed that the whole of the French First Army and the whole of the British Expeditionary Force north of the Amiens-Abbeville Gap would be broken up in the open fields or else would have to capitulate for lack of food and ammunition. These were the hard and heavy tidings for which I called upon the House and the nation to prepare themselves a week ago. The whole root and core on which and around which we were to build – and are sure to build – in the later years of the war, seemed about to perish upon the field, or be led into an ignominious and starving captivity. The enemy attacked us on all sides with great strength and fierceness, and their main power, the power of their far more numerous airforce, was thrown into the battle or else concentrated on Dunkirk and the beaches. Pressing in upon the narrow exit, both from the east and from the west, the enemy began to fire with cannon upon the beaches, on which alone the shipping could approach or depart...they sent repeated waves of hostile aircraft, sometimes more than 100 strong in one formation, to cast their bombs upon the one single pier that remained and upon the sand dunes on which the troops had their only shelter...for four or five days, an intense struggle raged. All their armoured

335

divisions, or what was left of them, hurled themselves in vain upon the ever narrowing, ever contracting appendix in which the British and French armies fought. Meanwhile, the Royal Navy, with the willing help of countless merchant seamen strained every nerve to embark the British and allied troops. Two hundred and twenty light warships and six hundred and fifty other vessels dared to operate upon the difficult coast often in adverse weather under a ceaseless hail of bombs and an increasing concentration of artillery fire...It was in conditions such as these that our men carried on with little or no rest for days and nights on end, making trip after trip across the dangerous waters, bringing with them, always, men whom they had rescued. The numbers they have brought back are the measure of their devotion and their courage. The hospital ships which brought off many thousands of British and French wounded, being so plainly marked, were a special target for Nazi bombs. But the men and women on board them never faltered in their duty.

"Meanwhile, the Royal Air Force, already intervening in the battle, so far as their range would allow, from our home bases, now used part of its main Metropolitan fighter strength, and struck at the German bombers and at the fighters which in large numbers protected them. This struggle was protracted and fierce...

"The crash and thunder, for the moment, but only for the moment, has died away. A miracle of deliverance, achieved by valour, by perseverace, by fervid discipline, by faultless service, by resource, by skill, by unconquerable fidelity is manifest to us all.

"The enemy was hurled back by the retreating British troops. They were so roughly handled they did not harry our departure seriously.

"Sir, we must be very careful not to assign to this deliverance the attributes of a victory. Wars are not won by evacuations. But there was a victory inside this deliverance. It was gained by the airforce. Many of our soldiers coming back have seen the air force at work...this was a great trial of strength between the British and German air forces. Can you conceive a greater objective for the Germans than to make evacuation from these beaches impossible, and to sink all of these ships, which were displayed almost to the extent of a thousand? ... They tried hard, but they were beaten back, they were frustrated in their task. We got the army away...

"Nevertheless, our thankfulness at the escape of our army...must not blind us to the fact that what happened in France and Belgium is a colossal military disaster. The French army has been weakened, the Belgian army has been lost...the whole of the Channel ports are in his hands with all the tragic consequences...

"We shall go on to the end. We shall fight in France. We shall fight on the seas and the oceans, we shall fight with confidence arid growing strength

336

in the air. We shall defend our island whatever the cost may be. We shall fight on the beaches, on the landing grounds, in the fields, in the streets, we shall fight in the hills. We shall never surrender..."

I landed in Washington on July 22, 1940.

PART THREE

Warning: This document may not be published before August 1st, 1995. Prior publication will lead to confiscation, and to prosecution by His Majesty's Government.

Germany surrendered in May, 1945, and I flew back to London at the end of June.

My father, mother and sister were at London airport – I had not seen them for five years. My German mother wept and my father clasped me to his bosom. Not a thought that we were in public. My sister wept, and then I burst into tears. We got home distraught, and then constraint battled with unbelieving, dizzy happiness. My father said huskily, "You went away my young teenager, and now you come back a mature matron," and I gave him a glare so that my mother and sister burst into uncontrollable laughter.

My sister said, "You haven't put on any weight. You must have had all you wanted to eat over there. At least the war has made us all slim in Britain."

* * *

We talked till two o 'clock in the morning, and went on most of next day. They had told me that despite the Official Secrets Act, I could tell my family what had happened, but they requested me not to talk to anyone else.

340

Two days later, I talked to Graham Bunton, and begged him to find Prince Bernd and his family. "If they are not in the Russian Zone, can you get them cards to shop in Allied Forces shops, or to receive the same rations? If the Prince needs a car, or petrol, could he be provided with that too?"

Five days later, he called me. Prince Bernd had a schloss in the mountains, in Bavaria, close to the Austrian border and the Austrian town of Kufstein. It was a mile-and-a-half from a small village. Bunton had arranged with the Americans for them to receive full rations, petrol, and American medical attention.

Bunton said, "They were going to billet American soldiers on him, using his schloss as a Rest and Recreation Centre, but now they'll leave him alone"

I said very carefully, "Could I go there and debrief him? Could you send me with a shorthand typist?"

He sat looking at me for a full two minutes,

"I'll go and chat to some people and see what they say. You were going off our payroll next month, but for the moment you stay."

I nodded gravely.

Out in the street, I found a corner tea shop, and decided to think about my finances.

The British government had paid me in America, with an extra cost of living supplement. I had received a good salary in the American State Department. The Germans had deposited $500 a month in a bank in Mexico City, and the balance stood at almost $30,000. How much tax would 1 have to pay, to bring that rnoney back to England? The Secret Service had paid me £50 a week for five years, and my balance stood at about £12,500

For two years, in 1932 and 1933, we had gone on holidays to a small village in Wiltshire. Could I afford a house in the countryside there?

I finished my bun and tea, and left the Lyon's Corner House.

* * *

Graham Bunton called me to his office.

"Do you remember you made friends with Albert Speer, the architect? You invited him to the Prince's home for dinner, and afterwards, when you had left Germany, he came again. Hitler named him Minister of Armaments, and as the Prince was in raw materials procurement, Speer finally brought him in to work with him. Speer is now a prisoner and will be hanged —"

The Russians wanted to, but the British arranged for a 20-year prison sentence, which Speer served at Spandau Prison in Berlin.

"– but the Prince will be in possession of considerable knowledge. His son-in-law, Richterin Prieguity, was in Luftwaffe Technical Planning, and Speer made him a liason officer with his Ministry. We shall send Prieguity to the Bavarian schloss, They will talk to you, that is certain, and if at a later date we need more technical knowledge, we can send some boffin or the other, provided they will want to talk to the boffin. And well they might not."

"Richierin arid Doris got married?"

"As did Thoma and Graf Walter Vellinghauaen," he smiled. "Claus rose to Generalleutnant. We have located them, and all are being taken to the schloss with commendable American efficiency.

"Another man who will be most important – well, it will be most important to talk to him – is the Prince's brother.

"Count Axel Hohenlinden has been at the schloss since they arrived. What mouthfuls these people's names are."

"Is the grandmother there, and I'll bet you can't say her name if she is?"

Bunton drew a deep breath, assumed a solemn expression and said "The Princess Gabriele Pfaffenhofen is there," and I giggled.

Bunton said, "Now, there is another matter. You have signed the Official Secrets Act, but the war is ended. Your experiences outside Britain and its territories are secret – and they are *not*. So let us look at it this way. We will have a big trial of the top Nazis, and of lesser fry too, so that while that is going on, you would be well advised to keep a very low profile. This trial business could drag on for ten years, so whatever the technicalities, I would observe the Secrets Act at least for that time. After that, if you enquire, some officious bureaucrat will make your life a misery, but if you decide to publish something without consulting anyone, I don't see why anyone should bother to pull you up or come after you.

"However, in the case of this debriefing, the British Government is footing the bill. We will send you with three shorthand typists, so they can work for an hour at a time each, and then they can type up their notes while another one takes their place. We have sent someone to see the Prince and he has insisted that he receive a copy of every page that the girls type up. We cannot ask him to sign the Official Secrete Act, because he is not a British national, but he has signed an agreement with us under which the British Government claims ownership of the international copyright for fifty years, until August, 1995, and he and the other family members – who have had to attach their signatures – recognise the British Government claim. Of course, if they want to write their memoirs, there's nothing we can do about it, but the exact content of your debriefing becomes our property, and your signing of the Official Secrets Act does apply to you in your debriefing of those people in Bavaria now."

"That's perfectly clear. However, I don't see myself sitting down and writing my story."

"The ways of the Lord are enigmatic and mysterious to behold," he said piously.

"Aren't they just," I said.

The two American jeeps drove the three shorthand-typists in uniform and myself through forests, the road winding upwards. We crossed a mountain village, with US jeeps and an armoured car parked outside the inn, and climbed higher. The air was cool and braced us after the summer heat in Munich. At a post with a sign, we turned right along a narrow road, the trees crowding us. Abruptly, the trees gave way to wide, unkempt gardens, and we drove along a meandering gravel drive to the front of the schloss, a wide, two-storey, imposing and silent pile. The American drivers unceremoniously blew their horns as we approached the towering front door with pillars on each side.

We pulled up, and Prince Bernd opened the door, with Reinhard behind him.

The Prince was taller, thinner, even more erect than I remembered him. His face was gaunt, in granite, and he smiled when he saw me.

The girls stayed in the jeeps as I ran across to the stairs, and the Prince came down them, and we met on the gravel.

He took both my arms.

"You are the truest friend we have ever had," he said huskily. "Cards for unlimited food, and use of the American Army hospitals."

He looked most Germanic and severe, and smiled again. "They have 'liberated' a Nazi Mercedes, brought it to me yesterday, and given me a card for petrol."

He took my elbow, and led me up the steps. Reinhard greeted me warmly.

"Thank you, madam," he said. "Thanks to you, we can start eating again."

344

He was thin, and very drawn.

The Prince led me through a marbled foyer, through carved wooden doors into a sitting-room. All the family stood there, Princess Jutta weeping, in most un-Germanic fashion. Their clothes, none too clean, hung loosely on them. Then Thoma and Doris were embracing me, laughing and crying. I hugged Princess Jutta, and crossed to the grandmother, hungry but unbowed, who took my hands and said, "Bless you, child, for what you have done for us."

The men stood stiffly, dressed in their uniforms, but with all insignia gone. They looked haggard, very worn.

Claus picked me up, and whirled me around.

He put me down, and the Count Hohenlinden, Richterin and Walter shook my hand.

Claus said, "As you can, see, we are still alive, but most of our friends are dead, a few killed in enemy action, but most by the Gestapo after the attempt on Hitler's life a year ago."

The Prince said, "We can offer you a very good lunch, because I took the Mercedes to an American PX Store, and loaded it up with food."

* * *

At lunch, they told me they had heard I had been shot down at Dunkirk; then that I was 'working' for the SD in Washington.

"Were you sending misinformation? What sort of thing?"

"Everything. That the real Allied landing was to be at Calais."

I asked Thoma, "What happened to my things?"

Doris said, "I and my sister did alterations, and we wore your dresses."

I said, "Now they're out of fashion. There's a new fashion called the New Look."

The women bombarded me with questions about the New Look.

Over coffee – real Yankee coffee – the Prince said, "I've made an agreement that I will receive a copy of all the debriefing. I'll have another copy made for you."

"Don't send it through the post," I said. "Wait till I come back here."

I asked, "What has happened to the house in Berlin?"

The Prince said, "It was never hit. Bombs fell in the parks, in the lakes and the river, but the houses are so scattered there – it was the rare house that was bombed. The Russians have it now, until they divide the city into its four sectors."

I looked at them in horror, "The looting!"

"Well, no," said the Prince. "We bricked up the door to the wine cellar, and spent a day every month rubbing dirt into the whole wall. As you will remember, we have large cellars, but below them, are large, secret halls. One of the stone walls of the cellars – three large stones open one way, and three more the other. Behind, is a ramp leading down to the secret halls. We carried everything down there before we left. Princess Gabriele, my wife, my brother, myself and the two servants got passes to go, thanks to Speer. We have been here five months. I went back, and joined Speer till a few days before the Russians reached Berlin."

* * *

Half-an-hour later, the three English shorthand-typists came in, and I introduced them to the family. They said their bedrooms were "luvely", and were pleased with the small room and the typewriters,

At 4 o'clock that afternoon, we got down to work.

All the family were there, in the sitting-room, with myself, and Mavis, the first short-hand secretary.

To my surprise, she didn't have a notebook, but a small machine she set up on a folding stand. It had a large roll of narrow paper, and the ribbon unfolded on another spool.

* * *

Prince Bernd said, "The first thing to understand is that England and America did NOT win this war. Hitler won it for them; in Hitler, they had an ally without par."

Oh, goodness, I thought. London *is* going to bury this for fifty years.

"Hitler found the German people in despair – without food, money or employment. He primed the pump with the autobahns, public housing and modest rearmament, and the German people went delirious. Exactly what Roosevelt did in America; and both men led their countries to the edge of catastrophe."

Roosevelt? What was he talking about? We had come on a wild-goose chase.

"Roosevelt was a high-born aristocrat, with Red ideas, and so it was easy for him to have the American government intervene, and pull the country out of the depression. But at Yalta, he let Stalin come within a hop, skip and a jump of the North Sea and the English Channel, of France. Future American historians will say that Roosevelt was dying and the decisions taken did not reflect Roosevelt's will. They did! Roosevelt wanted to give Western

347

Europe to communism, eventually, as he gave Eastern Europe, to make communism wealthier, but also to drag back Western Europe, so that for hundreds of years it could never compete with the United States. In a backward world, the United States would advance till it stood centuries ahead of the rest of the world. The man was mad."

I stuttered, "That can't be right!"

"Go to Spain! The Republican Spaniards in the streets are blessing the name of Roosevelt – they think it's his legacy for them. They are counting the days till Stalin takes Europe. Franco is beside himself, and the half of Spain that's with Franco."

I said feebly, "It's not that bad. He can't take Europe."

"Now Stalin has Poland, Czechoslovakia, Romania, Hungary, Yugoslavia, Austria and half of Germany. How do you think he got there? Do you think he *took* it? Hitler warned again and again that Roosevelt wanted this. When Stalin takes Greece, he's got ports on the Mediterranean. He's at the gates of Italy. He holds Vienna, and is an hour's drive from Switzerland. Two days of fast tank penetration from France. Thank God Roosevelt died when he did –"

(he had died three months before, on April 12)

"– and now we have a draper from Missouri as President. Truman is no aristocratic megalomaniac with dreams of steering the destinies of us all. He must see that Stalin with Western Europe's industry threatens the life itself of the United States. I tell you, that if America reacts in time to save Europe, America will spend the rest of this century sword to sword with Russia. America will not sleep easily in the next fifty years, thanks to Roosevelt."

The British government would not thank me for giving them this expense. They would bury this 30 fathoms deep.

"Churchill carries equal blame. He *lusted* to destroy Germany, to flatten it, to turn it into a cow pasture. He used every ounce of his strength for the allies to demand unconditional surrender. The greater part of the German Army High Command would have executed Hitler on an offer from the Allies, and that was Stalin's nightmare. He had to depend on Roosevelt's madness and Churchill's blind hate to bring his armies to where they stand today. An agreement with Germany would have stopped Stalin at the Russian frontier. But Churchill never distinguished between the Germans and the Nazis. Yet the Nazis had us prisoner!"

I said hurriedly, "I know that as well as you do. If you haven't lived under a dictatorship you can't believe what it can do. If only every Englishman could live one month under Franco and protest against him publicly – some holiday and some education. We live in a sort of European paradise in England."

The British government would shut this away for fifty years.

348

The grandmother said, "Stalin was mad. He had already killed twenty million Russians before the war began. Roosevelt was mad. And Hitler the maddest of them all. Mankind lets its leaders murder them in its millions, as Napoleon did. We are a lot of monkeys up in the trees, obeying the strongest male monkey. And don't you think democracy is any better. People think their leaders are going to make things better. Eighty five out of one hundred leaders are corrupt and fools, and take people's money off them, telling them it is for roads and old age pensions. Democracies let them stay in power for four or five years, and let them be re-elected."

London would have my scalp for this.

Claus said, "The bombing swung the whole of German people behind Hitler. Churchill and America weren't bombing factories. They were bombing housing – bombing women and children. They made sure the German soldier would fight like a tiger. And he didn't surrender till your armies pushed him up to the Baltic, until the Russians entered Berlin. When our defeats came and multiplied, people would have turned against Hitler. And the widespread Resistance which went back to 1933 could have taken over when Hitler no longer hypnotised the ordinary German. But with the bombing and the unconditional surrender the ordinary German knew that Hitler was the lesser evil. We used to joke, 'Have a good war because the peace will be ghastly.'"

Count Axel Hohenlinden said, "To understand this whole mess, we have to go back to day one. Hitler's father beat him, bullied him, and dominated him. I believe Hitler hated his father with all the strength of his mad brain. Hitler was an Austrian, and Austria is the small German-speaking nation, Germany the giant. I think within his psychotic brain, Hitler came to see himself as Austria, identify himself with Austria, and to see Germany as his father. Taking revenge on Germany, destroying Germany, he tore apart his father. Because from the beginning, he encompassed the smashing of Germany. He led Germany to war, rearmed it – but so half-heartedly, it was a joke. In 1939, we produced about 1,500 planes. In the last two years, we turned out about 45,000 war planes each year. We really only used our potential for two years, not twelve. Imagine if we had produced to our limits for twelve years. In the first years, Hitler wasted steel on battleships – afterwards, he confessed his mistake. He needed that steel for U-boats. But the U-boat techniques came from the Great War. Within a year, the Royal Navy was sinking our subs everywhere. Men wanted to build revolutionary submarines – Hitler blocked them. Men wanted to build jet fighters. Hitler ignored them. He ignored rockets. And above all, he gave us that crazy mystique of the German mother-animal, producing babies, and did not let women into factories until 1943. Imagine if the full labour force of women bad gone into the armanemt factories from 1933! Hitler was the best ally Britain and American ever had."

Claus said, "At first, he won only victories. The German people already loved him for lifting them out of their misery – now he assuaged the shame of the Great War defeat with incredible victories in Europe, in eastern Europe, in Greece, Crete and North Africa. After that, each of his interferences with our generals was wrong. Everything he did was wrong. We gave the world the blitzkreig and tank warfare. The Russians, the British and Americans learned – somewhat. They never came near to equalling us. But Hitler blocked the generals, and we no longer had an invincible military machine. Without Hitler, and with full armament production years earlier, no one could have stopped Nazi Germany – we would have had a 1000-year nightmare. It would have needed a new bomb that killed one million people, or some sort of rays that killed one million at one sweep. Just take the Normandy landings. It's childish the logic – just childish. If the allies hold their beachhead, if it grows, THEY DON'T NEED TO LAND AT CALAIS. It doesn't matter whether they may land at Calais – YOU HAVE TO STOP THEM IN NORMANDY OR THEY ARE NOT GOING TO NEED CALAIS. Hitler gave Eisenhower his Normandy landings on a plate."

I trembled. London would muzzle this! So long as they didn't muzzle me too, shut me up in the Tower.

Count Axel Hohenlinden said, "Churchill knew what Roosevelt was doing, but all he cared about was that the Russians took half of Germany. Didn't he fear a Russian invasion of Britain? I think he shrewdly guessed when Roosevelt would die, and that he felt he could count on Truman to leave a huge American Army in Europe. Because mark my words – the Americans will have to keep a powerful army here for the next fifty years. And what was the alternative? The British and American army leaders make a pact with the German Army High Command, who shoots most of the Nazis, and allows the allied armies to land peacefully. Then British, American and German troops stand together on the Russian frontier. That would have saved hundreds of thousands of lives, and changed the next fifty years. But for Churchill and Stalin, this idea was a nightmare. Churchill wanted to destroy Germany. Stalin wanted to reach the North Sea. The insane megalomania of Roosevelt served them both well. But if Stalin seizes Western Europe's industry, he can invade the United States through Alaska and Canada, with an army of 20 million men. Millions and millions of Americans will die, and he will bomb American cities to rubble before America finally stops him – if America can...Americans, British and Germans had to stand watch on the Russian frontier, shoulder to shoulder,"

I said weakly, "Let's call it a day. Tomorrow, could we talk about German armanent production?"

The Prince nodded. "After working alongside Speer, I can tell you about that."

Thoma interrupted. "Ray, your jewels are in a box, in one of the secret, underground halls."

"They were cheap jewels," I said wryly. "And some, imitations."

"Jewels don't make an aristocrat," said the grandmother sharply. "But an aristocrat can make jewels appear far more precious. And Ray, your modest jewellry took on a splendour when you wore them."

I blushed, and everyone laughed.

The Prince said, "Let's go for a walk in the forest."

* * *

Next morning, after breakfast, we sat down in the summer drawing-room.

The Prince walked up and down, rubbing his fingers.

"The whole thing is a bit unbelievable. Different Reich Ministries were warring fiefdoms, and how anything got done between 1933 and 1943 is thanks to the German industrialists themselves. In 1933, when Hitler said he wanted hundreds of millions of marks for rearmament, the Reich bankers said the money wasn't there. He told them to print it, and they drew horrifying pictures of citizens with wheelbarrows full of paper money to go shopping. With everyone at work, and building everywhere, there was no danger of that, but the hidden demon deep within Hitler saw his excuse, and he did not press forward. With limited goods available, people banked their money, and the banks lent it back to the government. In the last year of the war, America produced 95,000 war planes – in that last year, Germany 45,000. In 1939, Germany produced about 1,300 war planes. Our war production was a joke, and we conquered all Europe, invaded Russia and North Africa. With 45,000 war planes every year from 1935, Hitler's nightmare world would have fallen on us all. But until 1943, German war industry worked ten hours a day, no more, on Hitler's insistence, and non-vital production went on to keep the ordinary German in his comfort. British factories ran 24 hours, seven days a week. There was rationing in Germany – but no serious scarcity on the home front till 1943. Britain mobilised every adult immediately, men AND women. Women were NOT to do factory work in Germany, Hitler dictated. Until 1942, when he named Speer Minister of Armaments Britain had already outproduced Germany for three years – tripling and quadrupling what we produced in some arms, such as planes.

"Up to February, 1942, German roads and war production were in Dr. Todt's hands. Speer had been in Russia, trying to put together Russia's railways which the Russian Army had completely wrecked in their scorched-earth retreat. Sepp Dietrich let him use his plane to fly back to Berlin, but the plane had to put down at Rastenburg, Hitler's east Prussian headquarters. Speer had not chatted with Hitler for months, so he went to headquarters and sent Hitler a message. This was February 7, 1942.

"Hitler was closeted with Todt all afternoon, until late at night. Todt emerged, much the worse for wear from a clearly strained couveration with Hitler. Speer and Todt were good friends, but their conversation limped badly as Todt sipped a glass of wine. He told Speer he was flying back to Berlin the next morning, and had one free seat on his plane. Spear took him up on the offer. Todt said goodnight, and went off to get a bit of sleep before the early flight.

"At one o'clock in the morning, an adjutant came to Speer and asked him to join Hitler. Speer found Hitler as much put out as Todt had been, but they talked about grandiose architectural plans to build a new, gigantic Berlin, and quickly Hitler's mood changed to one of energy and enthusiasm. His face regained its color. His headquarters were deliberately spartan, with only hard chairs – no upholstery anywhere. They talked about Russia, and Speer told him the troops were singing 'hard-luck' songs, and loving them. He had written down the words, and Hitler took the sheets. Hitler scowled, talking about undermining morale, and later Speer found he court-martialed the officer who had printed the songs. Speer didn't leave Hitler until 3 am. The plane left within five hours, but Speer left a message that he wouldn't catch it. All he wanted was to sleep.

"The phone ringing shrilly woke up Speer. It was Dr. Brandt, of Hitler's entourage. 'Dr. Todt's plane has crashed and killed him.'

"We all liked Todt. He was canny, cautious and very experienced. Todt loved the outdoors – skiing, sleeping in alpine shelters with the mountains white with snow. He had a solid technical background. He had a simple house at Hintersee near Hitler at Berchtesgaden – the small house of the man who built Germany's autobahns. Among the warring fiefdoms, he steered this way and that, never to meet trouble. He stayed away determinedly from the Nazi bigwig dinners, meetings and parties, an abiding, patient recluse. So Germany's war production stumbled ahead, now this way, now that, with Göring keeping air-production in his hands, and Göring together with everyone else interfering with Todt when they could. Todt had written Speer a letter, speaking of his 'bitter disappointment with all the men with whom I should actually be cooperating.'

"Debate raged at the breakfast table – who would succeed Todt? What everyone agreed on was that he was irreplaceable. Not only had he been Minister of Armaments and Munitions, but had built the Todt Organisation for the construction of the West Wall and the U-boat shelters on the Atlantic.

"Speer did not leave for Berlin, but waited, and at one o'clock in the afternoon, after Hitler had risen and breakfasted, an adjutant told Speer he would be Hitler's first appointment that day. Chief Adjutant Schaub came for him, his face solemn, and when Speer went into Hitler, Hitler received him officially as Führer of the Reich, standing. After listening to Speer's condolences, Hitler said curtly, 'Herr Speer, I appoint you herewith as the successor of Minister Todt in all his functions.'

"Much later on, Speer told me that he heard the words as a thunderclap. He was an amateur. Hitler always appointed amateurs – Ribbentrop had been a wine-salesman. Where did Hitler think Germany would go with all this desultory dilletantism? An ex-fighter pilot, Göring, ran the Four Year Plan.

"Speer said, 'I will do my best in Dr. Todt's construction work,' because Speer was an architect.

Hitler said severely, 'In all of his functions, especially that of Minister of Armaments.'

"Speer stammered, 'I know nothing of that!'

"Hitler said, 'I have total confidence in your ability. I know you will be able, and will shine. Can't you see? I haven't got anyone else. Now, on your way to the Ministry at once and take over.'

"Speer made one last try. 'Mein Führer, you must make that a direct command, because in no way can I attest to my capability to handle this.'

"Hitler stiffened, raised himself to full height, and barked out the command.

"They had always had a close, personal, informal relation. Now, without a personal word, Hitler dismissed him. Now Hitler treated him as a subordinate Minister."

I interrupted.

"How did the plane crash?"

"Planes flying over Russia had a self-destruct mechanism, and this one had a lever beside the pilot. Well, the throttle was beside the pilot, and the lever beside that... If I remember, Todt had to fly on to Munich. The plane landed in Berlin, I believe, then took off, suddenly veered tightly and tried to land straight on to the runway. A tall flame shot up high from the top of the fuselage, and the plane went in on its nose. I seem to remember that's what happened..."

I glanced about me, and everyone stared at him in fascination. No one else knew...I couldn't check.

"What happened to Speer?" prompted Thoma.

All this would interest London. At least I was earning my keep, and they were not throwing away their money.

The Prince said, "Speer received the direct order, Hitler dismissed him, and Speer turned to the door. But Chief Adjutant Schaub came in, blocking his way. Schaub said, 'The Reich Marshal is here and asks to speak to you most urgently, mein Führer. He has no appointment.'

"Göring was outside!

"Hitler's face darkened with vexation. 'Send him in.' He turned to Spear. 'You stay.'

"Göring barrelled in, gave his condolences, and without more ado, said, 'Best I assume Dr. Todt's job within the framework of the Four-Year

353

Plan. With one stroke, this would end all the wrangling and conflicts in the past because no one's field was properly marked out.'

"Göring had his hunting lodge at Rominten about 60 miles away. The accident had happened at half-past nine, so Göring must have jumped into his special train in pyjamas and dressed on board.

"Hitler told him coldly, 'I have already named Reich Master Speer here as Dr. Todt's successor. He has just taken up all of Dr. Todt's responsibilities,' Hitler said it so baldly and incontestably that Göring stood there dumb, staggered and clearly daunted. After some seconds, he bounced back, as always, and talked about Todt's funeral. 'I hope you will forgive me, mein Führer, if I don't attend, after my wars with him.' That shook Speer to his core – an augury of what was to come? And to say something so secret in front of him!

"Hitler said, 'You must come to the funeral. Your fights cannot become public. These public spectacles are basic to our Nazi regime.'

"Speer suddenly suspected that Hitler knew Göring would try to storm in, and had rushed Speer's appointment. Speer guessed that Todt had given orders directly to industry, but Göring, with his Four-Year Plan, believed his task was the whole German war economy. Ray, can you imagine? Göring! Speer then remembered that two weeks earlier, in January, 1942, Göring had so railed at Todt, Todt had told Funk he would resign that afternoon."

I asked, "Who was Funk? I knew, but now I don't remember."

"Walther Funk was Minister of Economics and President of the Reichsbank. Of course, Todt always made the mistake of wearing a uniform of brigadier general of the airforce, which put him at an enormous disadvantage with Göring in *his* uniform with *his* medals."

At Nuremberg, Funk passionately protested his innocence and ignorance. The Court decided he deliberately closed his eyes, and sentenced him to life. They released him in 1957 because of ill-health, and he died in May, 1960.

"Speer was appalled at the heedless temerity, at the folly of naming himself to the post. How could Germany wage war? And he would have to contend with Göring. He thought this was leadership run amok.

"In the end, Hitler backed him against Göring. When I worked with Speer, it was like the Red Sea opening before us, and allowing us to walk on dry land. We moved inside a magic bubble, where there was no resistance, right through the war.

"Not straight away, of course, and you had to see Hitler fix matters. Everyone knew that Speer had never even fired a rifle, but Hitler did choose men with whom he got on well, and who did not argue with him. Todt's personal assistant, Oberregierungsrat Konrad Haasemann, was first to arrive at Hitler's headquarters, minor fry – an intended disrespect by Todt's more powerful associates. Hassemann probably thought he could have Speer for breakfast, and offered to tell Speer about his future colleagues. Speer curtly told him he'd make up his own mind; and took the night train for Berlin. Speer had gone cold on air travel."

"Me too," I said.

"Speer once told me that when the train ran through the suburbs of Berlin with their factories and railroad yards to Schlesischer Station he felt his legs fail him and his bowels turn to water, to use the words from the bible.

"Göring summoned him, and said what good friends they had been while Speer was Germany's first architect, and overwhelmed him with the charm for which Göring was famous. Then, hardening, he said he had a written agreement with Todt, and had brought a copy for Speer to sign...to wit, Speer could not poach upon the Four-Year Plan in seizing raw materials for the Germany Army. Speer didn't answer, and excused himself cordially. How had Germany managed to wage war up to February, 1942?

"Field Marshal Erhard Milch, state secretary for the Air, invited Speer to a conference in the huge hall of the Air Ministry, on Friday, February 13. People from the three services and top men from industry would be there. Spear tried to beg off, but Milch wouldn't have it.

"Lucky for Speer, Hitler had come to Berlin for Todt's state funeral. Speer told Hitler that they were setting him up, and Hitler said, "Well, then, if you feel they are moving against you, interrupt the conference and request everyone to join you in the Cabinet Room. Then I'll deal with those gentlemen.'

"Thirty people came to the conference, all top men, especially Wilhelm Zangen and Albert Vögler from industry, Walther Funk, the Reich Minister of Economics, and Göring's biggest men from the Four-Year Plan. Milch took the chair, and told of conflicts in the needs of the three services. Vögler, of the United Steel Works talked of orders and counter-orders, unending shifts in priorities and interference with industrial production. Unused reserves stayed untouched. One man was needed with overall command.

"Funk stood up and told Milch, 'It is clear one man must take over, Who better than yourself, my dear Milch! I feel I speak in the name of all present, moreso as you enjoy such close confidence with our dearest Reich Marshal, Göring.'

"Speer heaved himself to his feet, and announced, 'The conference will be adjourned to the Cabinet Room. The Führer wants to speak to you about my authority.' Quick as a flash, Milch saw what was what, and told Funk he was honored but could not accept.

"Speer went ahead and briefed Hitler on what had happened. A grim

355

Hitler then strode into the Cabinet Room, and standing, talked for an hour. He said plainly of Göring, 'This man cannot handle armaments and the Four-Year Plan at once.' Of Speer, he said, 'Armaments are now in his hands' but was careful not to say 'with absolute authority'. He said he was counting on their total cooperation and that they would treat him 'as a gentleman', using the English word. As, up to that moment, Hitler had never stood behind a Minister like this, the message was clear.

"So, German armament production turned around – but ten years too late."

The Prince stood at the windows, looking out at the forest beyond the lawns. We waited in silence.

He turned around, and sat down. "I'm not being clear. By 'too late' I mean that the war in Russia would have ended in 1942 had we invaded with 70,000 tanks. The Allied invasions would never have happened.

"But Speer still could have saved Germany!

"Who it was who baulked him was Hitler. As Hitler blocked the decisions of the generals and field-marshals, time and again.

"And all his decisions were wrong, and led Germany inexorably to catastrophe.

"With Speer freely in charge, the allied air fleets over Europe would have perished, to the last plane. Bombers and fighters alike. The invasion fleets would have been sunk by very fast jet fighters, firing rockets, two years before the Allies built jets.

"Hitler's declaration of war on the United States was pure insanity. Without Hitler, we would never have gone to war with America, The United States Congress and Senate would have not agreed to Roosevelt declaring war on us, as ardently as Roosevelt wanted it.

"Today we would not have the Red Army poised to take the ports of the North Sea and the Channel. But we could have still had a Nazi Germany, unless Roosevelt and Churchill were overruled, and the German Army was persuaded to kill the Nazi hierarchy."

He paused, and rang a bell.

A girl came in, and he asked for coffee.

"So, what did happen to Speer?"

"Speer had been working in an offshoot of Todt's set-up, in construction. As is the case, often the corporal sees more than the general – he had long ago made up his mind about what was wrong with German war production. So he prepared a plan of vertical columns of rings. Each column meant tanks, artillery, planes, submarines and so on. Each circle meant the components – electrical units, ball bearings, turrets, forgings, and the rest.

"Next day, February 18, he met the top men in war industry and the armaments bureaucracy in the conference room of the Academy of Arts. Spear talked to them for an hour, and they accepted his new organisation map. He handed around a paper, repeating the agreement for one leader, made on February 13, and accepting his new 'map', for them to sign.

"Some made a fuss, but Milch had them sign. Admiral Witzell from the Navy was last, and signed under protest.

"Next day, February 19, Speer went to the Führer's headquarters with Air Field Marshal Milch, and from the Army, General Thomas and General Olbricht, to show Hitler the new organisation. Hitler approved.

"No sooner had Speer got back to Berlin, than Göring ordered him to his hunting lodge, Karinhall, some 45 miles north of Berlin. This had been a nice old hunting lodge till Göring saw Hitler's new Berghof in 1935. He rebuilt the small lodge into a great country mansion, with a large saloon like Hitler's but an even bigger picture window. This pretentiousness irritated Hitler.

"Speer had a lot to do, was pressed for time. He arrived, chagrined, and Göring made him cool his heels for an hour. He materialised from the upper floor in a sweeping green velvet dressing gown, and majestically came down the stairs.

"They greeted each other cooly, and Göring led him to his gargantuan desk. Göring sat, clearly enraged. Speer had not sent him an invitation to the conference, and across the prairie of his desk top, he pushed a tendentious report from the director of his Four-Year Plan. He heaved his huge bulk to his feet as lithe as a cat and paced the wide office in a frenzy. Spear watched in alarm. Göring's underlings had put their signatures to Speer's paper! He vituperated them, phrenetically, but directed not one word against Speer himself. Speer suddenly saw how inviolate his own position was, with Hitler right behind him.

"Then Göring tossed his bombshell. He would resign.

"Speer thought like lightning. That was the best that could happen. Humpty-Dumpy didn't like work. He wavered, changed his directives...by 1942, his Plan was thought torpid.

"But Hitler would never allow Göring to resign. And he would not forgive Speer putting this crisis in his lap. Hitler would seek a compromise, one of his famous compromises that solved nothing but created a new swamp in which people struggled against each other. Hitler never chose what was important. He evaded giving clear lines of demarcation, but made people and offices overlap on jobs, 'so the stronger one comes out on top, like in Darwinism.'

"Speer hastened to tell Göring that the new organisation had Hitler's personal approval, and that of the industry, but in no way did it touch upon his Four-Year Plan. Göring relaxed perceptibly, and Speer hurried on to say how happy he would be to become Göring's subordinate within the Four-Year Plan.

"Three days later, Speer went back, with a decree that named Speer as

357

Chief Representative for Armaments within the Four-Year Plan. Göring half-heartedly tried to limit Speer's powers, but signed it as it was, on March 1, 1942. This decree gave Speer the right 'to give armaments...within the total economy the priority which is proper for them in wartime.'

"Speer rubbed his hands. This gave him even more power than the paper of February 18, which had made Göring rabid.

"On March 16 – after Hitler's approval, Hitler being all too happy to get Göring off his back – Speer told the German Press the news.

"Göring kicked up another fuss over this, and Speer at last saw that Göring's luxurious life hung on lavish handouts from industry. Göring feared the money would dry up if he lost standing, so Speer suggested to him that he invite fifty of the biggest industrialists to Berlin, and in the conference, Speer would make clear his subordination. Göring grabbed at the idea. Speer delivered a short introduction, and Göring talked to then for an hour.

"Thereafter, Göring faded into the background, and showed no more interest. He had kept the money coming in.

"On March 21, fearing comatose activity from Göring, Speer had Hitler sign another proclamation: 'The needs of the total German economy must always take second place to armaments.'

"This was the best Speer could hope to get. Hitler would not draw lines of authority; Speer would have to navigate uneasy waters, dealing with everyone. What Speer did do was to set up directive committees, each one for a different weapon. Then he set up directive pools for supplies. In all, 13 of them. He set up commissions, so that army and air force officers met with the best designers. The designers worked with the directive committees, and each committee had to make sure that each factory produced but one item. He guaranteed permanent orders to all factories. Before, with stopping and starting, factories would try to get half-a-dozen orders for different items to cover themselves. After a spell of blitz warfare, the Army would stop ordering ammunition, so factories tried different lines, or suffered financial loss. Speer saw that in these lulls, Germany had to build up reserves of ammunition and one factory should make only one sort of bullet or shell.

"He gave thousands of technicians freedom to organise as they wanted to. They revolutionised armament production. They joked that Speer was re-introducing Parliamentary democracy.

"Speer set up guarantees that no one working in armaments could be arrested except against Speer's own signature. This raised the hackles of a jumpy Gestapo. After the July 20, 1944 Plot against Hitler's life, Ernst Kaltenbrunner, the Gestapo Head (who the Allies hanged at Nuremberg), wanted to arrest Bücher of the AEG, Vögler of the United Steel Works and Reusch of the mining Gutehoffnungshütte, for 'defeatist' remarks. Speer told Kaltenbrunner that if people couldn't talk out plainly and get what bothered them off their chests, they couldn't produce arms for the fronts. A distrustful

Kaltenbrunner had to depart without victims to club to death in the Gestapo cellars.

"By August of that same year, the Index Figures for German Armaments End-Products showed a 27% climb over February in guns, 25% for tanks, and ammunition an astonishing 97%. Armament production as a whole rose by a steep 60% over two and half years, in the heavy bombing, production of arms went up from the index of 98 in 1941 to 322 in July 1944, the peak. The labor force grew by 30% only – the Nazi hierarchy blocked Speer from getting more labor,"

The prince paced up and down.

"Ray, what you have to understand is that Hitler asked little of the German people on the home front. Churchill offered 'blood, toil, sweat and tears', and that is exactly what the British people got. Roosevelt's demands on American industry were colossal. His supplies to Russia were gigantic – 18 million pairs of boots to mention one item. Hitler told the Germans over and again, 'Victory is sure.' The popular feeling, the morale in the street, obsessed Hitler. Hitler and the top Nazis had lived through the Collapse of 1918. And the allies had that collapse within their grasp. With the trapping of the Sixth Army in Stalingrad, the destruction of the Africa Corps, and the allied landing in North Africa, the man in the street knew the war was lost, What snatched the German collapse from the allies was the heavy bombing of women and children, of the residential areas in German cities. Roosevelt wanted the bombing. Churchill and your 'Bomber Harris' wanted it from psychopathic hatred. When, with dull resignation, the German people saw there was to be no mercy, they decided to kill every last British, American and Canadian soldier they could, in revenge, every last pilot. All those who died on the Second Front, in the Invasion of Europe, died needlessly."

I thought, my God, London will seal this with Seven Seals.

"Speer wrote an analysis in Spring, 1942. '...we must end the war in the shortest time possible. If not, Germany will lose. We must win this war by the end of October, before the Russian winter, or we have lost it once and for all. Thie means we must win with the weapons we have now, not with those we will have next year.'

"I gave this to Rubén Zorreguieta in the Argentinean Embassy, and he encoded it in your code, and sent it to London. The Times of London published it on September 7, 1942.

"Speer saw that all building had to stop, to free men and materials. He prevailed upon Hitler to stop the building at Obersalzberg, and then he made a speech to the assembled Gauleiters and Reichsleiters – the Nazi district bosses. They agreed enthusiastically, and afterwards, came up to him asking for special exception in their personal cases.

"Reichsleiter Martin Bormann easily persuaded Hitler that the Obersalzberg need not stop. The Führerprotokoll of March 5-6, 1942, Point

17.3, ordered that 'work at Obersalzbarg be halted. Compose appropriate memorandum to Reichsleiter Bormann.' Two and half years later, work still went on, and Bormann wrote a letter to his wife, which somebody managed to purloin. It reached my hands, and I passed the copy on to Speer."

The Prince rang the bell and when the maid came, asked for mineral water. She brought it, and he drank it.

He said wryly, "I need to wet my throat. I can't drink just coffee."

He put down the glass.

"The letter said, 'Herr Speer, who I see time and again has not the remotest respect for me...asked for a report on the Obersalzberg construction. A crazy way to go about things! Instead of going through correct channels and addressing himself to me, the God of Building, without further ado, has ordered my men to report directly to him!'

"The man in the street knew the war was lost.

"But not the top Nazis. They would not see the writing on the wall, the hangman's noose waiting for them.

"Well, I finally decided Hitler knew. Speer thought Hitler was mad, but I had decided that Hitler wanted to encompass the pulverisation of Germany. I could not say that to one single soul, or I was a dead man. Hitler led us all to Germany's tomb."

After a long pause, he went on. "He rebuilt a derelict castle called Klessheim, near Salzburg, robbing armaments of millions of marks. Himmler built a lodge for his mistress near Berchtesgaden. Hitler backed a Gauleiter to renovate Posen castle, heavily draining key materials. In 1942-1943, Ley (he strangled himself in his Nuremberg cell), Keitel (hanged) and others built special trains for themselves, a grave drain on materials and technicians.

"Hitler tenaciously defended production of consumer goods, even 'rug factories and producers of other artistic products', even 'a Munich manufacturer of picture frames.'

"Top Nazis had big houses, hunting lodges, palaces, rich menus and select wines. The man in the street learned of this, and only Bomber Harris and the American air force kept him in line. The man in the street also learned that Hitler was ever increasing the thickness of the roofs of his bunkers, up to sixteen and half feet, more than five metres. Air raid bunkers multiplied like mushrooms – at Rastenburg, Obersalzberg, Munich, at a guest palace near Salzburg, at Nauheim headquarters and on the Somme. In 1944, Hitler had thousands of specialists blasting underground headquarters into mountains in Silesia and Thuringia, all at the cost of armamants. Göring built bunkers along the road from Berlin to Karinhall, although the road was but 45 miles long, and wound through empty forests. Ley built a deep bunker by his house in Grunewald suburb, in Berlin, where hardly a bomb fell."

"And you were all right, in the bombing?" I asked him.

"London kept its word. A bomb would fall in a nearby park, in a lake, in the river, when a plane had to jettison its load and couldn't reach its target."

He stood up restlessly, then sat down again.

"When we were winning the war in 1940 and 1941, we never got near the output at arms we had in the autumn of 1918. Three years later, as we neared our summit in manufacture, our total in ammunition – taking in Austria and Czechoslovakia as well as Germany – didn't come near that of the First World War.

"One reason, as I've just told you, was crazy production by Nazi bigwigs. Robert Ley pushed for a pigsty on his model farm, because "it would be vital for future food production." Speer refused and addressed his letter: 'To the Reich Organisation Chief of the Nazi Party and Chief of the German Labour Front: Subject – Your pigsty.'

"Late one evening, we inspected one of the first-line Berlin arms factories, Rheinmetall-Borsig. On the great factory floors, advanced machinery stood silent. They didn't have enough men to run a second shift. We came back to my home for dinner, and decided to visit more factories at this hour. Everywhere the same.

"We had to find millions of workers.

"Speer had managed to interrupt the crazy construction work and free several hundred thousand building workers. But now the boss of the 'Business Department for Labour Allocation within the Four-Year Plan', Dr. Mansfeld, told us he couldn't move the building workers from one part to another because of the refusal of the Gauleiters. They were jealous of loss of men from their districts. Speer sought an ally in Karl Hanke, Gauleiter of Lower Silesia. Hitler agreed, but Bormann stepped in. Bormann thought Hanke was Speer's man, and Speer threatened Bormann's rank in the Party ladder.

"Hitler suddenly wavered, with transparent excuses. He said, 'I've talked to Bormann, and decided to take Sauckel.'

"Bormann had hit at Göring and Speer, putting Sauckel into Göring's Four-Year Plan. Göring cried 'foul!', Hitler ignored him, and called Speer and Sauckel to his headquarters. Hitler handed over the anthorisation and said that as Germany now commanded two hundred and fifty million people, Speer could put all the millions he wanted into the labor force.

"I had decided that Hitler was encompassing Germany's destruction –"

I interrupted, "He confused Germany with his father?"

"My brother suggested that," and we all looked at Count Axel Hohenlinden, who moved his shoulders in a deprecating gesture.

"As I had decided that Hitler was leading us to Germany's undoing, and as I knew that millions of new workers would turn the war around, I wondered what Hitler would do next. Speer never saw those workers. By their millions, they vanished into the forests, joined the partisans, fled labour

361

service in Germany. When foreign workers did arrive, loud cries arose. They would sabotage the factories! Spies would fill Germany! No one could find interpreters!

"Speer had to shift his ground. The solution was German women. Speer circulated photos of workers leaving the factories in 1918 and 1942. The difference? In 1918, they were all women. In 1942, all men.

"In England and America, countless millions of women filled the armament factories – the munitions factories, as they called them there. American and British newspapers and magazines made that abundantly clear.

"At the beginning of April, 1942, Speer went to Sauckel about getting women. Sauckel told Speer that getting whatever workers was his business, not Speer's! That as a Gauleiter he answered alone to Hitler!

"Finally, he offered to submit the business to Göring, who ran the Four-Year Plan. At Karinhall (where Göring was only 4 years and 6 months away from his cyanide pill, taken 2 hours before they were to hang him), Göring was most gratified, scarcely heeded Speer and listened to every word from Sauckel on the moral risk to German womanhood, the danger to their 'psychic and emotional life' and their capacity to bear.

"Göring could not have agreed more (and advanced his noose in one giant step). Sauckel then hastened to Hitler, and after talking to him, was able to declare, 'To give the German housewife – and above all mothers of several children – relief from her tasks, the Führer has ordered me to bring into the Reich from the eastern territories some four or five hundred thousand carefully chosen, healthy and strong girls.'

"In 1943, England had cut the number of maidservants by two-thirds; in Germany some 1.4 million women worked as household maids. Another half a million girls from the Ukraine worked for Nazi Party members – and how the ordinary people talked about that!"

At Nuremberg, they hanged Fritz Sauckel for what slave labour he did import into Germany. High on the gallows platform, on October 16, 1946, in a sweater without a coat, he looked around the gymnasium and shouted, "I am dying innocent. The sentence is wrong. God protect Germany and make her great again! God protect my family!"

They hanged about a dozen from those gallows on October 16, and next afternoon, they gave Speer a mop and a bucket and told him to try and clean the great stain on the polished boards underneath. It would not go away.

The Prince said, "My voice is getting tired from so much talking. That's

362

enough for this morning. Let's go down to the village, to the inn."

He laughed.

"The Americans have taken over the inn, and we couldn't use it. But with this card, we can go back into the inn where we have been going all our lives."

We walked down without talking, and inside the inn, sat down at a table by a window. We ordered beer, and Axel said in a low voice, "That's the captain in charge of the village, over in the corner."

He was talking to two soldiers, and handling papers. The soldiers left, giving us women a good look, and then the captain sauntered over.

"Can I join you?"

We ordered for him, and he asked me, "Are you settled in comfortably?"

We chatted, and he said he was from Michigan. He used to go hunting; for half-an-hour, the men talked about hunting.

We left, and took a longer way back, through forest trails. We passed a *pightle*, a sort of croft with an enclosure cleared in the forest. Two children ran out to us, and a peasant woman stood in the doorway and exchanged greetings.

Princess Jutta said, "Her husband will be working somewhere in the forest. They hardly know we have had a war."

She had American chocolate in her bag, and gave it to the boy and girl.

* * *

After lunch, we rested; and then gathered in the drawing-room.

We waited for Lucy to set up her shorthand machine, and make herself comfortable.

I asked the Prince, "Did Speer still feel so friendly towards Hitler – did he admire him so much as before?"

"Hitler became Speer's bane. As I explained, Speer tried to cut back heavily on consumer goods - at the beginning of 1942, their production ran at only 3%...less than peacetime. All Speer could manage was a 12% cut. With three months austerity, Hitler was dithering and worrying, and on June 28-29, 1942, ordered that 'the manufacture of products for the general needs of the population must hereby be restored.' Imagine Speer's repressed anger."

I asked, "Did Speer come to see that Hitler was undermining Germany's ability to wage war?"

"Speer thought Hitler did that from weakness, blindness, from vacillation. He never thought of it as being deliberately pathological, as obeying a pathological need to destroy Germany."

"Destroying his father," I mused.

"Do you find that hard to believe?"

"Perhaps. What I am sure of was how he must have hated his father. And that he was pathological too. Absolutely. I think I told you once that I found that he didn't seem to connect with the outside world directly. The world seemed to register with his senses and then everything went deep down inside him. There, he churned it all up, and that deep part of his mind sent a non-stop stream of ideas and interpretations to his conscious mind. As though he got everything secondhand. That inner stream seemed to be real for him. You and I react straight off to what we've got in front of our noses. God only knows what those deeps in his mind were telling him about Germany and mixing it up with his father. Count Axel told me Hitler had several sorts of insanity, perhaps because his parents were cousins."

"Good enough," approved the Prince. "Coming back to Speer, then, he said over and again what Hitler had once told him: 'Speer', Hitler said to him, 'who will win this war is he who makes the least blunders.' And Hitler multiplied his blunders beyond belief. Churchill did have his blunders, one of which threw away the British Empire in one stroke, an Empire built over three hundred years. Churchill conceived the idea that Russia had no aircraft industry. During the Spanish Civil War, Russia had about three dozen factories working full-out, one of them I understand turning out tens of thousands of propellers alone. He insisted, as so often he did, overruling his military advisers as Hitler did, that Britain must send thousands of Spitfires on the Murmansk convoys – and you know how many of those ships we sank, with their Spitfires. In the Spanish Civil War, the Russians sent up their Mosca against the Me-109, and it easily held its own. They produced tens of thousands of Moscas, but by 1941, they had more advanced models, again produced in their thousands, While the Russians admired the Spitfire, they made no effort to build it themselves. In a word, Russia did not need the Spitfires to stay in the war.

"But Malaya and Hong Kong *did* need those Spitfires, and without them the *Prince of Wales* and the *Repulse* went straight to the bottom with high-level Japanese precision bombing, using the Norden bombsight which we had stolen from the Americans before the war. Churchill gave the captains permisson to sail without air cover – Churchill didn't believe this nonsense of planes sinking heavy battleships.

"So, 68,000 British and Australian defenders – more Australians than British, Tokyo tells us – faced some 300,000 Japanese troops, with full control of the air. What a fight they gave the Japanese! Twenty thousand Japanese dead and 5,000 wounded, while the allies – 7,000 died and 2,000 wounded.

"Churchill proclaimed that 30,000 Japanese had overcome 100,000 British and Australian troops, not to take the blame for his criminal blunder with the Spitfires. Whenever this war with Japan ends, those soldiers will go

364

back to England and Australia in shame – men who let '30,000 Japs'walk all over them, so people will believe."

I said, "Praise be to God for Hitler's blunders. How these politicians interfere with the military experts!"

"You've just put your finger on what Speer thought. Speer found Hitler, above all, an amateur. He told me that the man had never studied for a profession and tried to be jack-of-all-trades as Führer, and master of none. People who teach themselves lack that mental discipline, that rigour of thought, a University education bestows. Self-taught people ignore the complexities, and that gave him stupendous successes from 1933 to 1942. He ordered rearmament, the building of 2,500 miles of autobahns, the building of workers' housing – ordered the Reichbank to print paper money and extend credits without a thought for the danger of inflation. Unwittingly, he was right – huge activity sopped up the paper money. The generals read Lidell Hart and de Gaulle on the lightning, mechanised war, but the few exceptions like Guderian were far, far outweighed by the cautious, fearful generals who had fought the Great War. Hitler took it at its face value, and ordered them to attack, attack, attack. He was right. By accident, because he knew not what he did. He had a horror of static trench warfare from what he lived through in the First World War. But he knew nothing of handling great armies. He wanted heavily armoured tanks with high muzzle velocity guns. Designers hated putting long barrels on tank turrets, and wanted speed, not armour. Again, Hitler was right. Every time he scored, a mean shine came into his eyes as he looked around his experts. After 1942, came the defeats, and he could no longer stare around him as before. He must have wondered whether he could dominate them now – and found he could. The Gestapo behind him was too great a danger for a single general, industrialist or minister, like Speer, to challenge him.

"Speer saw in him a lightning intelligence to grasp salient points. He was audacious, and loved showing a layman's originality. No rules encumbered him as they did his educated companions, so over and again he leapt to unheard-of ideas, ideas which the others could never have thought of because the rules blinded their thinking.

"But when things went wrong, his ignorance caused defeat upon disaster. He could win against a reeling opponent – but not against powerful military counterattacks, He needed to know the rules for that.

"Speer told me many times that mishaps are what undo the untrained. Reverses sort them out. And as this happened to Hitler, Speer insisted that his obdurate dilettantism grew obsessive. His decisions got wilder and wilder. He got more obstinate in believing his intuitions would finally work again. He would not accept, Speer said, that disaster after disaster confirmed the rules – rules that he barely understood.

"As I say, I don't necessarily agree. I think deliberately he sought the obliteration of the German people, to bring down upon them such a wrath as history had never seen."

His brother, Axel, said, "Perhaps we don't need to complicate this so much. Think of Hitler as a killing machine. Like 85% of leaders, democratic or not, they are at the bottom, killers. They attract killers, as Hitler did, and he gave them rein. Most leaders are closer to the criminal classes than to the middle-classes in their instincts and intuitions. People are all looking for a daddy to solve their problems for them, and history shows that our leaders don't solve many problems, mostly they make them. Simply, then, Hitler outdid the lot."

Silence fell on us.

I prompted the Prince, "What else did Speer think?"

"Speer said his problem was that Hitler had a childish glee in shining in questions of armaments. He had a big book, a red cover with wide yellow stripes, full of statistics. He would proudly recite streams of figures, not realising that he showed himself as a rank, uninformed amateur. He kept it on his night table, and had it brought up to date. He knew fifty different calibres of ammunition, and Speer had bad moments trying to keep conversations on the rails. Sometimes, in haste, someone would make a mistake in a calibre – of no importance – and Hitler would stop the conversation, get a servant to bring the book, to show up the general, manufacturer, or whoever. This petrified people, and imposed a constraint on meetings which was damaging, What Speer had to do was go to his Führer conferences with a 'bodyguard' of at least a score of technicians and experts, and Speer scarcely opened his mouth; they were known as 'Speer's invasions'. Nothing could shake these experts. The tone of the conversation might rise, they usually forgot whom they were arguing with, but Hitler took it with humour, and rare courtesy. Hitler couldn't win, but he impressed them with his speed in going to the core, his speed in making the right choices. But they led the way – Hitler had to follow. He found his way instantly through technical processes and drawings. His questions showed he had understood the most complicated reasonings. But Speer said that here was Hitler's lethal failing – he understood the essence too easily, but never the details, never the full question.

"What made Speer despair was that Hitler's technical ideas were circumscribed by his personal life in the First World War. The Great War was Hitler's mental outer horizon...the war and its traditional arms. His intuitions responded sluggishly to the atom bomb, jet fighters, radar and rockets. He didn't like flying in planes with retractable landing-gear. He was afraid the landing-gear wouldn't go down when he had to land, and tried to make planes keep fixed wheels."

The Prince paused, and Claus said, "At the Führer's Headquarters, Hitler took his meals with generals and staff officers, so he tried to keep a more elevated tone to his table-talk. They sat at a long table for 20 people on hard chairs, and these people weren't the high-level Nazi louts at the Chancellery lunches. In that year of 1942, Hitler launched a new offensive in Russia. Many generals back in the OKW warned against it, but at first it roared ahead. Hitler was exultant, and lorded it over his generals, Again, he had been right, But the left prong east of Kiev got longer and longer, approaching Stalingrad. Hitler moved to advanced headquarters in the Ukraine, at Vinnitsa. Guderian had told Hitler, to the point of weariness, that tanks could not go on running without spare parts, but Hitler refused to manufacture them because that cut back the new tanks by 20%. Designers warned that tank tracks were good for only 500 miles. So the offensive ran itself into the ground – without spares, and supplies couldn't keep up."

The Prince said, "In those months, we manufactured only one-third of the tanks we would in 1944.

"Faces grew longer at Headquarters, and Hitler's certainty, his effrontery, wavered. He stopped taking his meals with the others, and Keitel moped like a pet dog that had been locked out. Hitler ate alone, for the very first time.

"The generals warned we had to pull back. But for years they had fawned on him, and fostered the belief that he was a godlike figure with preterhuman capacities; and he ordered the worn-out army to push ahead,"

The Prince said, "Speer by this time attended the daily two-hour situation meeting in the map room, and he said Hitler's brushing aside the lack of spares and supplies showed him as the utter amateur. *I* think Hitler knew exactly what would happen."

I said, "His inner voices – if that's what they were – told him this was the way to begin the destruction of Germany?"

Claus said, "I don't understand how my superiors obeyed him. The German character has this fatal rent – we are almost *proud* of obeying. When they hang Germany's leaders, most of them will plaintively claim they only obeyed Hitler – you'll see. They'll claim that not from hypocrisy but because it is the very greatest virtue here. Grandmother has made me think – how everyone *obeyed* in this war. Millions of Russian infantry ran upon our machine-guns. When you were 'working' for the German Secret Service in Washington, you sent us two reports – one of a US captain in New Guinea who refused to obey an order for his men to charge a Japanese bunker. They withdrew him from the front – I wonder what happened to him? You also reported that Eisenhower had shot two or three deserters. The allies don't forgive disobedience, but they won't hear of it when they come to hang Germany's leaders."

The grandmother said, "The day will come when the common people will rise up against their leaders, even the democratic ones, who are nothing but a pack of thieves who rob them blind."

"When?" I laughed.

"In a hundred years – two hundred. Today, about 15 people in every hundred have a far better education, know far more, than their elected leaders. The ancient Romans made you finish the *causus honorum* before you could enter politics. Today, fifty million will have gotten themselves killed by one leader or another before Japan surrenders, you'll see."

I turned to Claus.

"So what happened in the Stalingrad debacle?"

London would devour every word.

Richterin said, "Can I interrupt?"

We all turned to him.

"Stalingrad was at the end of the year, in winter. On November 8, Hitler went to Munich to celebrate the Beer-Hall Putsch, and news came from the Luftwaffe of an unbelievable convoy sailing through the Straits of Gibraltar. Hitler was flattered. 'The biggest landing force in the history of the world', he said proudly. But where were they going? Hitler said, 'I would land on the Italian coast near Rome, cut Italy in two, and take Rome. We would lose Italy, and Rommel too. We could not supply Rommel. They would defend a narrow front that they could hold.' And Hitler was right. This was more than a year and half before the abortive Anzio Landing, that Churchill described as a 'beached whale'. The allies lost countless thousands of dead in Sicily and in the cruel fighting upwards in Italy, through the easily defended mountains. The allies were stodgy in their thinking, and had no one like Hitler who grasped in a flash what had to be done. What the allies and the Russians had was a tidal wave of guns and planes and men. In 1943, the Russians produced more planes than we did. And thank God for that. Hitler would have defeated them all."

A heavy silence fell.

Finally, I asked, "Stalingrad?"

Claus said, "Hitler told the generals, 'Our generals are committing their old, old mistakes. They always overestimate the Russians...they are weak, they've lost far too much blood... Besides, the Russian officers train so badly! ...' He was enjoying the false quiet of the Berghof, but as the appalling news flooded in, he rushed back to Rastenburg. The Russians advanced on a front of 125 miles across. Between the forest of red Soviet arrows, the maps showed blue circles on entrapped Germans. Red enclosed Stalingrad. Hitler ordered up reserves to break through, but as his generals had warned him weeks ago, there were none. General Zeitzler swamped Hitler with facts – the Sixth Army had to break out. They had no rations, little ammunition. Göring said he would supply them from the air, then admitted that he could not. Hitler said, 'The counterattack I have ordered from the south will relieve Stalingrad...We've been in fixes like this before. We always ended up with things under our control.' No! said Zeitzler. The counterattack is weak, and will work only if it joins up with the Sixth Army that has broken out."

Claus paused. "Why did Paulus obey orders? How is it possible? Why didn't he break out and tell Hitler to go to hell?"

He shook his head.

"Back at Rastenburg, they argued more than half-an-hour. Then Hitler said, out of patience, 'We must hold Stalingrad at any cost. It's the key point. It cuts the Volga traffic where Russian grain from the south cannot reach the north.' This convinced no one. Day after day, a sleepless Zeitzler begged and pleaded. He beseeched Keitel to help him, and. Keitel said yes. But in the situation room, Keitel cried emotionally, pointing at the city engulfed in red rings, 'Mein Führer, we will hold on there!'"

"Hitler *knew!*" growled the Prince. "And the generals too. But he had them hypnotised ... I don't know what it was. Stalingrad and Montgomery's victory in North Africa! Most people knew the war was lost."

I said, "Churchill broadcast: 'This is not the end. It is not even the beginning of the end. But it is perhaps the end of the beginning.'"

Claus said doggedly, "Let me tell you about Generalfeldmarschall Eric von Manstein, probably the greatest general of the Second World War.

"On January 12, 1943, Hauptmann Behr, Paulus' top aid, flew out of Stalingrad with a letter for Manstein, demanding a free hand. Paulus described such atrocious conditions, Manstein sent Behr directly to Hitler.

"On the phone to Manstein, Hitler explained that the German Army would cross the Caucasus mountains and join up with Rommel, who would take Egypt and strike north. (At the end of last year – 1942 – the allies had decisively smashed Rommel at El Alamein.) The combined armies would march into India, whars the Indians would receive them joyously.

"The Field Marshal was sick to his stomach at this amateur strategy. The Sixth Army lay abandoned and moribund hundreds of miles behind the Russian Front. Several leaders hastened to Manstein, to draw him into the plot to depose Hitler. Manstein insisted that HE HAD SWORN AN OATH AND COULD NOT BREAK HIS ALLEGIANCE."

I said, "The German Achilles Heel. Their *loyalty.*"

Claus looked at me affectionately. He went on, "The problem was simple. The Russians were rolling westwards.

"Hitler had a single thought – to hold on mulishly to ground. Manstein thought in terms of movement and entrapment.

"Hitler travelled to Manstein's headquarters at Saporozhne in February, 1943, and the Field Marshall gave him his plan. Army Group South would withdraw behind the Don and the Dnieper rivers, and the Red armies would rush forward, outrunning their supply lines. The Germans would flatten them. The steep west bank of the Dnieper was one hundred and seventy feet high, and dominated the plain. That lay 125 miles behind the front, and Hitler had a fit, Hitler would lose Kharkov! That was the bait, cried Manstein. Kharkov would blind the Supreme Stayka.

"Hitler gave reluctant consent, and the Russians raced in. The Germans crushed them, and at last formed a strong front between the Sea of Asov and Byelgorod. For supreme generalship between November, 1942 and February, 1943, Hitler gave him the Oak Leaf to the Knight's Cross in March.

"When Manstein finally stalled the Russian winter offensive, a huge bulge thrust into the German line – the Kursk Salient. Manstein acted fast, before the Russians would build their classic in-depth defences of minefields and bunkers with heavy timber beams and earth. Forty-percent of the Russian army stood in the Salient, and its loss would strike mortally at the Red Army. Further, Manstein would shorten the German front by 500 kms, allowing him to build up a huge, mobile reserve with the freed-up troops.

"Hitler stopped him dead. He said that everything had to be in place before the attack. Each day, the feverish Russians built fortifications. Hitler was famous for his urging of fast, poorly premeditated attacks, crying for speed, speed. Now he hindered, blocked Manstein TILL JULY 5, when the Salient was almost impregnable."

Claus stopped, and I stared at him, stupefied.

Finally, I got out, "Have you got this right?"

The Prince, Richterin and Walter said together, "He has."

The silence lengthened.

The Prince said, "Hitler was leading Germany to its destruction – Germany and Europe. Deliberately. He was no amateur."

Our silence lengthened.

I glanced at Lucy, who was waiting.

"What happened in the Kursk Salient?" I asked.

"They attacked on. July 5, and got nowhere, but on July 11, the Third Panzer Corps burst through and was closing up with the Army Group Centre on the far side. The Russians counterattacked and stopped them. Then Stalin threw in the Guards Tank Army and the mightiest tank battle in human history took place.

"But Manstein made slow progress, and then told Hitler he was on the point of victory.

"HITLER CALLED OFF THE OFFENSIVE ON THE RUSSIAN 'ZITADELL' WITH THE EXCUSE THAT HE HAD TO PROP UP MUSSOLINI AGAINST THE SICILY LANDINGS.

"Manstein said, 'It's only a matter of a few days.'

"Hitler was adamantean. And the initiative went to the Russians, and they never lost it – they went all the way to Berlin.

"Filled with exuberant self-confidence, the Russians opened a *summer* offensive. Of course, all of this must have been in your newspapers."

"Not that Manstein needed only a few days to win the battle of the Kursk Bulge," I said.

The Prince said, "If Manstein said that, you can be sure, absolutely sure that it was true. Manstein would have won."

Claus said, "Hitler had refused permission to fortify the high west bank of the Dnieper. On August 27, Manstein said he could not hold the Donets Basin, and Hitler promised him prodigal reinforcements. Nothing came. On September 15, Manstein decided the Russians would overwhelm his men shortly. He decided to pull them back behind the Dnieper. The terrain was awful. The Germans held 700 miles under strong, Red Army non-stop attacks. Three Armies had to pull back, but had to be squeezed up to funnel through five narrow river crossings. On the Dnieper, they had to spread out for 700 miles again. It was one of the world's greatest military manoeuvres. Only Manstein could have done it and he did it for the textbooks.

"But he couldn't stop the Soviets. In October, they got across the river, and winter didn't stop their offensive. On January 4, 1944, Manstein flew to Führer Headquarters to tell Hitler he had to retreat from the Dnieper Bend. Hitler and his cronies refused, so Mastein asked for a private interview.

"In an angry conversation, Manstein told Hitler he had to appoint a Chief of Staff to guide the Führer to plans that were practical and that belonged in the real world. The weight of responsibility for the whole war was too much for one man – the war needed a separate Chief of Staff for the eastern and western battle fronts. Further, he said, a Supreme Commander was needed – that is, someone who would usurp Hitler's role, although he didn't say *that*. Hitler said that as his field marshals didn't obey *him*, a fat chance they would obey Manstein. An irate Manstein assured Hitler that any orders Manstein gave *would* be obeyed, even by all the other field marshals.

"On January 27, they held another conference, on a massive Soviet offensive against Army Group South. Manstein interrupted with a sarcastic remark on the whole conduct of the war.

"Early in March, Soviet task spearheads were thrusting into Poland, and if they joined up, they would encircle the 1st Panzer Army. Hitler announced the time had come to set up 'fortress cities' where German soldiers would fight to the last man and the last round. A disgusted Manstein, after a raging argument, dragged fron Hitler the authority to pull back the 1st Panzer Army.

"On March 25, at the Berghof, Hitler tried to blame Manstein for the whole military debacle. Manstein gave him better than he got, and the men separated, enemies."

I said, "What an amazing defect in German character. The German is 'not to reason why, the German is but to do or die.'"

"Back at his command, Manstein believed that with a free hand, he could manoeuvre to hold the Reds and gain time for Hitler to negotiate a peace in the west. He believed that Britain and America would be appalled at the Russians slavering at the outskirts of Europe. He knew nothing of the High Treason of Roosevelt's against the U.S.A. and against western

371

civilisation. Later, he would learn, and not be suprised when Roosevelt ordered Eisenhower to stop on the Elbe, and leave Berlin and the rest of Germany for the Russians.

"The man who would be appalled was the draper from Missouri, the powerless Vice-President, the future President Truman.

"On March 30, Hitler called Manstein to the Berghof yet again, gave him the Swords to the Oak Leaf of the Knight's Cross, and told him that Army Gronp South had a new commander, Field Marshal Model. He sacked Manstein, and told him that the days of strategic manoeuvre were long gone. The new world was one of dying to the last man.

"Manstein went home, and entered the eye clinic at Breslau, and then convalesced near Dresden. That summer, be watched from afar as the Reds destroyed Army Group Centre.

"In July, he had no part in the bomb plot to kill Hitler."

*

Comment: After the war, he wrote of the July Bomb Plot to kill Hitler, 'No top military commander can ask of his soldiers that they lay down their lives to gain victory and then cause defeat by his own actions."

In the third week of January 1945, Manstein knew that something had gone frighteningly wrong with Roosevelt and Churchill. He saw the Russians taking all Europe, to the shores of the North Sea. He took his family from Liegnitz in east Germany and set out to drive through Breslau to the west. Two Nazi Party men stopped the short column of vehicles at a village, and said that the local Gauleiter had forbidden evacuation. Manstein's aide de camp said he would personally shoot the two men. The Germans billeted the family in military barracks at Celle, west of Berlin.

After the war, the allies took von Manstein to Nuremberg, but he and other senior commanders presented such a skilful case that the General Staff was not condemned as a criminal organisation. In autumn of 1946, they took him to a special camp for top commanders in England. They sent him back to Germany in 1948, to stand trial with von Rundstedt, von Brauchtisch (who had been Supreme Commander till Hitler took over – the Field Marshal led the campaigns against Poland, France, Yugoslavia, Greece and the Soviet Union and was utterly subservient to Hitler) and Strauss (a minor figure), as war criminals. They only tried Manstein, in August 1949, and the world thought it an unfair trial brought out of spite. They gave him 18 years, but released him from Werl prison after three years because of his health. He lived in Bavaria till his death in 1973.

They called him out of retirement to help the German government set up a new army, to join the allied forces against the Soviet Union.

---

* * *

At five o'clock, we went for a long walk in the woods, to a tall, rock outcrop with natural steps, and we puffed our way to the top, where someone had cut a platform. We sat there, looking towards distant mountains swimming in a blue haze.

The Prince said, "The shorthand girls are very good. They are faithfully giving me a copy of every page. You can take another copy back with you. I'll have copies made."

"I don't dare," I assured him. "They might search me."

"We can miorodot it," he said comfortably.

I insisted, "I still wouldn't dare. They might find them. It might be ten years before I dare bring something like that into England. What I hope is to find work abroad, and then I'll come and see you. I can carry copies of all of this to another country without giving it a thought."

* * *

Next morning, half-an-hour after breakfast, we all settled down.

I asked the Prince, "What about the bombing of Germany?"

He said, "That shook us badly. We didn't think Britain and America would sink to such barbarism. They killed 500,000 civilians, mainly women and children. They used phosphorsus."

Dora said, in a harsh voice, "Have you ever seen a woman or child burn to death in front of you, from phosphorus? You don't dare go near. You can't put it out with water. It sticks to you and burns. If you're lucky, you can jump into water, if you don't have it on your head. While you keep it under water, it can't burn. When you step out of the water, it blazes again. When they could, people would jump into water, their families would come to say goodbye, and then the Gestapo would give them a mercy shot in the back of the head.

"We got thousands of the enemy flyers, thank God. We kept bits of phosphorus in airtight tins, and we'd open them, daub the end of a stick, and then daub the flyer. He'd jump into the water, screaming about the Geneva Convention, shrieking about goddam Krauts or filthy Huns. Some would think they had put the phosphorus out, and would climb out of the water. Then the reality would hit. They would last up to a week in the water, and

373

many went mad. Peasants for thirty miles around any city would round them up. When we didn't have water, we'd throw them into burning buildings in the next air raid, breaking their legs first.

"The Swiss Red Cross asked awkward questions. Twenty thousand airmen finally died, and that meant about two thousand planes, each with an aircrew of ten. How could so many aircrews die, the Swiss Red Cross demanded. We told them the planes spun, trapping the men by centrifugal force. They were not convinced. We said the anti-aircraft shells stunned them, and, they didn't recover before the plane crashed. That their parachutes caught fire.

"No. The German women, the mothers of the children who had died burnt alive, waited for them."

I whispered, "Nothing has been published anywhere."

"This was Churchill's doing, abetted by 'Bomber' Harris. They will *never* go to a War Crimes Tribunal, never be named as unspeakable monsters.

"So, nothing has been said. Nor will it. And when the Americans and British governments know, they will never say a word, not now, nor in one hundred years time. The bombing of Germany has covered them with ignominy. They sank to the level of the Nazis. All they did was fill the ordinary German with an iron resolve. It was mainly the British. The Americans went after our industry, and we treated American fliers over industrial cities more leniently. But for the British airmen – no mercy. After Hamburg, when tens of thousands died, 800,000 people were homeless. They had one thought – to work in a munitions factory, or get into the army. At Dresden, 120,000 civilians died. I understand that Churchill and 'Bomber' Arthur Harris planned the attacks, and that Harris told the newspapers that he could win the war alone just by terrorising the German population."

She broke into sobs.

"All our hopes were with Britain and America. They're no better than the Nazis, and they've betrayed us."

Claus said sourly, "Between American and European armies, we'll need 12,000,000 men standing to arms for decades to come. Stalin has twelve million men."

I turned uncomfortably to the Prince.

"How did the bombing affect production? Affect Speer, and the Nazis?"

Princess Jutta had her arm around her daughter's shoulders. She gave her a handkerchief to dry her eyes. The Prince looked at them uncomfortably, cleared his throat, and said, "When the raids got huge, and met almost no fighter resistance, Hitler was cursing and fulminating against Göring and all of Göring's mistakes. He told Speer over and again that the bombers would raze Germany's cities and pulverise the people's morale beyond any hope of recovery – he fell into the same blunder as the British strategists. The bombing kept him in power and brought the people behind him with a murderous passion.

"Not only did Göring fall out of favour, but air marshal Milch told Speer to look closely at the pupils of Göring's eyes. He had been a drug addict since 1933, and with years of morphine was sinking into a slow torpor.

At Nuremberg, they withheld morphine from Göring, and he recovered from his addiction.

---

*

"As Göring fell out of favour, Hitler intimated to Speer that he might name Speer as his successor."

The Prince stopped, thinking.

"Göring asked Speer to invite the leaders of the steel industry to Göring's home at Obersalzberg. Göring came in in a high good mood, his pupils sharply narrowed, harangued the steelmen for two hours, when his speech slowed, his face took on a faraway expression...and he put his head on the table and fell asleep! They went on talking till he woke up, and declared the meeting ended.

"This was the man who had to combat the bombers.

"The air raids devastated our cities and cost us 9% losses in production capacity. However, angry workers made productivity soar, so the more they bombed, the higher grew our output.

"We had a new weapon, the Waterfall rocket, about 25 feet long. It carried 660 pounds of explosives along a directional beam up to a ceiling of 50,000 feet, and hit the bombers on the nose. It sought their heat. It could destroy more than one at once. Neither fog nor cloud, night or day, affected it. We could have produced several thousand of these cheap rockets a month, and not an enemy bomber or fighter would have returned to its base. If Hitler had let us manufacture them in spring, 1944, the allies could not have landed in Normandy. Hitler decided to put everything into the V-2 rocket, and from July 1943 all our capacity went into this 46-foot long rocket, weighing 13 tons. Hitler wasted 900 of them a month. Each one carried to England 800 kilos of explosive, while the allies every day dropped 3,000 TONS of explosives on *us*. Thirty rockets would equal 12 Flying Fortresses, but the Fortresses could be used again.

"Without the Waterfall rocket, 10,000 anti-aircraft guns pointed vainly into the air instead of against Russian tanks, and trapped hundreds of thousands of young soldiers who were needed on the front."

"Men soldiers!" I burst out.

"Of course."

"In England, they were all women on the A.A."

Silence fell again.

I asked, "Was Waterfall tested against bombers?"

"It was, and it was unerring. When Hitler said 'no' to it, Speer at last saw he was mad. It was not just Waterfall. He stopped the most invaluable of our secret weapons, the M-262 jet fighter. In 1941, Speer had visited the Heinkel aircraft factory at Rostock, and the scream of a jet engine had deafened him. The designer was Professor Ernst Heinkel, who was frantically begging for this engine to go into a fighter plane.

"In September 1943, at the air force test field at Rechlin, Milch dumbly handed Speer a telegram from Hitler ordering a stop to all steps for large-scale production of the M-262. They ignored the telegram, but the work went on slowly without priority, under cover. On January 7, 1944, Hitler sent urgently for Milch and Speer; he had reports on British successes with jet planes. Now Hitler wanted the planes as of yesterday, but we could do no more than 60 a month from June, 1944. From January 1945, we could turn out 210 planes a month – but the Allies had landed in Normandy.

"But in this conversation, Hitler again put his spanner in the works. He planned to use the M-262 as a fast bomber – and take out all the weapons! It could defend itself by its speed. Perfectly true. Hitler had the mad idea of its flying in a straight line at great heights. The idea was one of drivelling fatuity, ludicrous, preposterous, self-annulling folly. Here was an invincible fighter that would wreak carnage and havoc, ravage the allied fighters and bombers. Hitler would have it with a 1,000 lb bomb and a tiny bombsight that would hit nothing.

"At last, Speer realised Hitler was destroying Germany, and he would have to kill him. He felt badly about it, because Hitler had advanced him, raised him up, treated him as his own father never had. I suggested that Hitler knew what he was doing, was deliberately leading Germany to the slaughter, but Speer dismissed that. Simply, something had gone wrong in Hitler's brain, independently of the man.

"He tried to convince Hitler that these jets could fly higher than the allied escort fighters to reach the unwieldy bombers, and with almost double their speed, blast them from the skies. Hitler fell back on sophisms – their high speed turns and sudden changes in great altitudes would knock out the pilots. Göring stepped in, and then Jodl, Guderian, Model, Sepp Dietrich and the top airforce generals. In autumn of 1944 he banned all further talk on the M-262.

"Speer talked openly with me. How much did he know? Did he know something about you? Had he realised you were a double agent there in Washington, and that knowingly we had had a British spy at our home? He *sensed* something because he put his life in my hands without an instant's hesitation. He told me that Hitler was deliberately committing high treason against his own *volk*, a *volk* which had made superhuman sacrifices for him, a *volk* to which he owed all he had, his position exalted above every other man.

"He told me that in his walks in the Chancellery gardens, he had spotted the air intake of the ventilation shaft for Hitler's bunker. It was flush with the ground, under a light grating, and a small shrub hid it. He knew that inside was an air filter, but he knew that no filter could handle the German poison gas 'tabun'.

"The Gestapo had gone after our head of armaments production, Dieter Stahl. He had said the end of the war was but a pace away. The Gestapo pulled him in, but Speer had made a good friend in Gauleiter Sturtz of Brandenburg, who rescued Stahl. In February, Speer found himself sitting down with Stahl in a small room in their Berlin air-raid bunker. The raid was heavy, but the drab room had thick concrete walls and a steel door. To Speer's consternation he heard his own voice calmly asking how could he get his hands on the new poison gas. Stahl answered, talking about the cataclysmic policies, and burst out, 'What's coming will be hideous, hideous!'

"Speer heard himself say, 'I want to get that gas into the Chancellery bunker.'

"Stahl said, in an approving voice, that he would cast about for ways to get the gas.

"Days later, he told Speer he had talked to a Major Soyka of the Army Ordinance Office. He had suggested ingenuously, 'Why don't we rebuild some artillery shells for poison gas experiments?' Then he found that middle-level managers all had easy access to tabun, because tabun worked only after an explosion. That was no good for Speer, because an explosion would have blown out the air ducts before the gas could get deep into the bunker. Stahl thought he could get the ordinary sorts of poison gas, and Speer realised be could kill Bormann, Goebbels and Ley too, when they had their nightly chats.

"Speer talked to the engineer who had built the bunker, Henschel, and told him the air filters had to be replaced. Hitler had made an official complaint about the stuffy air. But to Speer's chagrin, Henschel acted immediately, and took out the filtering system. Now the bunker had no protection against ordinary gas, but Speer didn't have any.

"Speer went to make a last check, and found armed SS sentinels all over the roofs, with lights. They had built a chimney ten-foot high over the air intake. Hitler had ordered it built because gas had temporarily blinded him in the war and he knew gas was heavier than air. He had this malign prescience of death – when Count Claus Schenk von Stauffenberg walked into his headquarters with the bomb, the attack was sudden and his tutelary demon had no time. But when the bomb lay for days in the Munich Beer Hall, when Speer worried about it for days on end, his intuition picked up something."

"So Speer didn't try again?"

"He realised it would have to be a suicidal murder. Stauffenberg made that mistake. They shot him short hours after he tried. Stauffenberg should have held the satchel in his hand and died with Hitler."

"But with the bombing, production went up?"

"In 1943, Speer had a labor force of 14 million. In late 1944, it doubled to 28 million. Most were bombed-out Germans, and German women. Sauckel brought in foreign workers but he plotted much more to frustrate Speer. Russian prisoners-of-war worked too, but they can't charge Speer with that because Russia never signed the Geneva Convention. One percent were concentration camp inmates – working, they got proper food and medical attention.

"We began the war with 771 fighters in 1939. In the last part of the war, we built 12,720 fighters, although Hitler interrupted production with the pretext of building more flak guns. Hitler would not hold the fighters back to protect the German skies, but sent far too many to the fronts. On the western front, the allies quickly shot them down, while over Germany *they* held sway.

"And Göring was good for nothing," I mused.

"He was a drugged whale of a man, in a sluggish stupor much of the time."

At Nuremberg, they cured Göring, and he quickly became the most aggressive and domineering of the accused men. The prosecutors and judges respected him for his strength of mind and personality. He was the old Göring of the early 1930's, and he took the highest score in the intelligence tests. Speer got a median score. With Göring's drug addiction, Hitler had his hands free to bring chaos to Germany's air war.

---

*

I remarked, "So Speer stayed faithful to Hitler to the end?"

The Prince shook his head.

"At the end, Hitler ordered a scorched earth policy. His final malignant smiting of the German people. He would leave them to starve among ruined cities, their industry back in the middle of the previous century.

"Before Hitler gave these orders, industrialists had come to Speer from the Ruhr, begging him to intercede with the Army High Command - so that they would not blow the Ruhr bridges as they withdrew. Without the bridges, coal could not reach iron ore, and ingots could not reach rolling mills, and the very heart of Germany would stop. Speer persuaded the generals.

"Hitler ordered destruction of all bridges, railway tracks, roundhouses, freight depots, workshops, installations, with the locks and sluices on the canals...all locomotives, passenger cars, goods wagons, cargo vessels and barges...sunken ships must block the rivers...all factories, including food producers...and on and on it went.

"Speer went to the ball-bearing factories, where they were ready to set fire to the oil baths and turn the machinery into melted metal. He persuaded them to stop. He persuaded Hitler to sign over to him all authority for the scorched earth, and then never gave the orders, or gave people a nod and a wink to hold their hand. Single-handedly, he saved postwar Germany."

The Prince got stiffly to his feet, and walked over to the tall picture window. He stood staring, then turned around.

"It was a damn close thing. Speer was trying to make Hitler see reason, and gave himself away. Hitler demanded angrily, 'Do you believe the war is lost!' Speer stuttered, and Hitler said, 'I give you 24 hours to answer me'. Speer spent a sleepless night. He knew he would not convince Hitler if he lied. Next day, he went back, and said, 'I'm with you all the way, to the end, as I have always been.' This brought tears to Hitler's eyes, and Hitler left him in charge."

I said in a low voice, "Then it's true. We didn't win the war. Hitler won it for us."

"Exactly," said the Prince. The grandmother nodded, with compressed lips, and Claus, Richterin, Walter and Axel said in unison, "Yes."

Walter said, "He was not fighting the allies. His victims were the German people, and western civilisation. He brought the Russians into Europe to finish off the German people and to wipe out our civilisation."

"That's fair enough," I agreed. "And the hero was Speer, not that the German people will ever remember."

At Nuremberg, Speer made a speech, which should be graven in marble, impressed in metal, in great plinths in every city of the western world.

He said, "Hitler's dictatorship was the first dictatorship of an industrial nation in this age of modern technology, a dictatorship which used to perfection the ways of technology to subject its own people...by such media of technology as the wireless and the public address system, the will of one man could dominate eighty million persons. Telephone, teletype and the wireless-tramitter made it possible to send the command of the highest levels directly to the lowest organisations, who executed those orders without question because of their high provenance. Many officials and squads got their evil orders directly. Modern technology made it practical to keep a close watch over all the citizens and hide criminal acts in a high degree of secrecy. To the outsider, it could look like the intricate tangle of wires in a telephone exchange but in fact a single will directed it. Dictators of history needed subordinates and go-betweens. The repressive system in the age of technology does not need such men. It creates unquestioning obeyers of orders."

We saw that in Franco's Spain. It was impossible to overthrow him. Months before his death, he put five men before firing squads, and impotent European governments withdrew their ambassadors from Madrid. In public speeches, Franco ranted against and excoriated those governments, with impunity.

It was the fairest of July weather; the sun was hot on the skin but the air cool in the high forests. The Prince suggested a picnic, beside a rock pool, fed by an icy mountain stream. Thoma, the three typists and myself changed into swimming costumes, in a forest glade. We walked back to find that Claus had changed too. The water was so cold, it stopped your breath. We stayed in about thirty seconds, then scrambled out, our skins burning and the typists shrieking, We went back in and out, and finally could stay almost a minute.

We sat on rugs for the picnic, and afterwards slept for some minutes. The Princess warned us against sunburn, and was right. We all had the beginnings of sunburn back at the house. Reinhardt drove down to the village, to ask the American captain did they have anything, and he gave us a bottle, a lotion he brought up himself in a jeep. The Prince gave him a bottle of wine from his cellars.

* * *

In the afternoon, after we were settled with our sunburn lotion, it was after four o'clock.

I said, "London wants to know about the German Underground. The occupying powers have to set up a German government and administration, and must find the authentic anti-Nazis."

The Prince said, "You will have to talk to Axel. We all know about the Resistance, but he was travelling to Switzerland, and plotted with them."

"Switzerland!" I exclaimed.

"Our family awoke suspicions in the Gestapo," said Axel. "But you made contacts so high up in the regime, you went to the Front, and then volunteered to 'spy' for us in Washington, you washed us whiter than snow!"

We all burst into laughter, even Jane, the third stenographer.

"As I knew a lot of people in Switzerland, I volunteered to work for the Deutschbank. I sometimes travelled with shipments of stolen gold – with guards too, obviously – and was back and forth with papers and paperwork. Switzerland had a blackout by then, so it was easy to meet people and escape from the Gestapo watchers. However, I wasn't strictly plotting with the Resistance."

Princess Jutta said,"I can make you a list of perhaps a thousand names, but almost all are dead."

I said, "London wants to talk to the family and relatives, to see who they suggest. Washington has a pretty complete list, thanks to an agent they had there, Allen Welsh Dulles, but London doesn't want to go hat in hand to Washington if it can avoid it. The British in Switzerland didn't do their homework as well as Dulles did."

Count Axel said, "I met Dulles several times – in secret, in the blackout. What the German Underground wanted from me was to sound out the British and Americans on signing a peace, and what I found was they didn't want it. I had very good Swiss friends, and among them I found a morose foreboding. I didn't connect the two things until slowly and reluctantly my Swiss friends told me what was going on. The Swiss Embassy in Berlin had a very good espionage system, for so small, dour and stolid a people as the Swiss, and their embassies in London and Washington were better. The Swiss paid you generously and offered refuge in Switzerland, or passports of other countries. People who talked to them now have solid

381

secret bank accounts in Switzerland.

"After some months, I finally got them to tell me what they were so ashen about. Roosevelt had given Stalin all Central Europe, all the eastern European countries – which, in fact, he now occupies – and half of Germany. The dividing line today runs south from the Baltic, just east of Hamburg; and north-east of Frankfurt; it turns at a sort of right-angle to the Czech frontier. The line was to run south, east of Frankfurt and Stuttgart to Lindau on the Swiss frontier. Further, Roosevelt gave him north Italy and all Austria."

Claus said, "The German army in Yugoslavia captured orders from Stalin to Tito, telling him the British would land at the top of the Adriatic, and when they did, he was to ally himself with the Germany army to throw then out. The British wanted to establish a line across the frontier between Italy and Yugoslavia to stop the Red army. Stalin would have had to attack them to enter Italy, and go to war with Britain."

Count Axel said, "Thank God, Roosevelt died three months ago. Truman repudiated this, and now we've got this awkward bend in the line dividing Germany. Truman also demanded that Austria be divided among four occupying powers, and refused to give Stalin north Italy. Of course, the Swiss saw themselves with the Red army on their Austrian, German and Italian frontiers. Roosevelt wanted to bring the Red army to the French frontier, and France has a huge communist party.

"The Swiss Embassy in Washington warned that Roosevelt, the *aristo* Red, had his sanity, his mind, warped by illness. And the Swiss Embassy in Moscow was far more busy than anyone imagined. They reported that Stalin was obsessed that Germany would make peace with America and Britain – that Stalin half-trusted Roosevelt, but none of the men around him. But the Swiss Embassy in Washington told us that Roosevelt had set his face inflexibly against any talk with any German. This was easier, because for the British and Americans, all Germans were bad Germans, and they wasted no time with the German Resistance.

"Not so Russia! Stalin set up in Moscow the *Free Germany Committee*, offering every concession should Germany overturn Hitler and negotiate with Stalin. Captured German generals broadcast from Moscow as members of the committee – most notably, Field Marshal Paulus, of the Sixth Army destroyed at Stalingrad. The German people saw that the Russians never bombed them, and wanted to talk. (They were too far away for their type of bombers to reach Germany). That the British and Americans bombed, and refused to talk."

"And Dulles?"

"He fought against the idea in Washington that all Germans were bad Germans, but they didn't want to listen. And it was Dulles, perhaps, who was first to see that the phosophorus bombing of Hamburg 'stiffened' the

German people, as he put it. At first, he told me that Hamburg would end the war. I think he saw what the bombing was doing before Speer and Hitler did."

"But how?" I cried.

"He was in touch with the Resistance, the German Resistance. Hitler was looking for signs of weakness, of a falling off. The Resistance feared a strengthening, a rallying, and they watched for *that*. They told Dulles they had seen it, and they were right."

"What was Dulles doing in Switzerland anyway?"

"They sent him there to contact the Underground, to help them assassinate Hitler. Then he got interested in the peace feelers, which Roosevelt didn't want to hear."

"And the German Army High Command?"

'Claus said, "They waffled and wavered, prevaricated, and no one could understand why. Yet it was simple enough. They feared chaos after Hitler's assassination and the killing off of tens of thousands of Nazis. Suppose supplies to the front stopped? Eight million people had joined the Nazi Party, and how many had opened their eyes? What the generals wanted but never said outright was a peace with Britain and America, in which they sent their best armies into Russia to cover their withdrawal, while American and British armies landed unopposed at the ports or were air-lifted in. Those armies would move up to the old Russian frontiers, and the German armies would withdraw through their lines. If Roosevelt had died in 1943 or 1944, Truman would have done it, I believe. What could Stalin do? Attack?

"If Stalin attacked, Truman and Churchill would agree on an invasion of Russia, the British and American armies backed by the German. With allied help, the German factories would be producing full blast. With the jet fighters, and Speer's rockets, we would have freed the Russian people."

I took a deep breath. I was well out of my depth. And how would they look upon me in London, knowing I knew all this? I would have to find work outside of England as quickly as I could, to feel safe.

I tried to order my confused thoughts.

"The Underground couldn't assassinate Hitler without the army?"

"They could, but the attempts were army ones, high officers who didn't waffle and vacillate," said Axel. "But these men weren't professional assassins – they were professional soldiers. As assassins, they were incompetent, unforgivably incompetent. Do you remember when the Germany army studied tanks? They *studied* them. They did war games. They looked for every argument against them, every danger in the changes. In 1943, Hitler flew from his headquarters to Berlin. An army officer gave one of his entourage a package of bottles of brandy to take to another officer in Berlin. On the plane, it didn't explode. When they opened it, they found the acid in the vial had eaten through the wire, the spring had worked, but the percussion cap did not fire. If the officers had taken up the role of Devil's Advocates and spent days and nights looking for reasons why the plan wouldn't work, someone probably would have pointed the finger at the percussion cap. Then they would have put in *three* vials of acid, with three percussion caps, and killed Hitler in 1943. They were not professionals. A man called Hassel had never attracted Gestapo attention, but the Underground had drawn up a document to show the West – you know, plans for government of Germany after they killed Hitler. This man wrote in a few words, an ammendment, in his own handwriting. The Gestapo captured the document, and finally traced down the handwriting. They hanged Hassel for his handwriting.

"The army mind is a bit 'hit or miss' – my apologies to Claus," and Count Axel looked at his nephew with a smile. "You put 40% of enemy troops out of action, and they may well withdraw. With the assassination of Hitler, it was 100% or zero. They couldn't understand that. He died – or they did, and Germany with them. Nothing, nothing could be left to chance, as in army manoeuvres. Germany prides itself as the most professional country in the world – and amateurism gave us the worst tragedy in all our history, the failure of the July 20 Bomb Plot, last year.'

We took that in, sitting there.

"After the Bomb Plot, the Nazis executed a thousand, two thousand of the best men in this country, the hope of Germany after Hitler. But hundreds of thousands had to die on the battle fronts."

Another silence followed.

At last, I said, "I know I'm an awful dunce, but what is this about acid vials and percussion caps?"

Walter said, "To explode a charge, you need first to explode a percussion cap, to set it off. You put a firing cap onto a spring, and pull the spring tight with a wire, and put the wire in a vial. When you pull a trigger, acid fills the vial and eats away at the wire. The wire breaks, the spring snaps open and drives the firing pin into the percussion cap."

I nodded.

After another pause, I said, "As I understand it, well, as everybody does, Count Claus Stauffenberg carried the bomb with a vial of acid in a briefcase into Hitler's headquarters."

Claus said, "The briefcase carried documents about the German Home Army. Hitler wanted to throw them into the Russian front. This was scraping the bottom of the German manpower barrel. Stauffenberg had already tried on July 11 and July 16, and, incredibly, his fellow conspirators were angry at his failures. Amateurs. He had suffered wounds in North Africa – lost his left arm, and two fingers of his *right* hand. Also, his left eye. He couldn't shoot,

384

which made him a bad choice. Field marshals von Kluge and Rommel had agreed to come into the plot if the conspirators could kill Himmler and Göring as well. Stauffenberg offered to make his third attempt a suicide one, but the other conspirators refused. They shot him hours afterwards anyway. If he had stood beside Hitler with the briefcase under his arm, as he wanted to, today he would be the world's greatest martyr, a saint! But the military men couldn't think in terms of 100% certainty."

I said, "He put the briefcase under the table, another officer pushed it out of the way with his foot and away from Hitler. Is that right?"

Claus nodded, "Yes, Ray. Claus waited outside with Colonel Fellgiebel, some hundreds of yards away. They saw the explosion. Stauffenberg got into his car, and caught his plane to Berlin. Fellgiebel had to knock out all the radio and phone communications with the outside – but he *did not*. Did he lose his nerve? Was there a technical failure? They shot him soon after, and his secret died with him. Had he cut off the headquarters from the outside, the revolt might still have prospered, but with Hitler's midnight broadcast all was lost. The bomb went off some 12 hours earlier."

Claus thought, then said, "It was the hot weather in July. Instead of working inside the bunker, they came out to this lightly-built wooden building with large windows. It didn't contain the explosion, where the bunker would have. Ho one would have escaped, inside the bunker."

I asked, "Do you know what happened all that afternoon in Berlin? What the plotters did?"

Claus nodded.

"Could you dictate that later on?"

He nodded again.

I said, "London asked me to find out about the churches."

Thoma laughed bitterly. "Good propaganda. Nazis torturing and hanging priests and clergymen."

Count Axel said, "It wasn't like that. Please, Thoma."

He got to his feet, and looked out of the window.

"I believe it was the example of priests, Protestant clergymen and believing laymen, men like Niemöller, Bonhoeffer, Wurm, Presing, Bodelschwingh – heavens, the list is unending – their example made a climate in which the conspiracy grew.

"You have to think that Hitler engulfed every organisation except the churches. Hitler sought a truce in which the churches worried about the afterlife and left him free with this life. But who saw the brutishness, the inhumanity, the cruelty of Nazism as no one did were the Christians. Today, the German people are living a fearful realisation of their sin, of the wages of their sins. Hitler ground down the Christian ethic of the dignity of man, and that stirred the opposition – brought together high army officers like Beck and Hammerstein, Admiral Canaris and Niemöller. Today, German churchmen must be the most hallowed, the most cleansed in the world. They have stood face to face with evil beyond comprehension, with death on a staggering scale.

"The German churches numbered thousands – but they were slow to wake up. Well, let me amend that – the foreign countries and the German people were just as slow. Hitler moved slyly, and very cleverly, and what hampered the churches was their teaching of 'render unto Caesar what is Caesar's'. Most churchgoers were lower middle-class, who blamed the Weimar Republic for the economic disaster, and blessed Hitler for pulling then out. The fact is that the Weimar Republic offered unemployment relief the same as the other western countries. But the ordinary German lived in a nation less than a hundred years old. The British, the French, the Americans, took things with patience, because they had centuries behind them of tolerance and human rights. The German people were more primitive – for centuries they had depended upon their kings, princes, dukes, counts...they were bred to live under a strong, paternalistic leader. Weimar offered then no strongman. The British, the French, the Americans abhorred strongmen. As in all the less civilised parts of Europe, the church was what pointed the way out of their primitive lives.

"Hitler gave the Protestants every reassurance. When their churches saw the truth about him, Pastor Niemöller and the Protestant Bishop of Württemberg, Bishop Wurm, with many others built the 'Confessional Church' to struggle against the Nazis.

"Some Protestant clergymen grew apathetic before the horror, others wanted to save their parishioners from the concentration camps, and the rest took whatever risk they could. Many went into concentration camps with Niemöller.

"These anti-Nazi pastors found themselves called-up, till in 1944 the conspirator, general Olbricht, ordered their exemption.

"Hitler's agreement with the Pope, a Concordat which Papen signed on July 20, 1933, and which let a Catholic join the Nazi Party, comforted the Catholic Centre Party. The Nazis threw Centre Party men out of office, and dissolved it in December, 1933. The Hitler Youth swallowed Catholic Youth groups.

"The Catholic clergy suffered the same as the Protestant pastors, but the higher Catholic dignitaries were somewhat spared, because Hitler was careful of the Vatican. The Catholic Bishop of Breslau publicly prayed that the Nazis send him to a concentration camp. Hitler gave instant orders that bishops should 'have no chance to enjoy martyrdom'.

"The Bishop of Münster – Count von Galen – opposed Nazism with every fibre of his being. They read his sermons aloud in other churches, sent them all over Germany in chain letters, and repeated them in allied broadcasts.

"Goebbels' assistant, Walter Tiessler, suggested to Martin Bormann that they *hang* Galon. His report said, as well as I remember –"

"You managed to get a copy?"

"I did. It went something like this: '...only the Führer himself can decide on this step. Goebbels fears that we would lose the populatian of Münster for the duration if we acted against him. And we might well add Westphalia...Goebbels argues we should keep up pretenses toward the church for the duration.'

"Neither the Protestants nor the Catholics directly joined the plots against Hitler, although Pastor Dietrich Bonhoeffer went to Sweden to tell the Bishop of Chichester details about assassination plots. I myself attended a secret church meeting in Geneva in 1941, and heard him pray. 'I pray for the defeat of my nation. Only through defeat can we atone for the dire crimes we have wreaked against Europe and the world.'

"In April, I learned that on April 9, drunken SS men at Flossenbürg concentration camp killed him, days before the Americans got there.

"Dr. Eugen Gerstenmaier, of the Kreisau Circle, and a layman high in the Evangelical Church, organised relief for war prisoners and slave laborers, and that let him travel abroad. On July 20, last year, he was in the War Office on Bendlerstrasse, when the Gestapo grabbed him. He still doesn't understand how they did not shoot him there and then, but after interrogation, sent him to trial. Everyone else was sentenced to death. He got seven years, and the Americans liberated him from Bayreuth prison.

"In Switzerland, I also met the famous Jesuit father, Friedrich Muckermann. He had escaped early, and published

The typescript ends here, suddenly, in mid-sentence.

Did the Prince give Raimunda a copy with the last pages missing?
Did she lose the pages herself?

Raimunda went to work in Italy in 1949, and in 1950, married an Italian film producer. They had two daughters.

In 1971, they returned to England with the second daughter, who never married, and lived in the house in Wiltshire.

A car accident killed her husband in 1973. He was working in British Television.

Her eldest daughter married in Paris, in 1975, and three years later died of cancer.

Raimunda died of cancer in 1981.

Cancer also claimed Wilma, whose marriage was childless.

Every winter, from 1951, they went to Belize for a five-week holiday.

Ray had slipped a letter from Princess Gabriele into the end of the typescript, but the first page only. The letter broke off in mid-sentence at the bottom of the page.

September 3, 1945

My dearest Ray, You ask me what can Hitler's war teach (sic) us, and suppose that no mind can encompass it.

I feel I *can* encompass with the temerity and insolence of my aged years!

One: Hitler at first wanted to exterminate all Europe, then decided he needed the 400 million Europeans as a counter-weight to America.

By the end of the century, I suppose the world population will be 10 billion people, and by the end of the next, perhaps 25 billion. The planet has not room enough, not water or soil enough.

A new weapon will come that can kill many millions at a stroke. A new Hitler will wipe out the world population, leaving alive perhaps 500 million people. This will come, I assure you, because Hitler showed the way to them.

Two: Hitler's war teaches us that we cannot trust our leaders. In democracies, we elect them for four years, to give them time to carry out their policies. That is what we do not want! We should elect them for one year, with no re-election ever, so they have not time to do anything!

Why?

When you get to my age, you realise finally that we know only the past. We try to second-guess the future, but can only find out the new and the unknown by trial and error. And our wrong tentative trials far, far outnumber our right ones.

Our leaders are only human like ourselves, so they make far more mistakes, just like the rest of us.

But leaders multiply their mistakes a millionfold...and we the people pay. It is better to let the people work out things slowly and the leaders simply keep the playing-ground level. Anything a leader does is going to hurt – hurt your pocket or hurt your living flesh.

To strike at our bestial oppressors, men had to steel themselves to commit high treason. In Germany, we have two sorts of high treason – Hochverrat, or treason against the Nazi leaders; and ranking army officers and others rose to commit Hochverrat.

But their conviction failed them before Landesverrat, to betray secrets to the enemy, which was primordial. Your courage never failed. Again and again, you committed Landesverrat, for a new Germany, yet to be born, but which will come.

As an elderly lady, may I venture to lay before you my feelings and thoughts about you and Claus,

(The first page ends here.)